Anonymus

Report and special Report from the select committee on the aged pensioners Bill

Together with the proceedings of the committee, minutes of evidence, appendix and index

Anonymus

Report and special Report from the select committee on the aged pensioners Bill
Together with the proceedings of the committee, minutes of evidence, appendix and index

ISBN/EAN: 9783742818553

Manufactured in Europe, USA, Canada, Australia, Japa

Cover: Foto ©Andreas Hilbeck / pixelio.de

Manufactured and distributed by brebook publishing software (www.brebook.com)

Anonymus

Report and special Report from the select committee on the aged pensioners Bill

REPORT

AND

SPECIAL REPORT

FROM THE

SELECT COMMITTEE

ON THE

AGED PENSIONERS BILL;

TOGETHER WITH THE

PROCEEDINGS OF THE COMMITTEE,

MINUTES OF EVIDENCE,

APPENDIX AND INDEX.

Ordered, by The House of Commons, to be Printed,
27 *July* 1903.

LONDON:
PRINTED FOR HIS MAJESTY'S STATIONERY OFFICE,
BY WYMAN & SONS, LIMITED, FETTER LANE, E.C.

And to be purchased, either directly or through any Bookseller, from
EYRE & SPOTTISWOODE, EAST HARDING STREET, FLEET STREET, E.C. and
32, ABINGDON STREET, WESTMINSTER, S.W.; or
OLIVER AND BOYD, EDINBURGH; or
E. PONSONBY, 116, GRAFTON STREET, DUBLIN.

1903.

AGED PENSIONERS BILL.

[*Friday, 22nd May* 1903]:—Read a second time and committed to a Select Committee.

[*Thursday, 18th June* 1903]:—*Ordered*, That the Select Committee on the Aged Pensioners Bill be nominated of Sir Alexander Hargreaves Brown, Mr. Channing, Mr. Crean, Mr. Doughty, Mr. Goulding, Mr. John Hutton, Mr. Lloyd-George, Mr. Grant Lawson, Mr. O'Brien, Mr. Pemberton, Colonel Pilkington, Sir Robert Reid, Mr. Remnant, Mr. Shackleton, and Mr. Skewes-Cox.

Ordered, That the Committee have power to send for persons, papers, and records.

Ordered, That Five be the quorum.

[*Tuesday, 30th June* 1903]:—*Ordered*, That the Report and Minutes of Evidence of the Select Committee on the Cottage Homes Bill, of Session 1899, and the Report and Minutes of Evidence of the Select Committee on Aged Deserving Poor, in the same Session, be referred to the Select Committee on the Aged Pensioners Bill.

[*Wednesday, 8th July* 1903]:—*Ordered*, That the Old Age Pensions (Friendly Societies) Bill of Session 1898, the Old Age Provident Pensions Bill of Session 1899, the Old Age Pensions (No. 3) Bill, Old Age Pensions (No. 4) Bill, and Old Age Pensions (No. 5) Bill of Session 1901, and the Old Age Pensions Bill, Aged Pensioners (No. 2) Bill, and Cottage Homes Bill of the present Session, be referred to the Select Committee on Aged Pensioners Bill.

SPECIAL REPORT.

THE SELECT COMMITTEE to whom the AGED PENSIONERS BILL was referred;——Have agreed to the following SPECIAL REPORT:—

1. In view of the very large amount of evidence on the subject of Old Age Pensions which has been accumulated by previous inquiries, your Committee have endeavoured, as far as possible, to confine the witnesses called before them to matters which have arisen since 1899, in which year Mr. Chaplin's Committee made their Report.

2. Such matters appeared to your Committee to include:—

(1.) The further experience gained by the continued operation of the Old Age Pension laws in Denmark, New Zealand, and Victoria.

(2.) The views expressed at conferences of Trades Unions, Friendly Societies and Co-operative Societies upon the proposals of Mr. Chaplin's Committee.

(3.) The result of recent investigations made in certain workhouses as to the number of aged inmates who could leave such workhouses if provided with pensions.

(4.) The value of the estimate made by Sir E. Hamilton's Committee in 1899, as tested by the census of 1901, and the extent to which such estimate would be affected by certain variations from the scheme upon which those estimates were based.

Upon all these matters your Committee have received evidence to which they desire to call the attention of the House.

Much additional information on the third matter mentioned above will be supplied by the returns moved for this Session as to the number and physical and mental condition of the aged indoor paupers. Your Committee have requested the Local Government Boards for England, Scotland and Ireland to take steps to supplement that information by inviting the Guardians of certain typical unions to ascertain the number of the aged inmates of their workhouses—mentally and physically fit to live outside an institution—who have friends with whom they could live if they had pensions. The result of these inquiries will be printed in the Appendix to this Report.

Your Committee have also had before them, as documents to be considered, the Bills on this subject and the subject of Cottage Homes, introduced in Parliament since the Report of the Royal Commission.

3. Your Committee do not think that any useful purpose would be served by their attempting at this late period of the Session to undertake the work more properly belonging to a Committee of the whole House, or a Grand Committee, of going line by line through the Bill referred to them and discussing the exact wording of the amendments to it which appeared to them to be necessary. They have accordingly agreed to report the Bill without Amendment to the House. They desire, however, to offer the following observations on the main features of the Bill, based on the evidence which they have received, or which has been referred to them.

(1.) If Parliament should decide to devote to the provision of Old Age Pensions the very large sum which would be required to carry out the provisions of the Bill in its entirety, the Bill, if modified as suggested below, appears to your Committee to afford a satisfactory basis for the distribution of that sum.

(2.) It does not appear to your Committee that it would be fair or reasonable to leave to an elected body the duty of deciding upon the merits of large numbers of its constituents. In the Colonies in which State Old Age Pensions are given, the duty of deciding whether an applicant fulfils the conditions necessary to entitle him to a pension is imposed upon Stipendiary Magistrates or Commissioners appointed by the State. Your Committee consider that any scheme adopted by Parliament should provide that the qualification of any person to receive a pension should be placed in the hands of Special Commissioners for suitable areas. If the money required for a Pension scheme is to come out of general taxation, an additional reason exists for declining to commit the management to a local authority. The temptation to relieve the rates by the grant of pensions instead of poor law relief might lead to grave abuses. To utilise the experience of poor law guardians in allocating pensions is one thing. It is a very different thing to leave the whole management in their hands. The Commissioners should consider any representations made on behalf of the Treasury or the local authorities.

4. Your Committee think that any person who has proved before the Commissioners the possession of the qualifications prescribed by the Bill amended as they suggest should, whether a pension is granted or not, be entitled as a "qualified pensioner" to certain privileges, *e.g.*, the retention of his civil rights even if he should receive poor law relief, and the right to outdoor relief should he, or she be compelled by destitution to apply for assistance to the guardians while in such a state of health as not to require admission into the workhouse infirmary.

5. The qualifications of pensioners dealt with in Clause 6 of the Bill should, in the opinion of your Committee, be amended in the following particulars:—

(1.) A fixed and long period should be required to elapse between the naturalisation of an alien and his application for a pension.

(2.) The disqualification arising from the receipt of poor law relief should be so defined as not to exclude from pensions aged persons who are in receipt of such relief at the time of the passing of the Act, but who had not received such relief for 20 years before they reached the qualifying age.

A definition of the "circumstances of a wholly exceptional character" under which poor relief may be given without invalidating a subsequent claim to a pension should be inserted in the Bill.

(3.) The transfer of property and collusive arrangements as to wages for the purpose of reducing the income of the applicant to a weekly sum below that which will disqualify for a pension should be guarded against.

(4.) Provision should be made against the transfer of the maintenance of aged parents from well-to-do children to the State, which is stated to have in some instances occurred in New Zealand and Victoria.

(5.) If any part of the pension is to be charged on the rates of a Union, the pensioner should have been a resident in that Union for a considerable period.

6. Your Committee desire to express their opinion that the provision of Old Age Pensions for the deserving poor is a matter which might well be proceeded with step by step. If it is not considered possible to provide by taxation the full sum which would be required each year in increasing amounts for the scheme of pensions contemplated by the Bill referred to your Committee, the provision of a considerably smaller sum would, in the opinion of your Committee, meet many of the most necessitous cases. This result might be obtained either by raising the age at which a pension might be claimed, or by reducing the amount of weekly income, the possession of which disqualifies for a pension.

7. There is some danger that those who are in a position to save money may be discouraged from saving by the reflection that the more they have the less they will receive in the form of a pension. It may be advisable to intrust those who have the distribution of pensions with a discretion as to amount, so that the pension awarded may not be so reduced as to deprive applicants of the fruits of their own thrift. In no case, however, ought any pension to be granted where it is not really needed.

8. Your Committee are of opinion that all the materials available, apart from actual experiment, for the purposes of enabling Parliament to arrive at a decision upon the subject of Old Age Pensions have been exhausted in the numerous inquiries that have already taken place. Nevertheless, it must be admitted that there is still much uncertainty upon several points. For example, the number of those in workhouses over a given age who could be properly attended to outside a workhouse, the number of those not now receiving poor law relief who require and deserve pensions, the possibility of obtaining reliable information in crowded communities if an applicant's antecedents are to be inquired into, the degree to which a pension scheme would transfer the cost of maintaining the aged poor from the rates to the taxes, and the sums needed for the various schemes propounded, are all matters of considerable doubt. Certainty upon these and other features of importance cannot be attained without actual experiment.

9. Your Committee are of opinion that the reduction in Poor Law Expenditure will be considerably less than has often been represented, inasmuch as the proportion of the aged poor who are now, or may in future be, in the workhouses, who could with advantage to themselves live outside with the help of a pension, will probably be found to be very small. Many inmates who would thus be compelled, from infirmity or lack of friends or homes outside, to remain in the workhouse, suffer great hardship from being compulsorily associated with other inmates who are imbecile or otherwise undesirable. Your Committee strongly recommend that the welfare and happiness of this class of in-door paupers should be provided for by the extension of the system of Cottage Homes.

27 *July* 1903.

REPORT.

THE SELECT COMMITTEE to whom the AGED PENSIONERS BILL was referred:——HAVE agreed to report the same without Amendment.

27 *July* 1903

PROCEEDINGS OF THE COMMITTEE.

Tuesday, 30th June 1903.

MEMBERS PRESENT:

Sir Alexander Hargreaves Brown.
Mr. Channing.
Mr. Flower.
Mr. Goulding.
Mr. John Hutton.
Mr. Grant Lawson.
Mr. Pemberton.
Colonel Pilkington.
Sir Robert Reid.
Mr. Remnant.
Mr. Shackleton.
Mr. Shaw-Cox.

Mr. Grant Lawson was called to the Chair.

The Committee deliberated.

[Adjourned till Monday next, 6th July, at Three o'clock.

Monday, 6th July 1903.

MEMBERS PRESENT:

Mr. Grant Lawson in the Chair.

Mr. Flower.
Mr. Goulding.
Mr. John Hutton.
Mr. Lloyd-George.
Colonel Pilkington.
Sir Robert Reid.
Mr. Remnant.
Mr. Shaw-Cox.

Miss *Edith Sellers* was examined.

[Adjourned till Wednesday next, 8th July, at Three o'clock.

Wednesday, 8th July 1903.

MEMBERS PRESENT:

Mr. Grant Lawson in the Chair.

Mr. Flower.
Mr. Goulding.
Mr. John Hutton.
Mr. Pemberton.
Sir Robert Reid.
Mr. Remnant.
Mr. Shackleton.
Mr. Shaw-Cox.

The Honourable *W. P. Reeves* was examined.

[Adjourned till Monday next, 13th July, at Three o'clock.

Monday, 13th July 1903.

MEMBERS PRESENT:

Mr. Grant Lawson in the Chair.

Mr. Goulding.
Mr. John Hutton.
Mr. Lloyd-George.
Mr. Pemberton.
Colonel Pilkington.
Mr. Remnant.

Sir *Edward Hamilton*, K.C.B., was examined.

[Adjourned till Wednesday next, 15th July, at Three o'clock.

Wednesday, 15th July 1903.

MEMBERS PRESENT:

Mr. Grant Lawson in the Chair.

Sir Alexander Hargreaves Brown.
Mr. Channing.
Mr. Flower.
Mr. Goulding.
Mr. Lloyd-George.
Mr. Pemberton.
Colonel Pilkington.
Mr. Remnant.
Mr. Shackleton.

Mr. *W. C. Steadman* and Mr. *William Crooks*, a Member of the House, were examined.

[Adjourned till Monday next, 20th July, at Three o'clock.

Monday, 20th July 1903.

MEMBERS PRESENT:

Mr. Grant Lawson in the Chair.

Mr. Channing.
Mr. Goulding.
Mr. John Hutton.
Mr. Lloyd-George.
Mr. O'Shee.
Mr. Pemberton.
Colonel Pilkington.
Sir Robert Reid.
Mr. Remnant.
Mr. Shackleton.
Mr. Shower-Cox.

Mr. *J. C. Gray* and The Honourable *Alfred Dobson* were examined.

[Adjourned till Wednesday next, 22nd July, at Three o'clock.

Wednesday, 22nd July 1903.

MEMBERS PRESENT:

Mr. Grant Lawson in the Chair.

Mr. Channing.
Mr. Flower.
Mr. John Hutton.
Mr. O'Shee.
Mr. Pemberton.
Colonel Pilkington.
Sir Robert Reid.
Mr. Remnant.
Mr. Shackleton.

Miss *Edith Sellers* and Mr. *E. Drake-Fuller* were examined.

The Committee deliberated.

[Adjourned till Monday next, 27th July, at Twelve o'clock.

Monday, 27th *July* 1903.

MEMBERS PRESENT:

Mr. Grant Lawson in the Chair.

Sir Alexander Hargreaves Brown.
Mr. Channing.
Mr. Flower.
Mr. Goulding.
Mr. John Hutton.
Mr. Lloyd-George.
Mr. Pemberton.
Colonel Pilkington.
Sir Robert Reid.
Mr. Renmant.
Mr. Shackleton.
Mr. Shaw-Cox.

DRAFT SPECIAL REPORT, proposed by the *Chairman*, read the first time, as follows:

"1. In view of the very large amount of evidence on the subject of Old Age Pensions which has been accumulated by previous inquiries, your Committee have endeavoured, so far as possible, to confine the witnesses called before them to matters which have arisen since 1899, in which year Mr Chaplin's Committee made their Report.

"2. Such matters appeared to your Committee to include:—

"(1.) The further experience gained by the continued operation of the Old Age Pension laws in Denmark, New Zealand, and Victoria.

"(2.) The views expressed at conferences of Trades Unions and Co-operative Societies upon the proposals of Mr Chaplin's Committee.

"(3.) The result of recent investigations made in certain workhouses as to the number of aged inmates who could leave such workhouses if provided with pensions.

"(4.) The accuracy of the estimate made by Sir E. Hamilton's Committee in 1899, as tested by the census of 1901, and the extent to which such estimate would be affected by certain variations from the scheme upon which those estimates were based.

"Upon all these matters your Committee have received evidence to which they desire to call the attention of the House.

"3. Your Committee do not think that any useful purpose would be served by their attempting at this late period of the Session to undertake the work more properly belonging to a Committee of the whole House, or a Grand Committee, of going line by line through the Bill referred to them and discussing the exact wording of the amendments to it which appeared to them to be necessary. They desire, however, to offer the following observations on the main features of the Bill, based on the evidence which they have received, or which has been referred to them.

"(1.) If Parliament should decide to devote to the provision of Old Age Pensions the very large sum which would be required to carry out the provisions of the Bill in its entirety, the Bill, if modified as suggested below, appears to your Committee to afford a satisfactory basis for the distribution of that sum.

"(2.) It does not appear to your Committee that it would be fair or reasonable to leave to an elected body the duty of deciding upon the merits of large numbers of its constituents. In the Colonies in which State Old Age Pensions are given, the duty of deciding whether an applicant fulfils the conditions necessary to entitle him to a pension is imposed upon Stipendiary Magistrates or Commissioners appointed by the State. Your Committee consider that any scheme adopted by Parliament should provide a similar tribunal for the decision of this question.

"4. Your Committee think that any person who has proved before such a tribunal the possession of the qualifications prescribed by the Bill amended as they suggest should, whether a pension is granted or not, be entitled as a 'qualified pensioner' to certain privileges, e.g., the retention of his civil rights even if he should receive poor law relief, and the right to out-door relief should he or she be compelled by destitution to apply for assistance to the guardians while in such a state of health as not to require admission into the workhouse infirmary.

"5. The qualifications of pensioners dealt with in Clause 6 of the Bill should, in the opinion of your Committee, be amended in the following particulars:

"(1.) A fixed period should be required to elapse between the naturalization of an alien and his application for a pension.

"(2.) The disqualification arising from the receipt of poor law relief should be so defined as not to exclude from pensions aged persons who are in receipt of such relief at the time of the passing of the Act, but who had not received such relief for 20 years before they reached the qualifying age.

"A definition of the 'circumstances of a wholly exceptional character' under which poor relief may be given without invalidating a subsequent claim to a pension should be inserted in the Bill.

"(3.) The transfer of property for the purpose of reducing the income of the applicant to a weekly sum below that which will disqualify for a pension should be guarded against.

"(4.) Provision should be made against the transfer of the maintenance of aged parents from well-to-do children to the State, which is stated to have in some instances occurred in New Zealand and Victoria.

"(5.) If any part of the pension is to be charged on the rates of a Union, the pensioner should have been a resident in that Union for a considerable period.

"6. Your Committee desire to express their opinion that the provision of Old Age Pensions for the deserving poor is a matter which might well be proceeded with step by step. If it is not considered possible to provide by taxation the full sum which would be required each year in increasing amounts for the scheme of pensions contemplated by the Bill referred to your Committee, the provision of a considerably smaller sum would, in the opinion of your Committee, meet many of the most necessitous cases. This result might be obtained either by raising the age at which a pension might be claimed, or by reducing the amount of weekly income the possession of which disqualifies for a pension."

DRAFT SPECIAL REPORT, proposed by Mr. *Chamming*, read the first time, as follows:

"1. YOUR Committee has had before them as documents to be considered in view of their Report:—

"(i.) the whole of the evidence taken by the Royal Commission on the Aged Poor, and by the various Select and Departmental Committees appointed for this purpose, together with the Reports made by these bodies;

"(ii.) the whole of the Bills on this subject introduced in Parliament since the Report of the Royal Commission, and which are printed in the Appendix.

"2. It has appeared to your Committee—

"(a) that the present inquiry should supplement not supplant the results of the previous inquiries;

"(b) that in making their Report regard should be had to the objects and proposals of the other Bills laid before Parliament, and to the extent to which those proposals represent the considered opinions of the classes more directly interested in the provision of Old Age Pensions; and

"(c) that, so far as was possible in the limited time at their disposal, the practical experience of the working of the pension systems of Denmark, New Zealand, and Victoria, and further information as to the probable number and physical and mental condition of those who might, under the Aged Pensioners Bill or other proposals, be held to be qualified for pensions.

"Your Committee has then taken and now submits to Parliament evidence on these issues of special and immediate relevance to the present inquiry.

"3. Your Committee have not attempted to examine or to amend in detail the Bill referred to them, but think it will prove more useful to the settlement of this question to indicate the broad lines of the solution which seems most desirable, the principles which must govern the working out of this or any other measure for making suitable and adequate provision for old age, and the limitations in the application of these principles and the special dangers and difficulties in the working of any such Act.

"4. Your Committee are of opinion that the social and moral advantages arrived at in any system of old age pensions cannot be fully secured unless the whole ground is covered by a practically universal endowment of old age; that it is difficult and administratively wasteful of the funds available to carry out with precision and justice discrimination between those who have and those who have not endeavoured to make provision for themselves and their families; and that the experience of New Zealand and of the Poor Law Authorities in this country shows that an income limit leads to serious and demoralising frauds.

"Your Committee attach, in support of this view, great importance to the unanimous demand of the Trade Unions and of the Co-operative Societies of the United Kingdom, who may be taken to represent a majority of the more experienced and thoughtful of the working classes, for a system of universal pensions.

"They would also draw the attention of Parliament to the fact that the 'Old Age Pensions' Bill introduced in 1902 and 1903, generally carries out the proposals supported by these important and representative bodies.

"5. If Parliament should decide that it is premature to attempt the immediate provision of universal pensions, your Committee are of opinion that in amending the Aged Pensioners Bill or any other Bill on restricted lines, the following changes would be made:—

"(a.) All persons over 65 years of age should be entitled, on personally making the demand, to be placed on the list of persons claiming to be qualified for pensions.

"(b.) The qualification of any person to receive a pension should be placed in the hands of a Special Commissioner for each county or groups of counties.

"(c.) A thrift test should only be applied by proof that the destitution of a person claiming a pension is due to his or her own fault or habits.

"(d.) Disqualification arising from receipt of relief should not be held to exclude aged persons who are in receipt of relief at the time of the passing of any such Act, but who have not been habitually or recurrently in receipt of relief during the previous ten years.

"(e.) The transfer of property, or collusive arrangements as to wages, for the purpose of reducing the income below the limit, should be guarded against.

"(f.) The Treasury and, if the local rates are applied for pensions, the County Council shall be entitled to be heard before the Commissioner, by Counsel or otherwise, and to offer evidence and ask questions.

"6. Your Committee are of opinion that the reduction on Poor Law Expenditure will be considerably less than has often been represented, inasmuch as the proportion of the aged poor who are now, or may in future be, in the workhouses, who could with advantage to themselves live outside with the help of a pension, is very small. Many inmates who would thus be compelled, from infirmity or lack of friends or homes outside, to remain in the workhouse, suffer great hardship from being compulsorily associated with other inmates who are imbecile or otherwise undesirable. Your Committee strongly recommend that the welfare and happiness of this class of in-door paupers should be provided for by the extension of the system of cottage homes, or, where the Union buildings permit, by better classification of those who are in the workhouse.

Question proposed, That the Special Report proposed by the *Chairman*, be read a second time, paragraph by paragraph.—(*The Chairman*.)

Amendment proposed, to leave out the words "the Chairman" and insert the words "Mr. Channing"—(Mr. *Channing*)—instead thereof.—Question proposed, That the words "The Chairman" stand part of the Question.

Amendment, by leave, withdrawn.

Question, That the Draft Special Report proposed by the *Chairman*, be read a second time, paragraph by paragraph,—put, and *agreed to*.

Paragraph 1, *agreed to*.

Paragraph 2:

Amendments made.

Another Amendment proposed, at the end of the paragraph, to add the words "which does not, however, materially alter the evidence already given in previous inquiries"—(Sir *R. Reid*).—Question proposed, That those words be there added.

Amendment, by leave, withdrawn.

Another Amendment proposed, at the end of the paragraph, to add the words:

"Much additional information on the third matter mentioned above will be supplied by the returns moved for this Session as to the number and physical and mental condition of the aged indoor paupers.

"Your Committee have requested the Local Government Boards for England, Scotland and Ireland to take steps to supplement that information by inviting the guardians of certain typical unions to ascertain the number of the aged inmates of their workhouses, mentally and physically fit to live outside an institution, who have friends with whom they could live if they had pensions. The result of these inquiries will be printed in the appendix to this report."—(*The Chairman*.)

Question, That the words be there added,—put, and *agreed to*.

Another Amendment proposed, after the words last added, to add the words "Your Committee have also had before them, as documents to be considered, the Bills on this subject and the subject of Cottage Homes introduced in Parliament since the Report of the Royal Commission"—(Mr. *Channing*).—Question, That those words be there added,—put, and *agreed to*.

Paragraph 2, as amended, *agreed to*.

Another Amendment proposed, after paragraph 2, to insert the following new paragraph: "Your Committee are of opinion that the social and moral advantages arrived at in any system of old age pensions cannot be fully secured unless the whole ground is covered by a practically universal endowment of old age; that it is difficult and administratively wasteful of the funds available to carry out with precision and justice discrimination between those who have and those who have not endeavoured to make provision for themselves and their families; and that the experience of New Zealand and of the Poor Law Authorities in this country shows that an inquisition leads to serious and demoralising frauds"—(*Mr. Channing*).—Question put,—That the proposed new paragraph be inserted in the Report.—The Committee divided:

Ayes, 3.	Noes, 9.
Mr. Channing.	Sir Alexander Hargreaves Brown.
Mr. Pemberton.	Mr. Flower.
Mr. Shackleton.	Mr. Goulding.
	Mr. John Hutton.
	Mr. Lloyd-George.
	Colonel Pilkington.
	Sir Robert Reid.
	Mr. Remnant.
	Mr. Shawe-Cox.

Paragraph 3:

An Amendment made.

Another Amendment proposed, at the end of the paragraph, to leave out the words "a single tribunal for the decision of this question," and add the words "that the qualification of any person to receive a pension should be placed in the hands of Special Commissioners for suitable areas"—(*Mr. Channing*)—instead thereof.—Question, That the words proposed to be left out stand part of the paragraph,—put, and *negatived*.

Question, That the words "that the qualification of any person to receive a pension should be placed in the hands of Special Commissioners for suitable areas" be there added,—put, and *agreed to*.

Another Amendment proposed to the paragraph, after the words last added, to add the words "If the money required for a Pension scheme is to come out of general taxation, an additional reason exists for declining to commit the management to a local authority. The temptation to relieve the rates by the grant of pensions instead of poor law relief might lead to grave abuses. To utilise the experience of poor law guardians in allocating pensions is one thing. It is a very different thing to leave the whole management in their hands"—(*Sir Robert Reid*).—Question, That these words be there added,—put, and *agreed to*.

Another Amendment made to the paragraph, after the words last added, by adding the words "The Commissioners should consider any representations made on behalf of the Treasury or the local authorities."

Paragraph 3, as amended, *agreed to*.

Paragraphs 4 and 5, amended, and *agreed to*.

Paragraph 6:

Amendment proposed at the end of the paragraph, to add the words "or, if that be considered a right course, by allocating a sum of money from which pensions might be conferred upon the most deserving of those who require them on a principle of selection. Your Committee are aware that grave objections may be urged, especially against the last of these alternatives, such as the danger of favouritism, and the apparent unfairness of bestowing benefits upon selected individuals out of national funds, while others, perhaps hardly less deserving, are excluded. It appears, however, that the choice now lies between three courses, one is to reject the idea of old age pensions and trust to an improvement of the Poor Law. Another is to decide upon and apply a scheme of Old Age Pensions. The third course is to make an experiment, which of necessity cannot possess the advantages of a complete scheme"—(*Sir Robert Reid*).—Question put, That these words be there added.—The Committee divided:

Ayes, 5.	Noes, 7.
Sir Alexander Hargreaves Brown.	Mr. Channing.
Mr. John Hutton.	Mr. Flower.
Mr. Pemberton.	Mr. Goulding.
Colonel Pilkington.	Mr. Lloyd-George.
Sir Robert Reid.	Mr. Remnant.
	Mr. Shackleton.
	Mr. Shawe-Cox.

Question put, That paragraph 6 stand part of the Report.—The Committee divided:

Ayes, 6.	Noes, 6.
Sir Alexander Hargreaves Brown.	Mr. Channing.
Mr. John Hutton.	Mr. Flower.
Mr. Pemberton.	Mr. Goulding.
Colonel Pilkington.	Mr. Lloyd-George.
Sir Robert Reid.	Mr. Remnant.
Mr. Skewes-Cox.	Mr. Shackleton.

Whereupon the Chairman declared himself with the Ayes.

Amendment proposed, to insert the following new paragraph in the Report:—"There is some danger that those who are in a position to save money may be discouraged from saving by the reflection that the more they have the less they will receive in the form of a pension. It may be advisable to intrust those who have the distribution of pensions with a discretion as to amount, so that the pension awarded may not be so reduced as to deprive applicants of the fruits of their own thrift. In no case, however, ought any pension to be granted where it is not really needed"—(*Sir Robert Reid*).—Question, That the proposed new paragraph be inserted in the Report,—put, and agreed to.

Another Amendment proposed, to insert the following new paragraph in the Report:—"Your Committee are of opinion that all the materials available, apart from actual experiment, for the purpose of enabling Parliament to arrive at a decision upon the subject of Old Age Pensions have been exhausted in the numerous inquiries that have already taken place. Nevertheless, it must be admitted that there is still much uncertainty upon several points. For example, the number of those in workhouses over a given age who could be properly attended to outside a workhouse, the number of those not now receiving poor law relief who require and deserve pensions, the possibility of obtaining reliable information in crowded communities if an applicant's antecedents are to be inquired into, the degree to which a pension scheme would transfer the cost of maintaining the aged poor from the rates to the taxes, and the sums needed for the various schemes propounded, are all matters of considerable doubt. Certainty upon these and other features of importance cannot be attained without actual experiment"—(*Sir Robert Reid*).—Question, That the proposed new paragraph be inserted in the Report,—put, and agreed to.

Another Amendment proposed, to insert the following new paragraph in the Report:—"Your Committee are of opinion that the reduction on Poor Law Expenditure will be considerably less than has often been represented, inasmuch as the proportion of the aged poor who are now, or may in future be, in the workhouses, who could with advantage to themselves live outside with the help of a pension, will probably be found to be very small. Many inmates who would thus be compelled, from infirmity or lack of friends or homes outside, to remain in the workhouse, suffer great hardship from being compulsorily associated with other inmates who are imbecile or otherwise undesirable. Your Committee strongly recommend that the welfare and happiness of this class of indoor paupers should be provided for by the extension of the system of Cottage Homes"—(*Mr. Channing*).—Question, That the proposed new paragraph be inserted in the Report,—put, and agreed to.

Another Amendment proposed, to insert the following new paragraph in the Report:—"Your Committee further think that the annual sums to be granted as Old Age Pensions should be differentiated in proportion to the incomes of applicants, but that no applicant shall (save as hereinbefore proposed) receive a pension which will raise his or her total income above the limit of ten shillings"—(*Mr. Goulding*).—Question, That the proposed new paragraph be inserted in the Report,—put, and negatived.

Question, That this Report, as amended, be the Special Report of the Committee to the House,—put, and agreed to.

Ordered, to Report the Bill, without Amendment, to the House, together with Minutes of Evidence and Appendix.

EXPENSES OF WITNESSES.

NAME of WITNESS.	Profession or Condition.	From whence Summoned.	Number of Days absent from Home under Orders of Committee.
James Clement Gray -	General Secretary to the Co-operative Union.	Manchester - -	[illegible]

MINUTES OF EVIDENCE.

Miss Edith Sellers .

Wednesday, 8th *July* 1903.

The Hon. William Pember Reeves . . . .

Monday, 13th *July* 1903.

Sir Edward Hamilton, K.C.B. . . . .

Wednesday, 15th *July* 1903.

Mr. W. C. Steadman . . . .

Mr. William Crooks (a Member of the House) . . . . .

Monday, 20th *July* 1903.

Mr. James Clement Gray . . . .

The Hon. Alfred Dobson . . . .

Wednesday, 22nd *July* 1903

Miss Edith Sellers . . . .

Mr. S. Drake Fuller . . . . . .

MINUTES OF EVIDENCE.

Monday, 6th July 1903.

MEMBERS PRESENT:

Mr. Ernest Flower.
Mr. Goulding.
Mr. John Hutton.
Mr. Lloyd-George.
Mr. Grant Lawson.

Colonel Pilkington.
Sir Robert Reid.
Mr. Remnant.
Mr. Skewes-Cox.

MR. GRANT LAWSON IN THE CHAIR.

MISS EDITH SELLERS; Examined.

Chairman.

1. You have made a considerable study of the subject of the treatment of their aged poor by various foreign countries, have you not?—Yes.

2. And also of the practice in England in the workhouses?—Yes, I have visited many workhouses.

3. You gave evidence before the Cottage Homes Committee in 1899, I remember. Since that time I believe that you have been in Denmark studying the question?—Yes. I spent the winter there in 1899.

4. And conversed with people who are receiving relief?—Yes, I did. I spoke with at least 100 of them, and probably more.

5. As well as to the officials who were administering it?—Yes.

6. I think that you have a short statement that you will kindly read to us on the subject of the Danish old age provision?—Yes. If I give you information for which you do not care, which is not really pertinent, will you kindly tell me, please? In Copenhagen the control of the administration of old age relief, as well as of pauper relief, hospitals, and public charities, is vested in the 3rd Section Burgomaster, who is responsible for the right doing of the work of his department to the Municipal Council, as the representative of the ratepayers, and to the City President, as the representative of the State. He is the official caretaker of the poor of all degrees, not only of the paupers, but of those who would rather die than become paupers. For poor relief purposes the city is divided into twelve districts, and each district is under the care of a District Superintendent, who is responsible to his Group Inspector, and through him to the Burgomaster, for the administration of the relief. A District Superintendent is always specially trained for his work, and devotes to it the whole of his time. He and his assistant officials are in close touch with the poor of the district; they go about among them in much the same way as the Charity Organisation officials go about among the poor in London, investigating the causes of poverty, as well as relieving distress. A District Superintendent has nothing whatever to do with old-age relief: it is only pauper relief that he distributes. His work, therefore, lies, for the most part, among the thriftless and the worthless; and when he comes across any of the respectable poor in need, he places them under the care of his Group Inspector, the official whose special duty it is to look after them. Infinite trouble is taken in Copenhagen to discriminate even among the destitute, and to relieve the distress of the deserving poor without subjecting them to the humiliation of being interfered with by the ordinary poor law officials. The twelve poor law districts are arranged in three groups, each one of which contains four districts. Just as a district is under the care of a Superintendent, a group is under the care of an Inspector, who is directly responsible to the Burgomaster for the poor law administration of the four districts. He watches over the Superintendents, sees that they do their work properly, and revises their reports and accounts. At the same time he is the chief of the special bureau that administers the old-age relief law in the four districts. It is to him that all claims for this form of relief must be addressed; it is he who examines them, who reports on them to the Burgomaster, and who decides practically whether they are or are not admissible. The three Group Inspectors are the special guardians of all the respectable aged poor

Chairman—continued.

poor in the city, just as the twelve District Superintendents are the guardians of the paupers, and on them falls the work of sorting the applicants for relief, of deciding which of them belong to the deserving section of the community, and which to the pauper class. Difficult work it certainly is, but Herr Wilson, one of the Inspectors to whom I applied for information on the subject, maintains that it is work that can be done, and that must be done if the poor are to be dealt with justly. As a point of fact, it is being done with fairly satisfactory results. He does not, however, underrate the difficulties that lie in the way of doing it; these are great, he admits, even in Copenhagen, and would be still greater, of course, in London. None the less he scoffs at the idea of their being insuperable. Criminals are already classified practically everywhere, and what the police can do poor law officials can do too, he maintains, if they choose to take the trouble. When an applicant for old-age relief presents himself at the Inspector's office, he is given a list of the questions which he must answer, and he is made to realise the importance of answering them correctly—to realise that inaccuracy in this case is a crime punishable with imprisonment. I have brought with me a list of the questions.

7. Those will be very valuable; I was going to ask for them?—Unfortunately, they are in Danish. I had not time to have them translated, because I had such very short notice. (*The paper was handed in; see Appendix.*)

8. Could you oblige the Committee by giving us a translation of them?—Practically, I give it here. Each question is simply a question relating to one clause of the law. It is, "Have you committed this offence?" The questions refer to certain things prohibited by the law.

9. Then perhaps you will continue your statement?—The object of these questions is to discover whether the applicant does, or does not, fulfil the conditions under which old-age relief is granted. One question relates to each condition. To be eligible for this form of relief he must have completed his sixtieth year, be a Danish subject, and be unable to provide himself, or those immediately dependent on him, with the necessaries of life. He must also not have undergone sentence for any dishonourable transaction, and not have squandered his means, either by extravagant living or by making undue provision for his children or others. He must have resided in Denmark during the 10 years preceding his application for relief, and he must not during that period have been found guilty of vagrancy or begging, or be known to have led a life of a kind to cause public scandal. He must not be a drunkard or an immoral man. That last clause, by which it is expressly forbidden to grant old-age relief to drunkards, was added to the law last year, because, in some few country districts, there was a tendency among the local authorities to regard drunkenness as too venial an offence to act as a bar to the receiving of this relief. When the first application for relief is made, either the Inspector or his representative questions the applicant closely, with a view to finding out what his past life has been, and, as soon as the official question form has been duly filled in and signed, the Inspector sets his Investigation Officer to work, to test the truth of the various statements which it contains. This officer visits the applicant in his own home; visits, too, if it seems good to him, his friends, relatives, and former employers, and obtains all possible information with regard to him. As he acts in concert with the police on the one hand and the Poor Law authorities on the other, he generally succeeds in arriving, sooner or later, at the truth. He then makes a report to the Inspector, who, after studying it carefully, has an interview with the applicant. If the Inspector then considers that the man has not established his claim to rank as a pensioner, he passes him over to the Poor Law authorities; but if he thinks that he has, he brings his case before the Old Age Relief Committee, of which the Burgomaster himself is the chairman. This Committee decides whether the relief shall or shall not be granted; still, as they act, as a rule, on the advice of the Inspector, the responsibility for the decision rests on him. It is he, practically, who classifies the whole of the aged poor in his group. As soon as an applicant's claim for relief has been granted, the question arises as to what form the relief shall assume. It must be sufficient, the law enacts, "for the support of the person relieved, and of his family, and for their treatment in case of sickness; but it may be given in money or in kind, or consist in free admission to a suitable asylum or other establishment intended for the purpose." In no circumstances, however, may this "asylum" be one where paupers are admitted. If an applicant be too feeble to live alone, and have no relatives with whom he could live, he is generally admitted to an old-age home, where the chance, at least, is given to him of passing his days in peace and comfort. These old-age homes are reserved exclusively for the aged deserving poor, and are delightful places. The cost per head in them, it may be noted, is considerably lower than in the worst of our workhouses, yet the cost of living in Copenhagen is almost the same as in London. The rule is that if a man is strong enough to take care of himself or has anyone to take care of him, he shall not be admitted to an old-age home, but shall receive a pension. In Copenhagen the average pension is about 7*l.* 10*s.* a year for one person, and 9*l.* 10*s.* for a man and his wife, and in country districts it is 3*l.* 11*s.* 10*d.* for one person, and 5*l.* 4*s.* 4*d.* for a family. I am not quite sure as to those figures. Only a few months ago the Copenhagen authorities raised their pensions a little. These figures are approximate, but I am not sure that they are quite correct. Last year an important alteration was made in the Old-age Relief Law owing to a misunderstanding that has arisen in certain country districts as to the meaning to be attached to the words "without the means of providing himself with the necessaries of life." When the law first came into force there were Communal Authorities who maintained that a man, to be eligible for old-age relief, must be destitute: and in one case, at any rate, an [illegible]

Chairman—continued.

and was actually told that he must go home and spend what savings he had before help could be given to him. The Home Office, however, the supreme authority in all that relates to the law, speedily put a stop to this state of things by decreeing that this was not what the law meant, whatever it might say. Still, in its original form the law certainly offered no inducement to save; for, if a man had saved, in most country districts it was the custom for the authorities, in fixing the amount of the pension which he was to receive, to deduct from the pension that he would otherwise have received the income derived from his savings. I do not know whether I have made that quite clear?

10. Perfectly?—Even in Copenhagen and other towns one-half of the income derived from his savings was deducted. By the law in its amended form, however, it is specially enacted that "in deciding the extent of the requirements of a candidate for old-age relief, any income or house accommodation which he may possess, derived from private sources, up to the value of 3l. 11s. 1d. a year, shall be left out of consideration. The Communal Authorities are, moreover, empowered, should circumstances recommend it, to leave out of consideration any income which the candidate may have from an annuity, a legacy, a pension, or any dwelling accommodation which he may possess, provided their value, in addition to the support which he may obtain from private sources, does not exceed 3l. 11s. 1d. a year." The most serious defect in the Danish old-age relief law—its offering no inducement to save—is partially removed by the new clause, and it will be removed entirely if the law be amended as Etatsraad Jacobi, the Third Section Burgomaster, now proposes to amend it. The law, as it stands, enacts that, to be eligible for old-age relief, a man must be without the means of providing himself with the necessities of life, but it leaves to the local authorities the duty of deciding what are the necessaries of life, and what means a man must have in order to procure them. Etatsraad Jacobi proposes that this shall be changed, that a certain standard shall be fixed, and that all whose means fall below this standard shall be regarded as being without the means of providing themselves with necessaries. He fixes the standard for a single person at 20l. a year, or property worth 222l.; and for a married couple, at an income of 28l. 13s. 4d. a year, or property worth 288l. This is the standard for Copenhagen: in small towns and country districts it would be lower. Then the law in its present form leaves the local authorities free to decide the amount of relief which they grant, decreeing only that it must be sufficient for the support of the person relieved. This, too, must be changed, Herr Jacobi insists. In his Bill he proposes that the pensions henceforth granted shall be fixed in amount and on a sliding scale. Should it become law, a pensioner, if a single person, would receive, when between 60 and 65 years of age, 7l. 6s. 8d. a year; between 65 and 70, 8l. 13s. 4d. a year; between 70 and 75, he would receive 10l. a year; between 75 and 80 he would receive 12l. 6s. 8d. a year.

Mr. *Lloyd-George.*

11. Is this for town or country?—This is for Copenhagen. It is to be rather lower for the country districts. Above 80 the figure is 16l. 11s. 4d. The pension of a man with a wife would always be 40 per cent. higher than that of a single person of the same age. These pensions are to be granted independently of any savings which the recipients may have made providing that the pension itself, together with the income derived from the savings, do not amount to more than 22l. 16s. 0d. a year for a single person. The pensioner's right to free treatment in case of illness, and to admission to an old-age home when too feeble to live alone, is left intact. Special interest is attached to Herr Jacobi's project owing to the fact that, as he is the chief administrator of the law, he knows, of course, exactly wherein the strength of the measure lies and wherein lies its weakness. I have brought a paper containing the form he wishes the law to assume, and also his reasons for the changes he recommends; but this, too, is in Danish.

Chairman.

12. I think the Committee follow his proposal, and I think the Committee must seriously consider it from the view of finance. The proposal, I gather, is a sliding scale?—Yes. He probably is the first expert in all Europe on the question, because he is the only man who has practically worked the law from the beginning. He devotes the whole of his time practically to working it.

Colonel *Pilkington.*

13. There are one or two things that struck me, with regard to which we might require an exact translation of the list of conditions and an exact translation of the list of questions. Are the conditions and the questions separate?—Yes, but the questions bear on the conditions in every case.

Chairman.

14. Each question is really a condition; they have to be answered in the affirmative or the negative, to comply with the condition of the law?—That is so practically. At the same time, there are certain additional questions with regard to where the applicants were born, and their ages, and also the amount of earnings received in the course of their lives at various stages.

15. In the course of their lives?—Yes, at various times what wages they have earned.

16. Is that a list of questions?—Yes.

Sir *Robert Reid.*

17. The inquiry as to wages bears on the question of whether they have been thrifty or not? —That is the reason for giving the questions.

Chairman.

18. If you will put it in in Danish, we will get it translated. (*The document was handed in; see Appendix.*) Now, you were telling us about what the Third Section Burgomaster suggested as a future improvement?—I have a note with regard to the financial part of the scheme which I should like to read. The figures it contains were given to me by Herr Marcus Rubin, who was at that time the head of the National

Chairman—continued.

Statistical Bureau in Copenhagen. He is now the Inspector-General of Customs. Unfortunately they relate only to the working of the law up to the year 1897. When I was there the other returns were not published. You can now obtain statistics for three years later, and I should have obtained them if I had had time; but I had no time to communicate with the Danish authorities. These statistics, as far as they go, are very striking, and they are worked out by a man of considerable weight and experience in the matter, only, unfortunately, they are three years behindhand, as I have said.

Colonel *Pilkington*.

19. Could we get them up to date?—Yes, you could, I suppose. I should have tried to get them up to date if I had had more time. In 1892, the first year in which the law was in force, the expenditure on old-age relief (on the administration of the relief, as well as on the relief itself) amounted to 142,108*l*.; in 1894 they amounted to 180,522*l*., and in 1897 to 233,747*l*. These sums must not, however, be regarded as representing the actual cost of old-age relief, namely, the actual burden imposed on the nation by the law of 1891; for, law or no law, the aged poor must be maintained, and a large part of the money that is now spent on old-age relief would have been spent on poor relief had the old-age relief law never passed. Of this we have proof in the fact that, no sooner was the old-age relief law in force in Denmark, than the expenditure on pauper relief decreased considerably. In 1890 this expenditure amounted to 457,142*l*. By 1894, three years after the introduction of the old-age relief system, it had fallen to 398,577*l*., and by 1896 to 376,187*l*. In 1897 it amounted to 384,108*l*.—that is to say, it was less by 73,034*l*. than in 1890. But meanwhile the population of Denmark had increased rapidly. The cost of pauper relief must, therefore, also have increased rapidly had the old-age relief law not been in force. Herr Rubin calculates that, had the cost of pauper relief increased during the years from 1890 to 1897 in the same ratio to the population as it actually did increase during the years from 1880 to 1890, it would have amounted in 1897, not to 384,108*l*., but, at least, to 495,220*l*. Thus the direct result of the granting of old-age relief is that a saving of some 111,311*l*. a year in the cost of pauper relief has been effected. But the full cost of old-age relief, as we have seen is, or rather was, in the year 1897, 233,747*l*. a year. The actual cost of it to the nation, therefore, was only 122,436*l*. a year, and towards this sum the State contributed 116,873*l*., that is half the full cost of the relief. So far as the local ratepayers were concerned, therefore, the cost of relief was only 5,563*l*. a year. Herr Rubin, indeed, is of opinion that at the present time old-age relief entails no burden whatsoever on the country communes, as the outlay on this form of relief is entirely covered, in some cases more than covered, by the money received as the State grant, together with the savings effected in pauper relief. What little burden there is falls entirely on the towns. It is interesting to note that the cost of old-age relief and pauper relief together, per head of the population, was in 1897 lower by 4*s*. 1*d*. in Copenhagen than is the cost of pauper relief alone in London. In 1897 there were in all Denmark 38,048 persons in the receipt of old-age relief, and they had dependent on them 13,240 more—wives as a rule. Thus the 233,747*l*. spent on the relief in that year was spent on securing the comfort in their latter days of no fewer than 51,288 persons, respectable old folk, old folk of the very kind that deserve to be helped; and, as we have seen, the sum really paid is not 233,747*l*., but only 122,436*l*. Whatever else it may have done, the working of this Danish experiment has certainly proved that an old-age relief system can be devised that entails no overwhelming expenditure on the country adopting it. I do not know whether you would care to know where the money comes from.

20. Yes; I was going to ask about that very point?—When the law first came into force there was a limit placed upon the money that was to be granted by the Government. What was to be paid by the Communes was not limited, but the other was limited. That limit was repealed by the law of the 1st July last year, and now the Government undertakes to pay one-half whatever the expenditure may be.

Mr. *Steuart-Cox*.

21. Part is paid by the State and part by the locality?—One half falls on the Communal or Municipal Authorities, and the other half falls on the State. The money that the State pays comes from the tax on beer. I do not know what would happen if the beer tax were not enough, but so far I think it always has been enough.

22. Is the beer tax allocated to old-age pensions?—Yes. It was the raising of the beer tax that led to introducing old-age pensions. When it was first proposed to raise the tax there was a dispute. It was maintained that the tax fell entirely on the poor; and that, therefore, the money it yielded should be given back to the poor. The Government agreed, and the pensions were introduced.

Mr. *Remnant*.

23. Does the whole tax on beer go to that?—I am not sure. I think there was a tax on beer, and an addition was made to it.

24. You do not know what the additional tax was?—No, I do not know the amount.

Chairman.

25. At any rate, it produces enough to pay the State contribution to old-age pensions?—Yes. The other half comes from the local rates, but it is specially enacted that it may not come from the poor fund. In Denmark there is no poor rate; there is what they call the "poor fund." The part of the money for the old-age pensions that falls on the Communes must not come from the poor fund. There is no rate levied exclusively for poor relief in Denmark. It is only when the money obtained from other sources proves insufficient that recourse is had to the rates.

26. What are the other sources?—Every town or Commune has a poor fund, the money for which is derived from whatever sources the local authorities fix upon, supplemented by grants out of the rates. In Copenhagen the poor fund consists

Chairman—continued.

consists of the yield of a tax on theatrical representations, which is 5 per cent. of the gross receipts of the company if it be Danish, 10 per cent. if it be foreign; a tax of ½ per cent. on the value of all property sold in the city, certain fees imposed by the City Courts, and Old Endowments; these are for Copenhagen alone. In the Communes it is a local tax on land. This tax on land they obtain the right to levy by surrendering the claim to certain grants out of the Royal Purse. Then there are certain fines, registration fees for forming companies and dissolving partnerships, and a ½ per cent. on the yield of public auctions. The money that goes to defray the cost of old-age relief is simply taken from the ordinary Communal taxes.

27. *From what would be called the rates in England?*—Yes, the rates. There is one more thing that I should like to say. I felt that the most important point with regard to the working of the law was its effect on thrift. It has been so very often stated that it was detrimental to thrift. The statement is very difficult to test, and one reason why I went to Denmark was to try to test it. There I found that the people who had most right to speak with authority on the subject maintain that the law has not acted in a way detrimental to thrift. Herr Rubin, the head of the Bureau of Statistics, and Professor Westergaard, Professor of Political Economy at the Copenhagen University, both maintained that the working classes are not one whit less thrifty now than before the law was passed. Herr Sörensen, the Inspector-General of the Sick Relief Funds, holds that they are more thrifty: "Never so eager to insure against sickness as now." He declares that they insure against everything now excepting old age; but, as the statistics that come to England relate, as a rule, to insurance against old age, they make it appear as if there had been a great decrease in all forms of insurance, whereas all the insurance companies have had an increase of work in other respects.

28. *Was there much insurance against old age before in Denmark?*—No, but certain companies used to grant annuities. It was purely private, I think.

29. *It was not a favoured form of thrift any more than in England?*—No, I do not think it was from the statistics one comes across. Herr Jacobi was in England only a few weeks ago, and I asked him then what the effect was now, and he said that the working classes are becoming more and more anxious to do without poor relief during the critical years between 50 and 60. There is one more thing. Of course, I felt very strongly when I was there that, as a stranger and a foreigner, I really could not trust my own judgment. I had formed my own judgment, and it was very favourable, but I thought it better to apply to the Danes themselves. Therefore, I asked various representative Danes to tell me what they thought of the working of the law. Herr Rubin was the first one. My question to him was: "Has the law worked for or against the common weal; is it doing good in the land or is it doing evil?" and his reply was: "The law has certainly brought about a very notable change for the better in the condition of the respectable poor. It is not so much that they are now materially richer than they were before the law was passed (although richer they undoubtedly are), as that they are more at ease in their minds, more contented with their lot, and this because they are no longer haunted by the fear of becoming paupers." Herr Jacobi, the head of the department, replied: "So far as the general comfort of the respectable poor is concerned, the law certainly works for weal, not for woe. Under the new system the worn-out worker class are undoubtedly better off than they were under the old." Then Herr Krieger, who is at the head of the Division of the Home Office that supervises the working of the law, said: "The law has done much good, and, so far, at least, very little harm." Herr Wilkens, the Inspector, and really the worker of the law, declared: "The law is decidedly popular among the poor themselves, and that, I think, is a strong point in its favour. No one who knows our people can doubt that they are, in many ways, more comfortable now than they were before the law was passed. The fact that they need never become paupers makes all the difference in the world to the more respectable among them." Professor Westergaard replied, "The law has undoubtedly brought about a change for the better; still, this change is by no means so great as it ought to be, or, at least, as I had hoped it would be." The Social Democrats' view of the case is that the law gives too little and asks far too much. Still, it is a measure to be thankful for, they admit. Colonel Richards, who is the head of the Salvation Army there, told me that nowhere in all Europe is there so much done as in Copenhagen to make the old folk happy. Could England have but some such law as this old-age relief law, what a difference it would make to the poor, he remarked. Herr Wilkens also remarked, in answer to a question as to whether the poor themselves made much difference between the two kinds of relief: "The respectable poor are keenly alive to the distinction our law now makes between them and ordinary paupers, and they are grateful that this distinction should be made. Many who would rather die than accept pauper relief, accept old-age relief gladly." In answer to the question, whether the people are content with the relief they receive or not, he told me that he gave out the relief papers for one-third of Copenhagen, and he made a rule of marking with a plus sign every case where the recipients expressed themselves contented, with a minus sign if they expressed themselves discontented, that he made no mark at all if they went away in silence. He found by referring to the papers that for every one where there was a minus sign there were at least 100, or more than 100, with a plus sign. There were some cases, but not many, where the people went away, and made no remark. He was surprised at the number of plus signs, because the amount the people receive is by no means large, but still there was no doubt that the overwhelming majority of them were content with what they received. That was my experience, too, when I talked with them.

30. *I am very much obliged to you for the account which you have given. There are one or two points I am not quite clear upon. The*

question

question whether an applicant complies with the conditions of the law comes before the Third Section Burgomaster, I understand?—At the end, when all the investigations have been made.

31. It first comes before an Inspector?—Yes; I believe in theory that all applications for relief must be addressed to the Third Section Burgomaster. In practice the Inspector represents the Burgomaster.

32. But neither the Burgomaster nor the Inspector are popularly elected, I suppose?—No, they are not.

33. They are State officials?—They are municipal officials. The Burgomaster is elected by the municipal authorities, and is confirmed by the King, but he holds office for life; they practically cannot dismiss him; at least, if they do dismiss him, they have to continue paying his salary until he dies, so they do not dismiss him at all.

34. He is indirectly elected in the first instance, not directly?—Yes, indirectly.

35. But has he power to say: "You shall be in this specially privileged class," or "You shall not;" is there any appeal?—Yes, to the Home Secretary, technically. There is a little Court of Representatives appointed. Appeals are very rarely made.

36. You mentioned an Old-Age Relief Committee: what are their functions?—It is a Committee formed of the distributors of relief, the Inspectors, the Burgomaster, a representative of the State, and two or three other officials, who, when each Inspector brings before them the cases, sift the evidence and decide. It is purely formal, they explained to me. Really, the man who decides, so long as things go smoothly and it is granted, is the Inspector.

37. But none of the Committee are persons popularly elected?—Not in Copenhagen. In the Communes the law is worked differently, as there the entire work that is done in Copenhagen by Inspectors is done by the Communal authorities.

38. The Communal authorities being popularly elected?—Elected by the people.

39. That takes place outside of Copenhagen?—Yes.

40. You mentioned that drunkenness under the new law would disqualify?—Yes.

41. Drunkenness how long before the application for the relief?—They really test a man by the last 10 years of his life. If he had been in the habit of drinking 11 years before, I do not think that would count. The words that they use in the new law are that he must not have lived a life to cause public scandal.

42. Within 10 years, or at any time?—Within 10 years. The law does not say so, but they certainly would not go back further than 10 years in judging him.

43. Do not the questions about his income go back more than 10 years?—Yes, certainly; the whole of his life is taken into account then.

44. Do you know how the applicants support the evidence that they have had a certain income? Are they required to call former employers, or anything of the sort?—No; they answer these questions themselves. Of course, it is a crime to answer incorrectly. The Investigation Officer does the rest. He goes and tests the answers. If he finds that one false statement has been made in the paper, the man cannot receive the pension. He loses all chance of the pension, and that in itself is a security that the applicants will speak the truth.

45. Then there must have been no vagrancy or begging. Do you mean a conviction for vagrancy or begging, or do you mean that there must have been no begging from anybody?—If it is known that they have been begging.

46. Do you mean if they have asked a neighbour for help?—No, it would not be so strict. You see, in interpreting the law, there is a good deal of latitude left. There are these delicate questions, but if a man has begged, and so on, had seen him beg, very well. It would practically mean having been convicted of begging.

47. As to the Communal authorities being the judges, do they in the country parts of Denmark leave the whole question of deciding who is to have poor relief and who is to have old-age relief to the popularly elected guardians, or whatever they are called?—Yes, but in that case the final appeal is not to the Home Secretary, but to the Amtmann, very much the same as our Lord Lieutenant. He is the supreme authority to whom they appeal.

48. They appeal to him to be put on the list, but is there any appeal to take them off the list? Supposing the ratepayers objected to a certain man as being on the list who ought not to be on, would there be an appeal to this State official on that subject?—Do you mean a pensioner as to whom they appeal.

49. Yes?—The law practically decides when he must come off. If he commits any of the offences that would have prevented his claiming the pension, he forfeits his pension at once. One of the clauses of the law is that you hold the pension only as long as you lead the same life after as you did before; and, further, if after you have received a pension, you marry and you require more relief owing to being married, then you forfeit your relief. You can get married as long as you do not ask for an increase of your relief, but if it leads to an application for increase in your relief you forfeit it and become a pauper.

50. The Communal Authorities, if they give the common ordinary out-door poor relief in Denmark, have to pay it out of their own local rates, I understand?—That is paid, in a very great measure, out of the poor fund.

51. But out of a fund locally raised in the Commune?—Yes, and that is the dangerous part of the law. It is a distinct inducement to local authorities to grant old-age relief rather than pauper relief, because they pay for the whole of the poor relief, and only pay one-half of the old-age relief.

Mr. Newnes.

52. I suppose that the pensions apply only to Danish subjects?—Only to Danish subjects.

Chairman.

53. Do you know anything about the qualification for naturalisation in Denmark?—No, I do not.

54. You do not mean Danish born?—Danish born or naturalised. You must be a Danish subject.

Chairman—continued.

subject; that is the test. Foreign women who have married Danish subjects can obtain relief too.

Mr. *Goulding.*

55. Has neither the Burgomaster nor the Inspector anything to do with the Poor Law?—Yes, the Burgomaster is the head of the Poor Law Department, but it is not only the Poor Law Department, it is the Old-age Department, the Hospital Department, and the Public Charity Department.

56. I understood you to say that it was a different individual from the Inspector who decided whether the applicant should come under Poor Law Relief or Old-age Pension Relief?—Yes, it is.

57. What is the difference?—You see, the Burgomaster is the head of the whole department. In Copenhagen the control of the administration of old-age relief, as well as of pauper relief, hospitals, and public charities, is vested in the Third Section Burgomaster, who is responsible for the right doing of the work of his department to the Municipal Council as the representative of the ratepayers, and to the City President as the representative of the City. He is the Head and Director of the whole.

58. The Inspector passes them on, I understand, with regard to Old-age Pensions, and she passes them on to the lower category of the Poor Law?—The Inspector. The Inspector really decides the point. The Inspector makes up his report. He is not only the Inspector for his own division, but he is also a member of the Old-age Relief Committee which decides it. If anyone wishes for old-age relief he applies to him for that relief; he collects the evidence and sees the man, and talks to him and finds out his circumstances. When he has made up his mind whether the relief ought to be granted or not, he places the case before the Pension Committee. But that, I gather, is rather a formal business. Supposing it is refused, the man himself is summoned before the Committee, and can appeal to them if he thinks that the report is unjust.

59. Does do applicants for an old-age pension feel any slur cast upon them because the same official decides as regards an old-age pension as decides as regards the Poor Law relief?—But I beg your pardon; it is not the same official. If you apply for pauper relief you go to the District Superintendent.

60. The Inspector only deals with the old-age pensions?—Yes.

61. And if he does not pass the applicants on they can go to the other officer?—Yes.

62. What is the name of the other officer?—One is the Inspector and the other is the District Superintendent, and that is a great point among the Danes. I hardly ever talked to them but that they impressed on me the fact that they were not only not paupers, but that they had nothing to do with paupers, and one old woman said to me: "We need never see a pauper now unless we choose."

63. The distinction is that there are two officials, one an Inspector and the other a District Superintendent under the Poor Law organisation, to deal with the two matters?—Yes, and they have separate offices—not in the same building; old-age pensioners and paupers are

Mr. *Goulding*—continued.

not brought into contact at all, and there is a very, very great distinction in the mind of the populace with regard to the two forms of relief: in fact, the old-age pensioners have the same thorough scorn and contempt for the paupers, I found.

Mr. *John Hutton.*

64. Have you any reason to think that the danger you spoke of just now about the Municipal or Communal Authorities handing over their paupers to the old-age pension fund is really a very substantial one? Is there much corruption of that kind?—Not much perhaps, but some, and that is really a reason for the alteration in the law. Some of the Communal Authorities did not behave particularly well about the matter. First of all, they were much too lax in some cases in their interpretation of the law. They undoubtedly gave the pensions in some cases to men who ought not to have had pensions, and then, in giving relief, they fixed it too low. Herr Krieger, who is at the head of the Home Office Department, which is the supreme authority for the Communes, is very strong on that point. He said that the law would have to be amended to bring the Communal Authorities to a sense of their duties in this respect.

65. Have you formed any opinion as to the usefulness or the unworthiness of local unpaid officials as compared with officials appointed by the State or by the Burgomaster, as in Copenhagen?—With regard to the working of this Act in Copenhagen there is no doubt about it that there is no such well-administered town in the world as Copenhagen, and the whole is in the hands of paid officials. They told me that in Copenhagen they had tried the other form, and found it too costly. They were obliged to alter it. They had a poor law precisely the same as our own up to 1888, and they had Poor Law Guardians, but they found the cost of the administration so very great when in the hands of amateurs, that they abolished it so far as Copenhagen is concerned, and appointed paid officials.

66. Then you mentioned that in the country districts, as well as in Copenhagen, there is the alternative scheme of Cottage Homes, or homes of some kind (old-age homes), to which these people have the choice of going?—It is not quite the choice of going. A great many of them are very anxious to go. If they are alone in the world they have the right to go to such places, and certainly there is nothing that makes the law so popular as the fact of having these places to go to as a refuge, so that whatever comes there is no fear of their ever being forced to go to the workhouse.

67. In the country districts are they small homes, or of considerable size?—Quite small as a rule. In one district there were three, hardly towns, but villages adjoining, and one of them I found had built an old-age home, a delightful place, another had built an ordinary workhouse, where it put the moderately good paupers, and the third village had built the Svenner Arbeits Hans, which is really a prison for paupers. The three villages shared in the expense, and they divided their paupers into three classes. All the

the first-class paupers—the pensioners—went to the Old-Age Home, the moderately good went to the ordinary workhouse, and those whom it was felt ought really to be in prison were sent to the Zwangs Arbeits Haus.

68. You do not mean that all the pensioners go to the home?—No, only those who have nowhere else to go. Those who choose to have the pensions have their pensions. No one can be forced to go into an Old-Age Home; it is quite voluntary.

69. With regard to those who went into the Old-Age Home, I suppose that the cost of that home was paid for by the Municipal Authority—that they were not paid a pension, and then allowed to keep themselves?—If you go into an Old-Age Home you resign your pension entirely and live in the home.

70. Must they necessarily be very infirm?—Oh dear no. Some of them were not at all infirm. If you are alone in the world, if you have no one to take care of you, you are allowed to go in. They are given 4d. a week pocket money, which adds to their happiness very much. The cost of living in Copenhagen is as high as in England, and yet, owing to the keeping down of official expenses, which are very often not more than 1-20th of the whole expense, the cost is marvellously small. It is only 11d. a day per head in a great many cases, and yet the people are surrounded with comforts of all kinds, and are really just as happy and comfortable as anyone could wish them to be.

Mr. Lloyd-George.

71. I could not follow all the conditions when you were reading. Is there any condition attached with regard to the capacity of the applicant for doing any work?—No.

72. None at all?—No condition at all is attached. Supposing you can work, you receive a smaller amount as the law stands at present, but with the alteration of the law that will be done away with. It is most important, because you will have the legal right to claim the pension corresponding to your years.

73. Irrespective of your capacity for working?—Quite irrespective, except that, if you are quite disabled you are reckoned as five years older than you really are.

74. That is important. Take the case of a man between 65 and 70 years of age really not able to do sufficient work to maintain himself, but able to potter about and earn a few shillings, would that incapacitate in Denmark now from receiving his old-age pension?—No, the only thing is that he would get a smaller pension.

75. But under the new law his pension would not be smaller?—No. It is not passed yet, but if it passes he will receive the amount corresponding to his age.

76. And if he likes to do odd jobs and earn a few shillings in addition to that he can?—Certainly.

77. Now who appoints the group inspectors? Are they Government officials or Communal officials?—The group inspectors are in Copenhagen alone; they are not in the Communes. There the Burgomaster, if it is a small town, or the ordinary communal Authorities, work the whole thing, because there is not much difficulty there in getting information.

78. Who appoints the inspectors in Copenhagen?—They are appointed by the Burgomaster.

79. Is the Burgomaster a State official or an official of the Municipality.—He is a municipal official. He is first of all elected by the Municipality; then his election is confirmed by the King, and from the day it is confirmed he cannot be dismissed without the consent of the King.

80. Is he always appointed on the nomination of the Municipality?—Yes.

81. As a matter of practice, is his appointment never vetoed?—It has been, but not in recent days. It used to be vetoed, and can be vetoed now.

82. But taking the practice there?—It is not so in the present days, certainly.

83. He is a municipal official really, then?—Yes.

84. For life?—Yes; unless they dismiss him, when they must still pay him his salary, which they must pay whether he is there or not; and they never do dismiss him, as a matter of fact.

85. His dismissal must be by the Commune and by the State?—No, the Municipality alone may dismiss him; but the State says: "If you do it without our consent, then you must pay his salary."

86. I think you said that the fund for old-age pensions was half contributed by the Municipality or the Communes and half by the State?—Yes.

87. Is the maximum amount of the old-age pension fixed by statute, or could a Commune increase the amount in any particular case at its own expense?—The accounts have to be revised by the Home Office, and, therefore, if the Commune chose to be extravagant, and the accounts were very large, the Home Office could come in and say, "No." They have the power of checking them, but it has never been used; in fact, the Home Office complain that they do not [illegible] enough.

88. Am I to understand that in Copenhagen the grant is fixed at 9l. 10s.?—No; I gave that simply as an average.

89. It is not a statutory maximum?—It is not statutory. The only thing is that the Burgomaster himself has practically made it so. The law has not fixed a limit at all.

90. It is the Burgomaster who fixes it, and not the Municipality?—The Municipality does not fix it at all. The matter is in the hands of the Commission, and the Committee, with the Burgomaster, fix the amount. The law only says that it has to be sufficient for the support of the man, and it does not say what it shall be.

91. The pension given in individual cases is not identical?—No, it is not.

92. More is given to one individual than to another?—Certainly. In point of fact, in Copenhagen very small difference is made. It is worked as a department, and the Burgomaster and all the officials have agreed on a certain standard; but in the country districts it varies enormously, from 1l. a year up to 10l.

93. In the same Commune?—In the same Commune, according to the circumstances of the case.

H 2

Mr. Lloyd-George—continued.

94. Is it not the idea contained in most Bills introduced here, of a fixed amount—say 5s.?—No.

95. Is it entirely in the discretion of the Committee?—Yes, it is; and Herr Jacobi maintains very strongly that it has a bad effect, and that is why he wishes to have the sliding scale introduced.

96. Will that act automatically?—Yes; it makes no great difference in a town like Copenhagen, but in the small Communes it is not safe to leave it in the hands of the local authorities to fix the amount which shall be given.

Chairman.

97. In the small Communes which you are speaking of do the same authorities administer both Poor Law relief and old-age relief?—Yes, they do. As a rule, they are kept apart, one officer taking one branch and another officer taking the other, but in very small places it is the same official. In Copenhagen and in the other towns they are kept rigidly apart, and I must say that even in the Communes the local authorities take a great deal of trouble to keep the reliefs apart. Supposing, for instance, it is the same man who is administering the relief, he will take care not to receive the applicants for old-age pensions in the same room as that in which he would receive the applicants for pauper relief.

Mr. Lloyd-George.

98. In the new law is there any disposition to curtail the number of inquiries, and to make the inquisition less severe?—No; it is rather otherwise.

99. Is the tendency to make it more searching?—Yes; the last clause of the new law in the paper which I have handed in—the clause with regard to drunkenness and leading a moral life—has been adopted from Herr Jacobi's law. The whole law has not been adopted. The tendency certainly is to raise the standard.

100. To increase the number of questions put?—I do not know about that, but certainly to raise the standard. There are additional questions.

101. With regard to the amount, the disposition is to make it a fixed amount?—Yes. Herr Jacobi says that there will always be a certain amount of injustice until that is done.

Chairman.

102. Has the Inspectors in Copenhagen other duties to perform?—The 12 Poor Law Districts are arranged in three groups, each one of which contains four districts. Just as a district is under the care of a Superintendent, a group is under the care of an Inspector, who is directly responsible to the Burgomaster for the Poor Law administration of the four districts.

103. The point is, rather: Is he an official with other duties?—He watches over the Superintendents. He sees that they do their work properly, and he revises their reports and accounts. He is the chief of the Special Bureau that administers the old-age relief law. His own office is for the administration of the old-age relief law, but at the same time he has the right to go into the other offices if he chooses.

Mr. Goulding.

104. He is a superior Poor Law officer?—Yes. His office is a new creation of the old-age relief law.

Chairman.

105. Could you tell us out of what fund the Inspector's salary is paid? Is it paid out of the Poor Law Fund?—No, none of those officers are so paid. The Inspector who showed me the working of the system told me that they are paid out of the ordinary rates.

106. With regard to the workhouse which you were mentioning in the villages, and which you said was really a prison, is it a system common to the whole of Denmark—that there are some workhouses which are prisons for refractory paupers?—At the time when the law was introduced for old-age pensions the Poor Law was reformed, and then it was enacted that every village, or every Commune rather, must have either a Zwangs Arbeits Haus or some portion of a building used as a Zwangs Arbeits Haus. As a rule, three or four Communes will join in building one.

107. Are tramps confined in these?—Yes, tramps and all those who go to the workhouse and behave badly; practically all the able-bodied who may be sent there. With regard to all the workhouses in Denmark, if you are once sent there you have to stay there until the authorities choose to let you come out. You cannot take your discharge without their consent, and they will not, as a rule, let you come out until you have earned enough money to start life again with, which is a most useful regulation.

Mr. Remnant.

108. Is the information obtained made public in any way?—No.

109. Can nobody get at it?—Nobody can get at it, and I must say that the people themselves have no fear with regard to that happening. I was present once or twice when the investigation was going on. The old people simply came in and sat down in the office, and seemed to have a little friendly chat with the Inspector, and there was nothing at all that implied any interference with them. They do not know much of the inquiries that are carried on in the background.

Chairman.

110. Are very rigid inquiries carried on in the background?—The investigation officer makes very rigid inquiries, and can, if necessary, appeal to the police to help him, and, in fact, frequently does.

Mr. Remnant.

111. Are the police consulted at all before pensions are granted?—Always, or, rather, as a rule, they are consulted. There may be cases where they are not; but it would be almost impossible in a place like Copenhagen to work the law without the help of the police with regard to classification. Only the other day I had strong proof of the possibility of working it even in London. I had a letter from a man in one of the London workhouses who had chanced to come across an article of mine in the "Nineteenth Century"—the very article which you have

Mr. Remnant—continued.

have there. He was quite convinced that his was one of the cases which ought not to be in the workhouse, and therefore he wrote to me to ask me to help him to come out; or, rather, to supply him with the clothes and money to enable him to come out. I referred his letter at once to the Charity Organisation Society. I knew nothing about the man, and the Charity Organisation Society knew nothing about the man. Within a week I was supplied by the society with full information as to the man's past life, even to the fact that upon more than one occasion he had been found drunk in the streets. If that could be done in this one case it could be done in other cases as well. All the officials in Copenhagen were very strong in insisting upon the fact that it can be done. Of course, it is troublesome work, and it requires a great deal of patience, but it can be done.

Chairman.

112. As regards Vienna, I do not think the Committee would wish you to go through the evidence that you gave before the Cottage Homes Committee, which we have all read, I have no doubt? But there were one or two points which you did not go into before that Committee. For instance, you said that there were usually more than four times the number of persons who wished to live in the cottage home or the institution than can be accommodated there; but nobody asked you how the authority in charge of the institution selected these favoured persons. Can you tell us how the one out of four who require this advantage is selected?—The selection lies in the hands of the Poor Law Department there. That department consists of all the officials for the city, together with the Poor Law Guardians. The city is divided into 19 Poor Law sections, and each has its own Board of Guardians. Supposing you wish to go into one of these homes, you apply to one of the Poor Law Guardians of your own district. He investigates the case, and finds out if you are suitable or not: then he takes the matter before the Poor Law Department of which he is a member, and they do what further sifting is considered necessary, and they place those whom they consider suitable on the list. You have to wait your turn. In some cases it is broken through. I am afraid that there are cases in Vienna where favouritism undoubtedly comes in.

113. Are the Poor Law Guardians popularly elected?—Yes. The orphans' fathers and mothers, as they are called, are not; they are nominated by the Burgomaster. In addition to the ordinary Poor Law Guardians, there are these subordinate officials who make inquiries and who take care of the children.

114. The Board before whom the question comes as to whether or not the privilege shall be granted to a certain person is composed partly of officials and partly of elected persons?—Yes. The first application is made to a popularly elected Poor Law officer in the district in which you live. He must report on your case, and he sifts the evidence as to whether you are quite suitable, and reports it to the Poor Law Department.

Chairman—continued.

115. Are the popularly elected persons in the majority of the Committee before whom the matter comes?—Yes, decidedly, but at the same time they do not possess the influence of the officials. The Burgomaster himself, for instance, has a great deal of power, especially at the present time.

116. The applicants must all be natives of Vienna, must they not?—No, they must have a right of settlement there.

117. So that their life and history would be fairly well known by the inhabitants of Vienna?—Yes. It would be sifted. When I was there in 1895 only one-third of the population of Vienna belonged to Vienna. The old law of settlement was still in force. About four years ago the law of settlement was altered, and now, by residence of two years, you can obtain a settlement. Recently they have decided to build a very large new almshouse, because the poor who can claim admission have increased so much.

118. I gather that the law has been altered since you gave evidence before?—The law of settlement has been altered completely.

119. So that now there may be people claiming to come into these houses who have only been in Vienna for two years?—Two, or it may be three, years, I am not sure, but it does not require more than three years' residence to obtain the right of settlement.

120. That has not been going on long enough for anybody to know whether the inquiry in such cases would be successful?—No. They have not been able yet to enlarge the houses, and very few cases have come up.

121. You have also examined this question in France, have you not, to some extent?—I have. With regard to France, a decision was arrived at the other day which has a great bearing on the Bill now before the Committee. In 1897 a law was passed for the same purpose as that which is before this Committee. It was decided that, if any of the Communal Authorities chose to give persons above 70 allowances varying between 200 francs a year and 90 francs a year, the State would come in with a contribution. The highest contribution was to be 60 francs a year. If the Communal Authorities would grant old-age pensions of 200 francs a year to these people, for each old-age pension that was granted the State would make a grant also of 60 francs a year, and half a million was set aside by the Government as money for doing this.

122. Half a million francs?—The Government was going to give up to 60 francs for each; but at the end of three years, instead of the half million being claimed by the Communes, only 95,000 had been claimed. The consequence was that last week, as you probably saw, it was decided by the French Parliament that the only thing to do was to build homes, because it was no good relying on Communes granting suitable allowances, and they have now passed a law insisting that a certain number of new Hospices, as they call them, shall be erected.

123. The persons in France who decide as to who is to be given relief are the Communal Council?—

Chairman—continued.

Councils?—In the country it is the Communal Councils; in Paris itself it is the officials.

124. The officials solely?—The officials solely. In Paris, practically, the working of the Poor Law is in the hands of officials.

125. In country districts, although some of the Communal Councils are elected, the majority are in the hands of the Prefect?—Yes, although the popular election element comes in there.

126. Did the State, in the law of 1897, lay down any qualifications for a pension?—No; excepting that the person should be above 70, and in need of help.

127. In other words, if his neighbours thought he was worthy of a pension, the State would help?—Yes, but it practically did not act. The cases were so few as to be of no importance at all. You have a right in Paris to claim 10 francs a month when you are 70.

128. Ten francs a month if you are 70?—You have a right to claim relief, and it may be 10 or it may be 30 francs a month. Very often an official permit to beg is also given.

129. That is peculiar to Paris itself?—Yes. As a matter of law, I believe you have the right to claim admission to the old-age homes, but so many people wish to go to these homes, and there are so many people in the homes, that while there are so few homes, that while you are waiting you are granted a small pension. Now the Government is taking up the question, and has decided that many more homes must be built, evidently regarding that, for the time being, as the solution.

Mr. John Hutton.

130. The homes are not ordinary workhouses, but they are a reward to the deserving poor?—They are homes for the old people, but there is no idea there of discriminating between the good and bad.

Mr. Kennaway.

131. I suppose the same officials who have to deal with the old-age pensions also have to deal with Poor Law relief?—In Paris?

132. Yes?—They may call them old-age pensions, or anything else but it is really pauper relief.

Chairman.] I am afraid we shall have to ask you to be kind enough to come again on the subject of the London workhouses and the country workhouses, which you have been over.

Wednesday, 8th July 1903.

MEMBERS PRESENT:

Mr. Ernest Flower.	Sir Robert Reid.
Mr. Goulding.	Mr. Remnant.
Mr. John Hutton.	Mr. Shackleton.
Mr. Grant Lawson.	Mr. Shown-Cox.
Mr. Pemberton.	

MR. GRANT LAWSON IN THE CHAIR.

The Honourable WILLIAM PEMBER REEVES; Examined.

Chairman.

133. You are the Agent-General for New Zealand, are you not?—Yes.

134. And, I suppose, in that position you have the opportunity of meeting with a good many New Zealanders, and of hearing their views on the operation of the laws of New Zealand?—Yes.

135. Have you been in New Zealand yourself since the Old Age Pension Act has been in force?—No.

136. You have, I suppose, conversed with a good many people on the subject?—Yes; but more than that, I have studied it very closely indeed, I think I may claim. I have taken a great deal of interest in it, and have written about it, and, in order to do that, have watched it as closely as I could from the outset.

137. I think that we need not go further back with regard to New Zealand than the year 1896, when, I think, a Bill was proposed which, if carried, would have given pensions to all persons over 65 whatever their income?—I think I may say without disrespect now that it was a somewhat crude Bill, and while it hardly went so far as that, it certainly was very loose indeed as regards any restriction with regard to income, and would have had almost that effect.

138. That Bill was not successful?—No. An amendment was carried in favour of universal pensions, and the Government dropped the Bill.

139. An amendment was carried in favour of universal pensions?—Yes; that is to say, to all persons irrespective of any amount of property or income that they might own. The Government Bill, although it was somewhat loose, certainly did not contemplate giving pensions to everybody, or to nearly everybody, but an amendment was carried in favour of a universal pension scheme. The idea, I think, was a scheme somewhat similar to that which Mr. Charles Booth advocates in this country, under which everyone would have a pension. The Government dropped the Bill. They would not go on with the thing at all.

140. In 1897 was that Bill introduced again?—It was modified. A Bill was introduced more carefully drawn. That was carried through the Lower House after considerable opposition, but was either rejected altogether or else wrecked by amendments in the Upper House, and it was not until 1898, the following year, that anything was really done.

Mr. John Hutton.

141. Was the 1897 Bill a Government Bill?—Yes. The 1897 Bill was Mr. Seddon's Bill, the Government Bill.

Chairman.

142. In 1898 the Old Age Pension Act was carried?—Yes. I have it here.

143. I think we may get the effect of it most shortly by question and answer. The principal conditions are that the recipients must be 65 years of age, and must have resided continuously in the Colony for 25 years, with certain concessions with regard to residence in favour of seamen and others that they must not possess an income in excess of 52*l.* a year, nor property exceeding 270*l.* in value; and there are other qualifications affecting good citizenship. Is that a correct short account of the Bill?—Yes, roughly. But a citizen may have been absent from the Colony for four years out of his 25, and as regards the 270*l.* worth of property, you must remember that they do not begin to reckon property until you pass 50*l.* Any man is allowed to have 50*l.* worth of property without its being brought into account—that is, 50*l.* worth of property over and above, of course, the amount of his debts and obligations. Then for every 15*l.* above that he begins to lose his pension. A deduction of 1*l.* a year is made from the amount of pension which he may claim, so that when eighteen amounts of 15*l.* apiece have been passed he has no right to any pension, the maximum pension being 18*l.* a year.

144. I must mention that I am merely taking a summary from this book, which I daresay you know, called "The Seven Colonies of Australasia"?—Yes, Mr. Coghlan's book.

145. With regard to the qualifications affecting good citizenship, would you tell us what those are?—There are a number affecting. First of all, what may be called the absolutely criminal class. Any serious crime committed within 25 years of getting to 65, a crime of what I may call the first magnitude, bars a man from the right to apply for a pension. A certain number of minor offences, if committed at any time within 12 years, bars him also.

Mr. Remnant.

146. Are all these under the Act of 1898?—They are all under the Act of 1898. Less serious offences committed within 12 years before applying for pension will disqualify a man, and, in addition to that, wife desertion disqualifies a man, and habitual drunkenness or flagrant immorality.

Chairman.

147. Wife desertion or husband desertion?—Yes; a woman, having the right to a pension like a man, is disqualified if she has deserted her husband and family.

148. For six months?—Yes, I think it is for six months.

149. It is the same in New Zealand as in Victoria, then?—Yes.

150. Desertion for six months within how long of claiming the pension?—It is probably 12 years. "The claimant has not at any time for a period of six months or upwards, if a husband, deserted his wife, or without just cause failed to provide her with adequate means of maintenance, or neglected to maintain such of his children as were under the age of 14 years; or, if a wife, deserted her husband or such of her children as were under that age." There does not appear to be any stipulation as to the time.

Mr. John Hutton.

151. Is not that governed by the general section?—I do not think so, because the stipulations with regard to 12 years and 25 are specially stated in the sub-clauses.

Chairman.

152. So that you think, as I think from what I have read, that wife desertion or husband desertion at any time in the life of the applicant would disqualify?—Yes, it appears to disqualify. Then, if I might explain what I said before with regard to immorality, Sub-section 5 of Section 8 of the original Act says amongst the conditions that the pensioner has to fulfil "of good moral character," and it goes on, "and is, and has for five years immediately preceding such date, been leading a sober and reputable life." That is a very generally worded clause, and I think, in practice, it amounts to this—that a man must not be a notorious drunkard or a thoroughly bad lot to the knowledge of the police.

153. Have you a law against habitual drunkards in New Zealand like we have in England?—We have an Inebriates Act dealing with the proposed establishment of Inebriates' Homes, and they are in theory dealt with under that; but in practice, at any rate, there is no law that deals with habitual drunkenness. Our laws as regards the offence of drunkenness are severe—more severe than in this country.

154. Is there any provision disqualifying a man because he has received Poor Law relief within any time?—No, quite the reverse. A number of the pensioners are people who have received Poor Law relief or who are receiving it. They may do one of two things: they may either take their pensions and cease to have anything to do with what are called Charitable Aid Societies, or, in the case of old people, they can live in the old people's refuges, but the authorities take the pension money. It is paid over to what you would call the Guardians in this country or the Charitable Aid Boards in New Zealand.

155. Are the Charitable Aid Boards elected by popular election?—No, they are elected by the local authorities—the different local bodies of a district.

156. Indirect election?—Yes, indirect or secondary election.

157. Do they dispense public funds—rates, for instance?—Yes, they do. It is about half and half, half of the money being derived from local rates supplemented by a pound for pound grant from the Government, the central authority.

158. These being the conditions, who is the judge as to whether an applicant complies with them?—The applicant, of course, makes his application to one of the Old-age Pension officers. There is a registrar in the capital, and there are Deputy Registrars, Government officers, in different towns in the Colony, and either to the Registrar or to one of his deputies the application has to be made. The application is sent on to a Local Magistrate, and the applicant has to appear before this Local Magistrate.

159. In open court?—Yes, in open court.

160. Are the Registrar's officials appointed by the Government or by the locality?—By the Government.

161. The Magistrates you are speaking of are the Stipendiary Magistrates, are they not?—Yes, the Resident or Stipendiary Magistrates.

Mr. John Hutton.

162. What is the difference between a Resident and a Stipendiary?—It is merely that once they were called Resident Magistrates, and then an Act, quite unnecessarily, I think, altered the name to Stipendiary Magistrates, and then again, I think, a more recent Act has called them by their old title.

163. They are all paid Magistrates?—They are all paid Magistrates.

Chairman.

164. That is what I wanted to bring out. They are not like Justices of the Peace, but more like Stipendiary Magistrates in this country?—They are paid Magistrates in the service

Chairman—continued.

vice of the Government, and I might add that, under one of the amending Acts, it is specially forbidden that Justices of the Peace shall hear these applications for pensions. They are not allowed to do it.

165. On account, do you suppose, of local influence?—Yes, local feeling and the idea that they would be too lax—too good-natured.

166. When the applicant appears before the Police Magistrate what sort of proof is required of him that he is a man of good moral character?—It depends a little bit on the individual magistrate, but they generally get the testimony of some respectable and fairly well-known person, for instance, clergyman, or some well-known employer of labour for whom they have worked. One or two persons of good character in the neighbourhood can give them a certificate.

167. Are those persons liable to cross-examination by the Registrar or his Deputy?—Under the original Act there is no doubt that that part of the law was not as strong as it might have been, and, under the amending Act of last year, the latest amending Act, a great deal of pains has been taken to give the Registrar proper authority with regard to cross-examining applicants and witnesses, and he can appoint anybody to represent him in Court who can do that. That is under Clauses 2 and 3; in fact, the greater part of the amending Act of 1901 has for its object to give the Registrar, or his officers, greater power to deal with these applications.

168. We have got the conditions and how the conditions are proved. Now if a man gets through this examination and gets a certificate from the magistrate that he complies with the conditions, has he, as of right, a pension?—Yes, as of right.

169. But the amount of that pension is variable according to what means he has been proved to have of his own?—Yes.

170. If he is absolutely destitute the State gives him 18*l.* a year?—18*l.*, or if his income from any source whatever is less than 34*l.* a year, he is still entitled to his full 18*l.*, the object being that the highest income to be made up is 52*l.* a year, or 1*l.* a week—34*l.*, plus 18*l.* Therefore for every 1*l.* over 34*l.* that he has of income he loses 1*l.* of pension. If his income is 52*l.* a year, 1*l.* a week, or anything above that, he is not entitled to any pension at all.

171. Do the magistrates go into the question of whether he has divested himself of property for the purpose of qualification?—There is a special clause in this amending Act of last year giving the Registrar power to go into that, and not only that, but into the whole question of his income, his property, or any steps which he may have taken to divest himself of property, and for that purpose the Registrar and his officers have power to ask questions, not only of applicants, but of bankers and officers of the Post Office Savings Bank, and so forth, in order to discover what the true means of the applicant are or have been.

172. That is the general effect of the Act of 1898 as amended at present, but I should like to ask you how soon after the passing of the Act was an amending Act brought in? Was it the very next year?—The next year but one. The Act was passed in 1898, and an amending Act was passed in the year 1900.

173. Are there just those two Acts on the subject, or more?—There is this more important Act of 1901.

174. What were the main provisions of the amending Act of 1900?—I have a summary of them in my book, if I might just refer to that.

175. It is on page 250?—It was passed, in the first place, to make the Act permanent instead of only for three years. The original Act had been for three years only. Then, of course, there was the clause dealing with the case of where a husband and a wife are pensioners. A clause was passed enacting that in no case should the joint income of the husband and the wife be made up by pensions to a higher sum than 78*l.* a year. Then there were clauses relaxing the conditions with regard to absence from the Colony during the 25 years. Up to that point a pension applicant had only been allowed to be away for two years from New Zealand out of 25, and the term was extended to four years. Then the restrictions as regards naturalised aliens were slackened, so that an alien who had been naturalised might get a pension almost directly after he had been naturalised instead of waiting for five years.

176. But only if he had resided for 25 years in the Colony?—Yes. He could not get it without. If it had been otherwise we might have had all the Australian old people coming over to get pensions. Then there was a clause forbidding a Charitable Aid Board—that is to say, a Board of Guardians, as it would be called here—to refuse to admit a pensioner to an Old Age Refuge. The Charitable Aid Boards are obliged to admit a pensioner if he wishes to be treated as a pauper, although he is a pensioner, but they take charge of the pension. There are, I think, now something over 500 pensioners living in the Government Refuges of the Colony whose pensions are paid to the Boards.

177. It was under that amending Act of 1900 that the case arose, which you mentioned in your book, of a person being prosecuted for unfairly obtaining a pension by divesting himself of property?—Yes.

178. He was fined, and the certificate was taken away?—Yes. Since the Act of last year they have been stiffening things up. They have been making use of the Act of last year, and the result, of course, has been rather marked in the effect which it has had on the increase in the number of pensions, and on the increased cost of the Act. The second amending Act (the third Act on the subject), which was passed in November, 1901, is almost entirely taken up with strengthening the powers of the Registrar and the Court in going into this question of the *bona fides* of applicants; into, for instance, the question of the amount of property or income a man may really have, or may have had, and any steps that he may have taken to divest himself of property. The whole object of this amending Act was to put a stop to fraud. There are

Chairman—continued.

one or two minor parts of the Act dealing with Maoris.

179. It came into force last November?—Yes, it was passed in November, 1901: "On the hearing of any application for a pension or renewal certificate, if the Magistrate finds that any real or personal property has been transferred by the applicant to any person he may inquire into such transfer, and refuse the application or grant a reduced pension." Then, again, if at any time after getting the pension the pensioner becomes possessed of property that is to be inquired into carefully. Then again, if a pensioner dies, and the probate or the proceedings for administration disclose that the pensioner has had more property than was supposed, that may be gone into, and the property may be seized and the amount of the pension taken from it; and, in fact, I think that double the amount of the pension may be seized and enforced.

180. Was that Act vigorously opposed in the House?—No. The truth is that in the previous year, 1900, the year of the first amending Act, some suspicions were already getting about that there was a certain amount of fraud. Several members, in debate that year, indicated cases that they had heard of of imposture. The Prime Minister, however, seemed unwilling to have any considerable amendments made in the year 1900, but in the year 1901 he had awakened to the position, and he proceeded to deal with it. He appointed a Committee to sit and examine into this question of imposture, and, before the Committee had sat very long, he proceeded to anticipate any Report which they might make by introducing promptly an Act which would deal with imposture; in fact, such an Act as the Committee might have recommended, and he made a speech, part of which I have quoted in my book, in which he frankly admitted that he believed that there was a certain amount of imposture, that he did not mean to stand it, that he meant to have the thing put down, and that he did not mean to have the Act brought into discredit.

181. Can you tell us about the number of pensioners and the cost of the Act?—The cost of administering the Act is not large. Taking the question of administration for a moment, which is the minor question, the actual cost of administration last year was about 2,333*l*. The officers are almost entirely persons who are already in Government employ, and who do the old-age pensions work in addition to other duties. The Registrar gets a small special fee, and then there is a certain amount for clerical expenses and legal and travelling expenses.

182. Perhaps you would tell us what other duties the Registrar has. Is he a Poor Law officer?—No.

183. My point is, have these Registrars or Deputy Registrars anything to do with the ordinary poor law?—No, the ordinary poor law in New Zealand is administered by the locally-elected Boards.

184. When you say "elected," you mean indirectly?—Indirectly. They are elected by the local bodies.

185. Now as to the number of pensioners, what do you say?—The Act came into force in November, 1898. The financial year in New Zealand ends on the 31st March. The result was that the first year, of course, was merely a piece of a year. The Government brought the Act into force at once, and there was a very considerable rush of applicants, so that, by the 31st March, 1899, five months after the Act was passed, 7,487 pensions had been granted, and the number of pensions in force was 7,443. I suppose it will be sufficient if you take the number of pensions in force at the end of each financial year.

186. You mean deducting those that have dropped?—Yes.

187. That will be sufficient, I think?—The number of pensions in force in March, 1900, at the end of the first complete year, was 11,285, a number which, it is only right to say, was considerably in excess of what had been expected when the Act was passed, and which gave rise to some anxiety. A year later, March, 1901, the number of pensions in force was 12,405. So that in two years and a quarter the pensions were 12,405, and it was then that a good many predictions were made that the Act would be extremely expensive and burdensome. However, in March, 1902, the number had only risen to 12,776, and in March of this year, 1903, it had dropped slightly, and the number was 12,557. That is 219 fewer than at the end of the previous year.

188. Might it not have something to do with the peculiar conditions of New Zealand—the men who first came on the pension list being old pioneers, whose health was undermined, and who died very soon after they were 65?—I do not think so. The number of aged, in proportion to the rest of the population, has been growing steadily, and rather rapidly. No doubt, the last few years have been exceedingly prosperous in New Zealand, and that I daresay has affected the number of pensioners; but I am inclined to think that it is the stiffer administration, and the use of the amending Act of last year.

189. Would the prosperous years have the effect that people would be able to acquire sufficient property to take them out of the right to their pension, and so losing their pension?—Yes, in some cases; but I have formed the opinion that the stopping of the increase is due to a somewhat stiffer administration of the Act.

190. As a matter of fact, is the pension withdrawn if the pensioner has acquired property since he got his pension?—Yes. Not only has he to apply for his pension when he first gets it, but he has to come up every year, and apply again, and he has to say that he has not got the property or income which would put him out of the Act. Once a year he has to run the gauntlet.

191. And the gauntlet as to his moral character, too?—I think that would be with the police or Registrar to suggest any objection to that, if he had once passed.

192. It

Chairman—continued.

192. It would be as well if you now told the Committee what the population is from which these pensioners are drawn. I understand that Maoris may participate, but that naturalised Asiatics may not?—That is so; no Chinese, whether naturalised or not, can have a pension.

193. Can you tell us what would be the numbers of the population out of which the pensioners are drawn?—The population in New Zealand, I suppose, to-day, excluding the Asiatics, would be, within a few hundreds one way or the other, 860,000. It might be a thousand or so over.

194. I see that the white population are put at 815,000?—That is deducting Maoris, half-castes, and Chinese.

Mr. Remnant.

195. The Maoris are included in the 860,000?—Yes; they are entitled to a pension.

Chairman.

196. Have you any means of telling us how many of those are over 65 years of age?—I cannot tell you the figure for to-day, but, according to the Census two years and a quarter ago, there were about 31,000 people over 65. The population then was 40,000 or 50,000 smaller than it is now.

197. In addition to the pensioners who are receiving aid from public funds, can you tell us how many over 65 are in receipt of the ordinary poor relief?—I could not tell you the number. I can tell you about the amount that is spent on charitable aid in the Colony. When this Act came into force it was about 90,000*l*. This Act reduced it by 10,000*l*. or 15,000*l*.

198. You are not able to state what proportion of persons over 65 are in receipt of aid from the State, either as pension or poor relief, are you?—No, I am not.

199. I see that you state in your work, on page 205, that more than one-third of the aged are almost altogether without means at 65?—They are.

200. That would apply to both pensions and poor relief?—Yes. You see, there are 12,500 pensioners, and I added to that, of course, a certain number, although not a very large number, of persons who are not pensioners, but are old people getting public or private relief, and I said that they would amount to more than one-third of the aged of the Colony (31,500), as they certainly would. If you take 12,500 old-age pensioners and 500 or 700 old people who are getting charitable aid, that is about 13,000 old people who are getting help, and that is more than one-third of 31,500, considerably.

Sir Robert Reid.

201. The 12,500 receiving pensions are not necessarily persons in a destitute condition. They may have 30*l*. a year apiece?—They may.

202. Therefore, I suppose, really you take some of the pensioners and the whole of those in receipt of charitable relief to make up your figure?—Yes. I should say that a considerable majority of the old-age pensioners would be nearly destitute—that is to say, people who had so little that you would call them in our country almost destitute.

Chairman.

203. You said that there was relief in the ordinary poor charges; is that considerable?—It is considerable from one point of view, and quite trifling from another. The proportion of reduction in the amount spent on charitable aid is considerable, because the amount was about 90,000*l*., and the reduction has varied from 10,000*l*. to 15,000*l*. Since this Act came in, it has pulled it down by 10,000*l*. or 15,000*l*. in different years. Of course, that is a considerable proportion of 90,000*l*., but then, on the other hand, a reduction of 10,000*l*. or 15,000*l*. brought about by an Act under which 210,000*l*. is spent, is small. That brings me to the point of the cost of the Act which I was just coming to. I gave you the number of pensions in force at the end of the different years. The cost of the Act went up, by March, 1902, to 207,000*l*., but this year, as you know, there has been a slight reduction of the number, although the cost, oddly enough, is 3,000*l*. more. It is something over 210,000*l*. for the financial year ending with March of this year. That is explained by the fact that there was some money spent this year which ought to have been spent last year, I believe. There was some overlapping. I think they have stopped the increase for the present; they think so.

204. The increase is much higher than the estimate, is it not?—The original estimate certainly was distinctly below what the Act cost, say, two years, or two years and a half after it had passed. There is no doubt that the cost of the Act at the end of 1901 was more or less of a revelation to people who had fancied that it would be about 120,000*l*. It had run up to about 200,000*l*. at the end of the second or third year. They thought it would cost something like 120,000*l*. That had been talked about. It turned out to be about 200,000*l*. The increase in the last two years has been slight. It is about 210,000*l*. They can claim that.

205. Under the law of New Zealand the relatives are compelled to provide for the poor, are they not?—Yes, when able to do so.

206. Relatives in the direct line?—Yes.

207. Is there a general opinion in New Zealand that relief is largely given to these relatives rather than the money being given to the Parliamentary Grant for Charitable Aid?—Yes. I can only give you my own opinion. My own opinion is that one of the effects of the Act has been to take off a considerable part of the 200,000*l*. a year from the shoulders of the near relatives of the aged poor.

208. Cases have been known in the Courts, have they not, of applications to be relieved from the burden of the relief of parents?—It is rather the other way, I think. Cases have been known where it has been pleaded, in defence against an application, that a son, say, should continue to support his parents, that the parent is now an old-age pensioner. I think that one or two cases of that sort have been known, and the magistrates have dealt with them in different ways. In one or two cases that I have noticed they have not exempted the children altogether, but they have

Chairman—continued.

have reduced the amount per week that they have had to pay. They have taken it into consideration.

209. The intention of this legislation was clearly expressed to be to discriminate between the deserving and the undeserving?—Yes.

210. How far do you consider that has been carried out?—I think, in a rough way, it has been carried out fairly well. It was undoubtedly the most difficult task, of course, that the framers of the Act set themselves to perform. There is no doubt there is some imposture under this Act, and that some people who are not deserving do get pensions; but, on the whole, in a rough sort of way, I think the pensioners are a very decent lot of people. As a class my own opinion emphatically is that they are a decent class.

211. I gather from your article on the subject that there is no great amount of intense poverty in New Zealand?—No, as compared with other countries there is not. There is poverty, but if you were to travel through New Zealand you would come away with the impression that there is no poverty. There is, of course, if you go behind the scenes and look for it, but there is not the horrible poverty that shocks one in old and populous countries.

212. I suppose that the condition of people who have lived for 20 years in New Zealand is fairly well known to the magistrates and the registrars and so on?—Yes, undoubtedly. I should say that it is one of the hopes of the Act, and one of our best aids, that we have no great masses of population. The largest town in New Zealand, with its suburbs, has about 70,000 people: the other three large towns vary from that to 63,000 people, and people are fairly well known to their neighbours therefore.

213. With regard to the finance of the scheme, do I understand that the whole of the money is taken from the revenue of the Colony and none from local rates?—Yes, that is so.

214. But the outdoor relief under the Charitable Aid Boards is drawn from local sources, is it not?—It is about half and half.

215. I should like to ask about the total revenue of New Zealand. Your total revenue is, roughly, five and a half millions, is it not?—It is now rather more than six and a half.

216. By far the greatest proportion of that is drawn from Customs duties and from the railways and post offices, is it not?—The Customs, railways, and what are called stamp revenues.

217. Would they make up between them about five-sixths. I am taking my figures from the "Statesman's Year Book," which represents that in 18[illegible] the revenue was five and a half millions:—from Customs, over two millions; from Post Office, stamps and railways nearly three millions; and only half a million from direct taxation. Is that a fair representation? —Yes, the proportion would be about the same. The Customs revenue now is about 2,300,000*l*.

218. There was a big balance in the year 1898 when the Bill was passed, was there not?—Yes, but not much bigger than this year. This year the surplus is 300,000*l*., or a little over.

219. You are in the fortunate position of having a balance in your exchequer?—Yes. They have been doing very well for some seven or eight years now. No doubt that has helped the Act too.

220. You say that all the Treasurer has to do is to impound part of his surplus for old-age pensions, instead of transferring it to public works?—Yes. What I mean is that if it had not been for old-age pensions, the surplus would have been considerably larger than it is unless they had reduced taxation, and in that way he may be said to have impounded part of the surplus. It has been reduced in consequence of that, or it would have been much larger. What is done with our surplus is that it is passed over and added to loan moneys, which are expended on developing the Colony.

221. Have you formed any opinion as to the effect upon thrift in the Colony of this Act?—No, I have not. It is not a subject upon which one could very easily form an opinion. Of course, you can only go on one or two general points, such as the effect on the swelling of the amount in the Savings Banks. It certainly does not seem to have reduced thrift, judging from the growth of the Savings Banks' returns. The Statesman's Year Book, or our Year Book, will give you those, and they show up very well.

222. But the Act itself does not offer any direct or specific encouragement to thrift?—No.

Sir Robert Reid.

223. As I understand it, the people who get the pensions may do work at the same time?—Yes.

224. And they may enjoy what means they have subject to the scale of diminution as their means increase?—Yes.

225. Has it given satisfaction in the way of reducing the privations and sufferings of the old people?—I think there is no doubt about the popularity of the Act. The country has gone through two general elections since it was passed. At the last General Election I watched the elections very closely, and read some of the speeches, and there was no suggestion that I could see from any quarter that the Act should be repealed or very seriously amended: in fact, there was very little said about it. It is absolutely accepted, and I think there is no doubt that it is distinctly popular with the poor, the class for which it was intended.

226. And you think that it is really a benefit to them?—Yes, I do, indeed.

227. It puts an end to scenes of misery?—I honestly think it is a good Act in the main.

228. Is there any practical difficulty in complying with the good citizenship conditions?—Not in the least. It is, of course, a very delicate thing for me to suggest what may be the weak points of an Act of my Government, but one or two points on the weaker side of the Act have had an effect quite the reverse of what you suggest. Instead of its having been made too difficult to establish good citizenship, I think it was made at first rather too difficult to bowl out imposition, and that is why these amending Acts were required.

Sir Robert Reid—continued.

229. That is rather what I was driving at. Supposing you have a good citizenship test, each particular country must draw up for themselves what is a suitable test, having regard to the conditions of the country. But the point is whether you can work any condition safely and feel that you are not being largely imposed upon?—I do not think we are largely imposed upon. That is my honest opinion. I think there is, and has been, a certain amount of imposition. Most of it has not been in the direction of notorious blackguards getting pensions, for they are too well known, but imposition upon the question of the amount of property that people owned, or the amount of income that they had; but I think that, thanks to the amending Act of last year, that has been grappled with. I do not think there was a large amount of imposition. A few cases were proved, and we can assume that there were some more that were not discovered. That is my sincere opinion.

230. There always will be some cases?—Under every Charitable Aid system you will have some imposture.

231. The persons who decide seem to be Stipendiary Magistrates?—Yes. A point upon which there is a difference of opinion is whether the ordinary Police Magistrate has the time or the energy to go into any elaborate inquiry into the merits of applicants, and it is a question whether this sort of thing ought to be given to the ordinary magistrate, or whether you ought to have some system under which a special judge or a special magistrate, a special person, should go into these things.

232. Has that difference of opinion been agitated in New Zealand?—In the debates on the Act there were arguments for and against the Stipendiary Magistrates. I took the Act of last year to be, to a certain extent, an admission that the inquiry wanted stiffening, and I think it is being stiffened.

233. Then it comes, practically, to this—that the Act is really working well, as far as you know, in New Zealand, and that, although it requires tests of good citizenship, it confers a right upon old people who comply with the conditions to have a pension?—Yes; I certainly consider that the Act is, in the main, working well; that is my opinion.

234. You anticipate, I imagine, that unless the population increases you have already now practically the maximum of pensioners you are likely to have?—I think that they will only increase in fair proportion to the increase of the population.

235. About 1 to 64 or 65 of the population, I make it, receive these old-age pensions, at a cost of about 17*l*. apiece, on the average, per annum?—Yes; a very large majority of the applicants get full pensions.

236. 18*l*. is the full pension?—Yes.

237. I work it out that the average is 17*l*.?—It is either that, or pretty near it, I should think.

238. If it is so, we can practically ignore the property which these people have. If 17-18ths of the total is given, it shows that, practically, those who get old-age pensions have nothing at all?—No; I will not say that, because you see they are allowed to have 33*l*. a year of income.

Sir Robert Reid—continued.

239. I beg your pardon; you are quite right?—Or anything less than 65*l*. worth of property and yet get the full pension.

240. That explains what otherwise did not seem to me to be quite intelligible—how there was a very small diminution, because it really is small, in the cost of the ordinary pauper relief. It is about 15 or 20 per cent.?—15 per cent. at the outside.

241. That diminution in the cost would practically correspond, I suppose, with the diminution in the numbers?—Yes.

242. I do not know the numbers, but they cannot be very great?—The Prime Minister stated a year or two ago that certainly not more than [illegible] per cent. of the pensioners were persons who had been getting Poor Law relief, and my own estimate is that it would be about 4 per cent. of the pensioners who were persons who had been getting relief.

243. Therefore, according to your experience, the class of persons who would receive pensions would be a class superadded to those who had been in receipt of either outdoor relief or of indoor relief?—Yes; and in a country like ours, where the amount of utter destitution is small, the great mass of the pensions goes to people who were not what you would call on the rates. In a country like this, of course, things might not be quite the same.

Mr. Goulding.

244. The cost of administration, I understood you to say, was 2,500*l*. odd?—Yes.

245. How is the pension paid?—It is usually paid at the Government Post Offices. It is made as easy as possible for the pensioner to get it. He can come to a Post Office to get it.

246. But does the sum of 2,500*l*., the cost of administration, cover the necessary expenditure in identifying the applicant?—Yes, it covers everything.

247. Absolutely?—Our system is better than the New South Wales one. They pay their pensions through a bank, and they have found it distinctly expensive, and they are going to alter it in that respect.

248. In cases of the very old and infirm, how do they get their pensions?—Allowance is made for a person who is very ill, or physically unable to come for his pension.

249. Is that covered entirely by the figure which you have given to us of the cost of administration?—Yes, it is covered entirely by the 2,500*l*.

250. You have great distances there?—Yes, but you must remember that very few of the aged live in the wilderness. The old people, naturally, flock into places where they can be fairly comfortable.

251. How is the money paid, weekly, monthly, or quarterly, or what?—Once a month.

252. Is any complaint raised there, as is often raised here with regard to soldiers' pensions, about the recipients getting the money in a lump?—Yes; but I do not think there is much in it. There have been one or two cases where someone has seen an old-age pensioner drunk and has written to the papers and said: "[illegible]

Mr. *Goulding*—continued.

old-age pension money goes into the pockets of the publican"; but I do not think there is much in that.

253. I do not mean drunkenness necessarily, but extravagance, and throwing it away?—There is a provision in the Act that, where a man is notoriously a spendthrift, his pension can be paid to a sort of a guardian for him, but I cannot offer an opinion on it.

254. Complaint has not arisen?—I have not heard much of that sort, and I cannot really give you an opinion.

255. With regard to the inquiries held before these magistrates, you said just now that the last Bill stiffened the inquiries?—Yes.

256. Would you tell us in what form it did that?—It gave the Registrar power to appoint somebody to represent him before the magistrate, and ask questions, which must be answered, and it also gave power to have witnesses brought up—relatives of the applicant or officers of the savings banks—who could be asked questions, which they have to answer, as to the means of the applicants.

257. Is there any limit as to the kind of people that can be inquired of? I understood you, in your statement, to say that it was limited to bank officers, and so forth?—It says here simply that it shall be the duty of every person to make true answers to all questions concerning any applicant for a pension or renewal, and then it says that any person who refuses commits an offence, and then: "This Section shall apply to any officer of any bank or other corporation carrying on business in New Zealand"—that seems to me pretty wide—"and to any officer of the Post Office Savings Bank, and of any other Government Department which receives investments of money from the public."

258. Has there been any complaint made by applicants against this inquiry?—I do not think so. Certainly, in the debates in the House, at the time the original Act was proposed, there were predictions that the Act would be harsh and tyrannical, and that really reputable people would not care to face the inquiry, while the brazen-faced impostor would swagger through and get his money, but I do not think there is much of that.

259. That very point has been raised over and over again in debate in this House?—I was not aware of it.

260. That the inquiry into the past character and the assets and qualifications of the individual would be objected to by the applicant?—My own opinion, from watching the law, is that the applicants have no grievance worth talking about under that head.

261. I gather that practically there are 31,000 of the population over 65?—Yes.

262. And 12,667 actually draw the pension?—Yes.

263. Then besides that there are some 600 who elect to go into the homes?—No, the people who elect to go into the homes are pensioners.

264. Are they included in the 12,600?—Yes. What I suggested was that there might be a few hundreds of people who might be absolutely destitute who were not getting old-age pensions. For instance, they may come under the head of people who do not deserve them, criminals and so forth, but they yet may be absolutely destitute. I was trying to give a rough estimate of the number of destitute aged persons in the Colony.

265. I wanted to know whether the 12,600 includes those who actually draw their pension and remain outside. I understand now it includes them, and those who go in?—Yes. The number of those who go in is about 550.

266. Can you give roughly the number of what you call non-deserving over 65 who would be in the workhouses?—No, I cannot, but it would not be large, I think.

267. That or prison would be the only resort, would it not?—They might be in prison, they might be in lunatic asylums, or wandering about outside, living as best they could—drunkards and so forth.

268. But would there be very many?—No, there would only be a few hundreds.

269. Can you give at all an estimate of what it costs per head for maintenance of an inmate of a workhouse? Take anyone except a child?—I would not like to give it offhand.

270. I want to know whether the State actually loses in cash by giving a pension outside instead of maintaining the person inside?—The pension is a shilling a day, and it goes to the Charitable Aid Board, and it must cost the Charitable Aid Board at least a shilling a day to keep its paupers. They pocket the shilling a day, and, as a matter of grace and kindness, they generally give a shilling a week back to the pensioners as pocket money. That is the arrangement that is followed.

271. At home here in England the cost per head in maintenance is largely over anything like 7s. a week?—I said it would cost them at least that, and I daresay it is more.

272. Now with regard to the money coming out of the revenue, is there any fund specially ear-marked for it?—No.

273. It comes out of the Treasury?—It comes out of the Treasury.

Mr. *Sharman-Crawford*.

274. Was it always the practice to have a yearly inquiry?—Yes.

275. A re-hearing?—Yes. They have to apply for what is called a renewal certificate at the end of each year.

276. Do you see anything against a private inquiry in this matter?—They have tried that in New South Wales, and I believe I am right in saying that the administrative Pensions Board there recommend now a public inquiry. I speak, of course, subject to correction, but my impression is that the feeling there is rather against a private inquiry. They have tried it.

277. Is it looked upon as a taint of pauperism if persons take pensions in New Zealand in anything like the way in which out-door relief here is looked upon?—I do not think it is. It would scarcely be regarded as an aristocratic boast socially to be either a pensioner or to have your father and mother as pensioners, but undoubtedly it is not looked upon as a disgrace.

Mr. *Sharman-Crawford*—continued.

278. Are all the provisions inserted in your public Acts, or are there rules and regulations?—All the provisions that I have referred to are in these Acts. Of course there are rules.

Mr. *Shackleton.*

279. Could you tell us what proportion the pension would bear to the ordinary earnings of a person just previous to the age limit, say from 60 to 65?—There, of course, it entirely depends on the occupation of the pensioner.

280. Take an average occupation?—I could not give you an average. Wages vary very much. Take a high-class mechanic in New Zealand who gets 11s. a day, take a general labourer who gets 6s. or 7s., take a woman who is earning perhaps 15s. a week—all these classes contribute. Wages, of course, are higher there undoubtedly than they are here. The only cases where wages are about the same might be with regard to one or two of the highest paid artisans here. Even for domestic servants I should think the wages are 40 or 50 per cent. higher out there than they are here.

Mr. *John Hutton.*

281. You told us about these old-age refuges. Can you tell us what they are like? Are they large or small, or scattered about?—They are not what would be called large here. In some cases they are almost cottages. In some cases, I think, they subdivide the houses. They have cottages or small houses scattered about in the same grounds, but under separate roofs; in other cases they have the usual sort of large barrack-like building in which the old people live.

282. And are they chiefly infirm persons who go into these Cottage Homes?—Yes, chiefly.

283. Do you know how they are cared for? Is there an attendant to look after them?—Yes. They are not at all uncomfortable. I have been into some of them.

284. Are they more popular, in the case of old people who have no friends to look after them, than is actually receiving the money as an old-age pension?—I think that where the old people had something else to supplement the pension, they would, in most cases, care to stay out.

285. But not in the case of infirmity, and so forth?—The very fact that you have over 500 pensioners who elect to stay in these places is the answer.

286. Are the different municipalities, or communes, bound to provide these homes for the aged and infirm?—They are bound to relieve destitution, and where there is a sufficient number of old destitute people they have these places.

287. They are bound to provide them?—They do provide them; they are bound to see that people do not starve.

288. Do you see any danger in New Zealand of an agitation, for political purposes or otherwise, for reducing the age from 65 to 60, or so forth, as the age at which an applicant shall become entitled to a pension?—Not now. The first year there was a good deal of talk about a universal pension scheme, which would have widened it in the way you speak of, but the last year or two it seems to have practically died out, and they take the Act as it is.

289. You stated that the officers who look after these people are practically appointed by the State and are Government officers?—Entirely.

290. Are you aware that that is similar to the system which they have in Denmark?—I did not know that.

291. In the opinion of the Parliament of New Zealand it would not be safe to trust the local officers with the selection of these aged poor for pensions, or they think it better, at all events, that they should be selected by a Government official?—The Government, the central authority, pay the pensions, and I think the power which finds the money should administer it.

292. In the case of the poor who are not selected for an old-age pension, in what way are they treated?—As I was explaining, there is a system of poor relief in New Zealand under which 70,000*l*. or 80,000*l*. a year is spent. It divides itself into this chiefly: There are these refuges for very old and infirm people and there are the cases of destitute children who are taken in by the Government; but, otherwise, it is chiefly an outdoor system of relief for old people, or wives and families who have been deserted. To paupers of that description the greater part of the money goes—more than half, I think—in outdoor relief.

293. Is that money raised by what we call a rate?—It is about half rate and half subsidy.

294. Is a rate in New Zealand levied on the ratable value of real property, or is it extended in any way?—It depends on where you are. Under our law a local body can either tax property simply as it stands, lands, houses, and improvements, or it can levy the rate on the unimproved value of the land, or what is called here the ground value. A number of the local bodies levy their rates on the ground value, and that number is increasing. It is under a new law that this is done. It is gradually spreading.

295. You have no means of taxing the general income of persons living within the district?—No. There is only one income tax, and that is by the central Government.

296. Therefore, the charge of the poor within the local districts of course is felt very much more heavily by those districts than in the case of the aged pensioners where it comes on the State?—It is more direct, of course. Half of it comes from the rates of the district.

297. Therefore, there is naturally a great tendency to place the charges of the local district on the national exchequer as far as it possibly can be done?—The answer to that is that the local bodies have nothing to do with the allocation of the old-age pensions. They have no power in that direction at all. I have described the system as far as I can. The local bodies have nothing whatever to do with it.

298. Are there any disabilities connected with your poor law—I mean is a person who receives poor relief disfranchised, for instance?—No.

299. Then there is no difference between the aged

Mr. John Hutton—continued.

aged pensioner and the recipient of poor law relief with regard to voting?—No, I think they can all vote.

Mr. *Shackleton*.

300. I should like to ask you a question which has arisen out of a question put to you. I suppose you have certain trades, as we have here, in which persons cannot work to 65, through defective eyesight, for instance. There are certain occupations which injure the eyesight rather sooner than others, and persons are not able to work at them from, say, 60. Do those people come under the ordinary poor law, or is there some arrangement for bringing them into the old-age pension?—In our country there is not. In Victoria and New South Wales people who have been disabled in the course of their trade, even if they are under 65, can come in for an old-age pension, but that is not the case in New Zealand.

Chairman.

301. I do not know whether you have examined the Bill now before the Committee?—No, I have not.

Monday, 13th July 1903.

MEMBERS PRESENT:

Mr. Goulding.
Mr. John Hutton.
Mr. Lloyd-George.
Mr. Grant Lawson.

Mr. Pemberton.
Colonel Pilkington.
Mr. Remnant.

MR. GRANT LAWSON IN THE CHAIR.

SIR EDWARD HAMILTON, K.C.B.; Examined.

Chairman.

302. You were Chairman of a Departmental Committee appointed in 1898 to consider the financial aspects of the proposals made by the Select Committee of the House of Commons in 1899 about the aged deserving poor?—I was.

303. Have you seen the Bill that is now before this Committee?—I have looked at the Bill.

304. Have you noticed how closely it follows the proposal of the Committee of 1899?—Yes. I saw that it was almost identical.

305. With the exception of (F) (2): "Has not an income from any source of more than: In the case of a married couple 15s. a week together"?—I noticed that.

306. Generally speaking, would the scheme of 1899 be applicable, as far as finance is concerned, to this scheme before the Committee?—Yes.

307. The method that you adopted before that Committee was, I think, to calculate the total number of persons over 65 in the three kingdoms who would be living at certain dates, and then you made deductions of the numbers likely to be unable to fulfil each condition in turn?—Yes.

308. You worked it out that the total number of people who would be alive and over 65 in 1899 would be altogether 1,979,000, and 2,016,000 in 1901. You may take the figures from me. That shows an estimated increase of persons over 65 in two years of 37,000?—Yes.

309. Now the point that I want to put to you is this: you estimated that in 1901 there would be 2,016,000 persons over 65 alive; working that out at the average pension of 6s. a week, I take it that it would cost nearly 31,500,000*l*. if they all had pensions?—That is so. I worked it out myself.

310. If everybody alive in 1901 over 65 had a pension of 6s. a week or 15*l*. 12s. a year, the cost to the country would have been 31,449,600*l*.?—Yes.

311. To that would have had to be added the cost of administration, I suppose?—Yes.

312. Having shown from your figures that you estimated that there would be an increase of

Chairman—continued.

37,000 in two years of these aged people, that would bring us, in 1903, to 2,053,000 persons. At 6s. a week I worked that out as being a cost for the present year, if the scheme had been in force, of 32,026,800*l*. Do you think that would be about right?—I think so. I did not work it out for the two years extra.

313. Plus cost of administration, that would be the cost of a universal pension scheme for everybody over 65. Now as to the accuracy of your figures, I think that since your Committee sat you have had an excellent opportunity of testing one of your most important figures. You know now how many persons over 65 there are in England and Wales?—How many there were in 1901.

314. That number is, I think, from the census return of 1901—1,517,753 for England and Wales?—Yes, that is so.

315. So that you were right within 753 as to that calculation as to the number of people who would be living in 1901?—Yes.

316. Whatever error there was was on the side of estimating that there would be fewer people over 65 rather than the other way?—Yes. I do not remember the exact figure arrived at. We took a round figure.

317. At any rate, if you did make a sub-estimation, even to a very slight extent, it was in the direction of making the cost smaller?—Yes. It was under the mark.

318. Rather than over the mark. Can you tell us anything about the figures as to whether they have been proved to be correct or incorrect for Scotland or Ireland?—I am sorry to say that I forgot to bring them up. They are very easily found. I will find them and send them to the Committee.

319. As showing the number of people whom you estimated would be alive at 65 in 1901, and how many were actually so?—Yes.

320. Ireland was more difficult?—It was very difficult.

321. In Ireland you may have wrongly estimated

Chairman—continued.

mated the number of people who would be of the pensionable age?—Yes.

322. As regards the census returns, do you think they are very reliable in the matter of the number of people of 65 and over. Do not you think there is a tendency to minimise the age on the part of people?—I believe the authorities on the subject who have to do with the census figures, like the Registrar-General, always think that it is the tendency of people.

323. As regards applicants for old-age pensions the tendency would be rather the other way—to exaggerate, I suppose?—I think it would.

324. There is a probability that the estimate of persons who would at any rate claim the age qualification is rather under than over the mark?—That is so.

325. Then as regards the expectation of life for future years and the cost in future years, is not the expectation of life growing with sanitary improvements at the present time?—Slightly I believe.

326. So that in future years it would seem probable that the proportion of persons over 65 to the total population would be higher than it has been in the past?—I think so. It is one of the considerations which we adduce at the end of the report—at page 49, paragraph 152.

327. Having arrived at the conclusion, apparently a very accurate one, that there would be in 1901 2,016,000 persons qualified by age, you proceeded to make deductions for want of qualification under the scheme. By those returns you reduced that number of persons to 655,000, did you not?—Yes.

328. So that your deductions were somewhat sweeping?—Very sweeping.

329. You reduced the cost from 31,449,000*l*., as it would have been for universal pensions, to 10,300,000*l*., for the year 1901?—Yes.

330. You knocked off two-thirds by the deductions?—Two-thirds.

331. You constantly speak of the risk of an under-estimate?—We did not wish to alarm people unnecessarily.

332. I will take it from you that you did not wish to alarm people unnecessarily. Now, taking the qualifications one by one, with regard to nationality you deduct eventually—on page 24—3,000 persons, on the ground that they would not be able to show that they were of British nationality. Was the fact brought to the notice of your Committee, and dealt with, that it is very easy to become naturalised in this country?—Yes.

333. Anybody can be naturalised in this country, can he not, unless he is a known criminal?—They have to reside here a certain specified time; I forget whether it is five years; I think it is five years.

Mr. Lloyd-George.

334. It is practically seven?—Yes.

Chairman.

335. If he has been here for five or seven years he can be naturalised?—I believe so.

Chairman—continued.

336. The Home Secretary may refuse to naturalise, but do you think that the Home Secretary would be justified in refusing to naturalise simply on the ground that the person, if naturalised, would come on the pension fund?—I think it would be one of the difficulties which the scheme would be confronted with.

337. That people would attempt to get naturalised?—Yes.

338. As to disqualification by conviction for serious crime, I think you say it is very difficult to make any estimate, but that you would take off 3 per cent.?—That was our rough figure.

339. Is not that deduction from the total number of people pensionable a sort of cumulative deduction, because are not these the same people, or part of the same class of people, who are already disqualified by having been in receipt of poor relief, or who would be disqualified for want of thrift?—I do not think a criminal would be in receipt of poor relief.

340. But would he not very probably have been in receipt of poor relief within 20 years of his becoming 65?—Of course, he might have been.

341. With regard to want of thrift, do you think a criminal could prove that he had endeavoured to support himself by his industry, to follow the words of the scheme?—No, I think that is highly improbable.

342. It is extremely likely, you think, that some of these 16,000 that you have taken off the pension list in the three kingdoms on account of criminal convictions, would be persons who were disqualified for other reasons as well?—That might be so. It is one of the difficulties which we had to deal with.

343. Do not you think that, if conviction and imprisonment without option of a fine led to disqualification for pension, it would have a great tendency to prevent magistrates committing without the option of a fine?—That might be so, but I should not like to express an opinion on that point.

344. That matter was not considered by the Committee, as far as I can see?—No.

345. Then, as regards non-receipt of poor relief, other than medical relief, except under circumstances of a wholly exceptional character, what do you take to be the meaning of the expression, "except under circumstances of a wholly exceptional character"?—I am not sure that I can say at this distance of time.

346. As a matter of fact, you do not deal with it in the report at all, and that is why I ask. You mention it, but you do not deal with it. At the bottom of page 8 it is mentioned that the applicants must show that they have not been in receipt of Poor Law relief, except in the case of illness, or under circumstances of a wholly exceptional character?—I think that these are the words used by the Select Committee.

347. Yes, and they are words which are in this Bill, and that is why I am asking about them?—I am afraid I have forgotten my lesson now. I know we went into the point at the time, and I think the words refer to circumstances such as a man having come to grief owing to something not his own fault at all. I think that is what

Chairman—continued.

what we took to be circumstances of a wholly exceptional character.

348. I think that your observations rather tend to show that you have deducted from the pensionable list all those who had been in receipt of relief during the 20 years before they were 65, and that you made no allowance for cases where the circumstances were of an exceptional character?—I think we did not.

349. Those words are a wholly indefinite description. Whether it was an exceptional case or not would depend on the opinion of the people administering the Act, I suppose?—Certainly.

350. And therefore, it would be impossible to calculate the effect?—Yes.

351. Then, as regards disqualification by receipt of poor relief, would it not cause a great hardship if you disqualified for pensions all those who are in receipt of poor relief now, but who never received poor relief until they became 65 years of age? Would it not be very unfair to disqualify them?—I think it would constitute a great hardship.

352. But you did take all those off your list of pensionable people?—Yes, we did.

353. So that there again you may have deducted too many?—Yes.

354. With regard to Scotland, you were in a very difficult position, were you not, because, in Scotland, there is no difference made between medical relief and other relief?—That is so.

355. So that you had to deduct the people who had received any sort of relief in Scotland, although some of them may have only been in receipt of medical relief?—Yes.

356. One of the qualifications in the Bill is that the person applying for the pension should be resident within the district of the pension authority. The man has to be resident somewhere?—That is obvious.

357. Do you consider that non-residence should be a disqualification? In your report you only deal with that matter in two or three lines. You apparently considered that it was a qualification which was no qualification?—It was laid down by the Select Committee that there was to be residence—I forget whether the number of years was stated.

358. No, the number of years was not stated. We will have on the notes the last few words of paragraph 51, page 14: "In short, we think that the number who will fail to comply with the residential qualification may be regarded as a negligible quantity"?—We felt that, if five years was the time laid down, a person would be sure to qualify somewhere in five years. The object of the Select Committee making a condition of residence was that a roving man should not be placed on the rates, but that the man would have to be qualified to the extent that he should be resident in one parish.

359. Now on a more important question, the question of means, you had to consider how many would be disqualified because they had more than 10s. a week. I want you to look at pages 26 and 27, and compare your estimate with regard to Scotland with that with regard to Ireland. As regards Ireland, you consider that 37 per cent. of the persons over 65 years of age would be disqualified because they were in possession of more than 10s. a week, but that only 35 per cent. would be disqualified in Scotland?—I think that that is explained on pages 16 and 17. We took the same figure for Ireland as we did for England—? per cent. for both.

360. You reckon that people in Ireland, at the age of 65, are, in proportion, as well off as people in England at the age of 65?—Yes; and we give special reasons why that is the case, in paragraphs 68 and 69.

361. That is based on the idea that the Irish, holding small holdings in a sort of family possession, the head of the family would have over 10s. a week if he was over 65?—Yes. It is in part due to that.

362. Do you not think that, stated broadly, it would somewhat surprise the world to know that a larger proportion of people in Ireland are in possession of 10s. per week at 65 than in Scotland?—I think it would.

363. The Scotch are a proverbially thrifty race?—Those are the two reasons which account for our figures.

364. Would you turn to page 71 of the Appendix, where you will find some figures for Ireland. Will you look at the third column: "Pensions from former employers." I notice that a large number of persons in Ireland are set down as having pensions from former employers. Is that a peculiarity of Ireland?—No, I should think not; but then we took no census in Ireland. We entirely depended upon the information which we received from the Public Departments. In Scotland and England we had a sort of test census.

365. In Ireland that was not a great census, I think?—We did not attempt it in Ireland: we were advised that it would be useless to attempt it.

366. So that your figures for Ireland are very largely conjectural?—Much more conjectural than those for England and Scotland.

367. Then as regards thrift, you make a reduction of 10 per cent. from those otherwise pensionable in respect of persons who could not show that they had complied with the thrift qualification which is required in the Bill?—Yes. I admit that that was a very rough and ready way of doing the thing, but we could not see how we could come to any more exact figure.

368. I submit to you for your consideration that this again is a cumulative deduction—that the persons who would be deducted for want of thrift are the same people who would be deducted for having been in receipt of poor relief. How does that strike you?—I remember that that question was taken into account, but I am afraid that it is one of the points which I have rather forgotten. I could look it up.

369. Should not you say yourself, if a person otherwise pensionable, that is to say, a poor person (because you have already deducted the people who have more than 10s. a week), has never received poor relief between the ages of 45 and 65, that should satisfy anybody as to his thrift?—It is awkward to get over. I am sorry to say I have rather forgotten some of the details of four years ago, but I think that was a point

on

Chairman—continued.

or took into account at the time—I am almost certain.

370. It is rather obvious what the answer would be to this question: The deductions which you made by which you brought down the number of pensionable people to 665,000 out of 2,016,900 were deductions of people who ought to be disqualified, but do you think that all those disqualifications would be detected by a committee of Guardians?—No, I think probably not.

371. Do not you think that a very large percentage would escape detection as to their disqualification owing to the fact that they had moved from one district to another?—I think that is very likely to be the case.

372. I think that, from what you have told me, I may take it that, in your opinion, the 10,300,000*l.* is not an over-estimate of the probable expense for 1901, but is rather the other way?—That is so. Perhaps you would allow me to say this also in confirmation of that: Mr. Brabrook, who was on this Committee, a very able public servant, as the Committee are aware, who is an expert on the subject, told me that he had been into the question by way of applying to England the New Zealand Act, which is in operation. I daresay the Committee are aware that the New Zealand Act has been in operation for four or five years now.

373. At our last meeting we had Mr. Reeves?—Mr. Brabrook told me that, assuming the conditions are similar, and I understand that in the New Zealand Act the conditions are practically similar—that is to say, that there is a poverty test, and there is some kind of test of thrift, taking the way in which it had worked out in New Zealand, the cost of the scheme in the United Kingdom would not be 10,300,000*l.* as we estimated it in 1901, but would be about 13,000,000*l.*

374. So that Mr. Brabrook also thought that the figure was under-estimated?—Yes, under-estimated.

Colonel *Pilkington*.

375. With regard to criminals, why should 3 per cent. escape?—It was a mere shot of ours: we had absolutely no information to go upon.

376. The escapes would very much depend, would they not, upon the length of time?—Yes. We had nothing to go upon.

377. With regard to 5 years, 10 years, or 15 years—if they had to reside in the district in which they receive the pension for, say, 20 years, that would make it exceedingly difficult?—Certainly. If the Honourable Member will turn for one moment to paragraph 28 he will see that we thought it was so uncertain that we only made a pure shot, more as a sort of reminder than anything else.

378. Of course, the longer the residence the less the escapes?—Yes.

Mr. *Goulding*.

379. I see that you do not estimate any saving in Poor Law expenditure until 1911, according to these returns?—No.

380. You then estimate for the first time a saving of a little over 500,000*l.*?—Yes, I admit that.

Chairman.

381. Are you quite sure of that?—I refreshed my memory yesterday by reading through the report. I could not remember that we had made any allowance before 1911.

Mr. *Goulding*.

382. I am afraid that it is not in the report, but it is in Clause 4 of the Bill before us, which we are now considering. Clause 4 is intended to remove the injustice that would otherwise be felt by those in the workhouse to-day of a deserving character. Do you think that their cases should be considered, and that they should at once receive the benefit of this Aged Pensioner's Bill? If there are people at present in the workhouse who have attained the age of 65 and would satisfy these qualifications if the Bill were in force, none of these have been taken into account. I see you make no estimate of saving at all in Poor Law expenditure until 1911?—I think you are correct.

383. You take a saving then of over 500,000*l.*?—Yes.

384. I understand you to deduct from the number over 65 years of age 741,000 for those whose incomes are over 10*s.* a week, and then you deduct for the whole of the United Kingdom 515,000. This is on page 28 of your report?—Yes.

385. That means to say that you leave people over 65 years of age at present in the workhouse on the same basis as they are to-day?—Yes.

386. I am trying to get at the cost. I see there is no saving allowed for an Aged Pensioner's Bill as against Poor Law administration. I have the figures for 1901 and 1902: "The foregoing table represents an average cost per head of the mean number of indoor paupers relieved of 33*l.* 11*s.* 7½*d.* in London, and 24*l.* 2*s.* 7½*d.* outside"?—Yes.

387. If the deserving out of that number over 65 years of age receive the benefits of this Bill, and receive from 5*s.* to 7*s.* a week, there will clearly be a large saving in expenditure, taking the sum of 15*l.* a year, the figures being for London 33*l.*, or for the whole of England and Wales 27*l.* 12*s.* per head?—I think there is some flaw in that, but I cannot tell you what it is now. I remember that point was discussed.

388. I am afraid that I have not made myself clear. You purposely in this return exclude all persons over 65 years of age who, at the time of this inquiry, are in receipt of Poor Law relief from participating in the Bill?—Yes.

389. And therefore their cost would fall on the ordinary Poor Law, and there is not the saving shown that we estimate will be shown if they receive an old-age pension instead of Poor Law relief. Do you not estimate any saving until 1911?—I think there is a saving, but if the Honourable Member would allow me, I would just look the thing up and let him know later on.

Chairman.

390. Look at the top of page 9 in Roman numerals. You will see there what the explanation is: "We take it for granted that all persons who may, on the introduction of the proposed pension

pension scheme, be found to be 65 years of age and upwards, and to be wholly or partly chargeable to the ratepayers, would *à fortiori* be debarred from making application to the pension authority. But we imagine that it might be by no means easy to defend the exclusion of those aged paupers who could give reasonable proof that, had they not had the misfortune to pass the Rubicon in 'pre-pensionable' days, they would have been able to satisfy the requirements of the pension authority"?—That is it.

Mr. *Goulding.*

391. They are debarred?—Yes.

392. As regards your expenditure of 10,000,000*l.*, you do not estimate any reduction in expenditure if these people receive old-age pension relief as opposed to Poor Law relief?—No.

393. The cost for London of every indoor pauper, according to the figures here, is 35*l.* 1*s.* 7¾*d.*, and your highest estimate of cost, including administration, is 15*l.* 12*s.* a year, so that there would be a saving of 20*l.* per head?—Yes.

394. The average for England and Wales is 27*l.* 12*s.* 10*d.* per head, whereas the extreme price here is 15*l.* 12*s.* Presuming, as many of us know, that there are some very deserving people in the workhouse at the present time, that would leave room for every one of those to come on the old-age pension list, and there would be a material saving to the country?—Yes.

395. And it would materially reduce the estimated expenditure of 10,000,000*l.*?—I do not like to admit that, because I know that we took the question into account.

396. I do not know whether you are aware that the estimate in Denmark, where the old-age pension comes into force at 60 years of age instead of 65, is that the saving in Poor Law expenditure has been one-sixth by reason of the Old-Age Pension Bill coming into force?—I was not aware of that.

397. I wanted to show that these figures were not really actually based on the Bill before us, and that the 10,000,000*l.* is rather an excessive amount if any saving is to be made on those in the workhouses?—I am afraid that, without going further into the matter, I could not answer you for certain.

398. Now, taking the New Zealand scheme to which reference was made just now, I do not know whether you are aware what the cost of administration of the New Zealand scheme is. It only amounts to 2,600*l.* a year?—Yes, it is about 1 per cent.

399. And your figure is very considerably in advance of that?—My figure is only 3 per cent.

400. The difference between 3 per cent. and 1 per cent. is a big difference?—I thought it was a very moderate estimate here, but I admit that if we take one into account we shall have to take the other into account. According to the figures that Mr. Brabrook got out, he makes it out that the New Zealand scheme has worked out infinitely more expensive than was allowed for.

401. That is not the evidence of Mr. Reeves, which he gave here last week, as to how it is

working. Now in fact the last year was [illegible] duced; it came down from about 210,000*l.* to about 200,000*l.* I see on page 25, in [illegible] figures, that, in giving your estimate for administration, you say the cost of every postal order is 3*d.*?—Yes.

402. Do I understand that on every postal order issued there is a loss?—That is what the Post Office estimate to be the cost.

403. But would you be justified in charging to a department 3*d.* on every postal order [illegible] is sold to the public at a penny?—If you are to pay the full cost.

404. But the postal orders are sold to the public at a penny?—Then there is a loss. This is the money order system. The costs are put at about 3*d.* per order issued and paid. There are two transactions, of course.

405. Then I see that you have estimated for fortnightly payments, which you consider enhance the expenditure. There would be no reason why there should not be monthly payments as in New Zealand, would there?—No. I thought it only reasonable that poor persons should receive the money every fortnight, but there is no reason why it should not be every month.

406. Now, if this Bill was modified to the extent of the pension which the applicant received only being limited to an amount that would raise his income to 10*s.* per week, would that materially alter the cost as estimated by you?—I should not like to say materially without going into the figures.

407. A great deal of discussion has been raised as to the hard and fast line of 10*s.*, and if the scheme was that a man having an income of 7*s.* or 6*s.*, it should be supplemented by 3*s.* or 4*s.*, which made it up to 10*s.*, instead of 7*s.*, would that materially alter the expenditure?—I should think it would, certainly.

408. As regards administration, do you mind my giving you these figures for expenditure exclusively relating to indoor relief: In London it is over half a million for officials, and for officials outside London 767,000*l.*, or a total for officials' salaries and other remuneration, rations and superannuation allowances, offices and servants, of 1,346,000*l.*, and then there are large sums for repayment of loans?—Yes.

409. If this Aged Pensioners' Bill came into force, you estimate just under 300,000*l.* for administration, I think?—Yes, about that; we took about 3 per cent.

410. 299,000*l.*?—Yes, 299,080*l.*—say [illegible].

411. If these officials were utilised for the purpose of old-age pensions, a large portion of that sum would be saved?—Yes, if it were practicable to utilise them.

Mr. *Pemberton.*

412. The proportion, according to these tables, of those over 65 is approximately 1-20th of the population. I see on page 25 that the total of those over 65 is put at 2,016,000?—Yes.

413. That is approximately 1-20th of the population now, is it not?—Yes.

314. From the figures given us by Mr. Reeves the other day, the figures in New Zealand are 31,080 over 65, out of a population of about [illegible]

Mr. Pemberton—continued.

414. Can you give us any information on that point, because there is a very considerable discrepancy between the two?—No, I am afraid I cannot. They are not figures that I am acquainted with.

415. Then do you think that your estimate for deductions is one at all to be relied on in practice? Do not you think that your deductions would be very much less when pensions come to be given to people?—I think in all probability that would be the case.

416. Your deductions were dealt with scientifically, if I may say so, and were rather in favour of keeping the costs of pensions down?—Yes.

417. Whereas, if the pensions were in force the tendency would be the other way?—I am afraid so.

418. The deductions would be very much less?—Yes.

Mr. John Hutton.

419. I take it that, when your Committee sat, your instructions were practically to ascertain the cost to the Treasury, without taking into consideration what the relief to the rates would be?—The cost of the scheme.

420. To the Treasury?—Not only to the Treasury; we did not draw any distinction between the Imperial funds and the rates.

421. But the total cost which you show here, of 10 millions odd, is on the bare cost of the number of people you believe will come on to the pension list, without deducting any saving to the rates?—Certainly; but I do not quite understand the saving on the rates. It would be an enormous increase of rates. The idea was that half the charge was to fall on the rates and half on the Imperial funds, if I remember rightly, so that half of the large cost would go on the rates.

422. But you did not estimate at all what the saving would be upon the present expenditure upon the rates; that does not appear in your estimate?—I know that the point was taken into consideration at the time.

423. It is not shown at all. With regard to the estimates of the number of the aged poor who are likely to come on to the pension list, may I ask did you use what is commonly called Mr. Ritchie's return?—Yes, Mr. Ritchie's return.

424. Mr. Ritchie's return in the year 1892 showed 376,427 persons of 65 years and upwards, and that you estimated would be increased, I presume, in 1901 to 410,000?—I think that is how we got at it.

425. Then after making all these various deductions in England and Wales, you came to the conclusion that there would be 469,000 persons probably available for pensions?—Yes.

426. You know Mr. Knowles probably as a great authority upon Poor Law matters?—Yes, I know him by name.

427. He is the Secretary of the Local Government Board. In the evidence which he gave before the Cottage Homes Commission in 1899, taking Mr. Ritchie's figures of 376,427 persons over 65 years of age in receipt of relief, he said that he came to the conclusion that there would be only about 100,000 of those who would be treated as deserving poor. Of course, the report of this Committee was not before the Treasury Committee?—No, but I know that we often refer to it.

428. Mr. Knowles stated that he considered that 150,000 deserving aged poor would be too high an estimate. Therefore, supposing that the number was only 100,000, the cost for pensions would be only 2,000,000*l.* at 20*l.* a year, or, if 150,000, 3,000,000*l.*?—Yes.

Mr. Lloyd-George.

429. I think you stated that someone made a calculation on the basis of the New Zealand figures, and that estimate was 13,000,000*l.* a year?—Yes.

430. Have you studied the New Zealand Act yourself?—No, I have not seen the Act myself.

431. Would you take this from a question put last week by the chairman to Mr. Reeves, that the conditions were that an applicant must not possess an income in excess of 52*l.* a year nor property exceeding 270*l.* in value. You are cognisant of the provisions of Mr. Goulding's Bill?—It is double.

432. So that the conditions are much more liberal in New Zealand?—Yes.

433. With regard to New Zealand, the latest returns show that there are 12,000 odd in receipt of a pension. Mr. Reeves says it was 12,403 in 1901?—Yes.

434. The total population of New Zealand is 830,000 according to Mr. Reeves?—Yes.

435. That means that only one-seventieth of the population roughly are in receipt of an old-age pension, even under these liberal conditions?—Yes.

436. Now supposing you apply that to this country, one-seventieth of 40,000,000 would be 571,000?—Yes.

437. So that, if even under the liberal conditions of New Zealand it is only one-seventieth of the population, would it not be fair to assume that it would be rather less here?—That is an assumption that anybody is at liberty to make.

438. Would you consider it an unfair assumption?—I think I should prefer my own figures.

439. Of course, your figures are naturally the result of a guess, and the best estimate you could make without having much to go upon?—I admit that, to a great extent, they are guesses.

440. The only practical experience which you could possibly have had would have been to have had the case of New Zealand before you, and it was not before you at the time, was it?—No.

441. Because your estimate was made before the Act in New Zealand had come into anything like practical operation?—I do not think it was passed even.

442. I think it was passed, but there was no experience of its working, if I remember rightly. Supposing that now you were making an estimate, you would naturally consider what the effect in New Zealand had been of a Bill, much more liberal, it is true, but more or less on the same lines?—Yes.

443. So, taking the New Zealand Bill into account, and how it has worked, would it not be

Mr. Lloyd-George—continued.

fair to say that not more than one-seventieth of our population would claim a pension under this Bill?—It would be a fair assumption to make, certainly.

444. Instead of 655,000 on the New Zealand basis receiving a pension, it would only be 571,000. Now that, at the rate of 5s. a week, would be a deduction of 1,300,000*l.* from your estimate?—Yes.

445. Supposing another condition of the New Zealand Act were put into operation here, that where you have husband and wife both over 65 years of age claiming the pension, you would not give the same pension to both; I mean that you would not give 6*s.* to each, but you would say: "We will give, instead of 12*s.*, say, 10*s.*, or 9*s.* 6*d.*" Would you consider that fair?—That would be quite reasonable, I think.

446. Supposing it were on the basis of giving less where two of the pensioners, being husband and wife, cohabited, would you consider 4*s.* 6*d.* an unfair estimate for the whole country instead of 5*s.*?—I am afraid I have not any figure at all to show me the proportion of married people to single over 65.

447. Do you think that one-third would be an unfair proportion?—I am afraid I cannot say.

448. Would you consider that excessive?—The figure could be obtained from the Registrar-General, I think.

449. Taking 5*s.* for each applicant, supposing that you make a payment in respect of married people, would you consider one-third as being a very extravagant assumption?—I think it reasonable.

450. Therefore, that would be 4*s.* 6*d.* instead of 5*s.*?—Yes.

451. Then I would also ask you to make a deduction in respect of the country. In London you might get 7*s.* per head given; in the country you would probably not get more than 5*s.* per head given; so, therefore, 4*s.* 6*d.*, taking everything into account, would not be an unfair average for the whole country?—Possibly not.

452. That would be a deduction of another third from your estimate if the Bill proceeded on those lines?—Yes. I am afraid it is rather a big "if," but it would be the case.

453. But in what respect—I do not want a conjectural estimate?—I think it is very much in the air.

454. But I want to know what is in the air?—Until I went myself into the figures more carefully, I could not answer. These are figures suggested to me orally.

455. But what is in the air, to begin with? The proposal of making a deduction in respect of two people cohabiting is a practical proposal, is it not?—Yes: but I do not know at all whether one-third is fair. The Registrar-General has got figures, and I should like to know them. If he gave me the figures I could deal with them.

456. Could you get the figures?—Yes, perfectly easily I could get them.

457. That is rather an important point?—No doubt, if the Honourable Member kindly wrote down exactly what he required, I could get it from the Registrar-General.

Mr. Lloyd-George—continued.

458. I will do so. That would be a very important deduction, would it not?—Yes.

459. It would be a deduction of one-third from the total estimate. The first deduction would bring it down from 10,300,000 to 8,800,000*l.* You would find a great difficulty, not in getting the proportion of married people to single people, but the proportion of cases where husband and wife were both over 65. There must be some husbands over 65 with wives very much younger.

460. I know. The whole thing at the present moment is purely guess; for instance, you can only guess the number of thrifty people?—Yes, it is a guess.

461. Could you not make a guess at the other figure, having first of all consulted the Local Government Board, whose inspectors might be able to assist?—The Registrar-General is the more likely person to supply the information.

462. This is really of the very essence of the estimate?—I do not know that the Registrar-General could give the information, but he is the only man who possibly could from the statistics which are collected from the centres.

463. Any estimate would be unreliable. Surely it is a most important element in the cost?—Yes, certainly.

464. And any estimate is exaggerated until we get that?—Yes.

465. There is another deduction; I do not know whether it was considered, and that is a deduction for soldiers and Civil Servants and policemen who are in receipt of a pension already from the State. I do not observe that there is anything in respect of those on the face of this document?—I cannot remember, but I hardly think it could have been left out of account.

466. I cannot find anything in the report which takes it specifically into account?—I will make a note of that.

Chairman.

467. Did you not, in your last estimate, have upon your card a question as to whether they were in receipt of pensions. If you look at page 8 of the Appendix you will find that your enumeration card sets out a question as to whether there is a pension from former employers?—I remember that now.

468. That shows that you considered the pension of Civil Servants in dealing with the question of how many had more than 10*s.* a week?—Certainly. I had forgotten that for the moment.

Mr. Lloyd-George.

469. I do not know what a policeman would get. I do not know whether you considered the pension of under 10*s.* There is no deduction on the face of this in respect of those. Now have you considered at all the question of how the money is to be raised?—No: I have never looked at it from a sufficiently practical point of view to have considered that question.

470. You have not gone into it at all?—No.

471. You did not go into it when you prepared this report?—No.

472. We had evidence the other day that in Denmark the money is raised largely out of local

Has

Mr. Lloyd-George—continued.

'or how much on beer would raise 9,000,000l. net?—I should not like to give you a figure to ne, but I should think from 3s. to 4s. extra per barrel.

473. To what extent would that increase the price of a pint of beer?—I am afraid I could not tell you.

474. What is the charge now on beer?—It is 7s. 9d., I think.

475. And it would mean an increase of how much?—Of 3s. or 4s. at least, I should think, as there might be a tremendous falling off in the consumption.

476. Now what do you say about a duty on sugar?—At present it is on an elaborate scale. The highest duty is 2s. 6d. a cwt. That produces 6,000,000l.

477. An additional 1s. 8d. would produce 4,000,000l.?—Yes, 1s. 8d., added to the present 2s. 6d.

478. You have not considered anything like the question of taxation of ground values?—Not in connection with this subject. I have always looked upon any taxation of ground values, if it ever came about, as a source of local revenue rather than Imperial revenue.

479. But, whatever it would be, it would have to be something that was likely to produce a permanent revenue?—Certainly.

480. And a growing revenue?—And a growing revenue.

481. How much does tea produce?—Tea produces about 1,000,000l. per penny. At present it is 6d. per pound, and it produces about 6,000,000l.

482. So that you would require 9d. per pound to produce 9,000,000l.?—Yes. That would not be a fair figure, because the consumption would be certain to fall.

Chairman.

483. A shilling tax on wheat produces 2,500,000l. a year?—Yes.

484. 4s. would produce, for the present at any rate, 10,000,000l.?—Yes.

Mr. Lloyd-George.

485. If the import decreased as the result of the tax, you would be left in the lurch, would you not?—Yes.

486. You have not gone into the question of old age pensions in Denmark?—No, I have not, beyond reading a book upon Denmark at the time when I wrote this report.

Mr. Goulding.

487. When you were estimating this expenditure here, did you take into account at all the evidence of Sir Henry Longley, who said that the Charity Commissioners control funds to the amount of nearly 1,000,000l. a year, taking almshouses, pensions, and doles?—No.

488. 611,000l. odd and 327,000l. odd, applicable for distribution to the poor, making a total of 938,000l. a year. That was not taken into consideration?—No.

Chairman.

489. Did not you take into consideration, in calculating the various incomes of the people, what they received from charity funds?—No, I did not take that into account.

490. But your card asks them to state all their earnings?—Yes; I beg pardon.

Wednesday, 15th July 1903.

MEMBERS PRESENT:

Sir Alexander Hargreaves Brown.
Mr. Channing.
Mr. Ernest Flower.
Mr. Goulding.
Mr. Lloyd-George.

Mr. Grant Lawson.
Mr. Pemberton.
Colonel Pilkington.
Mr. Remnant.
Mr. Shackleton.

MR. GRANT LAWSON IN THE CHAIR.

Mr. W. C. STEADMAN, Examined.

Chairman.

491. There was a Conference, I believe, held in January, 1902, at the Memorial Hall, Farringdon Street, convened jointly by the Trades Union Congress and the Co-operative Union Congress, was there not?—Yes.

492. Over that you presided?—The first day. If you would allow me I should like to go back to the reason why that Conference was called.

493. Certainly?—For several years past resolutions have been passed at our Trades Union Congresses dealing with this subject of old-age pensions, and at the Congress held at Swansea, in 1901, the following resolution, moved by myself, was unanimously agreed to: "That in the opinion of this Congress no scheme dealing with old-age pensions will be satisfactory to the whole of the workers in this country which seeks to subsidise existing pension societies, or which connects pensions with any institutions that will mark them with the stigma of pauperism. The only legislation that will solve the problem presented by age and poverty in modern industrial life is that which recognises the pension as a civil right which may be claimed by any citizen on reaching a given age. And we further call upon the Government to carry out the pledges given by its supporters at the general election of 1895, which up to the present time have been ignored. And we instruct the Parliamentary Committee" (that is, the Parliamentary Committee that is elected from the Congress) "to convene a National Conference of representatives of Trades Unions, Co-operative, and Friendly Societies to formulate a scheme which in its opinion would be practicable and approved by the people." That resolution was unanimously agreed to, and, of course, you see by the instruction in the latter portion of it, was the means of the calling of this Conference.

494. At Swansea, in moving the resolution, or in the course of the speeches in support of it, was anything said about the financial aspect?—Only by myself as mover of the resolution. I claim that it is the duty of statesmen to find the money that would be required for a general scheme of old-age pensions; but if asked my own opinion as to where the money should come from, I say from a graduated income tax.

Chairman—continued.

495. So that the people who pay income tax would provide all the money for those who are left without incomes at 65?—That is so.

496. Have you worked out how much money would be required?—Charles Booth worked out the total amount, and, of course, he bases it on the total number of persons over a given age. The Right Honourable Joseph Chamberlain, in addressing a meeting of Friendly Society men, said the total amount that would be wanted would be 30 or 40 millions. But my opinion is that all these figures are based upon hypotheses. It would be impossible for any man, however able he might be in calculating figures, to ascertain the total amount that would be required for a general scheme of old-age pensions until the scheme itself was in operation. By that time you would know the total number of recipients of the pension.

497. But if the pension was universal on coming to the age of 65, there is no hypothesis as to how many people are over 65. That is given in the census?—No; but then it does not follow that every person over 65 would take a pension. For instance, there are a number of Trades Unions that have a superannuation fund based upon membership of a society. When a man has been a member sufficiently long to entitle him to that superannuation, providing he can still get employment in his trade, he will not claim it.

498. You think that a large number of people would not claim them because they had pensions from their Trades Unions?—No, I am not now referring in a general sense to workmen; but what I say is that there are workmen to-day that will not claim their superannuation from their Trades Union if they can follow their employment. They prefer to follow their employment, and

Chairman—continued.

and receive their wages as mechanics to getting 7s. or 10s. a week from their society.

499. Would your scheme prevent a man working if he was drawing a pension?—The Union itself would not pay the man a pension if he was working at his trade.

500. But I mean if he was drawing one of the pensions that you proposed in your resolution at Swansea from the State, would he be allowed to work?—I should not think he would apply for the pension unless he was disabled from working.

501. But supposing he was drawing a pension, would you allow him to work, or would you not?—Yes, certainly. The Union would not interfere between the pension a man is getting from the State and his individual liberty to earn more money if he could.

502. As a matter of fact, the Trade Unions do not pay the pension if a man is still working at his trade, do they?—No, he does not apply for it while he is working at his trade.

503. Then in consequence of this resolution which you carried at the Swansea Congress, this other congress took place that I have mentioned in January, 1902?—Yes. We issued invitations in accordance with the resolution to the Co-operative Societies, the Trades Unions, and the Friendly Societies. Unfortunately, the Friendly Societies were prevented from taking part in that Conference, because they had got no mandate from their own members. You see, they hold an Annual Conference, the same as the Trades Unions do, and their Conference was not held in time for them to take part in our Conference.

504. Had the reason which they gave anything to do with that part of your resolution which condemns the subsidising of Friendly Societies?—No, they did not state that as a reason. They gave the reason which I have already given to you.

505. At the Congress, so that the people might know what they were going to discuss, you circulated several schemes of old-age pensions, did you not?—Yes.

506. I believe there were at least 10 different schemes circulated?—There were 12 schemes circulated.

507. Was one based upon the report of Mr. Chaplin's Committee, as this Bill is?—Yes.

508. And did that come on for discussion?—No.

509. A resolution was passed to take as the basis of discussion one of the other schemes, was it not?—Yes, one which the organising committee itself suggested. I might say in reference to the Conference, showing that it was representative in its character, that there were in all 394 delegates, representing a total membership of 2,441,000.

510. I should like to ask you upon that, do these delegates receive instruction from their Union or Co-operative Society before they come as to how they are to vote?—That all depends on whether the agenda is sent out in sufficient time for them to bring it before their members.

511. In this case a very full agenda paper was sent out, as I understand?—The only agenda that was sent out was the agenda with these 12 schemes, and you will notice, if you have read it, that the heading states that the Arrangements Committee for the Old-age Pension Conference, after due consideration of the terms of the resolution of the Swansea Congress, found that they had no authority to draw up any resolution on the subject. They decided, therefore, to draft a brief summary of the chief points of some of the schemes which had been suggested by different persons, which, in their judgment, would be the best way to deal with the problem of old-age pensions; that these should form the basis for discussion in the nature of an agenda for the use of delegates attending the Conference.

512. In your own Union did you discuss these 12 alternative plans which were before the Congress?—No, not those 12 plans, because we had already discussed the question of a general scheme of old-age pensions, and the members of my Union are unanimously in agreement with the resolutions which have previously been passed by various Trade Union Congresses.

513. They declared that the scheme must be non-contributory, universal in its application, that the pension age should be 60, and the amount of pension 5s. a week?—Yes.

514. You took the chair, and in making the opening remarks, did you deal with the financial side of the question at that Conference?—I do not think I dealt with it there at all; but I have dealt with it at a Trades Union Congress, and that is the line which I take; and I still adhere to the view that the money should come from a graduated income tax.

515. Do you remember whether any of the speakers at the Memorial Hall Conference dealt with where the money was to come from?—No; only that it should come from the Government.

Mr. Channing.

516. It was not to come from the rates?—Not to come from the rates. I will deal with the various resolutions which were passed at that Conference.

Chairman.

517. We came, on the second day of the Conference, to the question of the rates; but on the first day certain resolutions were proposed, and perhaps you would kindly read first Mr. Rogers' resolution?—I do not know if you notice this, but on page 4 of the schemes which were printed and sent round to the delegates, under No. 10, there is this: "Note.—The Joint Committee, after giving considerable attention to the schemes and suggestions foreshadowed above, favourably agree in recommending the provisions of No. 10 to the consideration of delegates attending the Conference." Now No. 10 is: "That the scheme be non-contributory, universal in its application, and that the public should pay; that the pension age should be 60, and the amount 5s. per week." There are five principles embodied there.

518. With regard to Clause 3, which you have just read, stating that the public shall pay, do you read that as meaning not the whole of the public, but only income-tax payers?—We meant by that that the Government should pay.

519. Because

Chairman—continued.

519. Because you put it as an interrogatory, "Who shall pay?" and then, in brackets "the public"?—Of course, we claim that the public pay for everything at the present time. I might say, because I want to be perfectly fair in giving my evidence, that there were two Friendly Societies represented at this Conference, one the Sir Robert Peel Provident Society, of 1,400 members, and the other the Royal Hearts of Oak Benefit Yearly Dividing Society, of 16,000 members. This was our first resolution, and this, of course, would deal with the first point—that the scheme be non-contributory: "This Conference affirms the fundamental necessity of any national scheme of old-age pensions being entirely non-contributory, and is strongly of opinion that such a pension scheme based on any proportion of direct contributions to the funds would be unsatisfactory and unworkable." That resolution was carried unanimously.

520. Was there some discussion?—None against it. Those who spoke, spoke for Mr. Rogers, who moved it; he is a Trade Unionist. Mr. Aldridge, of the Guildford Co-operative Society, seconded it.

521. But there was no discussion against it?—There was no discussion against this resolution.

522. This was in January, 1902?—Yes; the dates were the 14th and 15th of January, 1902.

523. That was a scheme dealing with the question of contribution?—Yes.

524. Then we come to the next resolution, proposed by Mr. Maddison, and will you read that?—"That any scheme, to be acceptable to this Conference, must be universal in its application, and this Conference further believes that, quite apart from any consideration of cost, to attempt to discriminate between the needy and the affluent would stamp it with the taint of pauperism and lower the dignity of the recipient, and that inquiries into the character of individuals would reduce it to the level of charity, which would be repugnant to the feelings of the country generally." There was an amendment moved to that resolution. The amendment was moved by Mr. Medhurst, who represented the Royal Hearts of Oak Yearly Dividing Society, and this was his amendment: "That no scheme can meet with the approval of this Conference which does not distinguish between the thrifty or otherwise deserving and the dissolute and deliberately thriftless members of the community." When that amendment was put to the Conference only the mover voted for it.

525. The mover represented the Royal Hearts of Oak Society, which you have just mentioned to us as having 16,000 members?—Yes.

526. Was he supposed to speak for the 16,000, or as an individual?—He was supposed to speak for the 16,000, the same as a miners' representative would speak for the 300,000 which he was representing.

527. There was another friendly society gentleman present, you said just now?—Yes.

528. He was a member of the Sir Robert Peel Friendly Society?—Yes.

529. And do you happen to remember whether he took any part in that discussion?—No, he did not.

Chairman—continued.

530. As you know, from your experience in this House, and as we know, the voting does not always quite clearly indicate the trend of feeling. Did many people walk out, as it is called in the House, and not vote?—No.

531. The whole meeting voted?—I have something else to say on that point. After this Conference was over, in January, the Co-operative Societies held their Annual Conference at Easter the following Whit week. I think, speaking from memory, they had perhaps 1,200 delegates. They had had ample time, from January until then, to bring the whole matter before every branch of the Co-operative Union, and unanimously they endorsed the principles arrived at at the Conference.

532. We are having a witness to say what they did at their Conference, and what the feeling was there. We may take it that your Conference, with the exception of this gentleman representing the Royal Hearts of Oak, were unanimously of opinion that you should not distinguish between persons on the ground of their character?—That is so.

533. So that we may take it that the working men of the country, as represented at this Congress, would be willing to give a pension to a man who has just come out of prison?—Yes. I will read the speech of Mr. Maddison, who is a gentleman well known to yourself, as ex-Member of this House. You will find that he even advocated that a common prostitute, if she lived to 60 years of age, should be entitled to her pension.

534. That shows very clearly what the line taken was. After that, you came to another resolution, which appears to have been of a financial description, dealing with the question of who shall pay?—Yes. This settles the point which you raised "about the people" in brackets: "That in the opinion of this Conference of Trade Unionists, Co-operative and other Societies, it is the duty of the State, by means of Imperial and local taxation, to meet the expenditure involved in the establishment of a scheme of old-age pensions."

535. To that an amendment was moved?—To that an amendment was moved by Mr. Curran, of the Gas Workers' Union, to substitute for the words "local and Imperial taxation" the words, "the taxation of land values and the appropriation by the Government of royalties on minerals."

536. To provide the 30,000,000*l.* or so which would be required. In other words, to produce the money that would be required for a universal scheme?—Yes. Mr. Curran withdrew his amendment. There was strong opposition to it; and then Mr. Lewington, of the Barge Builders' Co-operative Society, moved to omit the words "and local," so that, of course, left it as the duty of the State by means of Imperial taxation. The words "and local" being deleted, that was agreed to. So that the resolution, as amended, was that it was the duty of the State, by means of Imperial taxation, to meet the expenditure.

537. Did anybody take the point of the cost of the administration which would be involved

b

Chairman—continued.

in making the whole thing manageable from a Central department?—No, I do not find that.

538. Of course, what we want to know is whether stress was laid on these matters. If stress was not laid on them probably you would not remember them?—The only financial reference that was made was made, I see, by the mover of the resolution, Mr. Smillie, of the Miners' Federation. He states that "there were 20 or 30 different ideas as to how the money could be raised. There was the taxation of land values, of mining royalties, the graduated income tax on incomes of over 400*l.* or 500*l.* a year, etc. But they should not shut their eyes to the fact that so long as the social system continued as now, by whatever means the money was raised, the worker would have to pay for it." That is the only reference.

539. Then there was no stress laid on the question of the expense of administration of a centralised system?—No.

540. You then carried that with the amendment to leave out "and local"?—Yes.

541. And you proceeded to another resolution?—Yes; that would be the second day, when Mr. Ben Jones, of the Wholesale Co-operative Society, was in the chair.

542. You were present?—Yes, I was present. I was the Chairman of the Organising Committee of that Conference. The fourth resolution was: "This Conference desires to strongly affirm the principle that each citizen should be entitled to receive a pension from the State on arriving at the age of 60 years." And that was agreed to.

543. Was it not proposed by Mr. Rogers to strike out 60 and substitute 65? The "Times" report says that Mr. Rogers, of the Vellum Binders' Society, proposed as an amendment to delete "60" and substitute "65"?—Yes, Mr. Rogers did move an amendment to raise the age to 65.

544. And did some discussion take place upon that?—Yes, there was some discussion; Mr. Mitchell, of the Carlisle Trades Council, and Councillor Richards, of Leicester, and Mr. Orbell, of the Dockers, spoke. This is a verbatim report of that Conference, and it says: "A motion having been made 'that the question be now put' was adopted, and only a few hands held up for the amendment." Then is the official report. "Upon being put to the vote the original resolution was carried by a tremendous majority."

545. The scheme of that Congress put it at 60 years of age, which would make it more expensive than a universal pension scheme at 65, of course?—Yes, certainly. There are more people of 60 than there are people of 65 years of age.

546. I am afraid that we do not know at present how many there are between 60 and 65, so I cannot take what the extra expense would be. You then passed a resolution as to amount?—Yes, No. 5: "That in the opinion of this Conference the amount of pension available for each citizen, male or female, on attaining the age of 60 years, should be at least 5*s.* per week."

547. To that an amendment was moved to substitute 7*s.*, was it not, and the Conference rejected the amendment?—Yes, Mr. Curran, of the Gasworkers, moved an amendment that it should be 7*s.*, but the amendment was withdrawn. It was not voted upon, and the original resolution was carried. Then there was a concluding resolution, if I am not boring you?

548. Not at all?—"That this Conference urges upon the Government the urgent necessity of establishing a national system of old-age pensions which shall be universal in its application to all citizens, male and female, on attaining the age of 60 years, the pension to be at the rate at least 5*s.* per week; and that the entire cost of such scheme be met entirely by means of Imperial taxation. That the Parliamentary Committees of the Trade Union and the Co-operative Congresses be requested to take such steps as may seem to them most desirable to work conjointly in bringing the resolutions of this Conference to the attention of the Government and the country, including the promotion of an Old-age Pension Bill in Parliament."

549. I think you told us that although it was upon the agenda paper the scheme, which is similar to the scheme before this Committee, was not discussed at the Congress. Have you discussed it since in your union?—No, we have not. We laid the twelve schemes before them, but the Organising Committee, of which I was the Chairman, recommended No. 10, and the delegates agreed to our recommendation, showing that they had no desire to discuss the other schemes.

550. Has scheme No. 5, which agrees with the Bill before this Committee, been discussed by your union since?—No, we should not attempt to discuss a scheme which we do not agree with. I dealt with the scheme in my opening remarks as Chairman on the first day of the Conference.

551. And the Conference agreed with you so thoroughly that no motion was made on the subject?—They did not agree with me so much as they agreed with the Organising Committee; and they preferred to discuss No. 10 to discussing the eleven other schemes which were put before them.

552. A copy of the Bill was sent to you, I think, by the Clerk of the Committee?—Yes, I have the Bill.

553. You were Chairman of the Organising Committee of this Congress?—Yes.

554. In that Organising Committee did you discuss each of these schemes, including No. 5?—We gave considerable attention to them, as we told the delegates, on the agenda.

555. Did you make notes on each of these, including No. 5?—No. We simply said: "The Joint Committee, after giving considerable attention to the schemes and suggestions foreshadowed above, favourably agree in recommending the provisions of No. 10."

556. Can you remember on what grounds you rejected No. 5, the scheme similar to this, and adopted No. 10?—Yes. But before I deal with that I should like to say that, following up the Conference, the Trades Union Congress was held last September in London; 500 delegates were present at that Congress. I was its chairman, and that Congress unanimously agreed to the scheme that was arrived at by the Joint Conference; so that practically now the whole of the Trade

Chairman—continued.

Trade Unionists and the Co-operators of the country are agreed upon the scheme that was adopted at the Joint Conference in the Memorial Hall. The Bill was not printed then, but we objected to the report of Mr. Chaplin's Committee, because it was not general in its scope. After making deductions for imprisonment, pauperism, etc., it practically boiled down the recipients who would be entitled to a pension to something like 655,000 persons. Now the Committee say that that would cost, after allowing 3 per cent. for administration purposes, 10,200,000*l.* per annum. Personally I think, roughly speaking, a pension for that number of 13*l.* per annum would mean in round figures about 8,000,000*l.*; that is leaving, according to the estimation, 2,200,000*l.* for administrative purposes.

557. But the words of the Bill are, "Not less than five shillings or more than seven"?—I will take it on its minimum—that is the five shillings.

558. The resolution of your Congress was, "Not less than five shillings"?—Yes, and the Bill goes for that, too. It gives from a minimum of five shillings to a maximum of seven shillings. I am dealing now with what would be the total cost of the minimum of five shillings per week for the number of persons who would be entitled to a pension under the scope of this Bill. I am going to show, if I can, that this Bill is a penny wise and pound foolish policy, and it is going to throw all the burden upon the poor people of the nation, and not upon the rich people, who are able to bear it. Mr. Charles Booth says that there are over 400,000 persons in our workhouses to-day over 65 years of age, and I should assume that if there is that number over 65, there is most likely to be more over 60. But, at any rate, the Local Government Board are always able to get those statistics.

559. The statistics for the 1st July, 1899, gave, outdoor and indoor combined, 274,718 over 65. That is the return before us?—Mr. Booth's figures are not quite correct, then. Now I will take it upon that basis.

560. That was on a given day—the 1st July, 1899—and not throughout the year?—It costs more for administration in a workhouse than it costs to keep the inmate himself, and, with the exception of 4*d.* per head which the Poor Law Guardians receive from the common poor fund, the whole of that cost falls upon the ratepayers. The proposed scheme of this Bill suggests that the Government should find 6*l.* and that the ratepayers should find the other 7*l.* Now, to take the parish where I am living, in East London—a very poor parish—the poor maintained in all our workhouses would not come within the scope of the Bill. We give 6,000*l.* a year away in outdoor relief, which is equal to a rate of 4*d.* in the pound, for which we do not receive a penny assistance from the Government; and on the top of that heavy expenditure which is coming out of the pockets of hundreds of men who do not average 25*s.* a week as an income, you are going to throw a further burden of 2*s.* 8½*d.* per week for every person who comes within the scope of this Bill for a pension, because the Government is only going to pay 2*s.* 3½*d.* per week, and the ratepayers have to find 2*s.* 8½*d.* to make up a maximum of 5*s.* per week. I was a Poor Law Guardian for three and a half years, and I know from experience that there are sons and daughters who are not in a position to assist their parents. You get a man up before you, and you charge him with non-maintenance of his father or mother, who is in the workhouse; he tells you he is a labourer whose money is, perhaps, about a guinea a week, and he has a wife and two children. You cannot expect that man is going to subscribe anything towards the maintenance of his parent in the workhouse. But supposing that parent was entitled, although a pauper, as he is termed to-day, through the law to 5*s.* per week, there are thousands of children in this country who would find a covering for their parent who cannot now find the covering and maintain the parent as well. You would save, under a pension scheme, the ratepayers of several millions per annum in that direction. But no. You say in this Bill that you are going to shut all that out, and you are going to pile up the expenditure upon the shoulders of those who cannot make ends meet at the present moment. And I say that is a penny wise and pound foolish policy.

561. Do you wish to say anything as regards the qualifications in Clause 6, which are identical with Mr. Chaplin's scheme, which was before the Organising Committee?—I can only say that I do not agree with the clause.

Mr. *Channing*.

562. I happened to be present at the Conference myself, and I remember what passed. Is it not the fact that the objections to what you might call the merit and the thrift tests, and also the objections to the fixing of an income limit, were freely discussed by a speaker on one of the main resolutions discussed on the first day, I think, by Mr. Rogers?—Yes, that was so.

563. In your opinion would it not be true to say that the Conference had considered the arguments against the possibility of usefulness of these tests and the income limit, and had deliberately rejected them in considering this resolution?—That is so. I should like to say that, although a Trades Unionist, I am equally strongly a Friendly Society man. I have been a member of the Hearts of Oak Benefit Society (not the Royal Hearts of Oak) for 30 years. I was four years on its Committee of Management and eight years a delegate. When I was a Member of this House a Bill came on one Wednesday afternoon—a private Member's Bill—dealing with this subject from the Friendly Society point of view, and the Bill was talked out; but I had an opportunity of saying a few words in opposition to it. When we come to discriminate between thrift and thriftlessness we have to ask ourselves the reason why men are not members of Friendly Societies, and when we take into consideration the circumstances of the average unskilled worker and his average workings, there is an answer at once why thousands and hundreds of thousands of men are not members of Friendly Societies; and we consider [illegible]

Mr. Channing—continued.

that those men have as much right to be looked after, because they are unable to help themselves, as any skilled workman able to join both a Trades Union and a Friendly Society.

Chairman.

564. That Bill made it a condition of receiving a pension that the applicant should be, or have been, a member of a Friendly Society, did it not?—I forget now the details of the Bill, but I know it dealt with Friendly Societies.

Mr. Channing.

565. To follow up my point, the Conference decided in favour of a universal scheme after the discussion of what were the principles of other schemes as regards contribution and merit and income tests. These were actually discussed before you arrived at the conclusion that a universal scheme is a desirable scheme, as far as I can remember?—There were no other schemes discussed excepting those that we suggested to the Conference.

566. You do not quite understand my question. My question is that the speeches of those who discussed the resolutions brought before Congress dealt with and condemned, with the assent of the Congress, the principles on which three other schemes are based?—The speeches travelled over the whole ground undoubtedly.

567. That is what I thought. Now the first resolution which your Organising Committee submitted contemplated a contribution from the local rates. That is, the striking out of the local rates was the act of the Congress on an amendment moved, I understand?—Yes. Our third resolution embodied the words "Imperial and local taxation." That was as drafted by the Organising Committee; but the Conference itself deleted the words "and local."

568. Your Organising Committee arrived at the conclusion that, on the whole, local taxation should not be excluded from the sources of revenue?—We arrived at the conclusion that we should contribute a certain amount from local taxation, but the Organising Committee was only five members, and the 400 delegates did not agree with us.

569. As a matter of fact, Imperial taxation more largely falls on the working classes who would receive pensions, does it not, than local rates do?—That is through the wretched system we have got of indirect taxation.

Mr. Remnant.

570. I should like to point out this: You say that this Bill was not in print at the time; but it was actually in existence; and, therefore, when you say that, it is very clear to my mind that this Bill was not considered by the Conference, but an absolutely different scheme altogether?—If I was in error there I will withdraw what I said.

571. As far as you are concerned, it was not in print: but it actually was, in print. This scheme was not before the Conference, although it was in existence?—Mr. Chaplin's Committee's scheme was before the Organising Committee,

Mr. Remnant—continued.

and this Bill is drafted upon that scheme; and in that sense it was discussed by the Committee, but not by the Conference.

572. Therefore the result of the Conference does not really bear on this Bill?—Only in this sense—that the organised workers and the members of the Co-operative Societies would be against this Bill to a man.

573. That is your opinion; but it was not settled by the Conference, was it?—I cannot see your point there. Certainly it was settled by the Conference; what else did it mean? They agreed to certain resolutions; they even refused to discuss the scheme upon which your Bill is based; and their resolutions have been endorsed at the Trades Union Congress and at the Co-operative Congress.

574. During the discussion of the cost, were any special taxes alluded to?—No more than I have read out. There was an amendment moved that the cost should be met by taxing land values, but that was withdrawn.

575. And by a graduated income tax?—Yes.

Chairman.

576. You read a passage from a gentleman's speech who said that there were 20 or 30 ways of providing the money?—Yes—taxation of land values and mining royalties, and so on.

Mr. Remnant.

577. You did not go into details in reference to it?—No, it was only in a general way.

Mr. Pemberton.

578. I want to ask you whether the objection which you have to the scheme before us in the Bill is one of principle or of practice—I mean do you think that these Pension Committees would find it in practice difficult to distinguish between those who should be aged pensioners and those who should not?—I think there would be a great difficulty, and I think the Conference felt that it would be a very difficult matter when they came to the question of discriminating between who should be entitled and who should not be entitled to a pension.

579. I want to know whether your objection to this Bill is one of principle only, or because of the fact that it would be in practice difficult to carry out its provisions?—My objection to it is one of principle.

580. But apart from principle, supposing you admit the advisability of the Bill, do you think the machinery of the Pensions Committee is a practicable one or not?—No. There are two or three ways. You have the machinery already in existence through your Poor Law institutions.

581. But I mean, do you think it would be easy or possible for the Pensions Committee to decide who should under this Bill be capable of receiving pensions or not: or do you think it would be too difficult?—I think they would have to go through a kind of Charity Organisation investigation before they found out who was really entitled to the pension and who was not, and in many cases they would find themselves deceived, I expect.

Mr. *Pemberton*—continued.

582. Do you think also that it would cause any jealousy between those who did not get pensions and those who did?—I should think it would cause great feeling between those who did not receive a pension and those who were in receipt of a pension.

Mr. *Goulding*.

583. Can you tell me how many members of Trades Unions there are at present drawing old-age pensions under any Trades Union scheme?—No, I could not.

584. Have the Trades Unions, as a body, ever arrived at, or tried to arrive at, how many of their members receive old-age pensions under Trades Unions?—There is one society, the Amalgamated Society of Engineers, which I believe has about 4,000 at the present time in receipt of what they term superannuation. They do not call it a pension. It is based upon membership. I think, speaking from memory, it commences at a minimum of 5s., going up to a maximum of 10s. per week, according to the membership of a man in the society. I know the time is 40 years' membership; that means that if an engineer finishes his apprenticeship at 21 years of age, joins the Society of Amalgamated Engineers, and lives to 61, then he is entitled to a superannuation of 10s. a week for the rest of his life.

585. But are there 4,000 of those drawing at the present day 10s. a week?—According to what the General Secretary of the Union told me, I believe there are about 4,000 on that fund at the present moment. But, then, they have a membership of 90,000, and the cost of that superannuation is met by a weekly levy which amounts to 3d. a member per week.

586. I ask you because, as far as I have been able to gather from Sir Edward Hamilton's Committee, I can see no trace as to the number of members of Trades Unions drawing an old-age pension from Trades Union schemes?—I could not give the total number.

587. If there are 4,000 in one society drawing so much as 10s., there are probably others in some of the other Trades Union Societies?—There are a number of Trades Union Societies that have this superannuation benefit attached to their other benefits. I think before Lord Rothschild's Committee a number of Unions put in a statement, and if you look up the Blue Book of that Committee I think you will find it there. I believe it gives the total number that is in receipt of the benefit and the amount being paid.

Mr. *Lloyd-George*.

588. I am sorry that I did not hear your evidence. You will kindly tell me if I am asking any question that you have already answered. Have you reckoned up the probable cost of your scheme to the country?—No, I have not, because I say it is impossible to ascertain the total cost until the scheme is in existence, as it does not follow that everybody at 65 years of age or of 60 years of age, as the case may be, would apply for a pension, even if there was one. Take the upper and middle classes, for instance. I do not suppose, even if they contributed towards a

Mr. *Lloyd-George*—continued.

scheme, they would be mean enough to take 5s. a week from it.

589. Has the Trades Congress made any estimate as to what it would cost, or have you made any yourself?—The only information we have, got it from Mr. Charles Booth, who puts it at 26,000,000*l*.

590. The estimate of the cost under this Bill is about 8,000,000*l*., I gather?—That is only my own calculation. My figures may be wrong, but in round figures I think it would come about 8,000,000*l*. That is apart from administration.

591. Do not you think it would be better to proceed by steps with a proposal of this character, and to start with something a little modest to begin with?—With all due respect to you, those are the usual tactics of the politician, but they are not ours outside.

592. You would start with the 26,000,000*l*.?—We go for everybody.

593. That is the ideal at which you are aiming, anyhow?—Yes, that is our ideal, and a very good one.

594. You will take what you can get in the meantime?—We live to help those that cannot help themselves.

595. I am not quarrelling with it, but I am only thinking of the practical side of it. Would you mind taking the Bill which we have before us? I should like to ask you about the qualifications. Qualification (a) you would agree to, I take it—that the recipient should be a British subject?—Yes, I do not object to that.

596. "(b) Is of the age of 65 years or upwards"?—I adhere to the 60, as defined by the Congress.

597. What do you say about Qualification (d), as to having been convicted of an offence, and sentenced to penal servitude or imprisonment?—I do not agree with that.

598. Would you mind giving me your objection to it?—Supposing a man has been imprisoned, it is not to say once a criminal always a criminal, and even supposing he has been a criminal practically all his life, and he should live to a certain age, when he is no longer able, even by thieving or otherwise, to keep himself where does he go? He goes to the workhouse and whether you like it or not, you have to keep him.

599. That is so?—Then why should not you give him a pension, and keep him out of the workhouse?

600. You would not discriminate between the criminal and the industrious workman?—Certainly not. There is forgiveness for every man and woman too, excepting, perhaps, some of them.

Mr. *Channing*.

601. As a matter of fact, criminals over 60 are a very infinitesimal fraction of society, are they not?—I suppose they are. The same applies to the drunkard. I do not suppose many of them live to that age.

Mr. *Lloyd-George*.

602. Do you object to Qualification (f), "Has not received Poor Law relief, other than medical relief

Mr. Lloyd-George—continued.

relief, unless under circumstances of a wholly exceptional character, during 20 years prior to the application for a pension"?—Certainly; I strongly object to that.

603. Would you mind giving me your reasons?—We have 200,000 or 300,000 people to-day in our workhouses. Never mind what their past has been; they are there, and you have to keep them, and they are costing the ratepayers in administration expenses double what they would cost under a scheme of old-age pensions. You are going to exclude all these people under this scheme, and you are going to, as it were, intensify the system of rating by making it harder still for the poor people who have to pay their rates indirectly, through their rent, to live. You would make it worse than it is now, whereas if those people who are in receipt of Poor Law relief, or otherwise, could have a pension outside the workhouse, you would relieve the ratepayers of millions per annum.

604. You are putting it merely on the ground of relief to the ratepayers?—I am putting it on the ground of expediency and economy.

605. On this question of pauperism you know, from your experience as a Guardian, that there are scores of people who practically live on the rates all their lives, and sometimes it is almost hereditary, we find, in the country. Do not you find that?—Yes, to a certain extent that was my experience in Mile End. We would send them out, and they would come back again.

606. Would you really at the end of, say, 60 years, when they had been living on the rates all their lives, or, it may be, in the workhouse, treat them as pensioners, and put them on the same footing as an industrious working man who had broken down?—I should certainly, because it would be a saving to the ratepayers into the bargain.

607. But if it were not a saving to the ratepayers, you would not put them in the same category, would you?—I should.

608. Even if it cost more money to the ratepayers?—But it would not cost more.

609. But if you do not mind, that is a question of figures that you have not gone into, have you?—Yes, I have.

610. I thought you told me you had not gone into the figures?—Which figures?

611. The figures of what it would cost?—I have not worked out myself what it would cost, but I have taken my figures from Charles Booth. I did work out myself what it would cost under this Bill, assuming, of course, that the persons entitled under this Bill would be the number that was calculated by Mr. Chaplin's Committee.

612. But does Mr. Charles Booth say it would not cost more to give a man or a woman a pension than to give them something out of the rates, as they are getting now?—I have read four of his schemes, and he has not gone into this question at all.

613. That is what I am trying to get at. I want to ask you this: Do you mind assuming for the moment that it is found that it would cost more to the ratepayers to give a man a pension under this Bill, or under any other Bill, than to continue him as a pauper; would you still take him off the paupers' list and put him on the pensioners' list?—My answer to that is that it is no use supposing that a thing is going to happen that will not happen.

614. But why do you say it will not happen?—Because I say it is impossible for it to cost more.

615. But do you put it entirely on the score of cost?—I am not dealing with the question of cost now. You are dealing with the question of cost.

616. I will put it specifically, because I want to get at your real objections to these qualifications. I could give you many cases in the country where a pauper is in receipt of 3s. a week, and where he or she has been a pauper practically all his or her life. There are people of that sort. Do you mean to say that when he or she reaches 60 years of age you would take him or her off the category of paupers, and at once give a pension of 5s. a week?—Let me answer that question by asking you one.

617. No?—As far as my experience goes, we have no people in our parish who all their lives have been in receipt of 3s. a week in the shape of outdoor relief.

618. I can assure you that there are many in the country who have been practically all their lives paupers; that is, for 15 or 20 years receiving, say, 2s. 6d. a week?—What age would they commence at?

619. It may be at 30 or 40?—We do not give outdoor relief away in that form in my parish; we may to a widow.

620. I want to know what you would do in a case of that sort, where for 15 or 20 years a pauper has been receiving 2s. 6d. a week. Would you take him or her off the paupers' list the moment that he or she reached 60 and give 5s. a week?—Yes, and give full civil rights too.

621. Therefore, with you it is not a question of cost?—Not in the way you put it.

622. Residence in the district of the Pension Authority is hardly a qualification that I need deal with?—That is a matter of detail.

623. Now what about the income test?—You ask me in a general scheme where the money should come from; and I say from a graduated income-tax.

624. Pardon me; I have not made myself clear. I am taking you now to (f): "An income test for a recipient of a pension"?—I agree with that, certainly. I think that is a very fair proposal.

625. Then (g): "Has endeavoured to the best of his ability, by his industry or by the exercise of reasonable providence, to make provision for himself and those immediately dependent upon him"?—What test would you apply in that case?

626. Supposing there is a man in a district who has been a loafer all his life. In the country, at any rate, there is no difficulty in discovering it and ear-marking him. Would you put him in the same category of a workman who has worked himself out and has no strength left?—Certainly.

627. You would?—Loafer or no loafer he can

So

Mr. *Lloyd-George*—continued.

go into the workhouse; you cannot stop him from going in there.

628. I agree; but would you give him a pension?—Certainly.

629. And you would give him the same pension as a good workman?—Yes; but when you speak of a loafer, may I ask how the loafer, as you term him, is created?

630. I am not arguing now, but simply wanting to get at your views, if you do not mind. Now you suggest a graduated income-tax, and one or two other things, do you not?—I suggest a graduated income tax, and I do not suggest anything else.

631. I thought you suggested mining royalties?—One of the delegates suggested that in his speech.

632. What do you say to increasing, say, the duty on beer, as is done in Denmark, for the purpose of raising an old-age pension fund?—I should not agree to that.

633. Why should not you agree to that?—Beer is the poor man's beverage. I am a teetotaler myself; but, after all, beer is the poor man's beverage, and if you are going to increase the taxation upon that, you are going to make the poor keep the poor.

634. I put the same question about sugar, and no doubt you would have the same objection to that. Would you object to increasing the duty on sugar for the purpose of raising a fund for old-age pensions?—Yes, I should.

635. I take it that you would if you objected to the other?—For the same reason.

636. Do you not think that with regard to any fund of this character, which will be largely, if not mostly, for the benefit of working men, working men themselves would rather like to feel that they were contributing towards the creation of the fund?—My general experience of working men, at any rate, of their representatives, is, no.

637. You think they would object to contribute to a fund which would make provision for their old age? Would they not rather like to feel that this was a fund that they had been contributing to themselves, indirectly it may be, through taxation all their lives?—In expressing the views of organised labour as demonstrated at our annual Congresses, I should say they would object to contributing to a fund. They do not believe in it, and I personally agree with them.

638. You understand that I mean through taxation; I do not mean contributing directly to a fund for old-age pensions, but by means of a tax?—I should personally object to contributing in any sense towards a general scheme of old-age pensions in any way through taxation.

639. I think you said that the middle and the upper classes would not receive any benefit at all from an old-age pension scheme, because they would not claim the pension?—I do not suppose they would be mean enough to claim it.

640. I agree with you. Now would your notion be that the tax should fall exclusively on the class that would not benefit by it, and that the class that would benefit entirely by it should contribute nothing?—Certainly; for the simple reason that they are getting benefit every week of their lives from the labour of the working men who would be entitled to that pension.

Sir *Alexander Hargreaves Brown*.

641. I understood you to say that you have been a guardian?—Yes.

642. And you have been dealing with outdoor relief occasionally?—Yes.

643. The administration of relief?—Yes.

644. Is it not a very difficult matter to discriminate between the deserving and the undeserving poor?—Of course the relieving officer makes the investigation.

645. Even supposing that he does his very best, is it not very often a difficult matter?—No doubt he gets done at times.

646. It is abused at times?—I have no doubt of that, of course. The system under which we give outdoor relief in my parish is that the applicant has to show that he is in receipt of a few shillings or able to earn a few shillings per week, and that a few shillings from our Board to supplement his income will enable him to rub along without coming to the workhouse.

647. I do not ask you to go into details, but it is a difficult matter to discriminate between those whom I will call the well-deserving poor and those who are not well-deserving?—The abuses are likely to be had at times in a matter of that kind.

648. For that reason you say there should be no investigation at all?—No investigation for a pension; I think age should be sufficient.

649. With regard to any contribution from local rates, you are greatly against it, I understand?—I am, because I claim that we are paying enough now.

650. And your Congresses are, too?—Yes.

Mr. *Shackleton*.

651. First, with reference to the whole of the schemes that were before the Conference, the twelve schemes were sent to the various societies?—Yes.

652. Were they sent in good time for each society to consider the schemes?—Yes, ample time.

653. And no doubt the reason why only one scheme was considered was because the delegates had had instructions from the separate societies after a discussion in their own committee rooms as to which scheme they were to vote for? But whilst at the Conference none of the other schemes were spoken to as schemes, still the arguments underlying all the schemes were brought forward in discussion?—Yes, in the various speeches.

654. This was not a Congress of men coming to give their own personal views, but it was a delegate Conference, and many of them—almost entirely all of them, I should think—had received instructions from the various societies as to how to vote on the various schemes, had they not?—I should imagine so.

655. When these Conferences are called together that is the usual way in which the business is done?—Yes.

656. The

Mr. *Shackleton*—continued.

656. This was a Conference of representative men—not men expressing their own views; that is to be clearly understood?—Yes.

Mr. *Remnant*.

657. You cannot say for certain what the views of the members are?—It is impossible for me—and you as sensible men will realise it—to go round to 2,400,000 people and ask if these are their views. We can only get their expression of opinion through their representatives.

Mr. *Channing*.

658. They brought their credentials?—Certainly.

Chairman.

659. They represented the opinion of the majority of their different bodies?—Yes, they did. I want to be honest with the Committee. I have nothing to hide. The schemes were not sent to the Friendly Societies, because at the initial stage of the Organising Committee we had it from the Friendly Societies that they had no mandate from the members, and could not take part in the Conference. We only sent the schemes to those bodies who were going to take part in the Conference, so that, as Mr. Shackleton says, they could bring them before their members, and their delegates could come there with instructions as to how they were to vote. That is the usual way.

Mr. *Shackleton*.

660. This was a Conference mainly of Co-operative Societies and Trades Unions and one or two only of the Friendly Societies?—Yes, that is so.

661. You are not giving the opinion of the Friendly Societies?—No, I am not.

662. You said it was decided that the various resolutions should be put in a Bill and presented to Parliament?—Yes.

663. And that Bill stands now in the name of Mr. Channing, and, practically, the Bill includes the whole of the proposals?—Mr. Channing's Bill includes the whole of the five principles which that Conference agreed to.

664. Now, with reference to the Trade Unions which have superannuation funds, they are not old-age pensions, because the members have no claim upon them unless they pay towards them. It is not compulsory on them to pay?—No.

665. Some of them pay a bigger contribution for superannuation than they do for the ordinary benefits of the Society?—Yes.

666. What would be possible for an engineer to pay, earning 36s. a week, would not be possible for a labourer earning 18s.?—No, he could not do it.

667. And wherever you find superannuation, it is where higher wages are paid?—Yes; it is only large Societies that can have superannuation schemes. My own Society is a small one; we have gone into it by Special Committee several times, but we cannot touch it, because, the Society being so small, the tax would be too heavy for our members.

Mr. *Shackleton*—continued.

668. You would not get a reserve fund?—We have a reserve fund.

669. But you would not get one sufficient for the purpose?—That is so.

670. Now, why did the Conference refuse to specially earmark any particular form of taxation to meet old-age pensions? Could you give the reason of the Conference for that?—I think, speaking from memory, the chief reason was that they thought they were paying quite sufficient already towards the taxation of the country, without having any additional burden thrown upon them.

671. The chief reason given, so far as I remember it, was that if you specially earmarked any form of taxation for old-age pensions, in advocating old-age pensions you would also be advocating various reforms of the incidence of taxation. Taking, for instance, the taxation of land values, or any other form of taxation specially mentioned, the Conference thought that to specially earmark any particular forms of taxation would mean having to fight several other questions along with the one of old-age pensions?—Yes.

672. If I remember rightly, the chief speech on that point was really directed to that?—I think that is correct.

673. As to the question of its being somewhat of a relief to the rates, you estimate that 3 per cent. would cover the working expenses?—I do not say that.

674. But it has been estimated?—Mr. Chaplin's Committee did that.

675. That means that 5s. 3d. would cover each week each pension?—Yes.

676. Taking an average man or woman in the workhouse, the cost to the State is far more than 5s. 3d., is it not?—It varies in proportion with the treatment that is meted out to the inmates of a workhouse. I estimate it from a minimum of 10s. per week up to a maximum of 14s. In my own workhouse we give them good treatment—English meat, no margarine, Cork butter, and home-made bread, and all that. I had several letters sent to me, after that Conference, by various gentlemen from different parts of the country, which I have saved, and one in particular told me that in his parish it was 14s. a week.

677. That includes administration?—Of course, that includes administration. I would repeat that the administration costs more than the keep of the inmate.

678. Speaking as Chairman of that Conference, the expression of opinion given on that point was this, I understand it: That a large number, especially of the labouring classes (and what I mean by "the labouring classes" is those earning less than 22s. or 23s. a week—say those earning 18s.), if they could have some assistance, say 5s. a week, for the mother or 5s. a week for the father, could house them, but could not possibly maintain them?—That is so, and that is borne out by own experience as a Guardian.

679. With regard to the strong repugnance that there is to going into the workhouse, is it not

Mr. Shackleton—continued.

not a fact that many of them would feel relieved if it were possible to remain with their children under a scheme of this kind?—Greatly so.

680. That view was expressed at the Conference?—Exactly so. And the class whose earnings are below a guinea or a pound a week forms the greater proportion of the adult workers of the country.

681. With reference to the exemptions which we find in the Bill referred to the Committee, I want to put it in a general way, and that will save a number of questions. The question of being criminals, the question of being street-corner men, and all the matters taking them out of the Bill were considered by the Congress?—Every one of them.

682. The feeling of the Congress was that so few of that class live to the age of 65 that it was scarcely worth the expense of inquiry to weed them out?—For the few that would live.

683. For the few that would live to that age the expense of inquiry would be so much that it would cost almost as much for the inquiry every year as it would cost to pension those who lived to that age?—Yes.

684. A case was given to the Congress such as this: Supposing a man had during 20 years of his life, from 30 to 50, spent a considerable amount more of his money in drink than he should have done, but afterwards reformed, and for the next 15 years of his life was a respectable citizen, doing his duty, he would by the Bill be debarred from any benefits?—Yes.

685. The point was raised that any reference to a man's actions in his past life would be complicated by the question as to which part of his life you would take. If it was the nearest to the pension age, he would be disqualified; but if it was the furthest away from the pension age, he would come in; but still, taking two men, both might have spent a certain portion of their lives in a way which we do not desire to see?—Yes.

686. That view was placed before the Congress, I think?—Yes, very fully, both by Mr. Rogers and Mr. Maddison.

687. With regard to selecting these men, and considering what part of their life you would regard as being justifiable and which part unjustifiable, the feeling of the Congress, I gather, was that these cases were so few in number when the age was 65 that the question was scarcely worth considering?—Yes.

688. And that the cost of administration would be so enhanced by the inquiry that it would be more than it was worth?—Yes. The Committee should also consider on that point that every man who was a member of a Co-operative Society or Trades Union was, by the fact of his being so, in that sense a thrifty man.

689. In answer to Mr. Lloyd-George, on Clause 6, Section F, you said that you agreed with Sub-section (1), "In the case of a single pension 10s. a week"?—Yes.

690. But you would not say the Congress agreed with that. It could not be universal if they were excluded when they had an income of 10s. a week?—I do not suppose they did agree.

691. My point is that they did not agree. The point was not settled by them?—No, it did not come up before them.

692. I did not want you to seem to give evidence that the Congress had expressed an opinion on a point that was not considered?—That was not considered. Giving my own view of F, I do not think it intends to discriminate. A person may not have 10s., and still be entitled to the 5s., or he may not be fortunate enough to have anything.

Chairman.

693. Have you anything further to say?—I want to make myself clear upon that. Mr. Shackleton is quite correct. That question with regard to the income of 10s. or the per week has never been discussed by the Congress, although personally I have no objection to it.

694. If a scheme was put forward by which some of the most deserving and thrifty old people, say 200,000 or 300,000 of them, could get pensions, would you advise the Trades Union Congress to reject such a scheme?—They would have to decide that for themselves.

695. But I should like to know what your advice would be; would you advise them to reject it?—I should stand by the decision already arrived at by the Congress.

696. You would say, pensions for all or nothing—with the possible exception of those having more than 10s. a week?—Yes, that is the line I should take.

697. Even if it seemed impossible, for financial reasons, ever to get the scheme that you propose, you would not advise a Trades Union Congress to accept the more moderate scheme of this Bill?—I could only deal with that point when it arose. We sometimes ask for an increase in wages, and do not always get it all.

698. But this was one of the schemes put before your Congress on the agenda paper: and, therefore, it did arise?—Yes.

699. You would not advise them, if they could not get all that they wanted, to take all they could get?—No.

Mr. Channing.

700. I think that your answers to Mr. Lloyd-George were perhaps a little misunderstood. Did you wish to convey that, in your opinion, the whole of the old-age pension fund was to come from the taxation of the richer classes, or did you mean to adopt the position of the Conference, that it should come from Imperial taxation?—Broadly speaking, I agree with the principle laid down at the Conference, that it should come from Imperial taxation. That means everybody contributing towards it. But if more money was required, and I was asked where that money should come from, I should say from a graduated income tax.

Chairman.

701. Then it would not be correct to say that the view that you have set before us this afternoon is that the whole of the contribution for this purpose should come from the richer classes?—I say this: The Conference said that the money [illegible]

Chairman—continued.

money should come from Imperial taxation, which I agree with, and Imperial taxation is a fund that every person contributes to. But, say that the Chancellor of the Exchequer, who, after all, would have to find the money for old-age pensions, said, "Now I must have some other source of income for old-age pensions," then I say it should come from a graduated income tax.

702. This would be an additional charge; and, therefore, would require additional revenue?—If he said that he wanted another source of income, then I say it should come from there.

Mr. William Crooks (a Member of the House), Examined.

Chairman.

703. You are Chairman of the Poplar Board of Guardians?—Yes.

704. You have for a great many years made a study of the question of the administration of the Poor Law, have you not?—I have.

705. And you have actually been engaged in administering it?—Yes.

706. It has been stated before this Committee that if such a scheme of old-age pensions as is set out in this Bill was established a very large number of those over 65 now in the workhouses would go out and live with their friends. Have you any practical experience of whether that is so or not?—Yes, I have some practical experience, and I regret that it does not quite carry that out. In 1889 the Poplar Guardians appointed a Special Committee to go into that very point, and this is the report. The reference was: "To consider (1) any cases of inmates over 60 years of age who have relations or friends capable and willing to take charge of them. (2) The best means of providing additional accommodation, and to report thereon." I do not think it is necessary to read further. We went into it very carefully, and the words which we use are: "We are satisfied that they would not be as well looked after and cared for out of the workhouse as they are at the present time." We have got 1,000 inmates over 60. Having regard to the age and infirmity of such persons, some of whom are blind and others quite helpless, we are satisfied that they would not be as well looked after and cared for out of the workhouse as they are at the present time. This appears to be fully recognised by the inmates themselves, many of whom spoke gratefully of the attention they receive and the comforts they enjoy in the workhouse, and expressed a strong desire to be allowed to remain. We have, however, set aside for further inquiry all cases where there appeared to be any prospect of relatives or friends being able to provide suitable accommodation in the event of the Guardians agreeing to allow outdoor relief." Then our subsequent report runs thus: Adopted by the Board on July 12, 1898. Your Committee have now to report the completion of their inquiries in pursuance of the first portion of the Board's reference of October 18th, 1893. On the 4th April last we reported that we had seen and inquired into the circumstances of about 1,000 aged inmates of the workhouse, but that in the majority of cases, having regard to the age and infirmity of such persons, some of whom were blind and others quite helpless, we were satisfied that they would not be as well cared for out of the workhouse. This was fully recognised by the inmates themselves, many of whom spoke gratefully of the treatment they received, and expressed a strong desire to be allowed to remain in the workhouse, where they were happy and comfortable. We, however, set aside for further consideration all cases where there appeared to be any prospect of relatives or friends being able to provide suitable accommodation in the event of the Guardians agreeing to outdoor relief, the result of the inquiries into those cases being as follows:—We give the total result of our diligent inquiry into over 200 cases that we thought we might do something with. The result was that we recommended for outdoor relief 41, not considered suitable 130, and accommodation offered by friends, but not satisfactory, 11 cases. Fourteen persons were discharged from the workhouse altogether without any relief; sent to the sick asylum for infirmary treatment, 10; there died, 6; and we removed to the asylum two, making a total out of the 1,000 inquired into of 216. The number relieved at 5s. a week was 45; the number returned to the workhouse since that date out of that number, or to the sick asylum, is 21. The two inquiries that we held under the orders issued by your department, namely, that we should give wherever we could adequate outdoor relief, of course encouraged the Guardians to consider whether it was possible to get a number out of the house. I think the Committee is entitled to have it said of it that it was made up mainly of persons who were exceedingly anxious to get people out of the house—that is to say, they left no stone unturned—they did everything they could do; they gave outfits to people who had been in so long that they had no clothes; they gave them a working-day suit and a Sunday suit where they were men, and the same process was gone through where they were women. I have felt all along, speaking of Guardians generally, and I know a tremendous lot all over the country, that there is a general desire to get people out of the workhouse if it is at all practicable. The condition of things obtaining to-day is not the same as it was 12 or 15 years ago. Going back as I can to 1850 or 1860 I have a very lively recollection of everything that went on then.

707. Out of the 1,000 aged inmates you only had 201 for special investigation? How did you come down from 1,000 to the 201—what was the process by which you reduced it?—We have 1,000 persons over 60, and we had regard to age and infirmity; some of them were blind, and others quite helpless.

Chairman—continued.

708. On account of physical reasons they were reduced to 201?—That is so; we got down to that. I know you will agree with what I am now going to say, that there is a double obligation upon guardians, not only to see that people get sufficient to live upon outdoors, but that they are kept clean and generally well looked after. We have no hesitation in our Union in ordering people to the workhouse, even if 2s. 6d. a week would keep them out, if we find that their other circumstances as citizens are not all that we have a right to expect. 130 persons out of the 200 and odd had homes of such an unsatisfactory character that we could not allow them to go to them.

709. As regards the 130 "not considered suitable," was that on account of the accommodation that their funds could provide?—Yes, that is it.

710. Your experience is that not 5 per cent. of the old people in the workhouses could go out?—I do not think they could. In that little pamphlet I make that pretty clear. You see the system is so different now from what it was in the old times.

711. There is another point upon which you might, by your great experience, help us. It was suggested at the last meeting by Mr. Lloyd-George, in a question to Sir Edward Hamilton, that a great many of these old people are man and wife, and he suggested that one-third of the old people in receipt of help, or likely to require help, were man and wife. Would you say that one-third of the old people over 65 in a poor condition of life were man and wife?—That is a very large proportion; I should not think it was anything like that.

712. I do not know myself, and I was wondering whether you could help us?—I do not think it would work out at anything like that proportion. We have got, roughly speaking, 1,500 inmates to-day, and I should not think that we have 16 married couples. We have eight rooms set aside for married couples. We decided that those who were not living together in the house should have their meals together, and, looking in at the Dining Hall, I do not remember seeing more than four or five sitting down there, so I put the total at 16.

713. Of those over 65, the proportion would be very much less?—Yes. We do not consider any person aged at all who is not 60. We count those under 60 as able-bodied people, as you know, according to the Order of the Board, and put them out of consideration.

714. With regard to outdoor relief, are many men and their wives relieved?—Since I was asked the other day whether I could get any figures, I have obtained this letter, which practically covers the ground; it is very short:—"Dear Sir,—I herewith beg to hand you the information required by the Chairman of the Board as to the number of persons now on the Relief List having other sources of income, and who, with a pension of, say, 5s. per week, might cease to be chargeable to the rates. The figures as returned by the Relieving Officers are as follows." The precaution has been taken of asking whether 5s. a week for those people who are receiving outdoor relief and who have friends or relations to look after them, or who have a private source of income, would take them off the rates, and we find that we have over the age of sixty 1,824 persons receiving outdoor relief where such pension might have that effect. I absolutely agree that it would not be a fair average. It would be an abnormal amount, taking the country through—at least I think so, having regard to the fact that in some parts of Wales the workhouses are small, and they have no accommodation, and give outdoor relief to a very large extent. In manufacturing districts you get a congregation of poor; you perhaps obtain a reputation for being sympathetic, which will account for the large proportion of the persons coming for outdoor relief. They will come and qualify. I do not think I could deny it, although I sometimes like to.

715. They move into Unions where the Board are willing to give outdoor relief?—Why I plead for this is because I think the law of settlement is so awfully bad. Frequently you get a son and a daughter living in a district where they know the Guardians are fairly sympathetic. They go there and stop for the qualifying period. It would rather reduce the number if they were spread over a larger area. Take St. George's in the East and Whitechapel. Every man who knows the districts will declare that they are better off in consequence of the suppression of outdoor relief than a Union that gives it. St. George's in the East is an exceedingly poor place; they give very little outdoor relief: and the poor simply drift down to where outdoor relief is sympathetically considered—I will put it in that way.

716. You gave us the number of 1,824 over 60. Now what is the report of your relieving officers on the question that you put to them as to how many could maintain themselves if a little help was given by the Guardians?—We have a general relieving officer, and I asked through the clerk that it should be put in that way. It is perfectly natural, but sometimes Committees miss the all-important point. The Charity Organisation Society miss the point; they miss the fact that you do not give out relief to able-bodied persons at all, and persons under a certain age can only get relief if they are crippled or infirm. They may deserve the pension, but they are not within the four corners of the Bill, and for the moment we are dealing with the aged.

717. What was the result of the inquiry as to the 1,824?—The information asked for was "as to the number of persons now on the Relief List having other sources of income, and who, with a pension of, say, 5s. per week, might cease to be chargeable to the rates."

718. The answer to that question is "1,824"?—Yes.

Mr. Shackleton.

719. How many have you altogether on the list?—Probably 2,500, or something like that. I did not consider those figures were worth getting.

Mr. Goulding.

720. It is over half?—Yes. The Guardians bad as they are—and I have been associated with them

Mr. Goulding—continued.

them for 10 years—are fairly discriminating. You may have a tradesman come on who will help some person who should not be helped, but in a few weeks it is discovered that the person helped is not a proper person to be assisted, and he is given an order for the house, or got rid of altogether. I do not think you would find many getting outdoor relief who had no right to it. It is generally 4 or 5 per cent.

Chairman.

721. What do you mean by that, having regard to the applicant's circumstances or character?—I will put it in two ways. In the first place, they are people whose friends are sufficiently well off to be able to keep them, or, on the other hand, they are not the sort of persons that it is desirable to keep out of the house, and for the benefit of the community they should be in the house.

722. Inquiries are made by your relieving officer as to them?—Always.

723. Do you find the relieving officers have any great difficulty in distinguishing between deserving and undeserving cases?—No; I think it is the sort of thing that you get so used to by constant association as years go on, that you have very little difficulty in discriminating. For instance, you get an applicant, on Relief Committee day, and no one in the Committee knows the applicant at all. They say: "What do you know of this case, Mr. R. O.?" He says: "I have not had time to inquire; the statement is so and so," and he reads the statement out. We leave it in his hands for two weeks, and he gives food, so that the person does not starve while he is making inquiry into the conditions. At the end of a fortnight, if we have any difficulty in getting the information, we say: "We cannot find out about you; we are not at all satisfied; we will give you an order for the house."

724. You go into the question, not only of their destitution and having no friends, but also their previous history?—We say: "Who are you? What are you? Where do you come from? How have you been living?"

725. So that you really do look to see whether they have been good citizens or not?—It is part of our obligations to do that.

726. Is there anything else that you wish to bring before the Committee?—I do not disguise from myself the fact that the simplest way of dealing with the question, if the nation could bear it, would be a universal system of old-age pensions. But I want to go as far as ever I possibly can. I think that we have a good many thousands of respectable people who, with a little relief, might remain at home with their friends and relations, and if I know anything of the promoters of the Bill, I should say it is their desire to keep people out of the workhouses. Of course, the position in London is altogether different from that of other parts of the kingdom. For instance, in London we get 5d. a day from the Metropolitan Common Poor Fund up to the certified number of persons in the workhouse. There

Chairman—continued.

is a reduction made if there are any children in the workhouses, and very properly so; I have never complained about that at all. Then 4d. a day is given out of the County Council Fund on the average number of persons in the workhouse previous to 1888. That had this effect—that frequently people were ordered into the workhouse because it was cheaper to keep them in the workhouse than it was to give outdoor relief. St. George's-in-the-East are receiving money on a larger number of paupers than there are in the house at the moment. It draws 4d. a day on an ascertained number previous to 1888. It is 9d. a day altogether. Every farthing of outdoor relief, as you know, comes out of the local rates, and there was a tendency, therefore, to send people to the workhouse instead of keeping them out. Fourteen years have elapsed since that Act came into operation. It does not meet the case. Some of us have been arguing that, within the scope of a Bill of this character, we might extend the principle of the Common Poor Fund and the County Council payment, and give to certain people that the Bill would embrace the 9d. a day pension out of doors rather than indoors.

727. If you say it should be done within the four corners of the Bill, does that mean that you agree with the qualifications in Clause 6 of the Bill?—I think they are a great deal too much. Who is going to ask if a man "Has not within the last 20 years been convicted of an offence and sentenced to penal servitude or imprisonment without the option of a fine"? I want to put this perfectly clearly. I think I know men nearly as well as most other men know him, and I put it to you very plainly: supposing for a single moment you are going to give to any of these persons 5s., and they had absolutely nothing in the world, they would have to give you the 5s. back and go into the workhouse. They could not live outside. These people who have got to 65 years of age, and who have led a disreputable life, and have no friends, could not live outside; and your Act would not be worth a penny to them.

728. Then it is no hardship to exclude them?—Not at all. It is perfectly true that here and there you might get a man who really had reformed and was living a decent life. A case comes to my mind at this moment. I knew a man who was convicted of murder. He served 11 years and got out. He is now leading a proper life, and is certainly a very respectable man. Supposing he was over 65, it would be a little hard on him to say that he should be excluded from the benefit of the Act. And that is only one case in a million.

729. You really raise no objection to the exclusion on account of conviction?—I say that the 5s. a week will not be any good to some; they would not live on it. You want to help people who have already a little and want to help themselves and keep off the poor rates.

730. Would you put into this Bill a maximum limit of income?—I think I would.

731. On the principle of helping those who help themselves?—Yes. There are a variety of reasons why that should be done. One might say

Chairman—continued.

say, "What do you call thrift?" It might be said, "Belonging to a Trades Union or a Benefit Society." It is sufficient to know that the man has kept his head above water at a low rate of pay. That shows he has generally been a respectable man, all the crime he has ever committed being that of being poor all his life. I would not quarrel about him.

732. You would not make it a hard-and-fast line that he should succeed in acquiring an income for old age so long as he had tried?—That is so. Now what is the use of giving 5s. a week to a man who has no friends and relations to look after him, and no shelter at 65 years of age? It is too meagre; it is ridiculous. The fellow would have to be begging and cadging half the week to make two ends meet; he could not live on it.

733. Now I come to the point you wished to be asked about. Would you propose to allow the people in receipt of pensions to work?—Certainly not; I am very emphatic about that. I would refer to your own Local Government Board rules. If you departed from the principle you would land yourself in endless difficulties. If a person past the age claimed a pension and were allowed to use that pension as practically a subsidy, enabling him to go to work for somebody cheaper than the ordinary man, where should we be landed? I quote the case of a widow able to make shirts at 1s. 6d. a dozen because a sympathetic Board of Guardians gives her 4s. a week outdoor relief. She does not get the money at all; simply the fellow who sweats her gets all the advantage of the 4s. or 5s. as the case might be. He gets her to work cheaply because she has got some pension or out relief.

734. Would you put a proviso in Clause that they shall also be past work or shall not work if they receive the pension?—These are the words I would put in with regard to all grants made conditionally: "The recipient shall not be employed for wages or other hire or remuneration by any person." Otherwise I can see a pension going into the pocket of somebody who can do without it. A man could displace the 24s. a week man by taking a job for 18s., and live on the 18s. and 5s. which he got from the Government or from any other source.

735. You have studied the Bill; I do not know if you wish to make any remarks specially about the Bill?—There are one or two points I have marked. "An aged pensioner who elects to live in the workhouse, or special cottage home, or other suitable place provided by the Guardians, shall be classified as such, and receive special consideration and treatment to the satisfaction of the Local Government Board in lieu of an old-age pension." Where is the need to put that in?

736. I am afraid that we must ask you to attend again if it will be convenient?—Certainly.

Monday, 20th July 1903.

MEMBERS PRESENT:

Mr. Channing.	Mr. Pemberton.
Mr. Goulding.	Colonel Pilkington.
Mr. John Hutton.	Sir Robert Reid.
Mr. Lloyd-George.	Mr. Remnant.
Mr. Grant Lawson.	Mr. Shackleton.
Mr. O'Shee.	Mr. Skewes-Cox.

MR. GRANT LAWSON IN THE CHAIR.

Mr. JAMES CLEMENT GRAY; Examined.

Chairman.

737. You are the General Secretary of the Co-operative Union, are you not?—Yes.

738. What is the Co-operative Union?—The Co-operative Union is a voluntary federation of the Co-operative Societies of the United Kingdom, and it represents the opinions of the co-operators, as ascertained by their annual Congress and periodical Conferences throughout the country. It has been in existence for something like 40 years.

739. It includes a great many Societies, I presume?—The Union includes 1,169 Societies, with an individual membership of 1,814,118. Outside the Union there are 502 Societies, with an individual membership of 188,000. Therefore, we may say that we represent, out of 2,000,000, 1,800,000 of the co-operators of the country.

740. As regards the Annual Congress of Co-operators, it is attended by delegates, I understand?—Yes. The Congress is held at various places throughout the country. It goes from county to county, and it is generally attended by about 1,200 delegates representing the various Societies of the United Kingdom.

741. The Committee would like to know how far these delegates receive instructions from their Societies before they come to the Conference?—Three weeks before the date for holding the Congress we send out a report on all the matters which have been handled and discussed by the Board of the Co-operative Union during the year, and also the proposals which will come before the Congress. These are sent out to the Societies, with a request that they will instruct their delegates to meet, discuss the report, and take the opinion of their members upon them. Then they come up to the Congress prepared to vote.

742. Do you send round an agenda paper showing what questions will be put to the Congress?—We send round a rather big volume, which contains the agenda for the Congress, a detailed report of all that has taken place, and the work of the sub-committees during the year, and then the proposals which will be brought before the Congress.

Chairman—continued.

743. So that the proposals which they will be asked to vote upon are before the delegates before they come, and they receive instructions?—Yes, that is so; at least three weeks before Congress they are sent out.

744. There has been, I believe, a considerable development of opinion in your Union on the subject of old-age pensions?—Yes.

745. Would you briefly trace it?—The subject of superannuation and old-age pensions has received the attention of the Co-operative Congress for many years. It was first discussed at the Annual Congress held in Bristol, in 1893. At that time they dealt mainly with the question of superannuation and pensions for the employees of Co-operative Societies. It was resolved by that Congress "That the United Board of the Co-operative Union be requested to report to next Congress as to some scheme for old-age pensions." That meant for the employees of the Co-operative Societies only. That was brought up again at the Congress at Perth, in 1897, when a resolution was passed "That the Congress hereby expresses the opinion that the establishment of superannuation funds by all Co-operative Societies should be the least concession granted to the employees, and recommends, with the view of bringing the question prominently before the attention of Societies, that it be an instruction to the several sectional Boards to have this paper discussed at sectional and district Conferences during the year, to which employees' and Societies' representatives shall be invited."

746. You were still providing for your own members, and not for the rest of the community?—Yes. I am trying to trace how we began by our own people, and then worked up to the general system. I may say that the discussion was not satisfactory in the Conferences during the year, and then at the next the United Board were instructed again to take steps to have the question of superannuation more fully discussed during the coming year: "and that, in view of the various suggestions made at the Conferences of the past year, this Congress is of opinion that the

Chairman—continued.

the scope of the inquiry should be extended so as to include all phases of the superannuation question." That was in 1898, at Peterborough.

747. At what time of the year?—It is always the three first days in Whit-week. At Liverpool, in 1899, the following resolution was passed:—"That the United Board be instructed to inquire into the subject of superannuation and old-age pensions for co-operators, and that they be requested to prepare a special report for next Congress, such report to embody alternative methods, so that all aspects of the question may be fully discussed." That you will see was an advance upon the first Congress, when they were discussing only the application of pensions to employees. Now it is to include all members of Co-operative Societies.

748. But still to be provided by the Societies?—By the Societies. Following the Liverpool Congress, the Board of the Union appointed a Special Committee to devise pension schemes suitable for co-operators.

749. And that Board was sitting at the same time as Mr. Chaplin's Committee was sitting, in the year 1899?—Yes, that would be so, in the year 1899. A report was submitted on the schemes which had been prepared during the year. There were three schemes submitted, and this was only for co-operators I ought to observe again. The first scheme was that an old-age pension society should be established, to be composed of all Co-operative Societies willing to take part in the scheme; that each Co-operative Society, on becoming a member of the old-age pension society, should agree to contribute 6s. per year per member to the Old-age Pension Fund, and that this fund should be accumulated for eight years before any claim could be made upon it, and then it was proposed that a pension of 7s. 6d. per week should be paid to all members claiming it who had arrived at the age of 60.

750. Have you women members as well as men?—Yes. In some societies there will be at least two-thirds women. The scheme included the women members as well as the men, and also included a provision that, in the case of the death of the husband the wife might succeed to his claim for the pension.

751. That was the first proposal?—That was the first proposal. Then there was a modification of that proposal.

752. Did you make statistical inquiries to ascertain whether the 6s. per member contribution would be sufficient, when accumulated for eight years, to pay friends?—It was never tested by an actuary. This was my own scheme. The first two schemes were drawn up by myself, and the third by Mr. Greening, and we tested them, as far as we were able to, from our experience. There were many things to be taken into account. We worked it out in this way: According to the last returns there were 1,468 Distributive Societies in the United Kingdom. These 1,468 Societies had 1,535,000 members. At 6s. per member a sum of 460,535l. would be contributed annually to the funds of the Old-age Pensions Society. This sum, invested at 2½ per cent. (taking it as low as possible, to be on the safe side), would produce each year interest as follows—then I state what it would produce. At the end of eight years we should have a fund accumulated of 4,023,000l., which would then be permanently invested to produce an annual income of 100,569l. We could have really got a better interest than 2½ per cent. This, along with the annual contributions from the Societies of 460,000l., would give an annual revenue of 561,069l. available for pensions and expenses of management. I am on the 5s. scheme now; not the 7s. 6d. one.

753. It does not matter. May I take it that the second scheme was similar to the first?—Yes, it was based on the same proportionate calculations.

754. It proposed 5s. instead of 7s. 6d.?—Yes; subscriptions at the rate of 6s. per year per member, and 5s. per week pension on attaining 60 years.

755. The point which the Committee are interested in is that this is your calculation of the cost of supplying pensions to all your members at the age of 60?—At the age of 60.

756. You reckon that would cost 561,069l. a year?—I do not say all the members. I go on to say how many it would provide for, and then try to calculate whether there would be more than that number requiring a pension in a Co-operative Society. With this amount pensions of 5s. a week might be paid to 41,008 persons. This would absorb 533,000l., leaving a balance of 28,118l. for reserve and management of expenses. The membership of the Societies being 1,535,000, it would mean that the available funds would suffice to pay pensions to one member in every 37 of the total membership. Therefore, a Society having 3,700 members should not average more than 100 pensioners, and so proportionately. I tested that with one or two Societies in the country, and I was told by the secretaries and officials of those Societies that they thought that there would be an ample margin.

Sir Robert Reid.

757. 1 in 37 is a very low proportion of persons over 60?—The inquiries which I made led me to believe that it would be sufficient. Had the scheme been proceeded with we intended to submit it to an actuary to be tested, but the Conference would not have anything to do with it, as I say later on.

Chairman.

758. Are all your members over 21?—No; they can become members at 16.

759. Are there many young members?—Yes, a considerable number of young persons. According to the Act of Parliament they can become members at 16. Then there are some qualifications which would reduce the claimants considerably. "No claim can be made in respect to any member of a Distributive Society until he has been a member of such Society, or of some other Distributive Society, which has, for not less than 8 years, been a member of the Old-age Pension Society for a period of not less than 20 years in all, and has purchased" (to make, you see, a purchase qualification) "from the said Society or Societies, goods to the amount of 20l. as a yearly average during the whole of the

Chairman—continued.

the said period of 20 years." These conditions would make a considerable reduction in the claims, and, as the pensions would have to be paid out of the profits made from the purchases of the members, we intended that they should be loyal in their support of the Society in order to enable it to pay the pensions.

760. Is that the gist of schemes 1 and 2?—Of the three schemes. The third scheme by Mr. Greening provided that the members themselves should contribute something towards it.

761. As apart from the Societies?—As apart from the Societies. The Societies would contribute one-tenth of their profits annually to a pension fund, and according to the profits the rate of pension would vary. A society earning 3s. dividend would ensure 3s. per week, whereas a society only earning a 6d. dividend would ensure 1s. 6d. per week pension, and the difference was to be made up by the contributions of the individual members. That scheme was not discussed at all, so I do not think it necessary to enlarge upon it.

762. Those were brought before the Cardiff Congress?—These were submitted to the Cardiff Congress in 1900, and a resolution was passed instructing the Board to submit the schemes for the opinions of Sectional and District Conferences. It was overwhelmingly in favour of a national instead of co-operative system, and, as a statement of the feeling of those Conferences, I might read one resolution only.

Mr. Shackleton.

763. Will you explain what a Sectional Conference is?—The Union has one annual Congress, and for the purpose of organisation it is divided into six sections. We take Scotland as one section. The northern counties, Northumberland, Durham, and the northern part of Yorkshire, form one section. Then there is the north-west section, Lancashire, Yorkshire, and Cheshire; and then there are the Midland, the Southern, the Western and South-western sections. These sections each have a Board of their own subordinate to the Central Board of the Union, and each section holds four Sectional Conferences during the year. Then each of these six sections is sub-divided into District Associations. The North-west Section, which is the largest, has 15 District Associations. That is so as to have them in a smaller compass where each society can come into contact and confer with the others frequently. Each of these District Associations has four Conferences in the year, so that we have about 250 or 300 Conferences during the year by which we can ascertain the opinions of our members throughout the country.

Chairman.

764. You were going to read to us the resolution of one of these Sectional Conferences?—Yes. I take the first on the list as a sample of the rest: "That this Conference, recognising in the question of old-age pensions a subject of vast importance and charged with interests of a far-reaching character, hereby expresses the opinion that no solution on the basis of a National Old-age Pension Scheme will alone prove satisfactory, adequate, and just; and, further, thinks that any attempted solution on sectional lines for the benefit of co-operators only, through the medium of the co-operative movement, is unwise, ungenerous, and impracticable." The majority of the Conferences passed resolutions in that strain, believing that it would be wiser and better from every point of view to support a national system of old-age pensions rather than a sectional one for co-operators only.

765. They say in that resolution that it is "ungenerous." Can you explain how they make it out as ungenerous?—I think the idea would be that it would keep out a lot of poor people who have no connection with the co-operative movement, and whom it is very difficult to get connected with the movement.

766. They would not be subscribers to the scheme?—They would not be members of the co-operative societies. I am sorry to say that the great mass of the poor people who would benefit most by the co-operative movement do not take advantage of it. It is generally the working man and artisan who is better off who sees the advantages of the society, and joins it, and is able to save money by his membership of the society, whereas the very people who ought to have pensions more than the artisan are outside of the movement, and, in the opinion of many of our delegates, it was thought ungenerous to block the way for a general scheme of old-age pensions by adopting a partial one in our own favour only. I think that that was the leading idea.

767. You have told us that the opinion, as gathered in the way that you have described, is overwhelming in favour of a national as against a co-operative society scheme?—Yes, I have the report of the resolutions passed at various Congresses which all bear out what I say. At the Middlesbrough Congress, in 1901, when the resolutions of the Conferences were submitted to the annual Congress, a resolution was passed as follows: "That this Congress, strengthened by the overwhelming opinion as expressed by co-operative Conferences held during the year, hereby declares the urgent necessity of of Parliament providing an old-age pension for every citizen, male and female."

768. Were you at that Conference at Middlesbrough?—Yes. I have been at them all for the last 30 years.

769. Were various schemes of old-age pensions discussed there?—Not at Middlesbrough. I think you are referring to the one which was held afterwards in London.

770. We shall come to it gradually?—Following the Middlesbrough Congress, which was held in Whit week, 1901, in September of that year, the Board of the Co-operative Union agreed to join with the Trades Unions Parliamentary Committee in convening a National Conference of Representatives of Co-operative Societies and Trades Unions to discuss the question. At that joint Conference, held in London on January 14th and 15th, Mr. Steadman, Chairman of the Parliamentary Committee of the Trades Union Congress, presided on the first day, and Mr. Benjamin

Chairman—continued.

Benjamin Jones, as representing the Co-operative Union, presided on the second day.

771. We have had evidence of that from Mr. Steadman?—So I notice. I only wish to emphasise that it was a joint Conference of both bodies, both Co-operators and Trades Unionists. We were in equal force at that Conference.

772. At that Conference various schemes were submitted?—Yes, various schemes were put in the agenda before the Conference. The sub-committee which had the arrangements in hand for that Conference submitted these various schemes, and also submitted an outline of their own, which was the one mainly discussed there.

773. Did the Co-operative Union as such go into the relative merits of the various schemes on the agenda paper?—Through its representatives. We had three representatives on the Committee, and the Trade Union Parliamentary Committee had three.

774. But you had not a separate Conference of your Union to consider that agenda paper?—No, we had not, nor had the Trades Unions. We agreed to join in this one. It was arranged jointly by the Committees appointed for that purpose. The schemes were presented to the Board of the Co-operative Union, I may say, but not to the Congress.

775. That Board practically represents the opinion of the Co-operative Union, I suppose?—Yes, as ascertained through the Congress.

776. But I want to know whether you have had an inquiry at your Board on the relative methods suggested for providing old-age pensions?—The Congress has had the subject before it since this Conference in London, and unanimously approved. The Congress did not have all these details before them at first, but only the Board, but, following the Conference in London, it has been reported to the Co-operative Congress, and unanimously approved.

777. What action was taken by the Board subsequently to this Conference in 1902?—We appointed a sub-committee to continue to act with the sub-committee of the Trade Union Parliamentary Committee, and that Parliamentary Committee was instructed to prepare a Bill on the lines laid down in the resolution passed at the London Conference, and to seek an interview with the Prime Minister for the purpose of bringing it forward. We saw, however, that steps were being taken in this direction by other members of Parliament, and I think the opinion was that we had better wait, and see what developed.

778. So now you have traced before us the development of opinion in the Co-operative Union, from a small scheme providing for their own employees up to a national scheme providing for everybody?—Yes, that is what I have tried to do.

779. Would you tell us the reason for this growth of opinion, as it strikes you?—It is difficult to arrive, perhaps, at what were the reasons which guided people in voting, but it has struck me that the fact is that the Co-operative movement, being composed chiefly of working people in receipt of low wages, they object to providing old-age pensions for employees who are better paid than themselves. When it was proposed to provide pensions for our own employees, that was the objection in the first instance. The Co-operative employees generally are quite as well, or even better, paid than those who employ them. A large number of our members are agricultural labourers in receipt of 14s. or 15s. a week. Others never get more than 1*l*. a week by labour, and when a co-operative employee is getting 30s. or 35s. per week, or even more in the shops, these poor people object to any of their profits derived from their stores in country districts being taken to provide pensions for those who are better paid than themselves. That was stated commonly in our Conferences. It was said: "We are poor people. We cannot afford to lose anything that ought to come to us by reason of our dividends."

780. They thought, in fact, that the man getting 35s. a week ought to provide for his own old age?—That is so. It was plainly stated in agricultural districts where we held Conferences, "We are only getting 15s. a week, and the profits derived by our Society, according to rules, come to us in proportion to what we purchase from the Society, and we object to any portion of these being taken from us in order to provide for old-age pensions for employees.

781. When there was a universal scheme adopted by Congress in 1902, did not the poorer co-operators, who would be taxed, I suppose, to provide funds, raise the same objection to a universal pension scheme?—They objected altogether to any portion of their profits being taken to provide pensions. They said that it was the duty of the State to provide pensions for those who were unable to work after spending a lifetime in labour, and that they ought not to have anything taken from their scanty income at the present time to provide for their old age, seeing that they had so little to live upon.

782. There was, as you have just mentioned, an objection to a scheme for pensions for the employees of the Societies. Would you tell us what other objection was taken to it?—Under head (b) I say: "If the scheme suggested by the Report to the Co-operative Congress were adopted, the application would only extend to co-operators, and would not (except so far as co-operators were concerned) solve the problem of old-age poverty, which it should be the aim of any old-age pension scheme to do." They realised that it would only be a very partial solution, and a solution as regards those people really not so much in want of pensions as those outside the movement, as I explained before, and they believed that people having done a life's work and being worn out in that work, it was the duty of the State to provide for them in some way different from the present method of pauperising: that by right of their labour they had the right to live after they had ceased to labour.

783. By right of their labour? This was all based on the fact, I suppose, that they had been honest and industrious labourers?—Yes. I am giving, as far as I can, the gist of what was said in these discussions—that if a man had worked honestly for a lifetime, it must have been for the good of the community, and therefore the community should support him when he got past work.

784. That does not refer to universal pensions, but only to pensions to those who have been

honest

honest and industrious labourers?—That was as far as we discussed it. I am speaking now of its application to co-operators only.

785. But by your resolutions of 1902 you are pledged to a universal system?—We are; that was agreed to by the subsequent Congress, and it was so acceptable to them that they adopted it without discussion.

786. So that the question whether they were willing to give pensions to the wastrels was not gone into?—It was not at our Congress. It was gone into pretty fully at the London Conference.

787. What was your next Congress after the joint Conference?—At Exeter, Whit-week, 1902, at which the report of the London Conference was submitted and approved.

788. After discussion?—Without discussion. It was discussed very fully at the joint Conference, the London Conference, but not discussed at our own subsequent Congress.

Mr. Harold Cox.

789. But a full report had been sent round?—A full report was submitted with every detail of the scheme. Full reports of the joint Conference had been sent out in thousands to our members for their perusal.

Chairman.

790. May I take it that the Co-operative Union is pledged to a scheme of universal pensions at the age of 60 to all persons, whatever their previous history and whatever their means?—Yes.

791. Did you at Exeter consider the expense of that?—No, it was not discussed at all at Exeter.

792. Then what about the Congress in 1903, last Whit-week? Did you go into the question then?—No, there was nothing done in regard to it at that Congress.

793. There is one other matter on your proof which I should like to ask you about, and that is the suggestion which your Union make on the subject of the financing of the scheme. You object to local taxation being used, do you not? —We declare in favour of pensions coming out of the Imperial funds on account of the inequality of the burden on local taxes. It struck me in making this proof that there would be considerable inequality by reason of removals of working men from place to place, and I do not see anything in the Bill to provide against that. One district might be flooded with aged people who had been labouring there for years, or who had just gone out of the district before they ceased to work. There would be some difficulty in administration, and, I think, an unfair burden on the locality. At any rate, we declared at the Conference that it should all come out of the Imperial funds by Imperial taxation.

794. With regard to administration, how was it to be administered?—Local administration and, I think, the machinery provided in that Bill would answer our purpose.

795. When you say "that Bill," do you mean the one introduced by Mr. Channing or the Bill before the Committee?—Mr. Remnant's Bill.

796. You think that the machinery of Mr. Remnant's Bill, which is before the Committee, would be effective?—I should think so.

797. Local machinery to administer Imperial finance?—I am not a financier.

798. I did not know whether that question had been raised before your people or not?—No, it has not been raised.

799. Now I will put to you the same question that I put to Mr. Steadman: Do you think that the members of the Co-operative Union would reject a proposal by which a limited number of the most deserving of the aged poor would get pensions? Do you think that they would consider themselves pledged to a universal scheme and would reject a modified scheme under which some 300,000 might get pensions?—You ask my opinion?

800. Yes?—The opinion of the movement has not been ascertained. I say they are unanimously in favour of the universal scheme, but I should say personally that we should take what we can get.

801. You would use your influence, which is great, in favour of a modified scheme?—Certainly I am always in favour of that. When I cannot get all that I want I take what I can get, and trust to the future. I should think it a great thing achieved if we could get this, because I consider that this is a great advance on anything which has been proposed.

802. You having gone into this, may I ask you do you think there would be any very great difficulty in deciding out of, say, 20 or 30 applicants, all of whom were people who had resided for some time in the neighbourhood, which were the most meritorious and unfortunate cases?—I do not think there would. There are so many agencies at work now amongst poor people that it would be very easy to get at the facts.

803. Take one of your own co-operative societies, for instance?—In a country district it would be very easy indeed, because in a country district, as Mr. Shackleton knows very well, everybody knows everybody else in connection with these societies. They know almost what their belongings are and what their lives have been.

804. There are some cases, of course, even among co-operators, which are very sad cases of people over 65 who have tried hard all their lives, and whose only fault is that they have lived too long?—Yes, there are some, but not so many in co-operative societies as there would be amongst outsiders, because if a man and his wife have brought up a large family, and have been members of a co-operative society all their lives, they have generally what will keep them from want during the remainder of their days. If a man brings up half-a-dozen children, and they are all working as soon as they reach working age, his purchases from the society are large, and he shares in the profits of the society in accordance with his purchases, not his capital, and he is constantly accumulating funds in the society against the time when he is incapable of working by reason of his age.

805. It has been suggested here that a very considerable proportion of the people over 65 would be man and wife. Do you happen to know what sort of proportion of your own old members are man and wife as compared with widowers and bachelors

Chairman—continued.

bachelors and widows?—I should think a large proportion of them would be man and wife, because they generally lead careful lives. The class of people we have in our society are generally thrifty and careful, and I know hundreds of cases of the kind you mention of man and wife both being over 65.

806. Would you say the proportion of people over 65 that were man and wife would be one-third of the total?—I would not like to mislead the Committee. I have not calculated that at all.

807. I do not know whether you can get any evidence of it?—Had I known that this question was to have been put I should have made inquiries. We have an easy way of doing that by simply sending out a general circular to all our secretaries in the country, asking: "Can you give an idea of what your membership is over 65? How many men and how many women, and how many husbands and wives living together?"

808. It would be very important, on the subject of finance, and if you could give us a guide in that way we should be obliged?—Our organisation is such that we can get any information of that kind. I should write to the district where it was most likely that I should get the information, either an agricultural district or an urban district, and ask the secretary for information as near as possible, and if we got a score of returns in we could make a general average and get at what you want.

809. If you could it would be a great help to us?—I will do so.

810. Could you, when you are obtaining some figures on the proportion of people over 65 who are man and wife, also obtain some information as to how many of them have been in receipt of poor relief within the last 20 years?—Yes, I think that could be done.

811. You have seen the Bill now before this Committee. I think that a copy was sent to you?—Yes.

812. Do you desire to offer any observations in which you will feel that you are speaking the general view of co-operators in respect of the conditions?—Yes. On Section 6, Sub-section D, I should like to offer an observation: "Has not received poor law relief, other than medical relief, unless under circumstances of a wholly exceptional character, during 20 years prior to the application for a pension." I have no doubt that there are many sad cases in connection with co-operative members of perfectly respectable people who have had, through circumstances over which they have had no control, to obtain poor law relief during the last 20 years.

Mr. Remnant.

813. That is provided for by that same section. "Unless under circumstances of a wholly exceptional character"?—Then comes the question of who is to be the judge of the exceptional character. I have known members of Co-operative Societies refused relief by Poor Law officers because they were members of the Society, and had some little investment. In order to obtain the benefits of co-operative membership they have to become responsible for a 1*l.* share, but they have only to pay, on entrance, 1*s.*, and the rest can accumulate from the profits derived from the trading of the Society. They are not required to pay more than 1*s.* By doing this, and so obtaining the best value they could for the money they had to spend, poor people have been deprived of Poor Law relief when they only needed it, because the authorities have found that they have had 5*s.*, or 10*s.*, or 15*s.* invested in the Society. They have compelled them to withdraw every penny before they could give any relief. When the applicants have got over this temporary difficulty and got relief, they join the Society again. They get into difficulty perhaps shortly after, and have to withdraw everything again before getting relief. We think that a hardship of the Poor Law for one thing; and, having obtained Poor Law relief, we do not think it ought to be a disqualification for a pension.

Chairman.

814. As regards these qualifications in Clause 6, do you think the class of people who are members of Co-operative Societies would object to proving that they had these qualifications before magistrates sitting in the magistrates' room, as is done in New South Wales?—We do not like the necessity for having to prove it. We do not think that people ought to be called upon to have all the circumstances of their past lives inquired into. And again, we do not think that there should be any thrift test, because it is impossible for some persons in receipt of such small wages to exercise any thrift whatever, and what is thrift for one person is not thrift for another.

815. I suppose it is possible for everybody, however small his income, to use it wisely or unwisely?—Yes, to use it wisely or unwisely, but it is not always possible to save anything, and that is what people generally call thrift. "To make provision for himself and those immediately dependent on him," it says. I think that means saving.

816. There is nothing in this Bill, as there has been in other Bills, requiring a minimum income already existent. Would not your objection rather be to any requirement of the possession of some small savings?—Yes, it would. That is what I mean. I thought it was implied.

Mr. Goulding.

817. No, it simply says "to the best of his ability." Contribution to a Friendly Society would be an evidence of thrift?—Yes, but they cannot all afford to subscribe to a Friendly Society.

Chairman.

818. Have you anything that you wish to add? —I should like to say that I am with Mr. Steadman in this—that I think it will be cheaper for the nation to provide pensions for people, irrespective of these qualifications, rather than to compel them to go into the poor house or to take relief under the Poor Law.

819. On account of the expense of the present system of Poor Law administration?—On account of the expense, and also on account of the feeling that there is on the part of the aged poor.

820. But you said that it would be more necessary?

Chairman—continued.

mind?—It is certainly more economical, I think, on account of the expense of administration.

821. Do you think that all these people of 65 could live outside institutions; would the state of their health permit it?—They generally have someone belonging to them to take care of them.

822. Are not you contemplating, in the way of economy, having no further use for the workhouse?—Partly so.

823. But what about workhouse infirmaries? Could the very old amongst these people live without the infirmaries?—Some of them would certainly be better inside the workhouse infirmary, I should say, but others would be better under the supervision of their family connections. I know that in our part of the country they do not like to go into the workhouse, in fact, will not do so until they are compelled, and dragged away sometimes, as I think you know.

Sir *Robert Reid*.

824. As I understand, the idea that addressed itself to your Congress was universal old-age pensions—that is to say, pensions for everyone?—Yes, for everyone.

825. Irrespective of being well-off?—Yes.

826. And irrespective of previous character?—Yes; the resolution was with regard to a pension for every citizen, male and female, irrespective of character and irrespective of position or standing.

827. Did they think out, or was it discussed, how far it would be possible for some of the old people, quite apart from character, to live by themselves without being looked after; I mean those who had, for example, no home?—That was not discussed at all, but I do not think that would be any great difficulty.

828. You think not?—No. I am speaking of the northern part of the country at present. We generally find now that old people live with their connections, and are kept by them. If they have some little money, they will pay 2s. or 3s. a week towards their maintenance.

829. Do you think that 5s. a week, for example, would be sufficient inducement for connections, or even strangers, to take them in?—I think it would for very old people.

830. And look after them if they were in a very infirm state, and wanted a lot of looking after?—I am on one or two trusts for colliery disaster funds, and we find that for the allowance paid by those trusts for the maintenance of aged people, 5s. or 7s. 6d. a week, we can get people to take care of them, and take care of them well.

831. You mean even if they are infirm?—Yes.

832. Then your idea, as I understand, would be that workhouses, so far as old people were concerned, would cease to have any utility at all?—Not to the present extent. Perhaps the infirmary might be most useful, but, as a matter of fact, I find that many old people to-day prefer prison to the workhouse. I go round the Manchester Prison sometimes, and I find old people there who say they are more comfortable there than in the workhouse.

833. I was not desirous of discussing the relative merits of the workhouse and the prison, but your idea is that, substantially, people over 60 would prefer to live outside the workhouse, wherever they lived?—Yes; I feel sure that would be so.

834. It would be practicable, you think?—Yes.

835. A great element is cost?—Yes.

836. Did the Congress take the age of 60?—Yes.

837. The cost over 60 would be very great, would it not?—Yes, we acknowledge it. We know it would require increased taxation of some kind.

838. You say that it should come out of Imperial funds, and not out of local funds?—Yes.

839. I do not know if, in that connection, you have considered the relative incidence of Imperial and local taxation?—I do not think it has been very carefully considered by the bulk of the membership in discussing these questions, but we know that it would require increased taxation, and the workpeople would, no doubt, be prepared to pay their quota towards it. Perhaps it would require rearrangement of the Income-tax, whereby everybody in receipt of decent wages would pay something towards it.

840. It was not so much from that point of view that I asked; I rather wanted to suggest that, in the case of rates, they come, in the main, from a class of people who are better paid than the general taxpayer?—Yes, that is so.

841. I suppose that you did not really go into that aspect of the financial question?—We have not gone into details at all.

842. Now, supposing there were any limitations as regards, for instance, character, or limitations as regards income, and the pension was not universal, but only given to such as required it and deserved it, then, of course, the cost would not be very easy at present to ascertain. Do you think it would be possible to ascertain what proportion of the old people above 65 would bear the two tests, the test of income and the test of character, and would in that sense be eligible for pensions?—It would be very difficult to ascertain, and could only be done by a local body.

843. It would be easier in the case of the country?—Yes.

844. The Chairman asked you a question the substance of which, I think, was whether you would approve of an experimental Bill to begin with?—Yes, certainly. I should be pleased to see something of this kind brought into operation, although it does not go the whole length of what we asked for in our Congress.

845. The Chairman's question, as I gathered, imported something more than these tests in Section 6, which are specific tests. The question rather seemed to contemplate that a sum of money, for example, might be voted by Parliament for the purpose of providing one, two, three, four, or five millions of money, or whatever you like, for the year, and then it would be a case of selection from among those who were deserving. Do you think that would do any good?—I should not go quite as far as selection from the deserving. I do not know how you could select a portion of the deserving.

846. That is what I thought he asked you, and you said you did not see a difficulty?—I did not quite mean that.

Sir *Robert Reid*—continued.

847. I was rather interpreting what I understood to be the question?—I did not understand it then.

848. Take it, for the sake of argument, that the scheme of the Bill cost 10,000,000*l.* a year (this is mere hypothesis, of course), but Parliament was to say: "We should like to see how the thing works. We do not know how many people will come in. We will begin with 5,000,000*l.* a year," or "6,000,000*l.*," or whatever it is. Then in that way there would have to be a selection of those who were most deserving from among the deserving. You follow what I mean?—Yes, I follow what you mean, but I cannot agree with it. I understood the Chairman to ask: Would I be in favour of accepting a Bill of this kind with the qualifications and disqualifications existing in it, as against the claim made by the Co-operative Congress for a universal scheme? I said that I would prefer to have the universal scheme, but I would be quite content to accept this at present as a test.

Chairman.

849. I think that, in answer to another question of mine, you said you thought it would be possible to select the hardest cases, or words to that effect?—I did not mean that. I am very sorry that I misunderstood the question. What I meant was that it would be possible for the local administration to say which was a deserving case and which was not. That is what I meant to say.

Sir *Robert Reid.*

850. You mean, as I understand, that you would expect that a Board would be able to say: "This is a deserving case, and the other is an undeserving case"?—I think that a local Board would be able to say that.

851. But you would not think it competent to say: "From among three deserving cases we will select that which is most deserving"?—No.

852. Do you think that favouritism would come in?—I think so.

853. Supposing it was desirable to try an experiment, assuming, for the sake of argument, that that was done to find out how things stood, what would you say?—I think it would work very unfairly.

854. You mean that it would be unfair to those who did not get help?—Yes. Supposing they were all deserving, I do not like distinctions to be made between people who are really deserving, because favouritism is sure to come into the matter, and injustice would be done.

855. Injustice which consists of one getting the advantage and two deserving people not getting it; but do you think there will be corruption or favouritism?—I do not say corruption, but favouritism.

856. From political motives?—No.

857. Do you think that differences of Church, or that sort of thing, would operate?—That might come in.

858. Could you not have a tribunal, or a body, that would be impartial with regard to that? Would there be no means of selecting people who would be impartial?—I do not know. The difference between us is this, I think: It is suggested that Parliament might be willing to place a fixed sum at the disposal of a pensions scheme, whereas the Bill places a fixed qualification on people. Of the two I prefer the latter, and all people coming within that qualification should be entitled to a pension without regard to a sum. The difference is between fixing the qualification and fixing the sum.

859. Not necessarily. You might fix the sum, and also impose a condition in the form of a qualification, but you do not like a scheme of that kind?—I do not like a partial scheme at all.

860. You think that it would lead to injustice?—I think it would lead to injustice.

Colonel *Pilkington.*

861. You have rather discarded the idea of so much money being placed at the disposal of the authorities who administer this Old-age Pension Fund?—Yes.

862. But you might try an experiment on a much smaller scale by raising the age, might you not?—By raising the age or introducing other qualifications.

863. Nothing is so strong as the trying of an experiment if you want to introduce a new thing. If you can introduce it on a small scale and as an experiment, you try the system before you launch out into great expenditure. You see what I mean, do not you?—Yes, I see what you mean.

864. You approve of the Bill as a beginning—you go as far as that?—I approve of the Bill so far as it goes.

865. If we could find out some way of raising the standard, so to speak, by Act of Parliament, which probably might halve the expense of the present Bill, would you be in favour of that?—I should not like to reduce the scope of the Bill to any extent. I think it is surrounded by qualifications, or disqualifications, which go quite far enough, and if you make an experiment on a less scale than this I think it is most likely to fail.

866. But have you any idea what the expense of the Bill would be annually? It is supposed that it would be about 10,000,000*l.* Supposing that by raising the qualifications you can get an old-age pension scheme to try the experiment with with 5,000,000*l.*, what do you think of that?—I do not think you can do it by raising the age qualification. Sixty-five is quite high enough, too high in our view. A man is worked out long enough before he gets to 65 in the employments which he has to go through.

Mr. *Pemberton.*

867. Your objection is to those two Sub-clauses D and G?—Yes.

868. You think that they would not be easily worked? You think, in the first place, they are not fair, and, in the second place, you do not think they would be easily worked?—We think that D is not fair, and as to G, that it would not be easily worked, as you say, because it would throw on the Committee the responsibility of inquiring into the character for many years back, and it would also impose the exercise of thrift

Mr. Pemberton—continued.

upon a man whether he has been in a position to maintain it or not.

869. You said in answer to the Chairman that probably members of Co-operative Societies would be willing to have the income tax extended somewhat?—I think so.

870. In your opinion, if this scheme was made rather more wide by the elimination of those two conditions, the bodies that you represent would be inclined to agree with it?—That is my personal opinion gathered from general conversation with our members, but it has never been discussed by any of our Congresses.

Sir John Hutton.

871. In the three schemes which were placed before your Conferences and rejected, did you propose to allow the pensioners to work and to earn money themselves?—Yes.

872. To make what they could in addition to their pension?—Yes; it was apart from work altogether. They were not working for the society which gave the pension to them. They were merely individual members of the society, who might be working for somebody else. Immediately on attaining the age of 60 they would get the pension.

873. It did not strike you at all that if they received a pension and were allowed to work they would come into competition with workers outside?—No, that did not enter into our consideration at all.

874. Have you ever thought about that yourself?—That is done now. Police pensioners often take up other occupations after receiving their pension. If we had carried out our first scheme of superannuation of employees that would only have come into operation when they became incapable of work, but under this other scheme the pension is derived from profit on trade, and can be claimed by every individual member of a Co-operative Society as a matter of right. Having paid towards the pension, he would become entitled to it at 60 years of age, whether he worked for any firm or not.

875. Do any of the members receive poor relief?—Yes, they do, but I have no statistics.

876. Do they remain members?—Yes, but in some Poor Law Unions the members have difficulty in obtaining relief whilst they remain in connection with the Co-operative Society.

877. But relief in no case disqualifies a man from being a member of a Co-operative Society?—No, in no case.

878. You said in answer to the Chairman that there was no difficulty in getting at the facts with regard to a man's life, and I quite agree that there is no difficulty in the country, but what about a large London district, like Fulham say?—I cannot speak as regards London, but in Manchester I think there would be no great difficulty, because we have so many agencies at work amongst poor people that the officers of the several organisations concerned—temperance organisations and others—seem to be able to get at the people and know the inner working of their lives, as it were, and their condition for many years back.

Sir John Hutton—continued.

879. Is there more than one Poor Law Union in Manchester?—Yes; the Chorlton Union and the Manchester Union. I forget where the division comes in.

880. They would not have the difficulty, to the same extent, as in London, of a very shifting population always moving to their work?—No.

881. But you think there would be no difficulty in obtaining the history of the people?—No, I think not. In manufacturing towns they are more stationary.

882. What part of the north do you speak of yourself?—Manchester.

883. Now, you were saying to Sir Robert Reid that a certain number of persons could not be dealt with by annuities only, but they must have some kind of home to go to—a workhouse or some place?—Certainly, some of them.

884. A very small percentage?—A very small percentage.

885. There is a small percentage of the respectable poor who have really no friends, and who cannot shift for themselves?—That is so; they would have to go into some place provided for them.

886. In that case, supposing the workhouses were done away with, would you approve of paying out of the rates for the maintenance in ordinary hospitals of those people who were only fit for infirmaries?—I think so, because the proportion would be so much smaller of those who ought to be in the hospitals and infirmaries.

887. You approve of their being provided for in ordinary hospitals, and paid for out of the rates?—Yes.

888. Not relying on charity only?—Yes. The others who did not have to go to hospital could be found comfortable homes for the amount of the pension.

889. You think it would be safe to farm them out at 5s. a week?—5s. or 7s. 6d. We have no difficulty, as I said in connection with some of the trust funds I have to do with, in finding comfortable homes at 7s. 6d. a week.

890. Where?—In Yorkshire.

891. In the West Riding?—In the West Riding.

892. It has been found, in the administration of the Poor Law, that, with regard to boarding out children, there is very great danger of persons with whom the children are boarded out using the money, to a great extent, for their own purposes?—Yes, unless they are under strict supervision.

893. Would not there be the same danger, and very grave danger, with regard to old people?—There would not in country districts; there is too much supervision. They would be known too well by the Committees.

894. Do you know anything about the miners' homes in Durham?—I have heard about them, but have not seen them.

895. Do you know anything about the proposal to provide cottage homes in each Poor Law Union for the aged poor?—No, I have not studied that.

896. As is done at the present time in Sheffield. Do you not think that these people would be better provided for by the Guardians providing

Sir John Hutton—continued.

viding them with, say, two-roomed cottages, where they could be made to feel as much at home as they chose, and to feel themselves at liberty, with an attendant in a separate cottage, who could look after them?—Certainly I do; I believe in that.

897. With regard to the Income-tax, are you prepared to suggest that the Income-tax should be extended to those who earn weekly wages?—I do not see why it should not. I think they ought to pay their share on their income, as well as anyone else, and I think they would be willing to do it. If we could only get everybody to pay Income-tax on his full income, the working man would be willing to pay on his full income. The difficulty is that his income is known, and that of others is not known; therefore, it would not be fair, but I think he would not object to paying Income-tax in accordance with his income.

Mr. [illegible] Cox.

898. Do you see any objection to the Guardians being the administrative authority?—No, I have not heard any objection expressed to that at all, and I should imagine they would be as fair a body, and a body knowing as much about local circumstances, as any other body that could be appointed. I have not heard anything against it.

Sir Robert Reid.

899. If the Guardians were to be the persons to make the selection, to put it brutally, it would be their interest, as a local body, to shift the burden upon the Imperial Exchequer rather than upon the local rates?—Yes, it would, as matters stand at present.

900. I rather think it would be so under the Bill, whereas, of course, the public exchequer which found the money would not have a say as to the distribution of it?—No; we do not object to any better machinery which can be proposed. I was asked, Should we object to the Guardians being the administrative body. I do not think we should, but we should not object to any better machinery which could be proposed. There is, of course, the taint about it that the Guardians have been accustomed to administering the Poor Law, and it is rather derogatory to go before Guardians for relief. In some cases that relief has not been given with the best grace and administered by the officials as it ought to have been, and people do not like to go near them. It would have that taint, but I have not heard any objection raised against the proposals in the Bill upon that.

901. You do not object to the Imperial Exchequer being represented by a suitable person?—No; I think it should be represented. If the funds come from the Imperial Exchequer there should be some check on their part on the expenditure.

Mr. Lloyd-George.

902. Have you gone into the cost of the co-operative universal scheme?—No, not the universal scheme. We went into the cost of the scheme for co-operators only, but not into the universal scheme.

903. You know Mr. Charles Booth's scheme?—I have read that.

Mr. Lloyd-George—continued.

904. Does not he estimate the cost at about 26,000,000*l.*?—Yes, for a universal scheme for everybody who was entitled.

905. That is practically the Trade Union Scheme, is it not?—Yes.

906. The age is 60?—Yes.

907. But I gather from your evidence that it would be impossible to carry a scheme of that sort in the first instance?—I believe it would not be possible.

908. Therefore you would be prepared to work for something considerably short of that as an experiment?—Yes, to go just as far as we can get.

909. You do not object to any of these clauses, subject to what you have told us as to your ideal, except D?—We object most strongly to that, and to a less extent to G, but that is immaterial, I think, now.

910. Your objection to D, I understand, would be that a man who has received Poor Law relief under certain circumstances over which he has no control may be barred from a pension owing to that?—Yes.

911. But what sort of case would you suggest as a hardship?—I am not prepared to mention any particular case.

912. But can you mention any case which would not come under "circumstances of a wholly exceptional character"?—I have known widows have had to go for Poor Law relief whose husbands have been members of Co-operative Societies. They have lived on the little money which their husbands have left, and when that has been exhausted, and there have been a lot of young children, they have had to go for Poor Law relief, and those children have been brought up by means of relief.

913. Do not you think that that would be covered by "circumstances of a wholly exceptional character"?—I do not know what those words mean. They would mean whatever people who administered the Act chose to make them.

914. You think that they are too vague?—I know it would be a very great hardship on members of the Co-operative Societies if some people had to administer this, because it would be a detrimental fact if they had been members of Co-operative Societies.

915. You think that the words are too vague?—I think they are too vague.

916. If it were made perfectly clear that cases of special hardship were excepted you would not object to it?—I do not know any other cases. I come a great deal across poor people, and I cannot imagine any poor people going for Poor Law relief unless compelled to do it by stress of circumstances. They all tell me that it is the last thing they think of doing.

917. Do you mean to say that you do not have cases of application for Poor law relief where the resources have not broken down?—Not amongst the poor that I have mixed up with and inquired about. They tell me they will pawn everything they have got or go amongst their friends, or get what help they can before going to the Poor Law, which is the last thing they will do, because they have such a detestation of the idea of going for

Mr. *Lloyd-George*—continued.

Poor Law relief. I may not have come across the right people, but that is my experience.

918. Have you never known cases where a certain class of people take rather readily to Poor Law relief?—I have not come across them.

919. Not in the country?—No, I have not come across them.

920. I am sorry to say that I have done so. Now taking G, your interpretation of it was that it insisted upon thrift and saving?—I thought so.

921. I am not sure that you are not right, but I hope not. Supposing that that is not a proper interpretation, and that it merely means that a man has provided for his family and brought up a family by his industry and his labour?—And kept respectable.

922. Yes, without any condition as to his saving, would you object?—The words certainly to me mean that he must have saved something.

923. To provide for your family does not necessarily mean that you have saved money?—We do not necessarily object to this if there is no saving test. It was suggested once that he must have shown that he had been a member of a Friendly Society or Co-operative Society. We object to that altogether.

924. That is another thing entirely. This is rather an industry test I take it, not a thrift test?—I certainly thought it meant that he must have saved money.

925. If that is made clear you would not object to it?—No, I would not object to it then.

926. You do not object to the income test, do you?—No.

927. Have you seen the New Zealand scheme?—I read it just before we had the Conference.

928. Do you generally approve of it? I do not tie you to details?—I am afraid I could not say right off without reading it over again. This last week I have been confining my attention only to this Bill, leaving other things outside.

929. Then it would not be fair to press you about that. Now have the co-operators considered at all how the money should be raised?—The principal idea was that there should be a reconstitution of the incidence of taxation. Here I am contrary to Mr. Steadman's opinion. I think they might tax drink more. I am not a teetotaler, but I would make it more difficult for a working man to get drunk, and I should not object to a tax on drink.

930. In Denmark I understand from evidence we have had that for this purpose a tax is placed on beer. You would not object to that?—I should not object to that. I have considerable experience in the police courts in Manchester, and I find it is the custom of working men, or some of them, to spend a third of their income in drink. Out of 27*s.* a week they spend 9*s.* in drink, and give their wives 18*s.* I have asked them their reason for it. They have said: "We must have some enjoyment." When the 9*s.* is spent they have done. So evidently they spend the 9*s.*, no matter what amount of drink they get, so I would not object to making it dearer. They would spend the same money and get less drink for it.

931. And have the advantage of providing for old age?—Yes.

Mr. *Lloyd-George*—continued.

932. So you do not quite agree with Mr. Steadman?—No, not quite.

933. You are in favour of a contribution by working men themselves, through taxes, to a fund for old-age pensions?—Through a properly arranged income tax, where each would contribute according to his income.

Mr. *Skewes Cox*.

934. Do you think that there should be a special fund for the purpose?—No, I do not think so. If it came out of the Imperial Exchequer it would be out of the ordinary taxation, and would not require a special fund.

Mr. *Lloyd-George*.

935. How is that? We have no fund at the present moment available. You would have to raise the taxation of the country?—Yes, generally.

936. You suggest taxation of beer, or an extension of the income-tax?—Yes.

937. What is your view of a tax on corn?—We are most decidedly against it.

938. You would be opposed to that?—We object to all taxation of food most strongly. We are not divided at all on that.

Mr. *O'Shee*.

939. As to the workhouses, is it your idea that workhouse infirmaries ought to be preserved and that workhouses should be discontinued?—That would depend very largely on how the scheme worked out. It might or might not reduce the cases so much that as a matter of necessity the workhouses would not be required. I should not like to say.

Mr. *Shackleton*.

940. You said that you would ask certain questions from your Societies?—Yes.

941. As I understand the various systems, some Societies will take in the husband and wife and some the children, and other Societies will only take in the husband or the widow or the spinster?—That is so—one in a family.

942. In asking these questions you would be very careful to choose a Society where you can get the man and wife inside in order to get the figures?—No, it would not merely mean that. We want to know from the secretaries how far their membership would include cases of a man and wife living together whose ages are over 65. As far as I understand the Chairman's question, it does not matter whether both are members. You simply want, from a working-class point of view, to know how many couples live together after attaining the age of 65.

943. Do you think your staff on the various Societies would be able to furnish that information?—In the country districts only—not in the towns.

944. Would it be a fair test as to the number living over 65 to take a country district?—It is only so far as that particular class are concerned, you know.

945. Exactly. Now will you refer to Clause (c) of the Bill before us?—"Has not within the last 20 years been convicted of an offence and

sentenced

Mr. *Shackleton*—continued.

sentenced to penal servitude or imprisonment without the option of a fine."

946. Do you entirely agree with that clause? —No, I do not; but I did not like to raise any more objections. I thought that it was enough to deal with (d) and (g).

947. I take it that your opinion would be that if a person has suffered penal servitude or other imprisonment for a certain offence no second punishment should be put on him?—He has purged his offence, and ought to be on the same level as other persons.

948. That is your view?—That is my view. That is included in our resolution, which deals with every citizen, male or female.

949. With reference to the question put to you as to relief, you are speaking now of a class of the population who very rarely go for poor relief?—Very rarely.

950. You would not like to say that there is not quite a number in the lower population. Take, for instance, a person earning all his life no more than 18s. a week, having a wife and several little children to bring up; you can see it is possible for him to come for poor relief sooner than a co-operative member?—Yes, and there will be those, no doubt, in the Co-operative Societies who will have to go on to the Poor Law in their old age, notwithstanding their attempts to save in the Co-operative Societies.

951. Now take the industrial or thrift tests and 10s. a week; that would mean that a person earning 10s. a week, or having an income of 10s., would not have any assistance at all. Do you agree with that?—That would be so, according to this Bill.

952. Do you approve of that?—No; I was asked my own opinion, and I approve of it as a commencement; but the Co-operators or the Congress do not approve of the limitations. They claim that everyone attaining the pensionable age has a right to the pension, no matter what their circumstances.

953. Take (b): "Has endeavoured to the best of his ability, by his industry or by the exercise of reasonable providence, to make provision": how can that apply to a married woman who has to depend on her husband's earnings? Say, for 20 years and upwards she has been dependent on her husband?—A very large number of our co-operative members are women who practically maintain the families; some of them earn more than their husbands, I dare say, and are responsible for keeping their families. There are other cases where the woman is left alone, and it would be difficult to prove that she had exercised "reasonable providence" by the circumstances of her married life—that a woman left with 7s. or 8s. a week given by her husband on which to keep house was exercise providence. How a committee would deal with that I do not know. I do not think that these disabilities should be in, but I am prepared as a first step to accept them.

954. My point is that a large number of them would have no personal income?—No, they would not.

955. To apply any test to them would be difficult?—Yes, I think so.

Mr *Shackleton*—continued.

956. Your experience is of Lancashire and Yorkshire. A woman might be a weaver and her husband a joiner, or of some other trade?—Yes.

957. She would probably only be at work for a portion of the time. They do not work for anything like the 40 years—say from 20 to 65; it is only for a few years after they are married that they work?—It depends.

958. As a general rule, if a woman has no children she cannot go weaving?—No.

959. Therefore it would not apply to many? —No, it would not. We have cases where the man and wife earn very good incomes where they have no family; but they would not come under the Bill at all, because they would be provided for.

Mr. *Channing*.

960. You have considered this Bill pretty carefully, have you not?—I have.

961. Is it your opinion that the Bill, in applying the principle of old-age pensions, would make much difference in the ordinary system of Poor Law relief, except in regard to the fact that the discrimination is more definite and prescribed? —I think the fact that the pension is given in a different form from the Poor Law relief would make a vast difference in the minds of working people. They would appreciate receiving the pension as a matter of right on attaining a given age, and under certain conditions, as fixed in the Bill, rather than having to apply for Poor Law relief under present conditions.

962. You do not think that the people with whom you are concerned would regard it as still having the taint of Poor Law relief?—No; once the principle of pensions is adopted, I think that taint is taken away.

963. Have you been a Guardian yourself?—No, I have not.

964. But you are closely acquainted with the circumstances of working men. Is it your opinion that these tests could easily be worked? Taking, for instance, the income test; do you suppose that it would be perfectly easy to determine whether a certain person had 10s. a week or a married couple 15s. a week?—I think so. If the man or the woman happens to be in employment, you can get a return from the employer; and if not in employment, you would want to know what investments there were as a source of income.

965. Do you think that that information could be easily obtained?—Yes. In Police Courts where we want to know the income of a man in order to make an order upon him, we have no difficulty in getting a return from his employer for months back, as to what his income is.

966. Would there be no cases of fraud among working men?—There would, no doubt, be many attempts at fraud.

967. Do you think that those could be checked?—I think so.

968. Your Co-operative Societies joined in the Conference, I understand, with the Trade Unions?—Yes.

969. And approved of the results arrived at? —We approved entirely. Since that Conference was held, we have had a Congress of our own, at

[illegible]

Mr. Channing—continued.

which the report was submitted and unanimously approved.

970. Is it one of the arguments of practical ladies like co-operators that less money would be wasted in administration if you had the universal scheme?—We think so.

971. And more money would go to the pensions?—We think it would have that effect. If the administrative machinery was well organised, it would be cheaper and more economical than the present Poor Law system.

972. Have you considered the Old-age Pension Bill introduced into the House to carry out Mr. Booth's scheme?—This is the only Bill I have considered.

973. In your opinion, the only test should be the test of age and residence, I suppose?—Yes, age and residence and nationality; the applicant should be a British subject.

The Honourable ALFRED DOBSON; Examined.

Chairman.

974. You are, I understand, Acting Agent-General for Victoria?—Yes.

975. And as such, you will be able to give us, at any rate, the salient points of the Victorian Old-age Pension Act?—Yes.

976. That was passed in 1901, was it not?—It came into operation on the 7th day of December 1901. One Act was passed temporarily. That provided 10s. a week, and subsequently the Act which is now in existence, which is a much larger Act, and deals altogether more exhaustively with the subject, came into operation. It is 1 Edward VII., No. 1,761.

977. Before coming to that Act of 1901, can you give the Committee any information about the estimate formed of the cost of the previous Act of 1900?—The Government of the day thought that the whole system would be comparatively inexpensive, but they found that it cost just about double the amount that was estimated.

978. Would it be true to say that Sir George Turner's estimate of cost for the half-year was only 74,000*l.*, for which he took authority, and that in the six months it cost 181,000*l.*?—If you are quoting from Mr. Reeves' book, that would be correct.

979. There was also a Bill in 1900, to which I have seen a reference in some book, called An Act to Provide for the Registration of Claimants for Old-age Pensions?—Yes.

980. Is that a separate Act in itself?—That was a separate Act; and the idea was that those who would be, under the law which was contemplated, entitled to old-age pensions should send in their claims, so that the Government might have some idea of what those claims would amount to—that is to say, what it would cost the State.

981. That was the first step taken, was it not?—Yes.

982. The idea was to register the claims before a court of magistrates, was it not?—Yes.

983. In 1900 the measure was a temporary measure, and the longer measure, which you have just mentioned, came into force in December, 1901?—Yes.

984. Would you tell us the main points of that Act?—Under that Act, which is now the existing law, pensioners are eligible to a pension at 65. When first that subject was mooted there was a dispute between the Upper and Lower House. The Upper House insisted on the age of 65, and the Lower House wanted 60; but eventually the Lower House, or House of Assembly, gave way upon the point; and accordingly by this Act the age is fixed at 65. The rate of the pension is not to exceed 8*s.* a week.

985. Is the system a supplementary one, making the man's income up to 8*s.*?—Yes, that is so. The pension is at such a rate as will make the total income of the claimant from all sources not more than 8*s.* a week; but they allow him to have 2*s.* whether this sum be the whole or part only of the average weekly income derivable by him as wages.

986. Do not they allow him to have sick pay from a Friendly Society as well as the 8*s.*?—In the interpretation clause with regard to "income," it says that income is not to include any payment by way of benefit from any registered Friendly Society or any Trade Union or Provident Society or Association during illness, infirmity, or old age.

987. What other qualifications are there besides being 65? Is there any qualification with regard to how long he has been in the Colony?—Clause 8 contains a very long string of qualifications and conditions upon which he may receive the income. He must have been residing for 20 years in Victoria, and he must not have been absent from Victoria for more than five years at one time; and then there are disabilities in cases of conviction for drunkenness, and he must not have been in prison for six months during the period of five years immediately preceding the date. I propose, with your approval, to mention these things very rapidly, because if it is any convenience to the Committee I can hand a copy of this Act in.

988. If you would run through it briefly now I think that that would be the better plan?—Then there is a section with regard to desertion; in the case of husband and wife they must not have deserted one another. The net capital value of the applicant's accumulated property, whether in or out of Victoria, must not amount to 100*l.* or upwards. Then there is another provision, which seems almost peculiar—that he has not directly or indirectly deprived himself of property or income in order to qualify for or obtain a pension.

989. Was that provision put in as an amendment of a previous Bill, do you happen to remember?—The previous Bill only consists of five or six sections. It was passed in a great hurry, and it came into operation before this. It had very few

Chairman—continued.

few of these safeguards in it at all. The Premier of the Colony mentioned in Parliament a case where a man had 300*l.* in the savings bank, and he drew this money out, and paid it to his children, in order that he might become eligible for a pension. That is, I am afraid, an example of the fraud which is sometimes practised upon the Government in these matters; so that there is that safeguard with regard to his net capital not amounting to 160*l.*, and he must not have deprived himself of any property, either directly or indirectly, in order to qualify himself for a pension. Then he must have made reasonable efforts to provide for himself, or have brought up a family in decency and comfort.

990. Are those the exact words?—Those are the words. When the first Bill was brought in the Premier of the day tried to introduce some system of what your Committee would call "thrift," I suppose. It was recognised by a great many people that, although a man over the age of 65 years might well claim his pension without showing that he had made any provision, still it was a monstrous thing to imagine that young men and young women in full health and able to earn good wages and to live as working people can live only in the Colonies—that is with every comfort and convenience—should have a statutory right to claim a pension when they became 65, without contributing in any way towards that pension. However, although a great many people were of that opinion, the idea did not find place in the legislation of the Colony, and although by the contribution of a few pence, even 6*d.* a week, if a young man began soon enough, it might accumulate in the hands of the State to provide an old-age pension for him. That is not required of him. But if it had not been so much a matter of politics as it is in a democratic Colony like Victoria, some condition of that sort would probably have been insisted upon, I think. I do not know whether I am going beyond my text.

991. But do not you think that the working classes in Victoria do contribute very largely to the revenue of Victoria?—Yes, they do that, and indirectly give to the large grant which already exists for charitable institutions.

992. Your revenue in Victoria is raised very largely from Customs duties, is it not?—Yes.

993. Can you give the Committee any idea of what proportion of the revenue of Victoria is raised by Customs duties?—I should think three-quarters of it probably, speaking without book.

994. Roughly would it be true to say that a very large proportion of the total revenue comes from Customs duties on articles of general consumption?—Yes. Of course, since we have federated, the whole of the Customs duties are taken over by the Commonwealth, and no individual State has itself the right to tax as regards Customs; that is all in the hands of the Commonwealth, and the tariff which obtains in each State is enacted by the Commonwealth Parliament; so that we have only a right to tax ourselves by putting on a land tax or income tax. Excise is taken away.

995. Does not the Commonwealth contribute to the old-age pensions of Victoria?—No. The Act is in operation in New South Wales and in Victoria, but they contribute entirely out of their own revenue.

996. If the Commonwealth takes all the Customs duties and the excise duties, they leave you nothing to pay the pensions out of?—I have given you a wrong impression. They take the whole of the administration out of our hands, but they return all the money except a quarter. The quarter of the Customs duties which they keep is a very considerable amount, and that has accounted in some respects for the temporary embarrassment that has been found lately. The Commonwealth has only recently come into operation. As you say, the working classes pay a great proportion of the taxation, and they help to support, in Victoria alone, to the tune of something like 300,000*l.* a year, charitable institutions, lunatic asylums, and various institutions for helping the deserving poor and others.

997. Now will you simply continue the list of qualifications with regard to thrift?—Then there is another provision which I regard as one of the most important provisions in the Act, and that is, with regard to where the relatives of the applicant are able to maintain or provide for him. In Tasmania, which I represent as Agent-General, and in most of the other States of Australasia, that kind of legislation obtains always. If any man goes into a charitable institution, even a hospital, it is ascertained whether his relatives are able to provide for him, and if they are they can be brought up before a magistrate and be made to contribute to his maintenance, that is to say, they will not allow a man—say, a son—in wealthy circumstances, to leave his old father in a hospital or any charitable institution without making him pay what he is able to.

998. One of the conditions in that clause is that he shall have no relative able to support him?—Yes.

999. What are the exact words?—The husband, wife, father, mother, or children are the relatives picked out, and the exact words are: "of the claimant or any or all of them are unable to provide for or to maintain the claimant." On that point I learnt quite recently, from a telegram which I received from the Premier, that there has been a great deal of fraud, and he goes so far as to say that the sense of filial obligation has in many instances been lessened by the operation of this Act, that is to say, the relative thinks: "Very well, that is a matter for the State; I am not going to help my father or my mother"—or my wife or my husband, as the case may be—"I will let the State do it."

1000. Have you read to us all the conditions?—No. It must be shown that the claimant is unable to maintain himself, and also that he has not at any time within 12 months been refused by a Commissioner a pension certificate, except for the reason that he was disqualified on account of his age, or other reasons that are not in existence at the time of the further application. Those are the chief conditions, or disqualifications, as they may be called. Then there is rather an important section dealing with the

Chairman—continued.

the subject of what is meant by continuous residence. In Australia we have rather a floating population. Many people there, and I suppose more so in the United Kingdom, are absent. They may be away for some time, but still they may have supported their wives and families. In the same way with others. Say there is a rush to a new goldfield in Western Australia. They go away from other Colonies; a man may be three or four years away; his relatives are in Victoria, but if he remits money to them or helps to keep them, he is not disqualified, notwithstanding that he may have been absent for some time from the Colony.

1001. Would you tell us now how is it decided whether a man is possessed of these qualifications to receive a pension? What body deals with it?—The first portion of the Act provides for the administration, and it allows the Governor in Council to appoint a person, who is called the Registrar of Old-age Pensions; and subject to the control of the Treasurer of the Colony, that Registrar has the general administration of the Old-age Pensions Act. He, of course, is subject to removal or suspension, and his duties are prescribed by regulations made pursuant to the Act.

1002. But I want to know, before whom do I have to go, supposing I am a Victorian claiming a pension, to show that I have made reasonable efforts to provide for myself?—I am coming to that. Claims are sent in to the Registrar or his officials, and each claim is forwarded to a Commissioner, and in open court, in the locality where the claimant resides, or as near thereto as possible, his claim is fully investigated. There was a discussion as to whether the investigation should take place in open court or not. I think, having regard to our experience in the Colony of Victoria, that system is thoroughly appreciated, and thoroughly recognised as a perfectly sound and good one. Even although you assume that it is the duty of the State to provide these old-age pensions, it seems to be equally the duty of the State to see that the people come within the statutory conditions that are laid down. The claims, as I say, are investigated before a Commissioner, and the Commissioner sits in a court and exercises the same jurisdiction as a magistrate at Petty Sessions. He can call evidence and subpœna witnesses, and, in particular, he is authorised to obtain evidence from the police force, and the officers and members of the governing bodies of any charitable institutions—that is to say, people whose duty and business it is to know the circumstances of many of the poor people who receive relief.

1003. Who appoints the Commissioners?—The Government would appoint them.

1004. The Central Government?—Evidently the Government would appoint them.

1005. What sort of officials are they—are they like the stipendiary magistrates in this country?—Yes, they would be. They are not necessarily legal gentlemen, but they would be men chosen for their common-sense, and very likely they would be magistrates in the district they reside in. Most of them would be laymen, I should think.

1006. Are those the main points of the Bill, Sir, or is there anything else in the actual Bill itself to which you wish to call attention?—There is one other matter. The officers of the Savings Banks or of any Building Society or Friendly Society are expressly enjoined to give evidence if they are asked to do so, so as to assist the Commissioner. Of course, as the law stands now, not even the Government can compel any banker to reveal the business between him and his client. There are a very great many depositors in the Savings Banks in Victoria, and the ups and downs are very great. Sometimes a man is wealthy and sometimes he is poor, and these Savings Banks and all institutions of that nature are compelled to give evidence as to the circumstances of anybody whose business they may know, in order to assist the Commissioner and the Registrar in coming to a conclusion as to whether the claimant is qualified for a pension.

1007. Do they look back into his Savings Bank account to see whether he has made efforts to provide for himself, say, 20 years before?—I am not sufficiently well acquainted with the actual administration of the Act to say that, but I have no doubt they would do so if necessary; and I do not think that any exception, as I said before, would be taken to it. I think it would be recognised as perfectly natural that a man should court inquiry as to whether he is entitled to a pension, in order to assist the Government officials in doing their duty. Then there are further provisions, which I need not go into, about evidence, and saying that the strict rules of evidence need not obtain. They are to be guided by equity and good conscience. Then there is, after all this, a power to cancel any pension that has been granted, and many pensions have been cancelled for various reasons, without any complaint from the pensioners.

1008. Are the pensions granted for more than one year at a time?—Yes, and they are continued so long as recipient conforms to the regulations of the Act.

1009. They may be either cancelled or not renewed, I suppose?—I am talking of cancellation because the pension has been improperly obtained. Then there are special provisions to carry out the law, which I have mentioned, about the relatives, showing how proceedings are taken against them. Then there is rather a peculiar provision in Section 21, by which every pensioner signs an undertaking to transfer his real property or landed property, on demand, to the Government. I think that the idea of that is to prevent property passing to some distant relatives who have never at all assisted to maintain their relation. If it is found that the pensioner dies possessed of real estate, then, instead of allowing it to go to his relations, who may never have helped him at all, it goes to the State, to reimburse it for part of the moneys subscribed for the maintenance of the man. Then there are provisions by which, if it is thought desirable, the pension, instead of being paid directly into the hands of the pensioner, may be given to some clergyman or to some charitable Society, or, in fact, to anybody (the words are very elastic), to distribute the pension for him. That is to prevent a man spending his money in drink, or to prevent other people getting it from him.

1010. Is that a recognition, then, that there

Chairman—continued.

may be people who are qualified under that law to receive pensions, but who yet are not fit to have the money in their hands?—Yes, it is. If you put it in that way, "not fit," I must say yes.

1011. Is that part of an amending Act, or is it part of the Act which you are reading from?—I am only referring to the Act which is now in existence; there is no amendment to this Act yet; and although I telegraphed out, thinking it might be in the interests of your Committee to know whether there are any amendments to be passed to the Act, and they replied that amendments were desirable, unfortunately they have not told me the direction in which those amendments are to be made; but I apprehend that they are really in the direction of preventing fraud.

1012. I think that we have now got before us the gist of the Bill?—There is one other thing I should like to say. The last section provides for what may be done by regulation. There is very little indeed here left to regulation as regards the salient points of the Bill; they are all enacted by Parliament. An annual statement was made in accordance with the law under the Act, but unfortunately it has not been printed, or has not come to hand, and I am very sorry to say I cannot hand it in to your Committee, but when it comes to hand, if it is of any use to you, I will forward it.

1013. Would that statement give the number of pensions there are?—Yes.

1014. Would it give us, or could you give us, the total number of the population over 65? Perhaps you would begin by giving us the population of Victoria?—It is about 1,202,000 people altogether.

1015. Do you know about how many of those are over 65?—I am quoting from a Budget speech of Sir George Turner, in which he touched on the subject of old-age pensions. Speaking in 1900, he said that according to the report of the Old-age Pension Commissioners the persons over 65 were about 60,000.

1016. But that was speaking before the Old-age Pension Act came in?—Yes, it was, but there would not be so very much difference.

1017. That was an estimate, was it not?—It was an estimate made by the Old-age Pensions Commissioners.

1018. Has it not since turned out that the estimates were very much under the mark?—It does not follow that every man over 65 gets a pension. It is only those who are qualified. There is no doubt, to use the Premier's own words, that the Old-age Pension Act costs about double the original estimate on the faith of which it was brought into Parliament.

1019. Whose statement is that?—The statement of Mr. Irvine, the present Premier of Victoria.

1020. The present Prime Minister says that the scheme has cost twice as much as it was estimated it would cost when it was introduced?—Yes, this is in answer to a telegram which I sent; it was really received this month of July. That is his opinion now.

1021. The expenditure has risen to twice what was expected?—Yes.

1022. There are 60,000 people over 65, and how many pensioners were there in the last year?—The best information I can get on that point is from the Budget statement of Sir Alexander Peacock, made in December, 1901. He was then Premier, and he said that there were then 15,2[illegible] pensioners on the list.

1023. That again is before the Act came into force?—Yes, it was on the second reading of the now existing Act. You will remember that there was previously a sort of tentative Act, which came into operation in 1900.

1024. Which Act had very few safeguards in it, you said?—Very few. It was quite a short Act.

1025. Could you give us any further information as to the estimate of expenditure when this 1901 Act was brought in? Do you know what sum was taken in December, 1901, for the working of it in 1902?—No, I am afraid that I cannot give those figures.

1026. If you cannot give us the figures now never mind. We may take what you have just given us from the Prime Minister as being fairly conclusive that the Act has been very much more expensive than people expected?—I am very sorry that I cannot give more information; I have not grown up with this system in Victoria; it has only just come into operation, and the returns are not to hand, or you should have everything that we could possibly give you. I have telegraphed out to Victoria for additional information, but this is all I have got, unfortunately.

Sir John Hutton.

1027. Are the pensioners allowed to work and earn money when they are in receipt of a pension?—Yes. As far as I know they would be encouraged to work, I should think.

1028. They would be encouraged to work?—Yes, I should say so.

1029. There is no special tax allocated to the pensions, is there?—No, it comes out of the general consolidated revenue.

1030. What becomes of the aged poor who are not eligible for pensions; is there Poor Law relief?—Yes. We do not call it Poor Law; but over 300,000*l.* a year is spent in charity—that is to say, in general charitable institutions, and, I am sorry to say, also in lunatic asylums; that takes large rate. Then there are children's reformatories and other institutions which are supported by the State. That is in addition to the Old-age Pension Scheme.

1031. There are no local rates for Poor Law purposes?—No.

1032. Does the State maintain all the hospitals?—Hospitals for the insane are totally supported by the State, but other hospitals are mainly supported by public charity, supplemented by grants in aid from the Government which vary yearly.

1033. I think I understood you to say that they send the infirm aged poor to the hospitals at the expense of the State?—Yes. When you say hospitals they are called "charitable institutions." Of course, if a man wished to have medical attendance or needed medical attendance he would go into the hospital, and if he could not pay for it the State would pay for it for him.

1034. Do

Sir John Hutton—continued.

1034. Do the State give what we should call out-door relief in England to aged or infirm persons, other than the pension?—Yes, I believe they do in some cases.

1035. And does such relief disqualify those who receive it as citizens; that is to say, does it deprive them of their votes, and so forth?—No.

1036. Then there is no difference made between pensioners and others?—The outdoor relief is done on a very small scale; it is not the system that you have in England here.

Mr. *Lloyd-George.*

1037. For how long has this been in operation?—Our Act came into operation in 1900, and the existing Act came in on the 7th December, 1901.

1038. So that you have not had very much time?—No, we have not had very much experience of it just yet.

1039. It is more or less liberal than the New Zealand Act?—This is not exceeding 8s. a week. Of course, there may be a number of pensioners who only receive 3s. or 4s. or 5s. a week, according to their circumstances.

1040. Is there any income test?—Yes, there is an income test, and a property test also. I have given evidence of the provisions of the Act.

1041. If a working man was employed and receiving 1*l*. a week, say, would he be entitled to a pension then?—No.

1042. I think you said that he could work if he liked?—I do not think 1*l*. a week was mentioned to me. He might earn 2s. 6d. a week, or something of the sort, and *pro tanto* of course he would not be entitled to anything from the Government.

1043. That is why I am putting the question, because I was rather surprised. So that if he is earning 8s. a week he gets nothing?—That is so.

Mr. *Shackleton.*

1044. You stated in your evidence that if the relatives were able to maintain the father or mother there would be no payment at all from the State?—That is so; any relative—father, mother, husband, wife, or child.

1045. In the definition of "child" would be included, of course, a daughter?—Yes.

1046. With regard to a daughter without separate income, how would she be able to maintain her father, supposing she was a married daughter?—It does not follow that she would be able to do so.

1047. Could you in any way come upon the husband of the married daughter?—No, I should think not.

1048. So that in that case, if the daughter had no separate income of her own, supposing the daughter was the only child upon whom a claim could be made, the father would come on the fund in the ordinary way?—Yes.

1049. If the only person upon whom a claim could be made was a daughter, and she had no separate income, he would come on the fund?—That would be so. I take it you cannot go beyond the relatives that are defined in the Act.

1050. What is the real difference between your Charity Organisation or our Poor Law, as we call it, and this scheme at the age of 65?—They are taken into a charitable institution, and maintained there; that is the principal distinction. Under the pension scheme they would live out and be maintained.

Mr. *Shackleton*—continued.

1051. I may take it that there is very little outdoor relief given except by the pension?—Yes.

1052. In the case of a person under 65 still able to live somewhere else, to keep himself and not trouble any organisation at all, would there be any payment?—I am glad that you have reminded me of that. Except in an exceptional case which is mentioned in the Act, the usual age is 65; but the Act provides for any person of any age who is in permanent ill-health caused by having been engaged in mining or in any prescribed dangerous, unhealthy occupation; so that a man under the prescribed age can get an old-age pension if he is in ill-health caused by mining or other dangerous or unhealthy occupation. Those occupations are not specified by the Act; they are left to be named by regulation of the Governor in Council. On the point of the charitable institutions, I may mention that many men came out of charitable institutions, as they were entitled to do, in order to get their old-age pension; and when they had been out for a little time they went back again. They thought they would rather go back to the institution than remain outside and fend for themselves on this payment.

Chairman.

1053. Was it in Victoria that there was some complaint in the papers of the miserable conditions under which these men were living in huts, with their 5s. or 8s. pension?—I do not think so.

1054. Is the "Argus" published in Victoria?—Yes, that is one of the leading journals in Melbourne. That may be so.

Mr. *O'Shee.*

1055. Comparing the cost of living for working people in Australia with the cost of living in England, what would you say 8s. in Australia would represent in England?—I should not like to answer that. It is a very important point. Meat is very cheap, of course, in all the Colonies; but, on the other hand, there is a high tariff upon clothing and a number of other articles, and as to butter and eggs and bacon and milk, they are very much the same as they are in England, though just at present these articles are higher in price than usual owing to the recent drought.

Mr. *Lloyd-George.*

1056. What about bread?—Bread might not be. Bacon, butter, milk, and eggs, as I say, are much the same.

Mr. *O'Shee.*

1057. What is the wage of a working man, say a carpenter?—A good carpenter would get from 8s. to 11s. a day. There is plenty of money in that to save for an old-age pension.

1058. I understand you to say that meat and flour would be considerably cheaper in Australia than in England?—Meat would be, but I do not think flour would be considerably cheaper—not very much cheaper.

1059. Butter

Mr. O'Shea—continued.

1059. Butter and eggs and milk would be about the same price, you say?—I think about the same. Anything imported from England or Europe would, of course, be more expensive, because they have a heavy tariff with regard to most things. There is no duty now on tea. There was, but there is not now.

Mr. Channing.

1060. What would be the wages of an ordinary labourer a day?—From about 5s. to 6s., I think.

1061. That would be very nearly double what it is here?—I cannot very well speak about that. I think you would have to pay a man 6s., and in Sydney, unfortunately, some men would not work for 6s. a day, more is the shame to them.

1062. So that the payment with regard to unskilled labour would be considerably higher, as well as the payment for skilled labour?—Yes.

1063. With regard to Poor Law administration in the homes and institutions, what is the cost of maintenance in Victoria, as compared with this country?—Do you mean the cost per inmate?

1064. Yes?—I am afraid I cannot tell you that.

1065. You have no figures?—No; I could get them for you, I daresay, but without statistics at my hand I could not tell you.

1066. Do you think that the checks in these Acts as to residence are sufficient?—I think so; in the Victorian Act there are a great many safeguards which I do not notice at all in the Bill before the House.

1067. That would be more necessary in a Colony where you have constant immigration?—No. I think human nature is much the same all over the world. If you want to prevent fraud you must have these safeguards.

1068. I do not know whether you know anything about the Acts in New South Wales and New Zealand, but can you say whether these Acts tended to produce artificial immigration into the Colonies where they are in force?—No, I think not; I think they have hardly been sufficiently long in operation for such a thing to happen. It might happen, but I have not heard it suggested.

1069. With regard to the saving in Poor Law expenditure, or the equivalent in Australia, can you tell us anything about that?—No, I am afraid I cannot.

1070. With regard to duties, I am afraid that I could not catch what you said. Are there duties on food, except on tea and coffee?—Yes, on most food there is. We have inter-colonial free trade; that is to say, Queensland may import fruit from Tasmania, and New South Wales may import meat from any other Colony, duty free. New Zealand is not in the Federation.

1071. Is there a duty on wheat?—Not between the Colonies, but if brought from Europe, there is a duty of 1s. 6d. per cental.

Mr. Channing—continued.

1072. And a duty, of course, on sugar?—Yes, 6s. per cwt. on cane sugar, and 10s. per cwt. on other sugar.

1073. What would be the main source of revenue—would it be from that duty or from duty on manufactured articles?—Mainly from duty on spirits, wine, tobacco, and practically almost everything else that you use—clothing, and everything, in fact.

1074. But is the bulk of the revenue raised from those articles which you have last mentioned, or from articles of food?—No; the bulk is not raised from articles of food.

1075. There would be a small amount received from duty on articles of food, and a larger amount received from other articles?—Yes.

1076. The first Act was found to result in a great deal of waste and fraud, was it not?—Yes.

1077. There was great objection taken, was there not?—Yes, there was. It is found that, even under the existing system, fraud goes on.

1078. Is that fraud chiefly as to income and property?—Yes; and it must be so in any community, unless the safeguards put in are severe and complete. It is so, notwithstanding all the safeguards put in.

1079. These pensions go on from year to year, the pensioner having to stand questioning, if necessary; otherwise, the pension going on?—That was a question the Chairman asked just now.

Chairman.

1080. I asked whether they were granted annually or not?—The pensions go on without a fresh annual grant, but there is power to annul them at any moment. They may be challenged at any moment.

Mr. Channing.

1081. For improper conduct?—Yes.

1082. But supposing the conduct of the pensioner is not challenged, he merely has to appear and be ready to answer questions, and the pension goes on?—Yes, certainly.

1083. Is that so?—Yes.

Chairman.

1084. The Committee, I am sure, are all very much obliged to you for the trouble which you have taken. I wanted to ask you whether the money for the pensions and for what you have spoken of as charitable institutions both come from the same source, the State, or is any part raised from a local rate?—No, it all comes from the State.

1085. You will put in a copy of the Acts of the State of Victoria relating to old-age pensions?—Yes, I shall be very pleased to do that.

Wednesday, 22nd July 1903.

MEMBERS PRESENT:

Mr. Channing.	Mr. Pemberton.
Mr. Ernest Flower.	Colonel Pilkington.
Mr. John Hutton.	Sir Robert Reid.
Mr. Grant Lawson.	Mr. Remnant.
Mr. O'Shee.	Mr. Shackleton.

MR. GRANT LAWSON IN THE CHAIR.

Miss EDITH SELLERS; recalled.

Chairman.

1086. I believe that you have another observation to make about the Danish system of pensions with regard to cost?—Yes. The last time I was here I rather understated the amount granted in pensions. The average pension for Copenhagen for a married couple is 9l. 3s. 5½d.; for a single person, 7l. 9s. 3d.; for the whole of Denmark, 6l. 15s. 10½d.

1087. For a single person?—No, for a married couple; for a single person, 4l. 18s. 9¾d. That is, of course, the average. 16l. 16s. is the highest pension granted; and, of course, those that are simply supplementary grants decrease the average.

1088. Supplementary to the income already possessed by the applicant?—Yes. The last time I was here I was only able to give the statistics with regard to the cost up to the year 1897. Since then I have obtained the figures for three more years. For the year 1898 it was 252,850l.; for the year 1899 it was 269,539l.; for the year 1900 it was 285,491l. That is the full cost, without any deduction being made for the savings effected in the poor rate.

1089. Do you happen to know if the population of Denmark has been increasing very rapidly?—It is increasing. I have the Danish population for the year 1900, which is the last year that I have given the statistics for. It is 2,465,000 roughly. Therefore, as the English and Welsh population for the same year was 32,526,000, roughly, the cost of working out this scheme in England, at the same rate, would be 3,591,000l.

1090. But that is taking only England and Wales?—That is only England and Wales.

1091. Excluding Scotland and Ireland?—Yes, I left out Scotland and Ireland. I was thinking simply of England and Wales, and in that case the cost would be 3,591,000l. The pensions would have to be greater for England than for Denmark. If they were double it would only make some 7,000,000l.; and if the saving effected in poor law expenses was the same in England as in Denmark, it would mean a saving of

Chairman—continued.

3,000,000l. That would reduce the full cost of the pensions to 4,000,000l. for England and Wales.

1092. Denmark is a very prosperous country, is it not?—Yes.

1093. The people are small holders?—The majority are.

1094. The trade of Denmark, as probably you know, in agricultural produce has increased at a marvellous rate in late years?—It has.

1095. So we may take it that Denmark is an exceptionally prosperous country, with but few miserably poor people in it?—Yes, there is no very great poverty; I never saw anyone who looked hungry.

1096. So I understood?—May I just make one more observation with regard to Denmark, and that is, that it is, of course, rather startling to find that the people are so delighted and contented with what they receive, considering the small amount that they do receive. I made very careful inquiries among them as to why they were so delighted, because, after all, what they receive is not much more than they would receive as poor relief; and, as far as I could make out from their answers, the great thing was the distinction that was made socially between the old-age pensioners and the paupers. That made a great difference to them. It seemed as if they were willing to take a much smaller sum as pensioners than they would take as paupers.

1097. I think you told us that the fact that the two forms of relief were administered by totally different officials was a matter of considerable importance to the pensioners?—Yes, that makes a great difference. Then another thing that seems to add to the popularity of the system is that the old-age pensioners do not lose their votes. I hardly ever spoke to an old man in receipt of a pension who did not tell me that he had his vote. A third reason certainly is the fact of their having retreats, which are not workhouses, to retire to at last. They have no fear, whatever may happen to them, of being sent to the workhouse, because they have these old-age

homes

Chairman—continued.

homes to go to when they are too feeble to live alone.

1098. You take it, then, that their great fear is going into the Institution as apart from receiving outdoor help from the State?—I beg your pardon. I did not express myself clearly. It is a great comfort to them to have this Institution to go into.

1099. Yes, but that is an Old-age Pension Institution?—Yes.

1100. When you say they are afraid of going into the workhouse, you mean going into that form of institution—the workhouse form?—Yes.

1101. Rather than come to the State for help?—Yes. They have a very great objection to it.

1102. The other point on which the Committee were going to ask your assistance was this: It has been suggested that there are a very large number of old people in our workhouses who could go out and live with their friends if they had pensions. I believe that you yourself have made an inquiry into the circumstances of all the old people in one of our workhouses?—In eight workhouses—one large one, and seven of the very small rural ones.

1103. I was asking for the moment about the one in London. I think it was in Newington, was it not?—Yes.

1104. In 1902 you made, did you not, with the consent of the Guardians, minute inquiry into the circumstances of each of the old people over 65?—I did. I made no inquiries concerning the inmates under 65. I left them out.

1105. Would you tell the Committee what was the result of the inquiry? How many old people were there?—The number of inmates at that time above 65 was 725. There were 288 men and 437 women. Of these only 198 women and 100 men were strong enough to leave the workhouse, even if they had had friends to go to.

1106. Was that the opinion of the medical officer?—No, it was very easy to see that they were too feeble. Most of them were either blind, or quite deaf, or bed-ridden. It was the opinion of the Matron and the Master. I did not refer to the Medical Officer; but these people were manifestly much too feeble to leave.

1107. That accounts for 298 out of 725?—There were 198 women and 100 men, I found, who were physically in a condition to leave the house provided they had friends to go to. Of course, I felt very strongly that it was no good their leaving, even if they were physically able to leave, unless they had friends to go to. The Guardians in Southwark were kind enough to say that any who had friends to go to, and who were in such a condition that I could really recommend them as being suitable cases for out-relief should be granted 5*s.* a week. I was therefore a little more careful than I should otherwise have been with regard to their having friends to go to. Of the 198 women 62 I found had not a single relation in the world.

1108. They told you frankly that they had nobody whom they could go to?—They told me so frankly, and there was no reason to dispute the fact, because they were rather proud of having relations than otherwise, such of them as had. Many of them told me what relations they had had, and how they had lost them. Then there were 34 women who had practically no relations. If they had relations they were in America or in Australia, or they had lost sight of them completely. It is the women only that I am speaking of. Then 40 claimed to have relations with whom they could live. The first day 50 claimed, but day after day as I went I found a smaller number when I inquired about their relations; but 40 maintained practically that they had relations with whom they could live. They themselves, however, for the most part withdrew this claim in the course of about a fortnight after the relations were appealed to. I did not appeal to them, but they themselves did. On Wednesday the relations came to see them, and then, one after another of the inmates withdrew the claim to have relations willing to receive them. At the end of about three weeks I found that there were only 16 upon my list who said that they really had relations to whom they could go.

1109. I think you have not exhausted the 198 women yet. You took 62 who said at once that they had no relations, 34 with practically none, and 40 who claimed to have relations. That is only 136?—May I read this little passage, because it gives the numbers as I work them out?

1110. We have not yet deducted those who are too ill to go out?—I give the whole passage here if I may just read it; it is quite short.

1111. If you would?—Sixty-two women told me the first time I spoke to them that they had not a relation among them, and I found there were 34 more who for all practical purposes were in precisely the same position. Six of these had each no one but a husband who was also in the workhouse. Seven each only a sister, and in two cases the sister was in the workhouse. Ten had each only a lost son or a daughter, while 11, although sure that they had relatives, had no idea where they could be found. One woman claimed to rank with those having relatives on the strength of a sister whom she had not seen for 40 years, while seven would fain have secured the same position on the strength of certain memories they had of uncles, aunts, or cousins. After much sifting and sorting, and endless questioning, I found that of these 198 [sic] able-bodied women, 96 at the very least stood alone in the world, having no one on whom they had any claim whatever.

1112. You worked it down to 16 who had friends?—Yes, but when we sifted it further we found there were only three who had friends who could take them in. Forty claimed to have relatives, but only 16 had relatives with whom they could live, and only three had relatives with whom it was advisable that they should live. In some of the cases the house was too small, in other cases the relations were not quite satisfactory, and really only three came out of the workhouse with 5*s.* a week.

1113. The Guardians gave them 5*s.* a week, and they went out?—Yes. That was the state of things the last time I enquired.

1114. There were 437 women over 65 in the workhouse?—Yes.

1115. And only three out of the 437 could go out?—Yes.

1116. Now what about the men?—There were 100 men physically in a condition to leave; 24 of them

Chairman—continued.

them had not a relation in the world; 17 more were practically without any relations; 10 claimed to have relations with whom they could live. The others had relatives, but they acknowledged frankly that these relations would have nothing to do with them: and with regard to the 18, the majority certainly were not of the sort that could have come out.

1117. Did any of them actually go out on the offer of the Guardians?—No; the offer was made only with regard to the women and not with regard to the men.

1118. So that the men only produced 10 who could live with their relatives?—Yes, and of those 10 four were men that certainly could not possibly have been allowed to go out; they were evidently habitual drunkards.

1119. Were their relatives willing to take them?—No, I do not think they were. It was not tested in their case, because there was no offer.

Mr. John Hutton.

1120. They claimed to have relations with whom they could live?—They claimed to have relations with whom they could live, but there was no object in testing it because they were not to come out. Of course, these remarks would not apply to all workhouses, but they do apply undoubtedly to the small rural workhouses. May I read one or two of the little tables that I have made?

Chairman.

1121. Yes, I should like to hear about the other workhouses which you visited with the same object?—I went to seven in rural districts. In the first one there were 21 inmates—13 men, 6 women, and 2 boys. Of the 13 men the first was certified as an imbecile, the second was a dangerous lunatic waiting to be certified, the third was feeble-minded, the fourth was blind, the fifth was nearly blind, the sixth, seventh, and eighth were in the workhouse owing to illness, the ninth and tenth were habitual drunkards. The twelfth and thirteenth seemed respectable old men, but they had no relations. Then of the six women, four were certified as imbeciles, the fifth was a very disreputable old woman, and the sixth was a very respectable old charwoman. She was in the workhouse because she had broken her leg, and she told me that, whatever the doctor might say, she should go out the very day she could walk, because stay in the place she would not. I found that there had been a very respectable old man there a week or two before. He had been living there for some years. He was above 70, but he said that the dangerous lunatic would certainly do for them all soon, and he did not wish to be done for, and so he took his discharge, but he had nowhere at all to go to. When I went into the place it certainly struck me as being a private lunatic asylum more than anything else.

1122. Was there no respectable aged person who could go out on a pension except the woman who had broken her leg?—No, I do not think there was anyone else who could safely go out, than who had gone out, four, who ought not to be, but there certainly were three, and, with the lunatic, have been asked to live in this place, shut up with a lunatic.

1123. You are counting the charwoman?—Yes.

1124. They were all in the Infirm Ward?—No, only the old woman was going out because she could not live in the place. She was much too old to live alone. She had no friends to go to, and was only earning 1s. a day as a charwoman. She could not have been provided for properly by a pension. There was no one in the workhouse who could have accepted a pension with benefit.

1125. Nor to whom 5s. would have afforded a home?—No, certainly not.

1126. Would you tell us about the next?—In the next there were 15 inmates. This is also a rural workhouse. There were seven men, seven women, and one little girl. Of the seven men two were certified as imbeciles, two were feeble-minded, one was suffering from softening of the brain, one from chronic bronchitis, and one from liver complaint. So practically of the men not one could possibly come out. Of the seven women one was certified as imbecile, another was feeble-minded, two were disreputable, and then there were three cases of very respectable old women. One was a farmer's widow. She was 75, and it seemed that her husband had left her a little money, and she had stayed out and spent it all. It was very little. She had made it last as long as she could. She had no one with whom she could live. Whether she could have lived out if she had had 5s. a week was difficult to say. That certainly was one of the cases that ought to have been in a home of some sort.

1127. Had she no relatives who could have kept her?—She had no one, seemingly, that she thought would take her. The next one was a dressmaker. Her's seemed a very hard case. She was 74 years of age, and had worked as a dressmaker until she was about 71, and she then had nothing. She had no relation in the world, she told me, and she had not been able to lay by anything, so there was no alternative but to go into this place. Then the next was a hawker. She had been knitting stockings and hawking them until she was 68, and then she found she could not do it any more, and so she went into the workhouse.

1128. Had she no relatives at all?—She had no relatives at all.

1129. So that to offer her 5s. a week would not have met her case?—Not at all.

1130. How did you select these seven rural workhouses?—I went into one district in England. They are all practically in the same district. I do not think that what I say concerning these workhouses would apply to workhouses all over England. A little while ago I went into the workhouse at Eastbourne, and I do not think quite the same state of things obtains there.

1131. Do you mean that it was worse or better? Do you mean that there were more respectable aged poor in Eastbourne than in these workhouses, or less?—Yes, certainly more. For one thing, the state of misery in these other workhouses is so intense that it is only the very extreme cases that go in. No one will go in who can possibly avoid it; in fact, they almost prefer, I should say, to starve outside.

Chairman—continued.

1132. Is not that largely due to the fact that they are such very small establishments that the presence of one or two lunatics or imbeciles makes life unbearable?—I should say so. In one district I was told that all the lunatics were sent straight to the workhouse, and when I inquired why, I was told that it was so much cheaper than sending them to the Lunatic Asylum. This is very hard on the old people.

Mr. *Remnant.*

1133. Was there accommodation in those districts for lunatics?—There was the County Asylum, but the dangerous lunatic I came across had been in the workhouse for three or four years.

Chairman.

1134. Have you inspected in this minute manner any workhouses in small towns?—In one small town, also in the same district.

1135. We will take that case?—In this one there were 47 inmates—22 men, 9 women, and 16 children. May I mention, please, that in one workhouse that I visited I found the children playing with the casuals. That was also in this same district. In this small town workhouse two men and one woman were certified as imbeciles, two women and three men as feeble-minded, and three men and one woman were paralysed. Five out of the 22 men were, so far as I could judge, respectable, and three out of the nine women, which was a very high percentage, much higher than I found anywhere else. None of the eight had anyone with whom they could have lived if they had had pensions, and they were all too old to live alone; they were all above 70. In the seven rural workhouses I visited last autumn there were 148 inmates—115 adults and 33 children. Among the 115 adults there were, so far as I could judge, only two who would benefit if old-age pensions were granted to-morrow, providing, of course, that the pensions were reserved exclusively for the deserving, and even these two would be better in a home than living outside on a pension, for they are both alone in the world, and one of them, a farm labourer, is 77, while the other, a charwoman, is 66. They were both in the workhouse owing to illness, and, although penniless, they were both counting the days until they could take their discharge, and they were both going to take their discharge; and, therefore, of course, would have claimed pensions had there been pensions to claim.

1136. What has happened to the woman who hawked her knitting?—She had no relations. Those three, although all deserving women, had no relations to whom they could go. This woman, too, was leaving the workhouse.

1137. There were only two, in your opinion, who could profit by this Bill?—Yes, I think so. Among the other inmates I found a fair number of deserving old people—old people, some of them, whom it was positive cruelty to keep in a workhouse, for life in a rural workhouse is more often than not a terrible burden for a respectable old man or woman, a much more terrible burden than life in a prison. But they were all there not only because they were destitute, but also because they had no one with whom they could live, and were too feeble to live alone. So far as the inmates of these workhouses are concerned, an old-age pension law would have but little effect. In rural districts, at any rate, the persons whose lot it would better very considerably are not they, but the outdoor paupers. There are at the present time hundreds and hundreds of respectable old men and women who are living practically from hand to mouth, always within hailing distance of starvation, and this because they will not go into the workhouse. Poor Law Guardians cannot be induced to grant them more than, perhaps, 2s. a week, 2s. 6d. at most, as out-relief. It is such persons as these that an aged pensioner's law would benefit, as it would force Guardians to grant them something like adequate relief.

1138. You are aware that the Local Government Board sent out a circular in 1900, urging Guardians that if they granted out-relief it should be adequate?—I have made many inquiries, and I have never found one rural Guardian who knew that it was issued. Such circulars, I suppose, are sent to the clerk, and never read. Most Guardians never even see them. The chairman of one of the largest Boards in London, up to three months ago, had never heard that that circular was issued.

Mr. *Channing.*

1139. Did you inquire in Eastbourne?—I do not remember inquiring there.

Chairman.

1140. We can send circulars, but we cannot force Guardians to read them?—They never read them.

Mr. *Remnant.*

1141. Was the inquiry which was made before granting outdoor relief, in the case of the workhouses you have kindly given us information about, a very strict inquiry? I am sorry to say that I was not here at the commencement, but I rather gathered from what you said that at Newington they made an inquiry, and granted 5s. a week to certain people?—I made the first inquiry as to whether they had relations, and when I had finished the relieving officer went and tested the information.

1142. Was there any difficulty in arriving at a satisfactory answer?—No, I do not think so. I never found that any relieving officer had great difficulty in arriving at the truth when he wished to do so.

1143. I suppose many of the deserving cases that you came across in the workhouses could have been much better and more comfortably accommodated in homes such as have been suggested, if they were attached to workhouses. You found that they felt their position very keenly?—They did; but I think the homes ought not to be attached to the workhouses, because if they are, no difference comes in. The point is to have them away from the workhouse.

1144. Would there be anything against having them in the same grounds, providing they were distinct, and under distinct management?—I think it better not. In countries where cottage

Mr. *Remnant*—continued.

old-age homes are great successes they are always kept entirely apart, as in Austria and Denmark. They have no workhouses in Russia. There is no disgrace attached to going to the old-age homes there, but there certainly would be if they were in the same grounds as the workhouses.

1145. You would have them in different localities?—Yes; and it does not cost any more if they are. A very small number of old people have to be provided for, after all. When the inmates of the Sheffield Workhouse were classified, out of 200 men above 60 only 15 were put in the first class. I do not think there would be more than 4,000 altogether of those in the workhouse who would go into homes.

1146. In the whole country?—In the whole country altogether there are in the workhouses only 75,000 inmates above 65; nearly 35,000 of these are in the infirmaries, so that it only leaves a little more than 40,000 above 65 in the workhouse itself. If we take the deserving among them as 10 per cent.—that would be a very generous allowance, would it not? That reduces it to 4,000.

1147. During the discussion on this Bill the point has been the large expense that probably would be incurred by the country if this was undertaken, even at the age of 65, and it was suggested that if we chose we might, by way of an experiment, commence at 70 or 75. Do you think, if the age limit was extended to 70, for instance, it would meet the majority of cases of the 4,000 that you have given us?—In the country to a certain extent, but certainly not in London.

1148. Not in London?—Oh dear, no.

1149. So, on the whole, you think that 65 is, at all events, a fair limit of age to start with?—In Berlin they have fixed it at 70. Only eight in a thousand of the inhabitants of Berlin ever reach the age of 70, and only three in a thousand of the working classes. Thus only three in a thousand ever receive old-age pensions, and it is no good having an old-age pension scheme for three in a thousand.

1150. Does that apply to all the towns?—No; only to Berlin. In Posen it is much higher.

Mr. *Ernest Flower.*

1151. I gather from what you told us this afternoon that amongst these people would be a large number who might be accommodated by what is called the Cottage Home System?—Of the present inhabitants of the workhouses?

1152. Of those that you went through?—It is very difficult to fix on any number. I have tried very hard to get at a number, and the only conclusion I have been able to arrive at is that there would be about 4,000. Taking the whole of the workhouses in England, and comparing them with the workhouses that I know, I think there would be about 4,000 who would be able to come out of the workhouses and live in homes.

1153. Have you taken that on the percentage of the cases that you have actually investigated?—Yes, I have.

1154. I should have thought that it worked out rather higher than that?—I have made allowances for different districts. Although I have given seven workhouses, I have visited many

Mr. *Ernest Flower*—continued.

others that I have not given. It might be higher. It is very difficult to say, because, you see, one cannot always be sure of the information these people give. But it would certainly not be more than 5,000.

1155. And, on the whole, I think you said that you approve mainly of the Cottage Homes Bill?—I did not think it would work as the machinery then was.

1156. You have probably seen the Bill as it has been re-introduced?—Yes.

1157. In its altered state, do you see no objection to it?—I think it would work and do a great deal of good, in rural districts especially.

1158. You think that if the Bill became law it would work?—Certainly.

1159. But you think the extent of its working would affect about 5,000?—Yes, but it is worth doing to make 5,000 people happy. I do not think that you quite realise how very miserable it is in these small workhouses. You cannot understand, unless you have been there, how exceedingly unhappy the people are. One woman said: "It is very hard at my time of life never to hear a word of sense day in and day out," and it is very hard. You see, there is no attempt at separation in these small workhouses. Life is very much worse there than in an ordinary prison, and it is very hard that these old people should have to live there, and be treated worse than criminals, is it not?

Chairman.

1160. And infinitely harder in very small workhouses than in the larger ones?—No. I have been over the greater part of Europe visiting refuges for the poor, and I never saw such misery anywhere as in Newington Workhouse. It is infinitely worse than in the Russian prisons.

Mr. *Ernest Flower.*

1161. You have seen the Cottage Homes Bill, and you approve of it? You think that, to the limited extent of 5,000 people, it would be a very useful measure?—It would certainly. It would do a great deal to alleviate the condition of the respectable class of inmates, and the other Bill—the Aged Pensioners Bill—would do a great deal to alleviate the condition of outdoor paupers.

Mr. *John Hutton.*

1162. I would like to ask you whether you have formed any estimate of the cost of providing cottage homes such as are suggested in the Cottage Homes Bill?—It is a little difficult. I have worked it out on the supposition that there are only 4,000 persons to be provided for, and that they are lodged two in each room. We could build and furnish a one-roomed cottage and buy the land for it to stand on for 150*l.* Thus it would cost about 300,000*l.* for housing the people alone. But the cost would be less if, as in Denmark, you took an ordinary sized house; and, instead of building the cottages, you just rented that house and placed your paupers in it.

Mr. *Remnant.*

1163. It would be very expensive if you built these houses, and they cost 150*l.* a room?—It works out at 300,000*l.* for them all. I was thinking of one-roomed cottages in rows. There would be also the caretaker's house.

Mr. John Hutton.

1164. Have you considered further, since 1899, the difficulty of arriving at the previous history of the aged poor in town or country?—I cannot see where the very great difficulty comes in. It is always done in the case of criminals. I have never yet failed to discover the past history of any man or woman when I wished to know it. It takes a very considerable amount of trouble, but you can always do it if you wish, and certainly it is done in Denmark.

1165. I will read an extract to you which I will ask you to express your opinion upon. Is it your opinion that only in England the poor old folk who have toiled hard for long years, and pinched and saved, must pass their days in the workhouse, when even Russia has its old-age homes?—Yes.

1166. And is it not sheer waste of time to try to make decent old folk comfortable if we shut them up with folk who are not decent?—The head of a foreign Poor Law Department was in England a little time ago, and I went with him over Fulham Workhouse, which is certainly one of the best of our workhouses. When he came away he said: "It is sheer waste of time to try to make old people happy in such places as these." His idea was that the mere fact of a respectable old woman who had lived all her life in a cottage being asked to sleep in a room with 50 or 60 other people, and to sit down with 500 or 600 to dinner, and to share a sitting-room with 100 other people, entailed very great misery. Misery is entailed by the very fact of their being suddenly transplanted from their little cottage into the midst of such surroundings as these.

1167. How do you consider England ranks amongst other nations with regard to the care that she takes of her aged poor?—Very low down indeed, decidedly. I can certainly say that.

Chairman.

1168. Is there any country in the world where the fact that a man is destitute entitles him to be kept, as of right, by his neighbours?—Yes. For 600 years that right has been held in Denmark. In Austria there is the right not only to be kept, but, as far as the law goes, although it is not always observed, the right after you are 60 to one-third of your average earnings during your life.

1169. Is that under the law passed in the time of Joseph I.?—Yes. The law has never been repealed.

1170. But is it ever acted on?—It is not acted on as it ought to be, but in Denmark it is one of the fundamental laws that every man has a right to relief.

1171. Is there any Poor Law in Russia?—None in Russia. They have old-age homes there, however. I ought to say there is a Poor Law applying to the city of Moscow, and that they even have Boards of Guardians there, but it is really the only city where this arrangement exists. They have a very peculiar arrangement in force there. When Poor Law Guardians are appointed they are given a very small sum. The Board of Guardians is given possibly 10*l.* to defray the cost of the poor in the district. With that, of course, they can do nothing, and the Poor Law Guardians have to raise among their friends there as best they can whatever more money they need.

Chairman.

1172. This is in the nature of a Charitable Aid Board, as in some of our Colonies, is it not?—Yes, it is very much the same.

Mr. Remnant.

1173. In Russia there are old-age homes, you say?—There are old-age homes, exceedingly comfortable homes, in many places.

1174. How are they worked?—They are worked, as a rule, under the Crown. The Dowager Empress founded one of the best of them, and then some of the Royal Palaces have been turned into old-age homes. The City home takes in 6,000 inmates. That is worked by the Municipality. With regard to the saving that might be effected in the cost of workhouses, if the deserving poor were in homes, may I mention that the cost of the poor in one small union I know, amounts to 15,000*l.* a year; the full cost, with extra charges, etc., to 37,000*l.* For the maintenance of the paupers it is 3,986*l.* a year, while for the officials it is 3,702*l.* This is a country workhouse.

Chairman.

1175. But does it occur to you that if we attempted to group the workhouses and to effect large economies, we should have the local feeling of the unions very much against us?—Certainly.

1176. Are you aware that we hardly ever dissolve a union, and that where we do we are always very fiercely opposed by the local people?—Is that a reason for not doing it.

Mr. S. Dean Fuller, Examined.

Chairman.

1177. You have been a member of the Paddington Board of Guardians for many years, have you not?—Yes.

1178. The point upon which the Committee want some evidence from you is with regard to the method pursued by the Paddington Guardians for the purpose of ascertaining and recording the history of applicants for relief. I believe that you laid down certain rules for yourselves in 1880?—Yes. The law requires that the Guardians should come to a right decision after full information has been put before them, but we found by experience that the forms issued to us by the Local Government Board for that purpose were entirely insufficient. We therefore tried to improve upon the form, and the Local Government Board approved of the form which we have now in use. Shall I hand you over the form?

1179. I think that I can take it very shortly.—Our

Chairman—continued.

One of your rules is that you will not grant out-relief except to people who are deserving at the time of the application?—Yes, that is right.

1180. Another is that you will not grant out-relief unless the applicant has shown signs of thrift?—That is another condition.

1181. Those rules you have maintained from the year 1889 down to the present day?—Yes.

1182. The Committee desire to know what tests you apply with regard to a man's being deserving at the time of his application. Your Relieving Officer does it, I suppose?—I can best answer that question by showing this form. The application of the person is entered on the front page of this, and the decision of the Guardians is entered also on the same page in red ink. On the next page there are full particulars of the applicant and of his family, and the cause of his seeking relief, and further particulars of what members of his family are able to supply him with assistance or not. On the next page the Relieving Officer puts his observations. Here is a specimen of an actual paper, and I can give you a brief account of it if you wish. I should like to say, with regard to this case, as an illustration of the benefit of carrying out this practice, that we have the history here of a man who came to us 10 years ago, having lost his license through drink. We had to take him and his family in. We have the history of the case for the last 10 years, showing how, under our guidance, he improved, went out, became a steady, sober workman again, and took care of his family. He broke down, and came back again, and eventually, this month, we have adopted his children, and I hope the fact of adopting his children will be the saving of the man. We have often given him opportunities of going out to try to get work, leaving his children behind him. He has always come back to his children. He will be able to go out when he chooses, but he will know that he has lost his children till the age of 18, and the only hope of his getting his children again will be turning over a new leaf. Then we should let him have his children again on probation; and, if he behaved himself, would give them up to him. Having these papers before us, we should have no difficulty, five years hence, in seeing exactly what the character of the man was when with us during those 10 years, and what our best course in relation to his future should be.

1183. I can quite understand your keeping a history of a man who has been applying for poor relief for the last 10 years, but I want to know how you start the inquiry about the history of an unknown man coming and asking for relief?—According to this form, an unknown man has to answer a large variety of questions put to him by the relieving officer, who then makes the fullest inquiries into all the circumstances of the case. The applicant then comes before the Guardians. The Chairman has all these particulars before him, and he and the other Guardians ask what questions they wish, and very often record the answers on that form. It is only after full examination of the circumstances of the case that they decide what they shall do with regard to the case.

1184. Can you give us any idea of what test of thrift is applied? Do they ask him if he is a member of a Friendly Society?—Yes; and we scarcely ever get an answer in the affirmative.

1185. You mean that you hardly ever get a member of a Friendly Society?—Yes. We recognise that thrift does not mean, of necessity, putting aside money. If a man has brought up a large family, and had sickness in it, and spent money in educating them or in looking after a sick wife, we recognise that as equivalent to thrift.

1186. You have regard to how he has taken care of his family?—Yes.

1187. Are the Paddington Board of Guardians fairly satisfied that they get truthful answers to these questions?—We get answers that we can rely on very much more than we could in past days.

1188. I suppose, when you first started the system, sometimes the information was not very trustworthy?—We recognise that we are liable to be deceived, but with the growing experience of relieving officers and Guardians we are fairly able now to test cases.

1189. Even in a place like Paddington, where the population is, I suppose, to some extent shifting?—Yes.

1190. Do you refer to the man's previous parish, or the previous union that he has lived in, in making your inquiries?—That would depend upon the length of time he was in the parish. If a man had been for three or four years in the parish, and had had a good character in the parish, I do not think we should trouble much about the past. If he had been a bad man in the past, other things being equal, we should consider that he had atoned for the past by good behaviour in the four years.

1191. Have you a relieving officer whose special duty it is to make inquiries outside the union?—Yes, outside the union.

1192. What should you say was the proportion of people who come for relief to you whom you would consider deserving at the time of the application, and as having shown signs of thrift?—I cannot answer that. There used to be a statement made by Mr. Dodson, in 1871, that only one person in ten would accept an offer of the house, and go in, and that the other nine, having tried it on on the Guardians, would be able to get on without the workhouse, but I do not think that proportion would stand good at all with us now, and for this reason: The rules that we drew up in 1889 we print in large letters, and put up in our waiting-room where the applicants are, and whilst they are waiting to come into the Board room every one of them is able to read for himself or herself what will guide the Guardians in their decision on the case. A drunkard coming into the room and reading the rules would probably go out. He would know that there was no chance, and that knowledge for the last 15 or 20 years has been gradually spreading through the parish, and we have, comparatively speaking, very few applications now of the nature of a try on, and therefore the number of people deserving who apply to us would be much larger in proportion than it was some years ago.

1193. I believe

Chairman—continued.

1193. I believe that, if they are deserving people, you make efforts not to let them come on the poor rates at all, but to get for them private charity, do you not?—If a deserving applicant comes to us, we adjourn the case for two weeks, so that it shall not be lost sight of, and then we call the attention of either the Charity Organisation Society or the various clergymen and ministers of the union to the case.

1194. And you try to get a little pension for these people from private charity?—Yes; and we always tell them, in order that they may educate those outside, that our wish is, as they are deserving, that they should not become paupers. In other words, it encourages those that are deserving to come forward.

1195. I suppose that that, which almost amounts to a certificate of deserving old-age, turns charity into a right channel, and provides it with suitable objects?—Yes.

1196. But would it not be a great help to you in your work if you had some pensions, even if it were a limited number, which you yourselves could grant to the most meritorious case?—If, for any reason, charity says, "We cannot" or "We will not assist this case," and we think it deserving, we do not give a pension, but we give out-relief.

1197. Do not you think that people would like it better if it was called a pension, and administered separately from the Poor Law?—Other than by a Pension Committee of the Guardians do you mean?

1198. Yes. I would suggest to you its being managed by a different organisation altogether, as a sort of State Pension Charity?—What is proposed under this Bill can be done, and more than done, by Guardians. For instance, it is proposed that A. B., having 10s. a week, can have 5s. a week from the Pension Committee, but the Guardians have full power, and they could give out-relief to that person to the extent of 5s. a week, and also give an order for the doctor whenever he is ill.

Sir Robert Reid.

1199. Could they, if he had 10s. a week already, give him 5s. a week more?—Yes.

1200. But would they do such a thing?—They have done such a thing, but very rarely. By the Poor Law the Guardians are the sole judges as to what is destitution. Some years ago my colleagues thought it right that a mother and daughter in receipt of 15s. should have, in addition, out-relief. I considered the mother and daughter, who were of very good character, were not destitute in the eyes of the law, and I told my colleagues that I must communicate with the Local Government Board in the matter. The Local Government Board wrote back to me to say that the sole judges in the case were the Guardians themselves, and that they could not interfere.

Chairman.

1201. Destitution being defined not as being absolutely without means, but without the means to provide necessaries?—With all that is required to keep body and soul together.

1202. To return to the point that I put to you a short time ago—at present you go to private charity, and you try to get help given from private charity. I ask you, would it not be a great help to you if you had a certain number, even a limited number, of State pensions to which you could refer the most deserving of your applicants?—In some cases give out-relief, and in some cases give pensions, do you mean?

1203. In some cases refer them to a Register of Old-age Pensions, if such a Registrar was established in England?—In the first place, as I said before, we can give it, and in the second place I should very strongly deprecate that suggested action, because it would entirely remove from charity the exercise of its duty. For some years charity has been gradually developing. If you take away from the rich the duty which they have towards their fellow creatures by giving pensions from the State, you are entirely removing from them all feeling of the duty that they should undertake.

1204. Perhaps you could help us on a point which was raised by the last witness with regard to how many of the old people in the workhouse have friends with whom they could live if they had pensions. Have you made any inquiries in the Paddington Workhouse directed to that point?—Not the specific inquiries which have been made elsewhere, but without making specific inquiries we have fairly satisfied ourselves that the number who could be sent out would be very small. I have three cases here if you would allow me to quote them. It would not take a minute. Mr. Lockwood, the Poor Law Inspector, in 1898-9 called attention to the case of a London Board of Guardians who directed a call-over of the female inmates with a view to relieving the overcrowding in the workhouse, and giving relief outside. They, with one consent, besought the Guardians to allow them to remain in the house. At Poplar, in 1898, a committee of the Guardians went into the circumstances of 1,000 of the inmates, and eventually found that they were only able to send out, with outdoor relief, 47 cases out of the 1,000.

1205. Mr. Crooks told us that a good many of the 47 had come back to the workhouse?—Yes. At Whitechapel they made inquiries respecting 169 old men and women. Only 15 were found who could be at all considered further in the matter, and of those 15, 13 were in through intemperance or improvidence.

1206. You desire to make some observations on Clause 6 (f) of this Bill, do you not, with regard to the limitation on the amount of income which an applicant may have without being disqualified from receiving a pension? What is your observation on that?—By Clause 6, Section 2, the Guardians, through the Pension Committee, would have to deal with a class of people whom they at present have no knowledge of—that is, applicants for a pension having 10s. a week of their own if single, or 15s. a week if married. Those incomes would, in the eyes of Guardians, show that the applicants were not destitute. Yet even at the present time Guardians have full power to give out-relief to such

Chairman—continued.

such people. There is nothing to prevent Guardians from deciding that such people are destitute and deserving, in which case they could give them out-relief. In other words, Guardians could give now, if they saw fit, what this Bill proposes; and, in fact, a great deal more, but they do not think fit, and the effect of the Bill would probably be a total change in the present system. If the law required that a pension should be given by the proposed Pensions Committee of the Guardians to a suitable person having not more than 10s. a week, the Guardians would see no justification for withholding it from persons under 65 with similar incomes, who from ill-health or other cause could no longer earn their living. That means that the whole of the good work hitherto done by Guardians would be effaced. There would be no need on the part of applicants to exercise thrift beyond a certain point, no need for children to trouble about the future of their parents, and no need on the part of the public to exercise charity. There is another class that they would also be brought into contact with, a class which they are at present utterly ignorant of.

1207. We have agreed that we shall not go into the general question of whether there should be pensions, for this reason, that we consider that the House by passing unanimously the second reading of this Bill are adopting it. It would not be for the Committee to overrule that, so I do not think it is necessary for you to go into that. We may take it that your views are that a pension scheme would do more harm than good?—Yes. May I refer to the question of members of Friendly Societies coming before the Paddington Guardians?

1208. Yes, please. You said just now that you hardly ever had a case of a member of a Friendly Society coming before the Paddington Guardians?—There are two relieving officers, who have had experience of from 25 to 30 years, and I have had nearly 25, and we could only remember two cases. One is that of a man who applied, but who did not press his application. He had a son whom we found to be a lunatic, and we helped the man by taking the lunatic. The other is the case of a man, in receipt of 4s. 6d. a week, using our workhouse to come into to get rid of delirium tremens. Those are the only two cases in 26 to 30 years that three of us can remember, showing that we are almost utterly ignorant of a member of a Friendly Society applying to us. I spoke about our rules being posted up. We are always very anxious that nobody should be prevented from applying to us from the fear that he would not receive assistance if he was deserving. We virtually encourage deserving people to apply to us. If they are deserving, they know from the rules that we will try to get them pensions from charity, and that, if that fails, we will help them. But, instead of their being encouraged, people in possession of money in the Savings Bank or Building Societies or Friendly Societies, have not come forward. They have, as it were, co-operated with us, wholly ignorant of the principles which were guiding us.

Chairman—continued.

1209. They have kept their members from coming on the Poor Law?—They have done that, and if you asked for information about Friendly Society members and other people exercising thrift, we could give you no information at all.

1210. Because they have never come to you?—Because they have never come to us. They have got on without coming to the Guardians.

1211. Do you wish to say something about Clause 17 of the Bill with reference to State contributions?—In London there is a Common Poor Fund, that is, a poor fund raised by the whole Metropolis, and certain of the expenses of Poor Law Unions throughout London are payable out of that Common Poor Fund, and almost all Guardians, I think, would tell you that there is a very great temptation to consider: "Will this expense that we are contemplating come out of the Common Poor Fund or out of our own ratepayers' pockets." To show how it works, some years ago a certain union in London spent its money most recklessly. The money would have had to be paid, in the ordinary way, out of the Common Poor Fund. The Local Government Board were so impressed by the recklessness with which the money had been spent that they informed the Board that they would not allow it to come out of the Common Poor Fund, and it cost that union many thousands of pounds. The result has been most satisfactory. A certain number of the ratepayers objected to their money being spent in that way. They have got a different Board of Guardians, and they are spending now their own money in a proper way.

1212. The gist of the evidence is this, I suppose: That if pensions were paid, half by the State, and the selection of pensioners was left to Boards of Guardians, there would be very strong temptation to put people on to the pension list rather than to give them outdoor relief: is that the analogy that you draw from their present conduct towards the Metropolitan Poor Fund?—It would be a help towards corrupting Guardians.

1213. Is it not the case that the maintenance of a casual in a casual ward in London is a Common Poor Fund charge?—Yes.

1214. But if the casual goes into the workhouse, even for a night, the charge of keeping him for that night is not a Common Poor Fund charge, with the result that the Guardians will not, even when the casual ward is full, take casuals into the same building? Do you know of such a case at all?—I am afraid I forgot about that classification. We have no right to refuse the person.

1215. One of the London Police Magistrates said recently that you have no right to refuse to take them into the casual ward if there is room?—But if the casual ward is full, surely you have a right to take a casual into the main workhouse. I should say that, for humanity's sake, we are bound to take a man into our workhouse, there being no room in the casual ward, on a bad winter's night. Our casual ward is, perhaps, a couple of hundred yards from the workhouse. Strictly speaking, it would be our duty to send the man on.

1216. A

Sir Robert Reid.

1216. As I understand, you do not think there is any difference between out-relief and pensions?—I mean that, in substance, there is really no difference between the two, more especially if given by the same body of Guardians.

1217. As a matter of fact, what is the rate of out-relief that you give for a single man of 65?—I should say that it would be 3s. 6d. to 4s., plus his rent, which we should require to be of a proper amount. We should not accept a man's paying 5s. a week as rent for a room. We should tell him that he was extravagant, and that he should go into another room. I think, if all over London a single person had a maximum of 5s. a week, plus the rent, he would be perfectly well able to live on it. With regard to the views entertained by my colleagues, the relieving officers think that 5s. would be unnecessarily large, and, of course, they speak from considerable experience.

1218. Supposing that a man has got nothing, and he is 65 years of age and cannot work for himself, do you ever give him outdoor relief?—Yes; we should give him the full amount required.

1219. What would you give him, including rent and everything else?—From 7s. to 8s. a week.

1220. Outdoor relief?—Outdoor relief. It is not always very easy, but we try to carry out the proper principle, that if you give outdoor relief it should be adequate, and this is an excellent way of checking Guardians who are anxious to give outdoor relief very freely. If you can get them to give it adequately, it checks the number of cases in which they are willing to give out-relief.

1221. You think it desirable to check outdoor relief?—It is desirable to check a great deal of the out-relief that is given.

1222. Do you know that in Scotland it is almost entirely outdoor relief?—I do not know anything of the Scotch plan.

1223. Is it otherwise in London?—The larger proportion is indoor relief. You probably know Dr. Chalmers' views upon that. Might I quote them?

1224. If you please?—Dr. Chalmers said that the official relief of the poor had not only locked up the sympathy of the wealthier for the poorer classes of society, but it had also undermined the sympathy of the poor for one another, which he thought of far superior importance to the sympathy of the rich for the poor, for all which the rich give to the poor in private beneficence is but a mite and a trifle when compared with what the poor give to one another.

1225. The argument is that you should not check the flow of sympathy and of charity. I do not know the date when Dr. Chalmers said that, but I should like to ask a question about it. Supposing that a charitably disposed person can afford to pay 100*l.* a year, and does pay 100*l.* in charity, and gives it in relieving old people, and then supposing that the old people are provided for otherwise, is there any reason why the charitably disposed person should not find other objects equally deserving of his 100*l.*?—No.

1226. I do not know myself why you assume

Sir Robert Reid—continued.

that because one avenue of charity is closed by the action of the State, therefore human sympathy cannot find other outlets?—The sympathy with regard to charitable gifts is so very different from the—I do not know quite what word to use—with regard to money given by the State.

1227. That is true. However, I do not want to enter on the broad question, but I do not suppose that the only objects of charity in the world are people over 65. I think there may be many poor young people?—Yes, certainly, often money might be given in helping a young man to tide over his trouble until his sons and daughters have grown up and can help their father.

1228. You say that hardly any Friendly Society members come into your workhouse?—I cannot quite admit the word "hardly" even.

1229. May I ask are there many people coming into your workhouse who are, and who have been, total abstainers?—We never like to ask that question. If an applicant says, "I am destitute," we have no right to inquire whether he has been a drinker or not. The law requires us to help that destitute person.

1230. I understand that?—As far as our workhouse officials go, I think they would say that a great many of the people, or a very large number of the people, behave themselves while inside the house, but that the temptations are too strong for them if they go out.

1231. In other words, do you mean that a very large number of those in the workhouses have given way to drink?—I mean that they give way to drink when they go out.

1232. I am not talking about the legal obligation, but I am trying to get the social stratum which you tap, which is a different thing altogether. As regards the persons who come to the workhouses, do you think yourself that the bulk of them are people who have been brought thither partly in consequence of drink?—I will put it that it is almost entirely through their own fault.

1233. In the case of nearly all of them?—Yes. The only exceptions in our workhouse at the present time are those people who from infirmity could not be given out-relief.

1234. There are a number of persons in the workhouse, of course, to whom infirmity and affliction have come without any fault of their own; but, barring those who are infirm from affliction of some kind, do I understand that you think that the great majority of the inmates have been brought there by their own fault?—Yes.

1235. Do you think that they are brought there by their own fault to such a degree that they would not be in the class of deserving poor?—Persons deserving pensions later on, do you mean?

1236. You do not think favourably of pensions in any case, but you know the sort of persons one means by deserving people—people entitled to our pity and sympathy. Do you think that the great majority of those in your workhouse, apart from the cases that could not be removed, would not come within the nomination of "deserving poor"?—Certainly. At the same time, I should

Sir

Sir Robert Reid—continued.

like it to be quite understood that we never give up hopes of any person. When an applicant comes before us, we do not simply confine ourselves to the question of whether he is destitute, and what is the best thing to relieve the destitution, but we see how we can help. In that case that I instanced we sent the drunkard to the Church Army after we had kept him on probation with us. We always do what we can, if they are sufficiently young, to try to rescue them.

1237. I quite understand that, and I quite appreciate that, but I was not looking at how you discharge your duty, which is, no doubt, very well done. I was trying to get at what the source of your supplies is?—The people are people who have come in almost entirely from causes within their own control.

1238. And as regards persons relieved by outdoor relief, would you say that they were the same denomination of persons or not?—No. We should not give them out relief if they were.

1239. What is the proportion of cases of out relief to indoor relief in number?—At present we have, excluding 59 children boarded out (we always board out all we can), 275 men, women, and children out of the house, and 1,429 inside. That was on the 1st January, 1903. I could give you later information.

1240. No thank you, that will do very well. You say 275 outdoor cases?—Yes.

1241. Are they mostly old people?—Largely. Very often, if we are entirely satisfied that a woman (say a widow) has been a good mother, we do not take her children to the school, but we give her work, or give her assistance in some way, and watch over her to see if she continues to be a good mother and bring up her children well. If you give relief to one case and there are five in the family, that makes relief to six cases, so I cannot tell you the number.

1242. Did you only count that as one in the 275?—No, it would be more than one.

1243. It is not 275 families?—No.

1244. But 275 members of families?—Yes.

1245. What is the average that you give to each family out of the 275 in outdoor relief, roughly speaking?—That I cannot answer.

1246. But it is not always 7*s*. or 8*s*. a week?—No.

1247. Generally not?—Generally not. We take into consideration what they have. You put a case where a man applied to us having nothing at all, and in that case I say it would be 7*s*. or 8*s*.

1248. Do you remember many cases of persons who are total abstainers getting relief from you under any circumstances?—I cannot answer that question, because we do not encourage such a question being asked.

Mr. *Channing*.

1249. I understand that you refuse the outdoor relief to the people who obviously would be tempted to use it badly?—Yes.

1250. I think you were examined before the Aberdare Commission?—Yes.

1251. I notice that you say there that you make this test for outdoor relief—signs of thrift; no relations legally or morally bound and able to support them; unable to obtain sufficient assistance from charitable sources?—Yes; and there was a further condition with reference to children.

1252. But I am not talking of that just now. The question I wanted to ask was whether you consider it easy in practice to obtain satisfactory proof as to those points?—Under this form it is. The Local Government Board supply us with a large book, and it is quite impossible if one only uses that book to obtain, I consider, sufficient information. In this paper here we have the whole of the information from beginning to end, but if we had to turn over six to ten books to see the previous history of a case we should have great difficulty in coming to a right decision. The Local Government book is entirely insufficient for the purpose of enabling Guardians to do their duty, and it is for that reason that we have developed that form by which we are able to get all the information which we consider we ought to have.

1253. Does that involve the employment of more officials to enquire into the personal history and conditions of each case?—No. It checks people from coming forward who know that they cannot stand an inquiry. When we first started we had a great many cases, but as people learned that all these inquiries had to be made, and that the Guardians were guided in their decision by those inquiries, those who could not stand the inquiries ceased to come forward. Our proportion therefore of deserving people who come forward now is much greater than it was before.

1254. In your evidence you said it would be necessary to limit the number of cases dealt with by each officer?—Yes.

1255. Do you mean to say that the formularies which you adopt now render it unnecessary to employ a greater number of officers?—We have a sufficient number of officers now.

1256. Have you increased by the number of inquiries the expenditure on inspection?—No; we have an additional Relieving Officer since I gave that evidence, but that is owing to a part of Chelsea being added to our district.

1257. Putting it broadly, are you satisfied from your experience that the tests for ascertaining the real respectability and qualifications of applicants can be effectually carried out without a great increase of cost?—Yes, but primarily for the reason that it checks the undeserving from coming forward, and so the number of cases is comparatively small.

1258. I think you said that the greater proportion were people who had come into the workhouse from their own fault, but it is your impression that, say in Paddington, there is a very large number of deserving poor just on the border line who manage to struggle and to keep out of the workhouse, and a larger proportion of that class than you would find in the workhouse?—There are a good many people in poverty, as I think Mr. Charles Booth calls it. We have now something like 30,000 people with 31*s*. a week and under.

Sir Robert Reid—continued.

1259. And not on the rates?—Neither in nor out paupers. Our figures would be entirely taken from those 80,000, and not from the rich who live in the Parish of Paddington.

1260. But those that you are now speaking of would not be paupers, would they?—No.

1261. You are aware that there was a great deal of evidence given by other men of experience before that Commission to the effect that not only was outdoor relief inadequate, but that the inquiries were entirely insufficient, and the relief was given in places like Birmingham, for instance, and elsewhere indiscriminately. There was a good deal of evidence of that kind given before the Aberdare Commission, was there not?—Yes; and judging from the Local Government Board Inspector's reports now, that state of things continues.

1262. You think that that evidence was justified, and your methods have only produced relative relief in your own district?—Yes; I think those accusations are entirely justified, and there is no proof more clear than by going to Local Government Board Inspectors' reports.

1263. Do you think that the system which you advocate could be adopted everywhere without difficulty?—In large towns it could, but there would be great difficulty in carrying it out in small places. A chairman of our Board read a paper on this form, some years ago, at a large Poor Law Conference, and that objection was taken. Two places were mentioned, Atcham and Whitchurch, where a somewhat similar system was carried on, but on somewhat easier lines, owing to the different nature of a rural population from a town population.

1264. Do you not think that carrying out an adequate system of investigation with regard to relief which would really cover these cases, would involve a considerable increase in the cost of administration?—No. If people understand that you are to make full investigation into their cases before you relieve them, the undeserving will not submit their cases to inquiry, and they will not come forward.

Mr. John Hutton.

1265. What population have you in Paddington?—Going on for 144,000.

1266. How many people have you on the rates altogether, roughly—2,000?—No, not now. It was between 1,700 and 1,800 at the beginning of the year.

1267. How many relieving officers have you to look after these people?—Four, and a general relieving officer.

1268. Five altogether?—His work is outside the union.

1269. How many cases do you suppose one of your relieving officers would be able to inquire into in an afternoon, say, so as to get adequate information?—I could not answer that.

1270. I am asking these questions because in 1899, when the chairman of the Fulham Board of Guardians was before the Cottage Homes Committee, it appeared that they had 2,800 people on the rates, and only one relieving officer and a half for the whole of that number, who very often had to inquire into 14 or 15 cases. It was stated that they would have to increase their staff immensely if they had to make inquiry to try to sift the deserving poor from the undeserving. Would that be the case?—I do not know what their figures are now, but I should say that if they did their numbers would be very largely reduced. We consider it is good economy.

Mr. John Hutton—continued.

1271. Even with the increased staff which is required?—Yes.

1272. With regard to what you said just now about sifting your poor, has there been much alteration in the custom of your union since the year 1892?—No.

1273. I see by Mr. Ritchie's return of 1892, as to aged persons of 65 years and upwards, you gave to only 187 out-relief, and 874 were taken into the house?—Yes.

1274. Is that about the proportion now?—I am sorry to say it is not. For the last two years all over London pauperism has increased. Up to that time I should have said that ours was pretty stationary.

1275. You do not give, as a rule, out-relief unless you are practically compelled to do it, and the proportion, therefore, of out-relief is very small compared to the in-relief?—Yes; it was smaller at one time still.

1276. As a rule, you prefer to bring old people into the house, rather than leave them outside, and what are your reasons for that?—A deserving old person would have his case or her case submitted to charity first, and if charity would not give assistance, we should give out-relief. We never bring a deserving old person into the house unless for physical infirmity.

1277. You said that you had taken children away from a parent. In what sense did you mean you had taken the children away; would you explain that?—Under the Act of 1899, Guardians have the power to adopt children where the parents are unfit. In this case the man was a drunkard, and the wife was leading a bad life.

1278. Would you send them to either a Guardians' school or to an industrial school?—No, we should board them out. The power that we hold over the man is that we give no information as to their whereabouts. We are quite ready to tell him whether they are well or not.

1279. Do you find that people object to these inquiries being made?—Very few say that they object to the inquiries and withdraw their applications.

1280. It is not looked upon as insulting or derogatory?—No, that is quite exceptional.

Mr. Shackleton.

1281. When inquiring in respect to applicants for outdoor relief, do you ever put the question as to whether they are life teetotalers or have been teetotalers for a number of years?—The question is sometimes put, but it is rather objected to because some Guardians are teetotalers and some are not.

1282. But I mean does the Relieving Officer or any other person make that a part of the inquiry?—No. You see, we recognise that people who take a glass of wine can be respectable, and so we do not like to ask the question.

1283. Then if the question is not put to it by any

Mr. Shackleton—continued.

any way brought in as one of the points which can be marked against an applicant if there is excess in drinking?—Yes, we should have a report if he was a drunkard.

1284. And would it be considered one of his habits?—Yes, certainly.

1285. What other points would you put against him—laziness?—Yes, and want of thrift.

1286. Want of thrift in what way?—Either positive or negative—either not belonging to any club, or allowing his children to grow up in a bad way, unclothed; his wife helping him in his bad manners.

1287. And in dealing with the payment to a club, would you consider the wage he had earned and whether he was really able to pay towards a club?—No; but we should always accept a man's not belonging to a club if we knew that through ill-health he had been refused admission into a club.

1288. My point is this: in the case of a man earning 1*l.* a week in Paddington, you would not consider it a mark against him if he had not been able to pay towards a club?—It would be an item in the case.

1289. But would it be an item against him?—Not of necessity. If he was a good father, and had got children he was bringing up, we should recognise that as the same as putting his money into a very good club.

1290. You say you are against this Bill or any scheme for old-age pensions as pensions?—Yes.

1291. Will you give me your opinion as to one or two points in Clause 6? Take Sub-sections C and D. In applying those to your scheme of outdoor relief, how would you apply Sub-section C, for instance?—I think that we should apply it much more leniently than this Bill.

1292. You would not take 20 years?—No. If he had behaved himself well for the last 10 years we should be satisfied.

1293. With reference to D, a person might have been receiving Poor Law relief, and might have been inside the house for some short time. I will give an illustration. I know many cases where, during certain portions of the year, such as last winter in London, it was impossible to get work. I know hundreds who tramped the country to find it. Some of them had to go into the house, and to take the wife and children with them. Would you put that as against a man?—It would not be a point in his favour; but it certainly would be overlooked if his general conduct showed that it was quite unusual for him to do such a thing.

1294. You stated in your evidence, I think, in answer to the Chairman, that out of 2,750 cases you had only 16 per cent. (that is what it works out at) of outdoor relief. Now, is that rather a low percentage of persons on outdoor relief?—At present it is a high percentage.

1295. High for your district?—Yes.

1296. How does it compare with other Unions? Have you any information on that?—We are amongst those who have a small proportion of outdoor relief compared with indoor relief.

1297. My point is this: This appears to me to be a small percentage of persons on the Poor Law outside the house compared with a number of other Unions. Now is this higher or lower? Have you any information with regard to the other London Unions?—Yes, I see the figures every week, but I could not answer you offhand. As I said, our Union is amongst those who have a very small proportion. There are others who have a smaller proportion still.

1298. And Unions similarly situated with similar populations, and giving similar kinds of relief?—It varies so much in London that it is almost impossible to compare one with another.

Chairman.

1299. Have you anything else that you would like to add?—I should like to say that I hope the Committee will not think I am entirely opposed to the poor being considered. I think they are very much to be considered. All I wish to say to-day is that this Bill is not the best way of doing it, if the Committee will allow me to say so.

APPENDIX.

LIST OF APPENDIX.

APPENDIX.

APPENDIX No. 1.

PAPER handed in by the *Chairman*.

EXTRACT FROM THE LOCAL GOVERNMENT BOARD REPORT OF [illegible].

In connection with the half-yearly returns, we obtained from the clerks to the guardians of the several poor law unions in England and Wales returns showing the number of paupers of 60 years of age or upwards, excluding the insane, in receipt of relief on the 1st July 1889 and the 1st January 1890, distinguishing in the latter return the number of those who were 70 years of age or upwards.

It appeared from these returns that on the 1st July 1889 the total number of paupers aged 60 years or upwards, excluding vagrants and insane, was 278,718. The following table gives details as to the numbers of these paupers who were relieved in the Metropolitan and extra-Metropolitan unions respectively, and who received in-door and out-door relief respectively:—

Classes of Paupers.	Unions in the Metropolis.		Unions not within the Metropolis.		Total.
	Males.	Females.	Males.	Females.	
In-door.					
In Workhouse, exclusive of Infirm Wards or Infirmary.	6,435	4,808	17,163	7,[illegible]	[illegible]
In Workhouse Infirm Wards or Infirmary, separate Infirmary or Sick Asylum.	5,[illegible]	6,164	11,874	10,[illegible]	[illegible]
In Hospital or similar Institution	100	[illegible]	4	17	[illegible]
Total	[illegible]	10,[illegible]	[illegible]	17,[illegible]	[illegible]
Out-door.					
In receipt of Out-door Relief other than Medical Relief.	2,[illegible]	12,061	[illegible]	182,478	[illegible]
In receipt of Medical Relief only	[illegible]	[illegible]	[illegible]	1,[illegible]	[illegible]
Total	[illegible]	[illegible]	[illegible]	[illegible]	[illegible]
Grand Total (excluding Vagrants)	15,119	[illegible]	[illegible]	[illegible]	278,718

It further appeared that [illegible] vagrants, who were 60 years of age or upwards, were relieved on the night of the 1st July 1889, [illegible] being males and [illegible] females.

On the 1st January 1890 the total number of paupers, excluding vagrants and insane, who were aged 60 years or upwards, was [illegible], of whom [illegible] were 70 years of age or over.

The following table contains details regarding the paupers of 65 and 70 years or upwards who were in receipt of relief on the 1st January 1900, similar to those given for the 1st July 1899:—

Classes of Paupers.	Unions in the Metropolis.		Unions not within the Metropolis.		Total.
	Males.	Females.	Males.	Females.	
In-door.					
In Workhouses, exclusive of Infirm Wards or Infirmary:					
65 or upwards - - - -	7,[illegible]	[illegible],317	[illegible]	[illegible]	[illegible]
70 or upwards - - - -	4,[illegible]	[illegible]	[illegible]	[illegible]	[illegible]
In Workhouse Infirm Wards or Infirmary, separate Infirmary or Sick Asylum:					
65 or upwards - - - -	[illegible]	4,575	18,[illegible]	11,[illegible]	[illegible]
70 or upwards - - - -	[illegible]	[illegible]	[illegible]	4,[illegible]	[illegible]
In Hospitals or similar Institutions:					
65 or upwards - - - -	[illegible]	51	[illegible]	[illegible]	[illegible]
70 or upwards - - - -	[illegible]	[illegible]	[illegible]	[illegible]	[illegible]
Total:					
65 or upwards - - - -	11,[illegible]	10,[illegible]	[illegible]	[illegible]	[illegible]
70 or upwards - - - -	[illegible]	7,[illegible]	[illegible]	[illegible]	[illegible]
Out-door.					
In receipt of Out-door Relief other than Medical relief:					
65 or upwards - - - -	3,[illegible]	[illegible]	[illegible]	[illegible]	[illegible]
70 or upwards - - - -	[illegible]	[illegible]	[illegible]	[illegible]	[illegible]
In receipt of Medical Relief only:					
65 or upwards - - - -	[illegible]	[illegible]	1,[illegible]	1,[illegible]	[illegible]
70 or upwards - - - -	[illegible]	[illegible]	[illegible]	[illegible]	1,[illegible]
Total:					
65 or upwards - - - -	[illegible]	[illegible]	[illegible]	[illegible]	[illegible]
70 or upwards - - - -	[illegible]	[illegible]	[illegible]	[illegible]	[illegible]
Grand Total (excluding Vagrants):					
65 or upwards - - - -	[illegible]	[illegible]	[illegible]	[illegible]	[illegible]
70 or upwards - - - -	[illegible]	[illegible]	[illegible]	[illegible]	[illegible]

There were also [illegible] vagrants relieved on the night of the 1st January who were 65 years of age or upwards, [illegible] of these being 70 years or upwards.

From a comparison of the figures in this table with those in respect of the 1st July 1899, it appears that the total number of aged paupers, excluding vagrants and lunatics, on the 1st January 1900 exceeded the number on the 1st July by [illegible]. This increase is mainly due to the increase in the number of in-door paupers, of whom there were [illegible] more relieved on the 1st January than on the 1st July; it is practically confined to the male portion of the in-door aged paupers relieved on the 1st January 1900, on which date they numbered [illegible], as compared with [illegible], the number relieved on the 1st July 1899.

The following table shows the proportion which the total number of paupers of 65 years of age or upwards, excluding vagrants and insane, on the 1st July 1899, and the 1st January 1900, bore to the estimated population and to the total pauperism of the country, also exclusive of vagrants and lunatics, on the same dates :— Ratio of paupers 65 or upwards to population and total number of paupers.

—	Estimated Population in the middle of 1899.	Ratio of Aged Paupers per 1,000 of estimated Population.	Total Number of Paupers, excluding Vagrants and Lunatics.	Ratio of Aged Paupers per 1,000 of Total Number of Paupers.
1st July 1899 :				
Metropolis - - - - -	4,546,752	8·0	94,115	20·7
Extra-Metropolitan Unions -	27,195,[illegible]	9·6	580,153	21·3
Total - - -	31,742,[illegible]	9·5	674,848	21·3
1st January 1900 :				
Metropolis - - - -	4,546,752	8·6	109,633	23·8
Extra-Metropolitan Unions -	27,195,[illegible]	9·1	600,[illegible]	23·1
Total - - -	31,742,565	9·0	709,761	23·1

APPENDIX No. 2

Translation of PAPER handed in by Miss Edith Sellers.

Papers illustrative of the working of the Danish Old-age Relief Law, and of proposed Amendments to the said Law.

FORM OF APPLICATION.

Old-Age Relief No. ....

Schedule A.—For Men and Unmarried Women.

(*Two copies to be filled up and sent in.*)

APPLICATION for Old-age Relief under the law of 9th of April, 1891, to the Commune of Copenhagen, from

Full name and position ....

Living at ....

Born .... in .... Parish .... County.

The following questions must be answered as fully as possible, and certificates of identity and other documents procurable by the petitioner, in confirmation of the statements made, must be enclosed.

1. Has the petitioner during the last 10 years without interruption been settled in this country, and, if so, where and for how long at each place?

2. Has the petitioner during the last 10 years received any kind of parish relief for himself or his wife, his legitimate or illegitimate children, adopted children, or step-children? and, if so, in what form, when was it given, and by which commune?

3. Has the petitioner during the last 10 years been convicted of vagrancy or begging?

4. Has the petitioner ever been convicted of any crime, and, if so, when and how?

5. Which commune does the petitioner consider the commune from which he is entitled to relief? That is:

As a rule the commune where he has resided for five consecutive years without having received parish relief, and should he not have resided in such a manner in any commune, his native commune.

6. The number of members of the family and the age of each member of the family?

7. Does the petitioner live alone or together with relations or others, and, if so, with whom?

8. (*a*) What is the occupation of the petitioner and that of the members of his family?

(*b*) The approximate total amount of the income of the petitioner and the members of his family for the last year?

(*c*) How much of this income is derived from pensions, annual allowances, interest, legacies, real estate, gifts, or similar sources of income; as far as possible stated separately?

9. Has the petitioner any prospect of aid from relations or others, or any expectation of an inheritance?

10. The property of the petitioner? (Capital, real estate, right of yearly allowance, chattels, outstanding claims, etc., stating the approximate value.)

11. The debts of the petitioner?

12. How much has the petitioner's house-rent been for the last year?

13. The cause for the petitioner's poverty, with information about the health of himself and his wife, and their capacity for work, etc.?

14. How much the petitioner requires and in what form he wishes the aid to be given?

15. Other remarks which the petitioner himself finds reason for making.

I hereby declare to the best of my belief that all the above answers to the stated questions are correct and given without reservation, and in such a manner that they are in accordance with the truth.

Date ....
Signature ....
Dwelling place ....

We the undersigned, who know the position of the petitioner, certify that his poverty is not owing to acts by which he has deprived himself of his means of maintenance for the advantage of his children or others, or to disorderly or extravagant living, or in any other way owing to his own fault.

Date ....
Signature ....
Dwelling place ....

B. Please note:

That the aid which it may be necessary to grant the petitioner before the question of his claim to old-age relief has been finally settled, will be considered as poor relief should the claim be refused; and

That any person, when the law requires or allows a declaration concerning the truth of a statement made, is liable to punishment should this declaration be found to be false. This holds equally good respecting anyone who, for legal purposes concerning the public affairs, gives a false written declaration, and in writing certifies something of which he has no knowledge.

FORM OF APPLICATION.

Old-age Relief, No. .

Schedule B.—For Widows and for Divorced and Separated Wives.

APPLICATION for Old-age Relief under the Law of 9th of April, 1891, to the Commune of Copenhagen from

Full name and position ....

Living at ....

Born   in   Parish   County.

The following questions must be answered as fully as possible, and certificates of identity and other documents producible in confirmation of statements made must be enclosed by the petitioner.

1. The full name and position of the husband?

2. When and where he was born, and, if alive, where does he live at present?

3. When was the marriage dissolved? by his death? or when did the separation take place?

4. Has the petitioner during the last 10 years without interruption been settled in this country, and, if so, where and for how long at each place?

5. Has the petitioner or her husband while she lived with him as his wife, during the last 10 years received any kind of parish relief for themselves or for legitimate or illegitimate children, adopted children, or step-children, and, if so, in what form? when was it given, and by which Commune?

6. Has the petitioner during the last 10 years been convicted of vagrancy or begging?

7. Has the petitioner ever been convicted of any crime, and, if so, when and of what crime?

8. Which Commune does the petitioner consider as the Commune where she is entitled to relief (that is, as regards separated women the Commune where the husband is entitled to relief, and as regards widows and divorced women where the husband at the dissolution of the marriage was entitled to relief, unless they later on, by a five years' consecutive stay in a Commune, have entitled themselves there to relief)?

9. The number of members of the family and the age of each member of the family?

10. Does the petitioner live alone or together with relations or others?

11. (a) What is the occupation of the petitioner and that of the members of the family?
    (b) The approximate total amount of the income of the petitioner and the members of the family for the last year?
    (c) How much of this income is derived from pension, annual allowance, interests, legacies, real estate, gifts, alimony, or similar sources of income, as far as possible stated separately?

12. Has the petitioner any prospect of aid from relations or others, or any expectation of an inheritance?
    As regards separated or divorced women it has to be stated if the husband is bound to give alimony, and, if so, under what arrangement.

13. The property of the petitioner?
    (Capital, real estate, right to yearly allowance, chattels, outstanding claims, etc., stating the approximate value.)

14. The debts of the petitioner.

15. How much has the petitioner's house rent been for the last year?

16. The cause of the petitioner's poverty, with information about her health and capacity for work, etc.?

17. How much the petitioner requires and in what form she wishes the aid to be given?

18. Other remarks which the petitioner herself might find reason for making.

I hereby declare, to the best of my belief, that all the above given answers to the stated questions are correct and given without reservation and in such a manner, that they are in accordance with the truth.

Date ....
Signature ....
Dwelling place ....

We, the undersigned, who know the position of the petitioner, certify that her poverty is not owing to acts by which she has deprived herself of her means of maintenance for the advantage of her children or others, or to disorderly or extravagant living, or in any other way owing to her own fault.

Date ....
Signature ....
Dwelling place ....

N.B.—Please note:

That the aid which it may be necessary to grant the petitioner, before the question of her claim to old-age relief has been finally settled, will be considered as poor-relief, should this claim be refused, and

That any person, when the law requires or allows a declaration to be given concerning the truth of a statement made, is liable to punishment should this declaration be found to be false. This holds equally good respecting anyone, who for legal purposes concerning public affairs, gives a false written declaration, and in writing certifies something of which he has no knowledge.

Extracts from a Report drawn up by Etatsraad Jacobi, President of the Copenhagen Old-age Relief Department, concerning the lines on which the Copenhagen Magistracy, after the experience they have now gained, consider it desirable that the law for Old-age Relief should be altered.

The general conditions on which the law of the 9th of April, 1891, are based are accordingly the following :—

1. The proof of the existence of a certain indigence, arbitrarily decided, see Section 1 of the law.

2. The proof of a certain worthiness, see the title of the law and its Section 2 (a) and (b) and partly (c).

3. The proof of a certain negative self-help, see Section 2(c) of the law, but relief not of any positive one.

4. The condition that the assistance must comprise what at all times is required for necessary maintenance and medical treatment and nursing and consequently arbitrarily fixed, see Section 6 of the law.

To these general conditions we add the following observations :—

1. That indigency must be made a condition for the granting of old-age relief is evident, and that the question of its existence must be decided arbitrarily is probably right. An attempt to lay down fixed rules of such a nature, that all arbitration would be superfluous, as for instance to require that the petitioner should belong to certain classes of society or the like, would, as pointed out by others previously, probably lead to an unsatisfactory and unjust result.

It seems, on the other side, to be a defect in the law, that it does not give any indication how to find out or determine what is to be regarded as indigence in the sense of the law. The consequence of this must naturally be and has always been, for one thing, that the standard of indigence is fixed differently in the different communes, and for another that no one with certainty is able to know if he is entitled to old-age relief or not. The result of this is an uncertainty on the part of benevolent societies, private benefactors and others, as to whether any reason exists for them to render additional help or not. In other words, the basis of the law, the right to old-age relief is rendered doubtful by the circumstance, that its chief condition remains undefined.

It is therefore desirable that this part of the law should be altered in such a way that it be determined what in these conditions must be considered as necessary for maintenance, and directions be given for the calculation of the yearly income, so that he, whose calculated income exceeds the "standard of indigence," has no right to assistance whereas he, whose income falls below it, has a claim to it.

* * * * * * * * *

3. As regards the question of making old-age relief to depend upon evidence of self-help of some kind or other, opinions may be said to be most divided.

A negative proof of self-help, consisting in the person having kept himself free of poor relief for a series of years before he applied for old-age relief, is certainly required of all, but some consider that the law has gone too far in fixing the series of years at 10 years, and even in excluding him whose poor-relief has been repaid or remitted.

The Magistracy is inclined to believe that it would be justified in reducing the 10 years to five, but that it would in this case not be advisable to admit those who have paid back, or had the relief remitted. In each case, it would depend on fortuitous circumstances whether a claim to old-age relief could be established or not, namely, as regards the repayment, whether the petitioner could find a relation or benefactor, who would be willing to assist him with the amount owing, and as regards the remission, the entire accidental chance to retain the relief or not, as with a time limit of five years only, the cases, where, according to Section 33, first part, right to remission of the poor-law, relief, would not come under consideration.

Concerning the question of proofs of positive self-help, we are of opinion, that the demand for such as a condition for old-age relief ought not to be made, provided that the other conditions and the stipulations of the law generally speaking, are of such a nature, that by these the danger is sufficiently guarded against of old-age relief being granted to unworthy persons or individuals whose whole manner of life is identical with that of the special "clientèle" of the workhouse. If this should be the case, no reason seems to exist for excluding an honest and industrious man or woman, because he, owing to perhaps quite accidental reasons, such as unfavourable conditions of labour, illness, many children, etc., has been unable to put anything aside for his old-age, or even to pay in to a sick-club.

It must, on the other side be admitted, that the great defect in the present law is, that by making the relief proportioned to the want, and by not fixing a limit to its amount, it even tends to discourage an inclination to do something towards providing for old-age.

4. The stipulation, that the pension ought to amount to what at all times is necessary, is the weak point of the law and ought to be removed at any price. It is the one which necessarily involves that the pension, even if granted to a somewhat higher amount than poor-relief, very often entirely assumes such a character that it is impossible beforehand, even for only a few years, to determine what will be necessary for the person in question, so that it really suffices; and it becomes therefore necessary frequently to grant extra help, additional help, help for house rent, etc., each time after a carefully undertaken investigation.

It is furthermore this stipulation, which as shown in Section 3, tends to check the impulse to self-help; and in connection herewith it must be stated, that it likewise tends to loosen the tie between parents and children and other near relatives, and between families and former servants, employers and workers, and ordinary benefactors and the poor; as it is evident that if the law grants the indigent person what is necessary, and if what he receives from other sources must be deducted from the pension, no one then will feel any great inducement to help him. It has even actually happened that a benefactor frequently has withdrawn his support after the granting of old-age relief; and even that this has occurred, notwithstanding that the latter relief has been smaller than the benefactor's, and the consequence has been that it is really the benefactor who profits by the help, while the indigent person has suffered a positive loss by receiving it.

The worst results, however, of the stipulation is perhaps this, that what probably was principally aimed at, namely, conferring pleasure and satisfaction on the recipients, has in many cases not been attained, not because the assistance given in itself is too small, but because it has been fixed according to what is considered as being sufficient. This causes—not just at first after its being granted, but after a shorter or longer lapse of time, and especially when good friends have deplored and wondered at its smallness—that the recipients can never feel himself at ease about the question concerning the correctness of the amount of the assistance. At one time, it seems to him, that the assistance given is too small in proportion to what others, seemingly similarly situated, receive, and at another time it will—what is very natural for every indigent person—seem to him that after all he has not what he considers as necessary. And the result is therefore frequently an increasing dissatisfaction instead of the reverse. And from this results not only a largely increased amount of work, but also a diminished satisfaction to the administration, for whom, with the constantly-repeated demands for increase or extra help, often made several times yearly by the same person, at any rate in this city, the work becomes overwhelming, as part of it, from its nature, cannot possibly be distributed among many heads. That these drawbacks may be avoided, or at all events greatly diminished, has already repeatedly been proved, and needs hardly any demonstration.

On the other hand, we will make an attempt to fix the scale of relief grants, and must at once maintain that there ought not to be any attempt to fix them in such a manner that they correspond approximately with "what is necessary." Every attempt in that direction will of a necessity, if carried out logically, lead back to the arbitrary scale of assistance according to the particular circumstances. General rules for what is really necessary can evidently not be laid down, and if one wants approximately to arrive at something of the sort, it will be necessary to fix the scale very high, namely, in such a manner that they in some instances correspond to the greatest need. But if this be done, or if, generally speaking, it be attempted to take the need as the basis, the expenditure will probably be overwhelmingly large. But this basis is probably in itself not the right one either. The most natural and most considerate seems certainly to be, that the relief-principle, adapted to the special circumstances, be mainly taken as basis. And this adaptation should principally consist therein, that the rates, partly on account of the expenses not becoming too exorbitant, and partly on account of the relief being obtainable at a proportionally early age, commence with a rather low amount, but increase after a few years' interval, and further, in the circumstances, that extra assistance in certain cases is given to a home.

Against such a gradual increase, from a proportionately low initial rate (for instance, in Copenhagen 60 kr. increasing every five years with a like amount), may of course be objected, if the idea of "relief based on need" has not quite been abandoned, that persons, who have no other income, and are unable to work, already during the first or second age-period cannot live on the lowest or next lowest rate, and will consequently be obliged to give up the old-age pension and fall back on parish relief or the like.

But to this must be answered, that in any case it would have been impossible to prevent this with a fixed scale of relief, and that it would not be considered a misfortune in itself, but even quite natural, that a person, in so far as he belongs to that class whose whole way of living, as mentioned before, is identical with the special clientele of the workhouse, should be passed over to the guardians of the poor, but that, in the case of a respectable person, it is to be expected that relatives and friends or benevolent societies will find a special satisfaction in helping him over the lowest age-division, and finally, that so far as the want is owing to accidents, illness, or debility of some kind or other, which may equally befall anyone under 60 years as an older man, a remedy for this ought then not to be looked for in a law which, as the old-age relief law aims at giving a kind of supplementary wage for honourable work rendered, but in an invalidity-law which, should circumstances one day permit such a one to pass, would be a proper supplement to the old-age relief law, but does not concern this law.

And as a positive argument for the fixing of a scale for old-age relief and for a low initial-rate as standard, it may be stated (see remarks [illegible] self-help), that by this it is secured that old-age relief may without hesitation be granted to the person who already possesses an income approaching closely to the "standard of need," while he who possesses one rather higher gets nothing, and further, that with respect to him who possesses other resources than old-age relief it will always be possible, by a simple and easily-applicable process, to avoid letting him go beyond the fixed maximum by stopping the promotion at one of these stages.

On this point it would therefore be desirable to determine the relief according to a fixed scale, increasing according to age after the lapse of certain years.

The Copenhagen Magistracy, the 22nd January, 1902.

(Signed) H. A. Jacob.

DRAFT OF A BILL FOR THE AMENDMENT OF THE POOR RELIEF LAW OF 1891.

The aid which it may be necessary to grant the person in question before the final decision of the case will be considered, should he be found entitled to old-age pension, as a part of this, in the reverse case, as poor-relief.

SECTION 5.

The following yearly income is considered as necessary for maintenance:—

For a single person or head of a family:—

In Copenhagen and Frederiksberg	280 kr.
In the country towns	200 ,,
In the country	240 ,,

For the wife respectively 120, 100 and 80 kr. For the first unprovided for child the same as for the wife and for each following unprovided-for child the half of this.

Whether such a yearly income can be calculated on is shown by the information obtained and the judgment of the authorities granting the income, on a basis for which the Home Secretary will have to work out an instruction. Should the petitioner possess capital, the yearly income from this is calculated at an amount corresponding to what he, at the time he sent in his application, could have obtained by using his capital for buying a life-interest from the Government institution for life-assurance for his own lifetime, and if married for his wife's lifetime, as well, and he is thereby considered as possessor of such a life interest at any eventual later calculation of income, even if he meanwhile should have spent his capital or part of it.

SECTION 6.

A. Anyone whose calculated income amounts to the sums named in Section 5, or more, may, should it be considered necessary, be granted hospital assistance, or should the circumstances require it, medical attendance in his home, as old-age relief, but no other assistance.

B. Should the calculated income amount to less than the sums stated in Section 5, and should the case not come under Rule C, a fixed yearly income is granted according to the following rules:—

(a.) For a single person or head of a family, according to where he lives:—

	In Copenhagen and Frederiksberg.	In a Country Town.	In the Country.
In the age class 60–64 years	60	50	40 kr.
,, 65–69 years	120	100	80 kr.
,, 70–74 years	180	140	120 kr.
,, 75–79 years	240	200	160 kr.
,, 80 and thereover	300	250	200 kr.

Should the person in question, or if married his wife be considered quite incapable of earning anything, the authority granting the pension, may permit him to be considered as belonging to the next higher age division.

For the wife is added 40 per cent. and for each unprovided-for child 20 per cent. of the amounts granted, but no such allowance is granted to the man who has married during the last five years before his petition was sent in, and he is to be treated in every respect as a single person.

The higher rates which depend on increasing years are only to be granted in so far as the total yearly income is thereby not raised above the amounts stated in Section 5, with the addition of the rate for the lowest age-division (herein included the addition for wife and children), which consequently will be the maximum for the yearly income attainable as old-age relief.

The pension is either paid for one or three months at a time, in the latter case in the second month of the three months for which it is due.

(b) In case the person in question on account of weakness or chronic disease requires special treatment and attention, not procurable by himself, he will at his request be sent to a special asylum or home for aged or to a private home; but he will then have, if he is unmarried or has no unprovided-for children, to give up his income or capital to cover the expenses as far as possible.

Is he able to procure for himself the necessary attention, the higher or even the highest pension fixed for the age division may, according to the circumstances, be granted him should he even belong to a lower age-division.

Should his condition be such that it would be considered unadvisable to permit him to take care of his pension himself, he must be sent to a home for aged or an infirmary, or forfeit his claim on old-age relief, should he refuse to enter one of these institutions.

Apart from the case just mentioned, the authorities granting the pension have the right, at his request, to get him admitted into a home for aged, in so far as special reason thereto is found.

In the asylums (homes for aged) full board and maintenance has to be given to the persons having right to relief, including sufficient and suitable food and clothing, according to the state of their health and requirements; further, lodging, washing, light and fuel, and a small weekly allowance for minor necessities.

If a person, having a wife or unprovided-for children, is sent to a home for aged, the pension which he had, or had a claim to, when he entered the institution, may be granted in toto or partly to the above-named persons. Should it be found necessary to grant these poor-relief, the right of the chief person to remain in the home for aged is thereby not affected.

(c) Permanent relief carries with it the right to medical treatment at home or in a hospital, and burial expenses either in nature or in money, as fixed by the Home Office, provided the person does not belong to a sick or burial society or similar institution.

The rules referring to indigent persons in general, in respect to parish travelling, for treatment by doctors and midwives, and the fees fixed for these, and for burial expenses, hold good also for persons receiving assistance under this present law.

During hospital treatment of long duration the pension may be withdrawn in toto or partly.

C. Should it not be possible when the application is sent in, from the declarations made, at once to calculate with sufficient certainty the amount of the income; or should there seemingly be a prospect, or even a possibility, that this income may be considerably increased, a temporary pension may be granted, not, however, for a longer period than ½ a year at a time, until it shall be possible to fix the income in a permanent manner. Such a pension must, however, not go beyond the fixed rates stated above.

SECTION 7.

The person who is granted permanent old-age relief according to Section 6 B (a) receives on request, after being advanced to a higher age-division, from the beginning of the following month a pension according to the rate for the higher age-division, should his total income not thereby exceed the maximum stated in Section 6 B (a).

In case of death or other diminution in the number of the members of the family, in respect to whom the relief had been fixed, this will then be regulated on the basis of the altered conditions.

Should the male recipient of relief marry, he continues to be treated as regards the fixing and the increasing of the relief as before still unmarried.

Should a person receiving a fixed age-pension remove from one commune to another, he must, should he also there desire a pension, petition for it, and he continues then, should the rate of pension be higher in the commune to which he has removed, to receive and eventually to get the pension increased, according to the rate in force in the commune from which he removed, up to the time until he has lived without interruption at least two years in the commune to which he has removed, while the pension, in the reverse case, will be fixed by the rate in force at the commune to which he has gone.

SECTION 8.

Old-age relief when granted is forfeited, should the recipient commit acts which, according to Section 2, would exclude him from receiving old-age relief, or should he spend this in drinking, gambling, or similar manner, or if he goes to obtain and obtains poor relief.

The same rule applies likewise to the person who is admitted into a home for aged, should his conduct or behaviour be considered incompatible with the requirements of order or decency.

Besides the instances stated, relief granted may be forfeited in exceptional cases, at the request of the authorities granting the pension, by the decision of the Home Office, or the governor of the county.

SECTION 9.

Old-age relief is provided by the commune where the recipient dwells. Is the recipient not entitled to relief in the commune where he lives, this may claim to have the expenses incurred refunded by the commune where he was born, or, if none such is found, by the public funds, to whom the relief would be chargeable if it were poor-relief. Notification of the payment of the relief must, in such case, be given at once to the commune where he was born.

As long as a person receives old-age relief, his acquisition of right to relief in the commune where he lives is considered as dormant.

SECTION 10.

The expenses incurred by the commune in question, with deduction of the refunded outlays, are entered in the yearly accounts of the commune under a special heading.

After being audited in the usual manner by the communal auditors, and thereafter approved, a copy of this entry with accompanying vouchers must be sent to the chief authorities of the place, who, after perusing, and if necessary correcting, the received accounts, make a report to the Home Secretary of what each commune has spent. In Copenhagen, the accounts and the report is sent to the Home Secretary.

SECTION 11.

To the expenses of the communes for old-age relief in accordance with the regulations of this law, the Exchequer contributes half.

SECTION 12.

Complaints from desirous persons respecting the decisions arrived at in virtue of this law, by the respective communal authorities, cannot be referred to the courts of law, but must be laid before the authorities, whose decision may be referred to the Home Secretary.

Should the authorities by perusal of the accounts or otherwise, arrive at the conclusion that old-age relief has been obtained by unqualified persons, or that the regulations of the law had been eluded, the decision of the case rests likewise with them, which, however, may be referred to the Home Secretary.

Disputes between the communes concerning the obligations imposed upon them in accordance with this law are decided by the Governor of the County to which the commune belongs, against which the obligation is urged, or by the Home Secretary, if it is Copenhagen about which the dispute is.

The decisions given by the County Governors may be referred to the Home Secretary.

SECTION 13.

This law comes into operation three months after publication in the "Law Journal."

APPENDIX No. 2.

PAPER handed in by The Honourable *W. P. Reeves*, Agent-General for New Zealand.

1.—NEW ZEALAND OLD-AGE PENSIONS ACT OF 1898.

ANALYSIS.

1898, No. 14.

An Act to provide for Old-age Pensions. Title.

1st November, 1898.

WHEREAS it is equitable that deserving persons who during the prime of life have helped to bear the public burdens of the colony by the payment of taxes, and to open up its resources by their labour and skill, should receive from the colony a pension in their old age: Preamble.

Be it therefore enacted by the General Assembly of New Zealand in Parliament assembled, and by the authority of the same, as follows:—

1. The Short Title of this Act is "The Old-age Pensions Act, 1898." Short Title.

2. In this Act, if not inconsistent with the context,— Interpretation.

"Income" means any moneys, valuable consideration, or profits derived or received by any person for his own use or benefit in any year, by any means or from any source; and shall be deemed to include personal earnings, but not any pension payable under this Act, nor any payment by way of sick allowance or funeral benefit from any registered friendly society:

"Income-year" means the year ending one month before the date on which the pension claim is finally admitted, and at the same time in each subsequent year:

"Prescribed" means prescribed by this Act or by regulations thereunder.

DISTRICTS AND REGISTRARS.

3. (1) For the purposes of this Act the Governor may from time to time divide the colony into such districts, with such names and boundaries as he thinks fit. Districts.

(2) If any such district is constituted by reference to the boundaries of any other portion of the colony, as defined by any other Act, then any alteration in such boundaries shall take effect in respect of such district without any further proceedings, unless the Governor otherwise determines. Alteration of boundaries.

4. The Governor may from time to time appoint a Registrar, who, subject to the control of the Colonial Treasurer, shall have the general administration of this Act. Registrar.

5. The Governor may also from time to time appoint in and for every such district a Deputy Registrar and such other persons as he deems fit. Deputy Registrars.

6. Subject to the provisions of this Act, the Registrar and every Deputy Registrar and other person appointed as aforesaid shall have such powers and duties as the Governor from time to time determines. Their powers and duties.

PENSIONS.

7. Subject to the provisions of this Act, every person of the full age of sixty-five years or upwards shall, whilst in the colony, be entitled to a pension as hereinafter specified. Persons entitled to pensions.

8. No such person shall be entitled to a pension under this Act unless he fulfils the following conditions, that is to say:— Necessary qualifications.

(1) That he is residing in the colony on the date when he establishes his claim to the pension; and also

(2) That he has so resided continuously for not less than twenty-five years immediately preceding such date:

Provided that continuous residence in the colony shall not be deemed to have been interrupted by occasional absence therefrom unless the total period of all such absences exceeds two years; nor, in the case of a seaman, by absence therefrom whilst serving on board a vessel registered in and trading to and from the colony if he establishes the fact that during such absence his family or home was in the colony; and also

(3) That during the period of twelve years immediately preceding such date he has not been imprisoned for four months, or on four occasions, for any offence punishable by imprisonment for twelve months or upwards, and dishonouring him in the public estimation; and also

(4) That during the period of twenty-five years immediately preceding such date he has not been imprisoned for a term of five years with or without hard labour for any offence dishonouring him in the public estimation; and also

(5) That the claimant has not at any time for a period of six months or upwards, if a husband, deserted his wife, or without just cause failed to provide her with adequate means of maintenance, or neglected to maintain such of his children as were under the age of fourteen years; or, if a wife, deserted her husband or such of her children as were under that age:

Provided that, if the pension-certificate is issued, the pensioner's rights thereunder shall not be affected by any disqualification contained in this subsection unless the fact of such disqualification is established at any time to the satisfaction of a Stipendiary Magistrate; and also

(6) That he is of good moral character, and is, and has for five years immediately preceding such date been, leading a sober and reputable life; and also

(7) That his yearly income does not amount to fifty-two pounds or upwards, computed as hereinafter provided; and also

(8) That the net capital value of his accumulated property does not amount to two hundred and seventy pounds or upwards, computed and assessed as hereinafter provided; and also

(9) That he has not directly or indirectly deprived himself of property or income in order to qualify for a pension; and also

(10) That he is the holder of a pension certificate as hereinafter provided.

9. The amount of the pension shall be eighteen pounds per year, diminished by,— Amount of pension.

(1) One pound for every complete pound of income above thirty-four pounds; and also by

(2) One pound for every complete fifteen pounds of the net capital value of all accumulated property computed and assessed as next hereinafter provided.

Assessment of value of accumulated property.

10. The net capital value of accumulated property shall be computed and assessed in the prescribed manner, and for that purpose the following provisions shall apply :—

(1) All real and personal property owned by any person shall, to the extent of his beneficial estate or interest therein, be deemed to be his accumulated property.

(2) From the capital value of such accumulated property there shall be deducted all charges or encumbrances lawfully existing on such property, and also the sum of fifty pounds ; and the residue then remaining shall be deemed to be the net capital value of all his accumulated property.

Pension not to vary during year.

11. The rate of each year's pension shall not vary during the year.

Income for purposes of first year's pension.

12. (1) For the purpose of ascertaining whether the claimant for a pension is entitled thereto, and also of fixing the rate of the first year's pension, his income for the next-preceding income-year shall be deemed to be his yearly income.

Income for subsequent years.

(2) For the purpose of fixing the rate of the pension for the second and each subsequent year, the pensioner's income for the income-year next preceding each such year shall be deemed to be his income for such year.

General rules for computing income.

13. The following general rules shall apply to the computation of income for all the purposes of this Act :—

(1) There shall be deducted therefrom all income derived or received from accumulated property as hereinbefore defined.

(2) Where any person receives board or lodging, the reasonable cost of such board or lodging, not exceeding twenty-six pounds in the year, shall be included in the computation of the yearly income.

(3) In the case of husband and wife, the yearly income of each shall be deemed to be not less than half the total yearly income of both :

Provided that this rule shall not apply where they are living apart pursuant to decree, order, or deed of separation.

Pension payable pursuant to pension-certificate.
When to commence, and payable monthly.

14. With respect to every pension under this Act the following provisions shall apply :—

(1) The pension shall be deemed to commence on the date named in that behalf in the pension-certificate issued in respect of the first year's pension, being in every case the first day of the calendar month next after the date of the issue of such certificate.

(2) Each year's pension shall be payable pursuant to a pension-certificate issued in respect of such year, and not otherwise.

(3) Such certificate shall in every case specify the amount of the year's pension, and the instalments by which it is payable, being twelve equal monthly instalments, whereof the first is payable on the first day of the calendar month next after the commencement of the year.

PENSION-CLAIMS.

Pension-claim.

15. (1) Every person claiming to be entitled to a pension under this Act shall, in the prescribed manner and form, deliver a claim therefor (elsewhere throughout this Act called a "pension-claim") to the Deputy Registrar of the district wherein the claimant resides, or to the nearest Postmaster, who shall forthwith forward the same to the Deputy Registrar.

(2) The pension-claim shall affirm all the requirements and negative all the disqualifications under this Act.

(3) Every claimant shall, by statutory declaration, affirm that the contents of his pension-claim are true and correct in every material point.

(4) Such declaration may be made before any Justice of the Peace, solicitor, Deputy Registrar, or Postmaster, and shall not be liable to stamp duty.

Register of pension-claims.

16. The Deputy Registrar shall file the claim, and record it in the prescribed manner in a book, to be called "The   District Old-age Pension-claim Register," which shall be open to inspection on payment of a fee of one shilling.

Pension-claims to be numbered.

17. All pension-claims shall be numbered consecutively in the order in which they are entered in the register, so that no two pension-claims in the same register bear the same number.

Stipendiary Magistrate to investigate.

18. (1) The Deputy Registrar shall, in the prescribed manner, transmit the claim to a Stipendiary Magistrate exercising jurisdiction in the district, who shall in open Court fully investigate the pension-claim for the purpose of ascertaining whether the claimant is entitled to the pension, and, if so, for what amount in respect of the first year.

(2) The Clerk of the Magistrate's Court shall ascertain on what date the claim may be investigated, and shall notify the claimant of a date on which he may attend to support his claim, and the Stipendiary Magistrate shall on the day so appointed, or on the first convenient day thereafter, proceed to investigate the same :

Provided that where the Stipendiary Magistrate is satisfied that the documentary evidence in support of the claim is sufficient to establish it, and also that by reason of physical disability or other sufficient cause the attendance of the applicant should be dispensed with, he shall not require the personal attendance of the applicant, who shall be notified accordingly.

Witnesses and evidence on oath.

19. For the purposes of such investigation all the powers under "The Magistrates' Courts Act, 1893," shall be available for the purpose of compelling the attendance of witnesses, and every witness shall be examined on oath.

Evidence to be corroborated.

20. No pension-claim shall be admitted unless the evidence of the claimant is corroborated on all material points, except that in respect of the age of the claimant the Stipendiary Magistrate, if otherwise satisfied, may dispense with corroborative evidence.

How pension-claim to be dealt with.

21. The Stipendiary Magistrate may admit the pension-claim as originally made, or as modified by the result of his investigations, or may postpone it for further evidence, or reject it, as he deems equitable ; and his decision shall be notified to the claimant by the Clerk.

22. If the Stipendiary Magistrate is of opinion that, although the claim is not completely established, further evidence may be adduced in support thereof, or it may be proceeded by lapse of time, he shall postpone the claim if the claimant so desires, and in such case all matters as to which the Stipendiary Magistrate is satisfied shall be recorded as proved: Provided that this shall not be a bar to further evidence being adduced in respect of the matter recorded as proved.

Stipendiary Magistrate may postpone claim.

23. If the Stipendiary Magistrate decides that the pension-claim is not established, and cannot be assisted by postponement for a reasonable time, he shall reject it, and when doing so shall specify in writing all the material points which he finds to be respectively proved, disproved, and not to be proved.

Mode of rejecting claim.

24. In investigating any pension-claim, the Stipendiary Magistrate shall not be bound by the strict rules of evidence, but shall investigate and determine the matter by such means and in such manner as in equity and good conscience he thinks fit.

Strict rules of evidence not to be binding.

25. In disposing of material points against the claimant, the Stipendiary Magistrate shall distinguish between what he finds to be disproved and what he finds to be simply unproved or insufficiently proved.

Matters to be distinguished.

26. In respect of what is found to be disproved, the Stipendiary Magistrate's decision shall be final and conclusive for all purposes.

As to matters disproved.

27. In respect of what is found to be simply unproved or insufficiently proved, the claimant may at any time thereafter adduce fresh evidence on those points before the Stipendiary Magistrate, and in such case all material points previously found by the Stipendiary Magistrate to be proved shall be deemed to be established, and he shall dispose of all other points as in the case of a new pension-claim.

As to matters unproved.

28. In order to facilitate the adjustment of pension-claims they may be filed and provisionally investigated at any time not exceeding two years before the date on which the claimant alleges that his pension should commence; but no pension-claim shall be finally admitted, nor shall any pension-certificate be issued, until all the conditions prescribed in respect thereof by this Act have been fulfilled.

Provisional investigation of pension-claims.

29. The pension-claim may be amended from time to time on any point which has not been finally disposed of.

Pension-claims may be amended.

PENSION CERTIFICATES.

30. As soon as the pension-claim is established, and the rate of the first year's pension is fixed by the Stipendiary Magistrate, he shall, in the prescribed manner, certify the same to the Deputy Registrar, who shall, in the prescribed manner and form, issue to the claimant a certificate (elsewhere throughout this Act called a "pension-certificate") in respect of the first year's pension.

Issue of pension-certificate when claim established.

31. In respect of the pension for each year after the first, a fresh pension-certificate shall be issued as hereinafter provided.

Annual pension-certificate.

32. The Deputy Registrar shall enter in a book, to be called "The District Old-age Pension Register," the following particulars respecting each pension-certificate issued by him:—

Particulars to be entered in pension-register.

(1) The number of each certificate, and the name of the district in which it is issued.

(2) The pensioner's full name, occupation, and address.

(3) The amount of his income for the year, and the date on which the income-year ends.

(4) The date on which the year's pension commences.

(5) The amount of the year's pension, the instalments by which it is payable, and the due dates thereof.

(6) Such other particulars as are prescribed.

33. All entries of pension-certificates in the Old-age Pension Register shall be numbered consecutively so that no two entries in the same register bear the same number.

Entries in register to be numbered.

34. On application in the prescribed form, and subject to prescribed conditions,—

Transfer of pension-certificates to other districts, and duplicates.

(1) Any pension-certificate may be transferred from the register in one district to the register in another;

(2) The Deputy Registrar may issue a duplicate pension-certificate in any case where satisfactory proof is given of the loss of the original.

INCOME AND PROPERTY STATEMENTS.

35. For the purpose of ascertaining in respect of the second and each subsequent year, computed from the date of the commencement of the pension, whether the pensioner is entitled to any payment in respect of his pension for such year, and, if so, for what amount, the following provisions shall apply:—

Statement of income for preceding pension-year to be furnished to Deputy Registrar.

(1) Within the prescribed period before the commencement of each such year the pensioner, whether claiming any payment in respect of his pension for that year or not, shall furnish to the Deputy Registrar a statement in the prescribed form setting forth full particulars of his income for such year (being the income for the last-preceding income-year), and also the net capital value of all his accumulated property.

(2) If the pensioner has received no income for the year and has no accumulated property, the statement shall contain the word "Nil."

(3) The Stipendiary Magistrate shall investigate the statement, and shall ascertain whether the conditions of section eight hereof have been complied with, in the same manner, with the same powers, and subject to the same provisions as in the case of pension-claims.

(4) The Stipendiary Magistrate, when satisfied as to the amount of the pensioner's income, and the net capital value of his accumulated property, and that the conditions of section eight hereof have been complied with, shall certify the same to the Deputy Registrar, who shall enter the same in the Old-age Pension Register, and issue a pension-certificate in the prescribed form in respect of the year's pension (if any) to which the pensioner is entitled:

Issue of pension-certificate for year.

Provided that, in lieu of himself issuing such certificate to the pensioner, the Deputy Registrar shall forward it to the Postmaster of the post-office where the pension is payable, and the Postmaster shall issue it to the pensioner in exchange for the outstanding pension-

(3) When forwarding the pension-certificate to the Postmaster as aforesaid the Deputy Registrar shall, in the prescribed manner, notify both the Postmaster and the pensioner as to such exchange and surrender.

PAYMENT OF PENSIONS AND FORFEITURE OF INSTALMENTS.

Where pension payable.

36. Each monthly instalment of the pension shall be payable at the post-office money-order office named in the pension-certificate.

Change of place of payment.

37. On application in the prescribed manner, the name of such office may be changed from time to time, and every change of office shall be recorded by the Deputy Registrar on the pension-certificate and in the District Old-age Pension Register.

Instalment to be applied for within twenty-one days.

38. Subject to the provisions of this Act, each monthly instalment shall be payable at any time within twenty-one days after its due date on the personal application of the pensioner and the production of his pension-certificate to the Postmaster of the post-office money-order office named therein.

When instalment deemed forfeited.

39. In default of strict compliance with all the provisions of the last-preceding section in any such instalment shall be deemed to be forfeited, unless the forfeiture is waived under the provisions in that behalf hereinafter contained.

When and how forfeiture may be waived.

40. The Stipendiary Magistrate or two Justices of the Peace, by warrant in the prescribed form, may waive any such forfeiture in any case where, after investigation, he is or they are satisfied—

(1) That, if the forfeiture was occasioned by default of personal application for payment, or of application within the prescribed time, such default was due to the pensioner's illness, or temporary absence from the place (but not from the colony), or other sufficient cause; or

(2) That, if the forfeiture was occasioned by default in producing the pension-certificate, such default was due to its being lost or mislaid:

Provided—

(a) That, except in special cases of the pensioner's illness or debility, it shall not be lawful for the Stipendiary Magistrate or Justices to issue two such warrants in succession to the same pensioner; and also

(b) That in no case shall any such warrant be issued unless it is applied for within fourteen days after the forfeiture occurred.

Payment under warrant.

41. The instalment named in any such warrant shall be payable at any time within fourteen days after the date thereof, on the personal application of the pensioner or other the person named therein, and also the production of the warrant, and (except where the warrant otherwise provides) of the pension-certificate, to the Postmaster of the post-office money-order office named in the warrant.

When warrant deemed lapsed.

42. In default of strict compliance with all the provisions of the last-preceding section issued the warrant shall be deemed to have lapsed, and the forfeiture of the instalment named therein shall become absolute.

Provisions where pensioner in receipt of charitable aid.

43. The following provisions shall apply in every case where the pensioner is maintained in any charitable institution, or receives relief therefrom:—

(1) The reasonable cost of such maintenance or relief shall be payable out of the pension.

(2) For the purpose of procuring such payment, instalments of the pension shall, to such extent as is necessary, be payable to the governing body of such institution in such manner as is prescribed, and on production to the Postmaster of a warrant in the prescribed form.

(3) Any surplus pension-moneys remaining in the hands of such governing body after deducting such cost shall be paid to the pensioner.

(4) For the purpose of computing the amount of any subsidy or contribution payable by the Government to such governing body under any Act all instalments so paid shall be excluded.

Payment to other than pensioner.

44. Subject to prescribed regulations, and on production to the Postmaster of a warrant in the prescribed form, signed by a Stipendiary Magistrate, the instalments may be paid to any clergyman, Justice of the Peace, or other reputable person named in such warrant, for the benefit of the pensioner.

Such warrant may be issued by a Stipendiary Magistrate whenever he is satisfied that it is expedient so to do, having regard to the age, infirmity, or improvidence of the pensioner, or any other special circumstances.

Period for which pension not payable.

45. Every instalment which falls due during any period whilst the pensioner is in prison, an inmate of a lunatic asylum, or out of the colony, shall be deemed to be absolutely forfeited.

Procedure as to payments of instalments by Postmasters.

46. With respect to the payment of instalments of pension by the Postmaster the following provisions shall apply:—

(1) The Postmaster may, if he thinks fit, require the applicant for payment to prove his identity, but shall not be bound so to do, and may accept the production of the pension-certificate or warrant to which the instalment relates as sufficient evidence that the person producing the same is the person entitled to payment.

(2) When making the payment the Postmaster shall indorse on the pension-certificate or warrant produced as aforesaid the date and fact of the payment, and shall also require the person receiving the payment to give a receipt therefor in the prescribed form.

(3) Such receipt shall be sufficient evidence that the payment to which the receipt purports to relate has been duly made, and no claim against Her Majesty or the Postmaster shall thereafter arise or be made in respect thereof.

(4) Where the warrant produced as aforesaid relates to a single instalment, or to the last of a series of instalments, it shall be delivered up to and retained by the Postmaster on payment of such instalment.

I.

PENALTIES.

47. Every person is liable to imprisonment for not more than six months, with or without hard labour,— *Imprisonment for certain breaches of Act.*

(1) If by means of any wilfully false statement or representation he obtains or attempts to obtain a pension-certificate, not being justly entitled thereto, or a pension of a larger amount than he is justly entitled to; or

(2) If by any means he obtains or attempts to obtain payment of any absolutely forfeited instalment of pension; or

(3) If, by means of personation or any other fraudulent device whatsoever, he obtains or attempts to obtain payment of any instalment of pension; or

(4) If by any wilfully false statement or representation he aids or abets any person to obtain a pension-certificate, or any instalment payable thereunder.

48. In the case of any conviction under the last-preceding section hereof, the convicting Court, in addition to imposing the punishment thereby prescribed, shall also, according to the circumstances of the case, by order— *Additional powers of Court when convicting.*

(1) Cancel any pension-certificate which is proved to have been wrongfully obtained; or,

(2) Reduce to its proper amount any pension that has been proved to be too high; or,

(3) Impose a penalty not exceeding twice the amount of any instalment the payment whereof has been wrongfully obtained, and, if the defendant is a pensioner, direct the forfeiture of future instalments of his pension equal in amount to such penalty and in satisfaction thereof:

Provided that all proceedings under section forty-seven and this section shall be taken in a summary way before a Stipendiary Magistrate or two Justices of the Peace.

49. If any pensioner is convicted of drunkenness, or of any offence punishable by imprisonment for not less than one month and dishonouring him in the public estimation, then, in addition to any other penalty or punishment imposed, the convicting Court may in its discretion, by order, forfeit any one or more of the instalments falling due next after the date of the conviction: *Additional penalty for certain offences.*

Provided that if, in the opinion of the convicting Court, any pensioner misspends, wastes, or lessens his estate, or greatly injures his health, or endangers or interrupts the peace and happiness of his family, the Court may by order direct that the instalment be paid to any clergyman, Justice of the Peace, or other reputable person for the benefit of the pensioner, or may by order cancel the pension-certificate:

Provided further that if on any conviction the pensioner is deemed to be an habitual drunkard within the meaning of "The Police Offences Act, 1884," then, in lieu of forfeiting any instalment of the pension, the convicting Court shall, by order, cancel the pension-certificate.

50. If any pensioner is sentenced to imprisonment for twelve months or upwards in respect of any offence dishonouring him in the public estimation, the convicting Court shall, by order, cancel the pension-certificate. *Pension-certificate to be cancelled on imprisonment for certain offences.*

51. In any case where any pension-certificate is cancelled by order of a Court the pension shall be deemed to be absolutely forfeited. *When pension absolutely forfeited.*

52. In every case where any instalment is forfeited or any pension-certificate is cancelled by order of a Court, the Clerk of the Court shall forthwith notify the Deputy Registrar of such forfeiture or cancellation, and the Deputy Registrar shall record the same. *Notice of forfeiture to Deputy Registrar.*

MISCELLANEOUS.

53. The pension being for the personal support of the pensioner, it shall (subject to the provisions of this Act as to payment, forfeiture, and otherwise) be absolutely inalienable, whether by way of assignment, charge, execution, bankruptcy, or otherwise howsoever. *Pensions absolutely inalienable.*

54. Every Deputy Registrar shall, in the prescribed manner and at prescribed intervals, prepare and forward to the Registrar a return showing for each such interval,— *Returns to be prepared by Deputy Registrars.*

(1) All pension-certificates and warrants issued by him;

(2) All forfeitures recorded by him;

(3) Such other particulars as are prescribed.

55. The Registrar shall from the aforesaid returns compile a General Old-age Pension Register containing a record of all pension-certificates for the time being in force, and such other particulars as are prescribed. *General Register.*

56. The Registrar shall at prescribed intervals furnish to the Postmaster-General schedules showing for each such interval,— *Particulars to be furnished to Postmaster-General.*

(1) The names of the pensioners;

(2) The numbers of their pension-certificates;

(3) The dates on which and the post-office money-order offices at which the instalments in respect thereof are payable; and

(4) The amount of the instalments payable.

57. Copies of this Act shall be posted at the several post-offices in the colony, and a list containing the names of the pensioners whose instalments are paid at any post-office shall be kept thereat, and the same shall on application be open to inspection on payment of the fee of one shilling. *Act to be posted at post-offices. List of pensioners.*

58. The Colonial Treasurer shall from time to time, without further appropriation than this Act, pay out of the Consolidated Fund into the Post Office Account, by way of imprest, whatever moneys are necessary in order to enable the instalments specified in such schedules to be paid out of such account, and the Postmaster-General shall thereupon pay such instalments accordingly: *Payment of imprest money into Post Office Account.*

Provided that this section shall continue in operation until the fourteenth day after the close of the second session of the next next succeeding Parliament, but no longer.

Returns by Postmaster-General of all payments made.

59. The Postmaster-General shall, at such periodical interval as are from time to time arranged between him and the Colonial Treasurer, furnish to the Registrar a statement showing for each such interval—

(1) The balance of the aforesaid imprest moneys in the Post Office Account at the commencement and also at the close of such interval;

(2) The instalments paid;

(3) The pensioners to whom such instalments were paid; and

(4) Such other particulars as are prescribed.

Registrar to certify same for payment.

60. The Registrar, after satisfying himself that such statement is correct, shall certify to the accuracy thereof, and forward it to the Colonial Treasurer.

Expenses of administration.

61. All expenses incurred in administering this Act (other than the payment of pensions) shall be payable out of moneys to be from time to time appropriated by Parliament.

Annual statement to be laid before Parliament.

62. The Colonial Treasurer shall, within thirty days after the close of each financial year ending the thirty-first day of March, prepare and lay before Parliament, if sitting, or, if not sitting, then within fourteen days after the commencement of the next session, a statement showing for such year—

(1) The total amount paid under this Act in respect of pensions;

(2) The total amount so paid in respect of other than pensions;

(3) The total number of pensioners;

(4) The total amount of absolutely forfeited instalments; and

(5) Such other particulars as are prescribed.

Regulations.

63. (1) The Governor may from time to time make such regulations as he thinks necessary for any purpose for which regulations are contemplated or required, and, generally, for carrying out the intention of this Act.

(2) Such regulations shall be laid on the table of the House of Representatives within ten days after the commencement of each session, and referred to such sessional Committee for report as the House directs.

To whom Act not to apply.

64. This Act, in so far as it provides for the grant of pensions, shall not apply to—

(1) Aboriginal natives of New Zealand to whom moneys other than pensions are paid out of the sums appropriated for Native purposes by "The Civil List Act, 1863"; nor to

(2) Aliens; nor to

(3) Naturalised subjects, except such as have been naturalised for the period of five years next preceding the date on which they establish their pension-claims; nor to

(4) Chinese or other Asiatics, whether naturalised or not.

Act to apply to aboriginal natives of New Zealand.

Proviso.

65. Subject to the provisions of subsection one of the last-preceding section hereof, this Act shall apply to aboriginal natives of New Zealand: Provided that on the investigation of any such Native's pension-claim his evidence as to his age shall be required to be corroborated to the satisfaction of the Stipendiary Magistrate.

Rules for assessment of undetermined Native interests.

66. In determining the claim of any aboriginal native, in so far as the same may be affected by rights or property held or enjoyed otherwise than under defined legal title, the Stipendiary Magistrate shall be guided by the following rules:—

In respect of "income," any customary rights used or capable of being used in respect of land the title to which has not been ascertained, but which is enjoyed or is capable of enjoyment, shall be assessed and determined by such evidence and in such manner as the Stipendiary Magistrate shall in his discretion consider proper:

In respect of "accumulated property," the interest in land or other property held or enjoyed under Native custom, or in any way other than by defined legal title, shall be assessed and determined by the Stipendiary Magistrate in manner aforesaid, with the view of arriving as nearly as may be at a decision as to the net capital value thereof for the purposes of this Act, and the decision of the Stipendiary Magistrate thereon shall be final.

Pensions granted subject to any amending Act.

67. (1) Every pension granted under this Act shall be deemed to be granted and shall be held subject to the provisions of any amending or repealing Act that may hereafter be passed, and no pensioner under this Act shall have any claim for compensation or otherwise by reason of his pension being affected by any such amending or repealing Act.

(2) A notification of the last-preceding subsection hereof shall be printed on every pension-certificate.

"Registration of People's Claims Act, 1896," repealed.

68. "The Registration of People's Claims Act, 1896," is hereby repealed, and all pension-certificates issued thereunder are hereby cancelled; nor shall any fact proved, or entry made, or certificate issued thereunder be available for the purposes of this Act, anything in that Act to the contrary notwithstanding.

II.—NEW ZEALAND OLD-AGE PENSIONS ACT AMENDMENT ACT OF 1900.

ANALYSIS.

1900, No. 23.

Title.

An Act to amend "The Old-age Pensions Act, 1898."

[18th October, 1900.

BE IT ENACTED by the General Assembly of New Zealand in Parliament assembled, and by the authority of the same, as follows:—

Short Title.

1. The Short Title of this Act is "The Old-age Pensions Act Amendment Act, 1900"; and it shall form part of and be read together with "The Old-age Pensions Act, 1898" (hereinafter called "the principal Act").

Extended period of absence allowed.

2. Notwithstanding that the total period during which an applicant for a pension has been absent from the colony exceeds two years, such absence shall not be deemed to interrupt his continuous residence in the colony as provided by section eight of the principal Act if the total period of absence does not exceed four years:

Provided that he shall not be entitled to the benefit of this section in either of the following cases, that is to say,—

(1.) If he has been absent from the colony during any part of the year immediately preceding the date when the principal Act was passed; or

(2.) If the total period of his actual residence in the colony (exclusive of the total period of his actual absence) is less than twenty-five years.

Provisions where applicant is married.

3. If the applicant for a pension or a pension-certificate is married, the following provisions shall apply:—

(1.) In computing the amount of the pension of husband or wife the net capital value of all the accumulated property of each shall be deemed to be not less than half the total net capital value of all the accumulated property of both, and the yearly income of each shall be deemed to be not less than half the total yearly income of both:

Provided that this subsection shall not be construed to reduce the actual net capital value of the accumulated property, or the actual yearly income, of either husband or wife.

(2.) The amount of the pension of either of them for any year shall in no case exceed such sum as, with the total actual income of both of them for the year and the pension, if any, then already granted to the other of them, will amount to seventy-eight pounds for the year.

(3.) The foregoing provisions of this section shall not apply in cases where husband and wife are living apart pursuant to decree, order, or deed of separation.

(4.) Subsection three of section thirteen of the principal Act is hereby repealed.

Deputy Registrar, &c., may take declarations.

4. The power conferred by subsection four of section fifteen of the principal Act, enabling any Justice of the Peace, solicitor, Deputy Registrar, or Postmaster to take statutory declarations in support of any claim, is hereby extended to any statutory declaration required by the principal Act or tendered in proof of any particular required to be proved on the investigation of any claim or income and property statement.

Apportionment of instalment on death of pensioner.

5. In the case of the death of a pensioner, the instalment then accruing but not actually accrued due shall be apportioned up to the date of the death, and the apportioned amount, together with the previous instalment (if any) then payable but not actually paid, shall, without further appropriation than this Act, be paid to such person as the Colonial Treasurer directs, and shall be applied in or towards defraying the burial expenses of the deceased pensioner:

Provided that nothing in this section contained shall apply to any instalment which at the date of the death has become absolutely forfeited.

Extending time for payment of instalments.

6. (1.) The period during which instalments are payable as provided by section thirty-eight of the principal Act is hereby extended to one calendar month after the due date:

Provided that the Colonial Treasurer may further extend such period in any case where the provisions of that section are not strictly complied with owing to the pensioner's illness or temporary absence from home (but not from the colony), or other sufficient cause.

(2.) Sections forty, forty-one, and forty-two of the principal Act are hereby repealed.

Charitable Aid Boards not to refuse to admit pensioner.

7. It shall not be lawful for the governing body of any charitable institution to refuse to admit any person as an inmate of such charitable institution on the ground only that he is a pensioner under the principal Act.

Making the Act permanent.

8. So much of section fifty-eight of the principal Act as limits the time during which that section is to continue in operation is hereby repealed, and that section shall continue in operation in like manner as if such limit had never been imposed.

Power to cancel certificate improperly obtained.

9. (1.) If in any case the Registrar has reason to believe that any pension-certificate has been improperly obtained, it shall be his duty to cause special inquiry to be made before a Stipendiary Magistrate, and to give notice to the Postmaster through whom the instalments are payable to suspend payment of any instalments pending such inquiry.

(2.) Payment of every such instalment shall be suspended according to the tenor of such notice.

(3.) If on inquiry it appears that the certificate was improperly obtained it shall be cancelled by the Stipendiary Magistrate.

(4) If on inquiry it appears that the certificate was properly obtained the suspended instalments shall be payable in due course.

(5) Every such inquiry shall be conducted in manner prescribed by regulations.

10. For the purpose of enabling naturalised subjects (other than Chinese or other Asiatics) the more readily to obtain pensions, subsection three of section sixty-four of the principal Act is hereby amended by substituting the words "one year" in lieu of the words "five years."

11. In the case of pensions granted prior to the passing of this Act, the provisions of this Act shall apply to all pension-certificates hereafter applied for or granted.

12. The principal Act is hereby modified in so far as it is in conflict with this Act, but not further or otherwise.

III.—NEW ZEALAND OLD-AGE PENSIONS AMENDMENT ACT OF 1901.

ANALYSIS.

1901, No. 30.

An Act to amend "The Old-age Pensions Act, 1898."

[7th November, 1901.

BE IT ENACTED by the General Assembly of New Zealand in Parliament assembled, and by the authority of the same, as follows:—

1. The Short Title of this Act is "The Old-age Pensions Amendment Act, 1901"; and it shall form part of and be read together with "The Old-age Pensions Act, 1898."

2. (1) *Forthwith* on receipt of any application for a pension or a renewal certificate the Clerk of the Court shall (where he is not himself the Deputy Registrar) notify the Deputy Registrar of the fact and of the date fixed for the hearing of the application.

(2) The hearing may from time to time be adjourned by the Magistrate at the request of the Deputy Registrar.

(3) The Deputy Registrar, or some person appointed by him, shall have the right to appear at the hearing and to examine or cross-examine the applicant.

3. (1) It shall be the duty of every person to make true answers to all questions concerning any applicant for a pension or renewal, or any of the statements contained in any application for a pension or renewal certificate put to him by the Deputy Registrar or any officer authorised in that behalf by the Deputy Registrar.

(2) Every person commits an offence who—

(a) Refuses to answer any such question; or,

(b) Makes any answer knowing the same to be untrue.

(3) This section shall apply to any officer of any bank or other corporation carrying on business in New Zealand, and to any officer of the Post-Office Savings-Bank and of any other Government department which receives investments of money from the public.

4. On the hearing of any application for a pension or renewal certificate, if the Magistrate finds that any real or personal property has been transferred by the applicant to any person he may inquire into such transfer, and refuse the application or grant a reduced pension.

5. If at any time during the currency of a pension the pensioner becomes possessed of any property or income in excess of what is allowed by law in respect of the amount of pension granted to him, the Deputy Registrar may apply to the Magistrate, who may on inquiry either confirm or cancel the pension, or vary the amount thereof:

Provided that, should the excess of income so mentioned in this section cease, the pension shall be immediately restored to the original amount.

6. If on the death of any pensioner, or of the wife or husband of any pensioner, it is found that he or either of them, was possessed of property in excess of what is allowed by law in respect of the amount of the pension granted, double the amount of pension at any time paid in excess of that to which the pensioner was by law entitled may be recovered as a debt due to the Crown from the estate so found in excess:

Provided that, where the husband and wife were at the time of such death living apart pursuant to decree, order, or deed of separation, this section shall only apply in the case of the pensioner.

7. Every person commits an offence who receives any money in consideration of or in respect of the procuring of any pension or renewal certificate, and in the case of any licensed Maori interpreter so committing an offence his license as such interpreter shall be cancelled.

8. Every person who commits an offence under this Act for which no penalty is otherwise provided in any other Act is liable to a penalty not exceeding ten pounds.

9. The power conferred on the Colonial Treasurer by section six of "The Old-age Pensions Act Amendment Act, 1900," to extend the prescribed period during which instalments are payable, may be exercised by him at any time, notwithstanding that such period has then elapsed or that the instalment has then been paid.

[illegible] Payment of [illegible]
[illegible] [illegible].

APPENDIX No. 4.

PAPER handed in by Sir *Edward Hamilton*, K.C.B.

Copy of Letter (with enclosure) from Sir Edward Hamilton to the Chairman.

Dear Mr. Grant Lawson, 16 July [illegible].

I promised Mr. Lloyd George some further information, and I think the best way I can supply it is to send you the enclosed copy of a letter from Mr. Noel Humphreys, who is the Chief Clerk in the General Register Office and who served on the Departmental Committee, of which I was Chairman, in 1898.

Perhaps I may be allowed to supplement my evidence by an additional word or two. The conclusion I came to [illegible] years ago, after a very careful study of the Old Age Pensions question, was this: Any scheme, with conditions attached to it, must create hardships and inequalities, and be very difficult, if not impossible, to work; while any unconditional scheme, which would give Pensions to everybody—those who do not want assistance and those who do not deserve it—would be absurd.

Yours very truly,
Ed. Hamilton.

The Chairman of the Select Committee on the Aged Pensioners Bill.

Enclosure.—Copy of Letter received from Mr. Noel Humphreys, General Register Office.

General Register Office, Somerset House, London, W.C.

Dear Sir Edward Hamilton, 16 July [illegible].

I have carefully considered the two points in your evidence before the Aged Pensioners' Committee to which you called my attention.

Our Census Returns for England and Wales show that [illegible] married couples ([illegible] persons), aged upwards of 65 years, were living together in 1891; these [illegible] persons constituted [illegible] per cent. of the total number of persons at these ages enumerated in England and Wales. This information as to ages in combination of married couples is not, I believe, available for Scotland or Ireland, but if it be assumed that the proportion of married couples, among persons aged 65 years and upwards, was practically the same in the United Kingdom as in England and Wales (a tolerably fair assumption), it may be estimated that [illegible] per cent. (or [illegible]) of the [illegible] persons, calculated as qualified to receive pensions, would only be entitled to receive [illegible] instead of [illegible] per week. The aggregate amount of reduction of pension that would thereby result would be equal to [illegible] per annum, and would thus reduce the total calculated cost of pensions in the United Kingdom from [illegible] to [illegible].

With regard to the second point, the comparison between your estimate of the probable cost of pensions and the experience derived from the working of the New Zealand Act, I may state that the proportion of the New Zealand white population, aged upwards of 65 years in 1901, was only 4 per cent., against 5 per cent. in the population of the United Kingdom, and that this disparity invalidates any attempt to apply the New Zealand proportions for estimating the effect of an Aged Pension Act in the United Kingdom.

If, however, you are able to supply me with any official figures showing the results of the New Zealand Act, I should be very pleased to let you have my observations on them.

I am, faithfully yours,
(Signed) Noel A. Humphreys.

P.S.—I have shown this letter to the Registrar-General.

APPENDIX No. 5.

PAPER handed in by the Honourable *Alfred Deakin*, Acting Agent-General for Victoria.

I.—STATE OF VICTORIA: OLD-AGE PENSIONS ACT, 1900.

64 Vict.—No. 1702.

AN ACT to provide for the PAYMENT OF OLD-AGE PENSIONS.

[27th December, 1900.]

BE it enacted by the Queen's Most Excellent Majesty by and with the advice and consent of the Legislative Council and the Legislative Assembly of Victoria in this present Parliament assembled and by the authority of the same as follows (that is to say):—

1. This Act may be cited as the "Old-age Pensions Act, 1900." — *Short title.*

2. For the purpose of paying to any person who has attained the age of sixty-five years or who is permanently disabled or who is in permanent ill-health caused in either case by having been engaged in mining or any unhealthy or hazardous occupation and who makes a declaration in the form in the Schedule to this Act with such alterations and additions as may be prescribed a pension at a rate of not more than Ten shillings per week there may be paid a sum or sums not exceeding in the whole Seventy-five thousand pounds out of the Consolidated Revenue which is hereby appropriated accordingly. — *Appropriation of 75,000l. for old-age pensions. Schedule.*

3. The Governor in Council may make regulations as to the mode terms and conditions on which pensions may be applied for granted suspended or cancelled and paid out of the said Seventy-five thousand pounds, and for prescribing any alterations or additions to the form of declaration set forth in the Schedule to this Act, and generally for the purposes of carrying into effect the provisions of this Act, and such regulations shall be published in the "Government Gazette." — *Regulations. Schedule.*

SCHEDULE. — *Sections 2, 3.*

I, A.B. of   in the Colony of Victoria, do hereby solemnly and sincerely declare—

(a) that I am now residing in Victoria;

(b) that I have so resided for at least twenty years;

(c) that I have not been absent from Australasia whether continuously or not for more than five years during the time from which the said twenty years commenced to run;

(d) that I have resided in Victoria for not less than five years immediately preceding the date of making of this declaration;

(e) that during the period of five years immediately preceding such date I have not been convicted five times or upwards in respect of drunkenness and have not been imprisoned for any period or periods amounting in the whole to six months or upwards in respect of any offence or offences;

(f) that during the period of twenty years immediately preceding such date I have not for any offence or offences been imprisoned for any period or periods amounting in the whole to five years with or without hard labour;

(g) that (if a husband) during the period of ten years immediately preceding such date I have not for twelve months or upwards without just cause deserted my wife or without just cause failed to provide her with adequate means of maintenance or neglected to maintain such of my children as were under the age of fourteen years, or (if a wife) that during the period of ten years immediately preceding such date I have not for twelve months without just cause deserted my husband or deserted such of my children as were under the said age;

(h) that I am and have for five years immediately preceding such date been leading a sober and reputable life;

(i) that all my weekly income does not amount to   shillings or upwards;

(j) that the net capital value of my accumulated property, whether in or out of Victoria, does not amount to   pounds or upwards;

(k) that I have not directly or indirectly deprived myself of property or income in order to qualify for a pension;

(l) (in the case of a husband living with his wife) that my wife is unable to provide for or maintain me (or in the case of a wife living with her husband) that my husband is unable to provide for or maintain me;

(m) that I am unable to maintain myself;

(c) that I have attained the age of sixty-five years or (as the case may be) I am permanently disabled or in permanent ill-health caused by having been engaged in mining or any unhealthy or hazardous occupation.

And I make this solemn declaration conscientiously believing the same to be true and by virtue of the provisions of an Act of the Parliament of Victoria rendering persons making a false declaration punishable for wilful and corrupt perjury.

Declared at in the Colony of Victoria this day of 190 , before me—

A Commissioner, J.P. (or as the case may be).

II.—STATE OF VICTORIA: CLAIMS FOR OLD-AGE PENSIONS ACT, 1900.

64 Vict.—No. 1116.

AN ACT to provide for the Registration of Claims for Old-age Pensions.

[27th December, 1900.]

BE it enacted by the Queen's Most Excellent Majesty by and with the advice and consent of the Legislative Council and the Legislative Assembly of Victoria in this present Parliament assembled and by the authority of the same as follows (that is to say):—

Short title.

1. This Act may be cited as the "Claims for Old-age Pensions Act, 1900."

Pension claim. See N.S. Act, 1900, No. 34, s. 7.

2. (1) Every person of the age of sixty-five years or upwards or who is permanently disabled or who is in permanent ill-health caused in either case by having been engaged in mining or any unhealthy or hazardous occupation claiming to be entitled to a pension may not later than the first day of April One thousand nine hundred and one or such extended date as the Governor in Council either before or after the said day prescribes forward a claim (in this Act called a pension claim) to the Treasurer verified by statutory declaration.

Form of claim. See ib. s. 8. Schedule.

(2) The pension claim shall be in the form of the Schedule to this Act or to the like effect with all such additions and alterations as may be prescribed by regulations or as the particular circumstances of the case require.

Regulations. See ib. s. 22.

3. The Governor in Council may make regulations not inconsistent with this Act for the purpose of carrying the provisions of this Act into effect, and all such regulations shall be published in the "Government Gazette."

SCHEDULE.

EXAMPLE OF PENSION CLAIM.

Section 2.

1. My full name, occupation, and address are .. .. .. A.B., carpenter, of Daisily.
2. I was born at .. .. Bristol, England.
3. On or about .. .. 1st March, [illegible].
4. And first arrived in Victoria on or about .. .. .. 4th January, [illegible].
5. By the .. .. Steam-ship "Great Britain."
6. Since my first arrival in Victoria I have been absent three times and no more, namely—
   - (a) On or about 15th September, [illegible], I sailed to Hobart by the "Southern Cross," and returned to Melbourne on or about 1st February, [illegible], having been absent about four and a half months.
   - (b) On or about the 1st January, [illegible], I travelled from Melbourne to Brisbane by railway; and I returned to Melbourne, by the steamship "[illegible]," on or about the 1st July, [illegible], having thus been absent about six months.
   - (c) On or about the 14th June, [illegible], I sailed from Melbourne for London by the steamship "[illegible]"; and I returned to Melbourne by the steamship "[illegible]," on or about the 15th December, [illegible], after an absence of about six months.

I, the abovenamed A.B., do solemnly and sincerely declare as follows, that is to say:—

1. That, to the best of my knowledge and belief, the foregoing statements are true in every particular.
2. That my present means of support consist of and do not exceed the rate of shillings per week.
3. That during the year ending on the 31st day of December, 1900, my total income did not exceed and was derived from
4. That my property in Victoria or elsewhere does not exceed in value pounds.
5. That (if the case be so) I am permanently disabled or in permanent ill-health caused by having been engaged in mining or any unhealthy or hazardous occupation.

And I make this solemn declaration conscientiously believing the same to be true, and by virtue of the provisions of an Act of the Parliament of Victoria rendering persons making a false declaration punishable for wilful and corrupt perjury.

Declared at in the Colony of Victoria this day of 190
before me—

III.—STATE OF VICTORIA: OLD-AGE PENSIONS ACT, 1901.

1 Ed. VII.—No. 1781.

AN ACT to provide for the Payment of Old-age Pensions and for other purposes.

[18th December, 1901.]

WHEREAS it is the duty of the State to make provision for its aged and helpless poor: Be it therefore enacted by the King's Most Excellent Majesty by and with the advice and consent of the Legislative Council and the Legislative Assembly of Victoria in this present Parliament assembled and by the authority of the same as follows (that is to say):— *Preamble.*

1. This Act may be cited as the Old-age Pensions Act 1901, and shall be deemed to have come into operation on the seventh day of December One thousand nine hundred and one. *Short title and commencement.*

2. In this Act, if not inconsistent with the context— *Interpretation.*

"Benevolent Asylum" means any benevolent asylum which is partially maintained by contributions from the Consolidated Revenue, and which is proclaimed by the Governor in Council to be a Benevolent Asylum for the purposes of this Act. *"Benevolent Asylum."*

"Claimant," means any applicant for a pension. *"Claimant."*

"Commissioner" means any person appointed by the Governor in Council to be a Commissioner under this Act. *"Commissioner."*

"Hospital" means any hospital which is partly maintained by contributions from the Consolidated Revenue, and which is proclaimed by the Governor in Council to be a Hospital for the purposes of this Act. *"Hospital."*

"Income" means any moneys valuable consideration or profits earned derived or received by any person for his own use or benefit by any means from any source whatever, whether in or out of Victoria, and shall be deemed to include personal earnings but not any pension under this Act nor any payment by way of benefit from any registered friendly society or any trade union provident society or other society or association during illness infirmity, or old age. *"Income."*

"Paymaster" means any person appointed by the Governor in Council to be a Paymaster under this Act. *"Paymaster."*

"Pension" means an old-age pension under this Act. *"Pension."*

"Pensioner" means a pensioner under this Act. *"Pensioner."*

"Prescribed" means prescribed by this Act or by regulations made thereunder. *"Prescribed."*

Administration.

3. (1) Subject to the Public Service Acts the Governor in Council may appoint a fit and proper person to be called the *Registrar of Old-age Pensions* (hereinafter referred to as "the Registrar") who subject to the control of the Treasurer shall have the general administration of this Act. *Power to appoint Registrar.*

(2) Subject to the Public Service Acts the Governor in Council may also appoint such Commissioners Paymasters and officers as he deems fit and may remove or suspend the Registrar or any Commissioner Paymaster or officer. *Officers. Removal or suspension.*

(3) Every person appointed under this Act shall be a person who is a member of the Public Service or a person who having been in the Public Service is in receipt of a superannuation or retiring allowance unless the Public Service Board certifies in writing that there is no person already in the Public Service or receiving a superannuation or retiring allowance available and competent to fulfil the duties of such office. *Appointments to be made from Public Service or from superannuated officers.*

(4) Any office under this Act may be held in conjunction with any other office in the Public Service. *Offices may be held in conjunction.*

(5) In this section the expression "Public Service" includes railway service, service in the police force, service in any office of Parliament, service in any public office in the Commonwealth, or service in any office or employment whatever in Victoria for which payment is provided out of any special or annual appropriation of the Consolidated Revenue. *Meaning of "Public Service."*

(6) Subject to the provisions of this Act the Registrar and every officer appointed as aforesaid shall in addition to the powers authorities and duties provided for in this Act have such powers authorities and duties as are prescribed by regulations made pursuant to this Act. *Powers and duties of officers.*

4. No Commissioner shall exercise any of the powers or authorities conferred by this Act until he shall have taken, before a Judge of the Supreme Court or County Courts or before a Justice an oath of office in the form of the First Schedule to this Act or to the like effect. *Oath of office by Commissioner. First Schedule.*

Old-age Pensions.

5. A pension being for the personal support of the pensioner shall (subject to the provisions of this Act) be absolutely inalienable whether by way or in consequence of sale assignment charge execution bankruptcy or otherwise howsoever. *Pension absolutely inalienable.*

6. (1) Subject to the provisions of this Act the following persons whilst in Victoria shall be qualified to receive a pension, namely:— *Persons who may receive pensions.*

(a) every person of the age of sixty-five years; and

(b) every person of any age who is in permanent ill-health caused by having been engaged in mining or any prescribed dangerous or unhealthy occupation.

(2) A pension shall not be paid to any person who is under the age of sixty-five years unless and until such person's pension claim is certified by a Commissioner pursuant to this Act and is recommended in writing by the Registrar and approved in writing by the Treasurer.

(2) No woman having married an alien shall become disqualified to receive a pension under this Act in consequence of such marriage.

Persons to whom pensions not to be granted.

7. The following persons shall not be qualified to receive a pension, namely :—

(a) aliens ; or

(b) naturalized subjects of His Majesty unless they have been naturalized for the period of six months next preceding the date of their pension claims ; or

(c) Chinese or other Asiatics whether British subjects or naturalized or not ; or

(d) Aboriginal natives of any State of the Commonwealth of Australia or of New Zealand.

Necessary requirements. Residence. Twenty years.

8. No person shall receive a pension unless he fulfils the following requirements, namely :—

(a) that he is residing in Victoria on the date when he establishes his claim to the pension ; and also

(b) that on such date he has so resided whether continuously or not for at least twenty years ; and also

Absence.

(c) that he has not been absent from Victoria whether continuously or not for more than five years during the time from which the said twenty years commenced to run ; and also

Continuous residence for five years.

(d) that he has resided in Victoria continuously for not less than five years immediately preceding such date ; and also

Absence of convictions for drunkenness.

(e) that during the period of two years immediately preceding such date he has not been convicted three times or upwards in respect of drunkenness ; and also

Not imprisoned for six months.

(f) that during the period of five years immediately preceding such date he has not been imprisoned for any period or periods amounting in the whole to six months or upwards in respect of any offence or offences ; and also

Nor for three years.

(g) that during the period of twenty years immediately preceding such date he has not for any offence or offences been imprisoned for any period or periods amounting in the whole to three years or upwards with or without hard labour ; and also

Desertion.

(h) that, if a husband, he has not for twelve months or upwards during five years immediately preceding such date without just cause deserted his wife or without just cause failed to provide her with adequate means of maintenance or neglected to maintain such of his children as were under the age of fourteen years, or that, if a wife, during five years immediately preceding such date she has not for twelve months without just cause deserted her husband or deserted such of her children as were under the said age ; and also

Income.

(i) that his average weekly income during six months immediately preceding such date did not amount to Eight shillings or upwards ; and also

Property.

(j) that the net capital value of his accumulated property, whether in or out of Victoria, does not amount to One hundred and sixty pounds or upwards ; and also

Deprivation of income.

(k) that he has not directly or indirectly deprived himself of property or income in order to qualify for or obtain a pension ; and also

Reasonable efforts at self-support.

(l) that he has made reasonable efforts to provide for himself, or has brought up a family in decency and comfort ; and also

Relatives unable to support.

(m) that the husband wife father mother or children of the claimant or any or all of them are unable to provide for or maintain the claimant ; and also

Unable to maintain himself.

(n) that he is unable to maintain himself ; and also

Pension certificate not refused.

(o) that he has not at any time within twelve months been refused by a Commissioner a pension certificate except for the reason that he was disqualified on account of his age or for reasons which are not in existence at the time of the further application.

Occasional short absences.

9. (1) Continuous residence in Victoria shall not be deemed to have been interrupted by occasional absence from Victoria unless the period of such absence exceeds three months in all in any year, but in case of longer absence in any one year if the claimant proves that his home was in Victoria or that he was absent for a mere temporary purpose and intended on leaving and during all his absence to return to Victoria so soon as the object of his absence was accomplished, and in such case such year shall not be reckoned as one of the years of the period of continuous residence, or for the purposes of paragraph (d) of section eight, or for any purpose whatever under this Act.

Absence during any period.

(2) A person whether claimant or pensioner shall not be deemed to be absent from Victoria during any period of absence from Victoria if he proves that during such period his home was in Victoria and if married that his wife and family or his wife (if he has no family) or his family (if his wife is dead) resided there and were or was maintained by him, but no pension shall be payable to him for or during the time he is so absent.

Period of imprisonment not to count as residence.

(3) In calculating any claimant's length of residence in Victoria any time during which he was in prison for any crime shall be excluded.

When residence in any Australian State to count as residence in Victoria.

(4) Provided also that residence in any Australian State in which provision is made for granting old age pensions shall count as residence in this State if—

(a) The claimant has during the ten years immediately preceding the date when he establishes his claim continuously resided in this State ; and

(b) The State Treasurer certifies to the Registrar that provision has been made by agreement with the Government of such other State as hereinafter mentioned.

And for the purpose of carrying out this proviso the State Treasurer on behalf of the Government of this State may agree with the Government of any other State for the payment by such other Government of any such pension in whole or in part or for the granting by such other State of concessions to a like amount under the old-age pension law of that State to persons who have been resident in this State.

RATE OF OLD-AGE PENSIONS.

Limit of pension.

10. (1) The amount of a pension shall in each case be at such rate as having regard to all the circumstances of the case the Commissioner who deals with the pension claim deems reasonable and sufficient, but shall not exceed the rate of Eight shillings per week in any event.

Provision where claimant physically capable of earning.

(2) Where a claimant who is sixty-five years of age appears to the Commissioner to be physically capable of earning or partly earning his living such Commissioner may either refuse to grant the pension claim or may grant the same for such lesser sum than Eight shillings per week as such Commissioner considers proper in each case.

Special cases for consideration of Treasurer.

(3) Where a Commissioner is of opinion that a claimant although unable to prove that he complies with all the requirements of this Act is owing to physical disability deserving of a pension such Commissioner may forward a special application to the Registrar to submit the case for the consideration of the Treasurer and if the Treasurer approves of the granting of a pension the Registrar on receiving such approval may issue a pension certificate accordingly, and the Clerk of Petty Sessions shall issue a pass certificate.

How rate to be determined.

11. A pension shall be at such rate as will make the total income of the claimant from all sources not more than Eight shillings per week: Provided however that to the extent of Two shillings per week, derivable by him as wages or earnings in respect of his personal labour or exertion, such sum shall not be considered or taken into account in the computation of the total income of the claimant from all sources but such pension shall be diminished by—

Sixpence for every Ten pounds of the net capital value of all accumulated property owned by the claimant (not including furniture and personal effects to the value of Twenty-five pounds) which does not return income, after deducting from the capital value of such accumulated property all charges or encumbrances lawfully and properly existing on such property.

Assessment of value of accumulated property.

12. The net capital value of accumulated property shall be computed and assessed in the prescribed manner, and unless otherwise prescribed the following provisions shall apply:—

(a) All real and personal property owned by any person shall be deemed to be his accumulated property, and

(b) From the capital value of such accumulated property there shall be deducted all charges or encumbrances lawfully and properly existing on such property and also the sum of Fifty pounds, and the residue remaining shall be deemed to be the net capital value of all accumulated property; and

(c) Where a valuation has been made for any municipality of any such accumulated real property such valuation being the last municipal valuation of such property, shall be taken by any Commissioner to be the net capital value of such property unless satisfactory evidence is adduced to the contrary; and

(d) In the case of husband and wife the net capital value of the accumulated property of each shall be deemed to be not less than half the total net capital value of the accumulated property of both after allowing only one deduction of Fifty pounds. This rule shall not apply where a husband and wife are living apart pursuant to any decree order or deed of separation.

General rules for computing income.

13. In the computation of income—

(a) where any person receives board or lodging or board and lodging the actual or estimated value or cost of such board or lodging or board and lodging not exceeding Five shillings per week shall be included in the computation of the income of such person; and

(b) in the case of husband and wife the income of each shall be deemed to be not less than half the total income of both. This rule shall not apply where a husband and wife are living apart pursuant to any decree order or deed of separation.

PENSION CLAIMS.

Pension claim.

14. (1) Every person claiming a pension shall in the prescribed manner and form deliver a claim therefor (throughout this Act called a "pension claim") to the Registrar, or to the nearest Paymaster or prescribed officer; and such Paymaster or prescribed officer shall forthwith transmit the pension claim to the Registrar.

(2) The pension claim shall expressly affirm all the qualifications and requirements and negative all the disqualifications under this Act, and shall set out the place of abode and length of residence therein of the claimant and the place or places of abode of the claimant during the previous twelve months and such other information as may be prescribed.

(3) Every claimant shall by statutory declaration affirm that the contents of his pension claim are true and correct in every particular, and if any person in any such declaration wilfully makes any false statement he shall be deemed and taken to be guilty of wilful and corrupt perjury and shall be punishable accordingly.

(4) Such declaration may be made before any Police Magistrate, Commissioner, Justice, barrister and solicitor, Clerk of Petty Sessions, Assistant Clerk of Petty Sessions, Paymaster, State School head teacher, or Commissioner for taking Declarations and Affidavits or any prescribed officer or person.

(5) A pension claim may be withdrawn at any time by a notice of withdrawal sent by the claimant to the Registrar.

Commissioner to investigate.

15. (1) The Registrar shall in the prescribed manner forward each pension claim to a Commissioner who shall in open court in the locality where the claimant resides, or as near thereto as practicable, fully investigate the pension claim for the purpose of ascertaining whether the claimant is entitled to a pension and if so at what rate. Such Commissioner in such Court shall have and may exercise all the powers and authorities of a Court of Petty Sessions.

Notice of investigation.

(2) The Clerk of the Court shall notify the claimant of a date on which he may attend to support his pension claim, and the Commissioner shall on the day so notified or on the first convenient day thereafter proceed to investigate the same.

Evidence of police, &c.

(3) In order to ascertain the circumstances of any claimant and of the relatives of the claimant, evidence may be taken at the hearing from members of the police force and officers and members of the governing bodies of any charitable institutions or societies or from any other persons whomsoever.

Notice to local police and charitable institutions. (4) The Clerk of the Court shall also give notice of the application to the police and to the prescribed officers and members of the governing bodies of any charitable institutions or societies in the locality and request them to furnish in writing for the consideration of the Commissioner any information in their possession regarding the claimant and to be present or to be represented at the hearing.

Confidential report from Savings Bank, &c. (5) Officers of the Savings Banks of Victoria or of any Company, or of any Building Society, or Friendly Society are hereby required on demand of any Commissioner to furnish such Commissioner with a confidential report as to any transactions in connexion with any such bank company or society as the case may be by any particular claimant or pensioner.

Evidence to be corroborated. (6) No pension claim shall be granted to any claimant unless the Commissioner is thoroughly satisfied as to the truth of the evidence given in support of the claim and unless the evidence of the claimant is corroborated on all material points, except that in respect of the age of the claimant the Commissioner if otherwise satisfied may dispense with corroborative evidence.

How pension to be dealt with. (7) The Commissioner may grant a pension claim as made or as modified by the result of his investigations or may postpone it for further evidence or reject it as he deems equitable, and his decision shall in every case be notified by the Clerk of the Court to the claimant and also to the Registrar.

Power to dispense with personal attendance of claimant. (8) Where the Commissioner is satisfied that the documents or evidence in support of a pension claim are or is sufficient to establish it, and also that by reason of physical disability or other sufficient cause the attendance of the claimant should be dispensed with, he may dispense with the personal attendance of the claimant, who shall be notified accordingly.

Strict rules of evidence not to be binding. (9) In investigating any pension claim the Commissioner shall not be bound by the strict rules of evidence, but shall investigate and determine the matter by such means and in such manner as in equity and good conscience he thinks fit.

Power to send certain claimants to benevolent asylums. (10) If in investigating any pension claim it appears to the Commissioner that the claimant although otherwise qualified for a pension is unfit to be intrusted with a pension, he may certify that such claimant instead of being granted a pension ought to be sent to a benevolent asylum or charitable institution and the Clerk of the Court shall at once notify the Registrar who may thereupon cause steps to be taken for the admission of such claimant into a benevolent asylum or any prescribed public or private charitable institution.

Power to distinguish in material points. (11) In disposing of material points against the claimant the Commissioner shall distinguish between what he finds to be disproved and what he finds to be simply unproved or insufficiently proved.

Decision of Commissioner to be final in matters found to be disproved. (12) In respect of matters found to be disproved the decision of the Commissioner shall be final and conclusive for all purposes; unless an appeal being made by the claimant to the Treasurer within the prescribed time and in the prescribed manner the said Treasurer causes an investigation to be made as to such matters by a County Court Judge named by him in that behalf, in which case the decision of such Judge shall be final and conclusive for all purposes; and such decision shall be remitted to the Commissioner and dealt with in the same way as a decision of the Commissioner.

Right to adduce further evidence in certain cases. (13) In respect of matters found to be simply unproved or insufficiently proved, the claimant may at any time thereafter adduce before the Commissioner fresh evidence, and in such case all material points previously found by the Commissioner to be proved shall be deemed to be established, and the Commissioner shall dispose of all other points as in the case of a new pension claim.

Notice by Registrar to relatives. 16. (1) In order to ascertain whether or not any of the relatives within Victoria (that is to say the husband wife father mother or children over twenty-one years of age) of a claimant or pensioner are able to contribute towards the support of such claimant or pensioner, the Registrar shall send a notice to every such relative requiring him to furnish in a prescribed form a declaration as to his means and ability. If such declaration is not received from such relative within a time limited in such notice, or if it appears to the Registrar that such relative is able and ought to contribute but is not willing to do so, it shall be lawful for any Justice on the complaint of the Registrar, or any person on his behalf, to issue a summons calling upon such relative to show cause to some convenient Court of Petty Sessions consisting of a Commissioner why such relative should not be ordered to contribute towards the cost of the pension of the claimant or pensioner. Such Commissioner shall have and may exercise all the powers of a Court of Petty Sessions. The onus of proving that a person summoned under this section is not a relative of the claimant or pensioner shall be on the person so summoned.

Relatives summoned to show cause. (2) When any such relative has been summoned as aforesaid unless he satisfies the Court that having regard to his means and the cost of supporting others dependent upon him he cannot afford to pay any part of the cost of supporting the claimant or pensioner the Court may make an order against any such relative or relatives to pay into Court fortnightly or monthly any sum or sums not exceeding in the whole the rate of Eight shillings per week until otherwise ordered by a Commissioner towards the cost of the pension of the claimant or pensioner, and all sums so paid to the Clerk of the Court shall be paid into the Consolidated Revenue.

Order against relatives. (3) The Court shall be at liberty to make an order against any relative or relatives although it may appear that other relatives may also be liable under this section for the support of the claimant.

Enforcement of order against relative. (4) Where an order is made under this section against any person it shall be the duty of the Clerk of the Court to recover all sums due and payable pursuant to such order before a Court of Petty Sessions; and if such person does not pay all arrears of the amount due forthwith when ordered by such Court, or within any time not exceeding fourteen days that such Court may fix, or prove to the satisfaction of such Court that he has not sufficient means and ability to pay such arrears or any part thereof and that he does not intend to go away with intent to evade payment, such person shall be liable to be imprisoned for any term not exceeding one month.

Cases may be heard in private. (5) Every case under this section may, if the Court thinks fit, be heard in private.

Temporary pension certificate. 17. If delay will be occasioned in having a pension claim investigated by a Commissioner the Clerk of the Court where such claim is to be heard may pursuant to the regulations if satisfied that there is an urgent necessity so to do issue a temporary pension certificate limited in operation to four weeks. A duplicate of such temporary certificate shall be forwarded by such Clerk to the Registrar.

Rehearing of pension claim. 18. At the request of the Treasurer or the Registrar any Commissioner may rehear a pension claim previously admitted or rejected by a Commissioner, and the Registrar may alter or amend any certificate so as to accord with the decision arrived at on such rehearing.

Pension Certificates.

29. As soon as a pension claim is granted and the rate of the pension is fixed by a Commissioner he shall in the prescribed manner and form issue a certificate (hereinafter in this Act called a "pension certificate") which shall be signed by the pensioner therein named, and the Clerk of the Court shall forward the same together with particulars for identification of the pension to the Registrar and the Clerk of the Court shall issue to the pensioner a pass certificate to the like effect in the form prescribed.

Issue of certificate where claim established.

30. (1) A pension certificate shall in every case specify the rate of the pension, and the office where payable and the pass certificate shall specify the instalments whether fortnightly or otherwise by which it is payable.

Particulars in certificate.

(2) A pension shall commence from any date named in that behalf in the pension certificate but shall not be dated prior to the date of the pension claim for such pension.

When to commence.

(3) A pension shall pursuant to the pension certificate and subject to this Act continue to be paid at the rate specified in the certificate whilst there is money legally available therefor or until cancelled or suspended or reduced or increased.

Continuance of payment.

31. No person shall receive a pass certificate or pension certificate until he has executed a deed poll undertaking on demand to transfer to the Treasurer of Victoria all his real property and authorizing the Treasurer to sell such property and deduct from the proceeds the total sum paid to the pensioner pursuant to this Act, and after such total sum is so deducted any balance remaining shall be paid to the pensioner, or where he has died previously to such deduction such balance shall form part of such deceased pensioner's estate. Such deed poll shall be in the form of the Second Schedule to this Act or to the like effect.

Undertaking to transfer property on demand.

Second Schedule.

32. On application in the prescribed form and subject to the prescribed conditions the Registrar may issue a duplicate pass or pension certificate in any case where satisfactory proof is given of the loss or destruction of the original.

Issue of duplicate certificate.

33. The Treasurer may at any time cancel or suspend or reduce or increase any pension if he considers it expedient to do so, and the Registrar shall alter or amend the pass and pension certificates accordingly.

Power of Treasurer to cancel or suspend or reduce or increase pension.

Payment of Pensions and Forfeiture of Instalments.

34. (1) Each instalment of pension shall be payable at the office named in the pass or pension certificate.

Where pension payable.

(2) On application in the prescribed manner the name of such office may be changed from time to time by the Registrar and every change of office shall be recorded by the Registrar on the certificate.

Change of place of payment.

35. (1) Subject to the provisions of this Act each instalment shall be applied for and payable at any time within twenty-one days after its due date on the personal application of the pensioner except as hereinafter provided and the production of his pass certificate to the Paymaster at the office named therein.

Instalment to be applied for within twenty-one days.

(2) In default of strict compliance by the pensioner with the provisions of sub-section (1) of this section such instalment shall be deemed to be forfeited unless the forfeiture is waived as hereinafter provided.

When instalment deemed forfeited.

(3) The Registrar may waive any such forfeiture in any case where after investigation he is satisfied—

(a) that if the forfeiture was occasioned by default of personal application for payment or of application within the prescribed time such default was due to the pensioner's illness or temporary absence not from Victoria but from the locality in which such pension is payable or other sufficient cause; or

(b) that if the forfeiture was occasioned by default in producing the pass certificate such default was due to its being lost or mislaid:

When and how forfeiture may be waived.

(4) Except in special cases of the pensioner's illness or debility it shall not be lawful for the Registrar to waive the forfeiture of a pension twice to the same pensioner; and in no case shall forfeiture be waived unless it is applied for within the prescribed time.

Restriction as to two instalments consecutive.

36. (1) Subject to the regulations, on production to the Paymaster of a warrant in the prescribed form signed by the Registrar or a Commissioner or Clerk of Petty Sessions any instalments of pension may for the benefit of the pensioner be paid to any Minister of Religion Justice or person named in such warrant as approved by such Registrar Commissioner or Clerk.

Payment to Minister, &c. for the pensioner.

(2) Such warrant may be issued by the Registrar or a Commissioner or Clerk of Petty Sessions whenever he is satisfied that it is expedient so to do having regard to the age infirmity or improvidence of the pensioner or any other special circumstances, and such Commissioner or Clerk shall forward a copy of every such warrant issued by him to the Registrar, and payment made to the person named in such warrant shall be deemed to be payment to the pensioner.

37. For any period during which a pensioner is in prison or an inmate of a lunatic asylum or in a hospital or out of Victoria his pension shall without further or other authority than this Act be deemed to be forfeited, but when the pensioner is discharged from any such asylum or hospital after having remained there for more than twenty-eight days, payment of his pension shall be resumed dating back for twenty-eight days previously to such discharge.

Period for which pension not payable.

38. In the event of a successful claimant of a pension being an inmate of a Benevolent Asylum the pension shall commence and be payable from a date not more than fourteen days prior to the claimant having been discharged from or leaving such asylum. No person while an inmate of a Benevolent Asylum shall draw a pension.

Benevolent Asylum inmates.

39. With respect to the payment of instalments of pension by a Paymaster the following provisions shall apply:—

(a) The Paymaster may if he thinks fit require the applicant for payment to prove his identity but subject to the regulations he may accept the production of the pass certificate as sufficient evidence that the person producing the same is the person entitled to payment.

(b) When making the payment the Paymaster shall indorse on the pass certificate the date and fact of the payment, and shall also require the person receiving the payment to give a receipt therefor in the prescribed form.

Procedure as to payments of instalments by Paymaster.

PENALTIES.

Imprisonment for certain breaches of Act.

[illegible]. Every person shall on conviction before a Court of Petty Sessions consisting of a Police Magistrate be liable to imprisonment for not more than six months with or without hard labour—

(a) if by means of any wilfully false statement or representation he obtains or attempts to obtain a pension certificate pass certificate or pension or to affect the rate of any pension for which he is a claimant; or

(b) if by any unlawful means he obtains or attempts to obtain payment of any forfeited instalment of pension; or

(c) if by means of personation or any fraudulent device whatsoever he obtains or attempts to obtain payment of any instalment of pension; or

(d) if by any wilfully false statement or representation he aids or abets any person in obtaining or claiming a pension certificate or pension or instalment of a pension; or

(e) if he wilfully lends his pass certificate to any other person.

Additional powers of Court when convicting.

31. In the case of a conviction under the last preceding section the Court in addition to imposing the punishment thereby prescribed shall also according to the circumstances of the case by order—

(a) cancel any pension or pass certificate which is proved to have been wrongfully obtained; or

(b) reduce to its proper amount any pension that has been granted at too high a rate; or

(c) impose a penalty not exceeding twice the amount of any instalment the payment whereof has been wrongfully obtained and if the defendant is a pensioner direct the forfeiture of future instalments of his pension equal in amount to such penalty and in satisfaction thereof.

Forfeiture of instalments for certain offences.

32. (1) When a pensioner is in any Court convicted of drunkenness or of any offence punishable by imprisonment for not less than one month, then in addition to any other penalty or imprisonment imposed the Court may in its discretion by order forfeit any one or more of the instalments falling due after the date of the conviction.

Order for payment of instalments to Minister &c. for benefit of pensioner.

(2) Where in the opinion of a Commissioner a pensioner misspends any part of his pension or misspends wastes or lessens any part of his estate or of his income or earnings or injures his health or endangers or interrupts the peace and happiness of his family, a Commissioner may on the complaint of the Registrar or any Paymaster or any member of the police force make an order directing that until further order the instalments shall be paid to any benevolent or charitable society Minister of Religion Justice or other person named by such Commissioner for the benefit of the pensioner or cancelling the pension certificate or directing the forfeiture of so many of the instalments as the Commissioner thinks fit.

Cancellation of pension certificate after two convictions, &c.

(3) Where a pensioner is twice within twelve months convicted of any offence punishable by imprisonment for not less than one month or of drunkenness, or where any pensioner is convicted of any offence punishable by imprisonment for twelve months or upwards, then in lieu of forfeiting any instalments of the pension the Court last imposing such punishment shall by order cancel the pass certificate and pension certificate.

When pension absolutely forfeited.

(4) In any case where any pass certificate or pension certificate is cancelled the pension shall be deemed to be absolutely forfeited, and the pass certificate shall be delivered up to the Clerk of the Court and forwarded by him to the Registrar.

Notice of forfeiture to Registrar.

(5) In every case where any instalment is forfeited or any pass certificate or pension certificate is cancelled the Clerk of the Court shall forthwith notify the Registrar of such forfeiture or cancellation, and the Registrar shall record the same, and give notice thereof to the Paymaster at the office where such pension is payable.

Power to cancel pension for drunken habits.

33. Notwithstanding that a pensioner has not been convicted of drunkenness a Commissioner may and if so requested by the Registrar shall at any time summon any pensioner to appear and show cause why his pension should not be cancelled reduced or suspended for a time on account of such pensioner's drunken or intemperate habits and at the time and place mentioned in such summons the Commissioner may, if he thinks fit, cancel reduce or suspend such pension accordingly.

MISCELLANEOUS.

Payment of money out of Consolidated Revenue.

34. The Treasurer shall pay out of the Consolidated Revenue (which is hereby to the necessary extent appropriated for the purpose) all such moneys as are necessary in order to enable the pensions payable under this Act to be paid; and payments shall be made in the prescribed manner. [illegible]

Annual statement to be laid before Parliament.

35. The Treasurer shall within sixty days after the close of each financial year prepare and lay before Parliament if sitting or if not sitting then within fourteen days after the commencement of the next session a statement showing for such year—

(a) the total amount paid under this Act in respect of pensions;

(b) the total number of pensions; and

(c) such other particulars as are prescribed.

36. Every pension shall be deemed to be granted and shall be held subject to all the provisions of this Act and to the provisions of any amending or repealing Act that may at any time be passed, and no pensioner shall have any claim for compensation or otherwise by reason of his pension being affected by the operation of this Act or by any such amending or repealing Act. Pensions granted subject to any future Act.

37. (1) The Governor in Council may make regulations not inconsistent with this Act with regard to all or any of the following matters, namely :— Regulations.

(a) the powers and duties of the Registrar and officers ;

(b) the form of pension claims, and any applications or declarations relating thereto and the times within which the same are to be made or given;

(c) the registering and numbering of all pension claims and particulars in regard thereto ;

(d) the form of pension certificates and pass certificates ;

(e) the mode of transmitting pension claims to a Commissioner ;

(f) the mode of valuing properties ;

(g) all proceedings of any kind before a Commissioner ;

(h) the certification of pension claims by a Commissioner and the obtaining of the recommendation of the Registrar and approval thereof by the Treasurer ;

(i) the form of receipt to be given for any pension ; and

(j) generally for the purpose of the more effectually carrying out the intent and objects of this Act.

(2) All such regulations shall be published in the "Government Gazette" and when so published shall be of the same effect as if they were contained in this Act and shall be judicially noticed and shall be laid before each House of Parliament within fourteen days after the same shall have been made if Parliament be then sitting and if not then within ten days after the next meeting of Parliament. Publication.

SCHEDULES.

FIRST SCHEDULE. Section 6.

I, of do sincerely promise and swear that as a Commissioner under the Old-age Pensions Act 1901 I will at all times and in all things do equal justice to the poor and to the rich, and discharge the duties of my office according to law and to the best of my knowledge and ability without fear favour or affection.

So help me God !

SECOND SCHEDULE. Section [illegible]

Old-age Pensions Act 1901.

I, of in consideration of being granted a pension under the Old-age Pensions Act 1901 do hereby undertake on demand to convey assign and transfer to the Treasurer of Victoria all [illegible] property of which I am now possessed or to which I am now or may hereafter be or become entitled, and I further undertake on demand to deliver to the said Treasurer all deeds documents and [illegible] of title in my possession or under my control relating to such real property, and I hereby irrevocably appoint the Registrar of Old-age Pensions for the time being my true and lawful attorney for me and in my name to sign seal and execute all or any conveyances transfers assignments receipts and acquittances for effectually vesting such real property in the said Treasurer, and also for me and in my name to demand receive sue for and recover all such deeds documents [illegible] of title as aforesaid and on receipt or delivery thereof for me and in my name good and sufficient receipts and discharges to sign and deliver therefor, and also to sell all or such real property by public auction and to deduct from the proceeds the total sum paid to me as a pensioner under the said Act, and after such total sum is so deducted any balance remaining shall be paid to me, or after my death to my legal representatives and no purchaser or other person body corporate company or institution shall be bound to see or inquire into the application of any moneys arising from any sale transfer or receipt of any such real property in any way whatsoever.

As witness my hand and seal this day of One thousand nine hundred and

Witness—

Short title and construction. No. 1768.

1. This Act may be cited as the Old-age Pensions Act 1900 further Amendment Act 1901, and shall be read and construed as one with the Old-age Pensions Act 1900.

Further appropriation of £50,000 for old-age pensions under Act No. 1768.

2. For the purposes of the Old-age Pensions Act 1900 there may in addition to the sums appropriated by the said Act and the Act No. 1782 be paid a further sum of Fifty thousand pounds out of the consolidated revenue which is hereby appropriated accordingly.

Provisions as to when pensions under No. 1768 are to cease.

3. All existing pensions granted under Old-age Pensions Act 1900 shall, from the seventh day of December One thousand nine hundred and one, be paid out of the consolidated revenue as a special appropriation under the Old-age Pensions Act 1901 No. 1781, and until altered or cancelled by the Governor in Council shall subject to this section be payable at the rates specified in the certificates issued thereunder, except pensions exceeding the rate of eight shillings per week which are hereby reduced to that rate; but no pension granted under the Old-age Pensions Act 1900 shall be paid to any person whatsoever after such day in the year One thousand nine hundred and two as may be determined by the Governor in Council, and published in the "Government Gazette."

North No.
South No.
West No.
North-West No.

Relief Office, [illegible] W.

Nature of Application and Order of Committee. (In black ink) (In red ink)	Date	Initials of Chairman or Clerk.

APPENDIX, No. 6—continued.

FIRST APPLICATION.

Paddington Relief Office, Harrow Road, W. 19

Names of Applicant and Wife.	Age.	When Born.	Where Born.	Religious Persuasion, and when and where Baptized.
Names of Children under 16				
Names of Children over 16				

Married, Single, Widow or Widower

When and where Married

Wife's Maiden Name

If a Widow or Widower, Name of late Husband or Wife

Occupation of ditto

Date and Place of his or her Death

When and where last Chargeable

Admitted to on the day of

If a Lunatic { Name of Magistrate Date of Order

Name of Asylum When sent

Examination Fees £ : Removal Expenses

Cause of seeking Relief

Residence, and how long there

Rent, and Amount due

Previous Residences and Rent owing (if any)

Occupation of Applicant, and earnings

Occupation of Husband or Wife, and earnings

If Applicant is in debt, nature of debts covered by bill of sale, pawn tickets, &c.

Club or Benefit Society

Trade Society

Nature and amount of other resources (if any)

Name of nearest Relative or Friend

Relationship of ditto

Address of ditto

Particulars of other Members of the family chargeable to this or any other Parish

Names and Addresses and financial circumstances of
(a) Liable Relatives.
(b) Other Relatives assisting or able to assist.

Source of Information

PARISH OF PADDINGTON, LONDON.

Guardians' Offices, 313-315, Harrow Road, W.

Report respecting Age

When born? Where born?

Name of Husband or Wife

When born? Where born?

Names and Ages of Children

When born?

Where born?

Date of Admission to Workhouse By whose Order?

Residence before Admission to Workhouse, and how long there?

Previous residences, given in order backwards, so far as may be necessary for deriving settlement.

Calling or Occupation Married or single

Able-bodied, temporarily disabled, or permanently disabled

If married, When?

Where?

Wife's Maiden Name?

	Christian and Surname.	*Address.*	*Occupation.*
Names and Addresses of Father			
Mother			
Husband			
Wife			
Children			
Friends, or any Relatives not above inserted.			

If Apprenticed, or if Father was Apprenticed

Name of Master

Address

Date of Apprenticeship?

Residence during last 40 days

G12. F 2

If rented a House, or if Parents rented a House before Pauper was 16 years old?

When?

Where?

Landlord's Name?

Address?

Rent?

Rates and Taxes?

If possessed of an Estate?

Value?

Where?

Parish Relief at any time?

When?

Where?

If removed before?

When?

From what Parish?

To what Parish?

Where was Father born?

When?

(If not known),

Where was Mother born?

When?

Where was father living at time when Pauper became 16 years of age?

No.

PARISH OF PADDINGTON, LONDON.

Guardians' Offices, [illegible], Harrow Road, W.,

To the Guardians of the Poor
of Paddington.

Sir,

I beg to state that I have made inquiry respecting the above-named, and to report that—

APPENDIX No. 1.

PAPER handed in by the Chairman.

COPY OF THE NEW SOUTH WALES OLD-AGE PENSIONS ACT OF 1900.*
64 Vict., Act No. 74, 1900.

AN ACT to provide for OLD-AGE PENSIONS, and for purposes in furtherance of or consequent on the aforesaid object. [Assented to, 11th December, 1900.]

WHEREAS it is equitable that deserving persons who during the prime of life have helped to bear the public burdens of the Colony by the payment of taxes, and by opening up its resources by their labour and skill, should receive from the Colony pensions in their old age: Be it therefore enacted by the Queen's Most Excellent Majesty, by and with the advice and consent of the Legislative Council and Legislative Assembly of New South Wales in Parliament assembled, and by the authority of the same, as follows:—

PART I.

PRELIMINARY.

Short title and definitions.

1. This Act shall take effect on the first day of January, one thousand nine hundred and one, and may be cited as the "Old-age Pensions Act, 1900."

2. This Act is divided into the following Parts:—

PART I.—PRELIMINARY—ss. 1-5.

PART II.—PENSIONS—ss. 6-36.

PART III.—PENALTIES AND MISCELLANEOUS PROVISIONS—ss. 37-52.

3. In this Act, if not inconsistent with the context,—

"Income" means any moneys, valuable consideration, or profits derived or received by any person for his own use or benefit in any year, by any means or from any source, and computed in accordance with the provisions of this Act, and includes personal earnings, but does not include any pension payable under this Act, nor any payment by way of sick allowance or funeral benefit from any registered friendly society.

"Income-year" means the twelve months ending one month before the date on which the pension claim is admitted, and at the same time in each subsequent year.

"Prescribed" means prescribed by this Act, or by regulations thereunder.

"The board" means the Old-age Pensions Board for the district.

4. The net capital value of accumulated property shall be computed and assessed in the prescribed manner, and for that purpose the following provisions shall apply:—

(a) All real and personal property owned by any person shall, to the extent of his beneficial estate or interest therein, be deemed to be his accumulated property.

(b) From the capital value of such accumulated property, there shall be deducted all charges or encumbrances lawfully existing on such property, and also the sum of fifty pounds; the residue then remaining shall be deemed to be the net capital value of all his accumulated property.

5. The following general rules shall apply in the computation of income for all the purposes of this Act:—

(a) Any moneys, valuable consideration, or profits derived or received from accumulated property as hereinbefore defined shall not be included in the computation of income.

(b) Where any person receives board or lodging, the reasonable cost of such board or lodging, not exceeding twenty-six pounds in the year, shall be included in the computation of income.

(c) In the case of husband and wife, the income of each shall be deemed to be half the sum of the incomes of both:

Provided that this rule shall not apply where they are living apart pursuant to a decree, order, or deed of separation.

---

* No amending Act to this Act has yet been passed by the New South Wales Parliament; but it is understood that the State Government will introduce an amending measure during the present Session.

DISTRICTS AND REGISTRARS.

6. (1) For the purposes of this Act, the Governor may divide the Colony into such districts, with such names and boundaries as he thinks fit, and alter such names and boundaries. Districts.

(2) If any such district is constituted by reference to the boundaries of any other portion of the Colony, as defined by any Act, proclamation, or notification, then any alteration in such boundaries shall take effect in respect of such district without any further proceedings, unless the Governor otherwise determines. Alteration of boundaries.

7. (1) The Governor may appoint a central board of three persons, who, subject to the control of the Colonial Treasurer, shall have the general administration of this Act. Central board.

(2) The Governor may also appoint a registrar for the central board, and for every other district a deputy registrar and such other officers as he deems fit. Registrar, and deputy registrars.

(3) The said appointments shall be subject to the provisions of the Public Service Act of 1895 and any Acts amending the same. Application of Public Service Act.

(4) Subject to the provisions of this Act, the registrar and every deputy registrar and other officer appointed as aforesaid shall have such powers and duties as the Governor determines. Their powers and duties.

THE BOARDS.

8. (1) There shall for each district be a board of three persons appointed by the Governor, subject to the Public Service Act of 1895, and any Acts amending the same, and called the Old-age Pensions Board for the said district, and such board shall have the powers and duties conferred and imposed on the board by this Act or regulations made thereunder. Constitution and powers of Board.

Two members of any board shall be a quorum.

(2) Each member of the board shall, before entering upon the duties of his office, make and subscribe a declaration in the form and in the manner prescribed. Declaration by members of Board.

PART II.

PENSIONS.

Persons entitled to and amount of Pensions.

9. (1) Subject to the provisions of this Act, every person of the full age of sixty-five years or upwards shall, whilst in the Colony, be entitled to a pension as hereinafter specified, if the following conditions are fulfilled— Persons entitled to pension. Residency qualifications.

(a) that he is residing in the Colony on the date when he establishes his claim to the pension;

(b) that he has so resided continuously for not less than twenty-five years immediately preceding such date:

Provided that continuous residence in the Colony shall not be deemed to have been interrupted by occasional absence therefrom, unless the total period of such absence exceeds two years; nor, in the case of a seaman, by absence therefrom whilst serving on board a vessel trading to and from the Colony, if he establishes the fact that during such absence his family or home was in the Colony:

Provided also that residence in an Australasian Colony, in which provision is made for granting old-age pensions, shall count as residence in this Colony, if—

i. the claimant has, during the ten years immediately preceding the date when he establishes his claim, continuously resided in this Colony, and

ii. the Colonial Treasurer certifies to the board that provision has been made by agreement with the Government of such other Colony as hereinafter mentioned.

And for the purpose of carrying out this proviso, the Colonial Treasurer, on behalf of the Government of this Colony, may agree with the Government of any such Colony for the payment by such other Government of any such pension in whole or in part, or for the granting by such other Colony of concessions to a like amount under the old-age pension law of that Colony to persons who have been resident in this Colony.

(c) that during the period of twelve years immediately preceding such date he has not been imprisoned for four months, or on four occasions, for any offence punishable by imprisonment for twelve months or upwards;

(d) that during the period of twenty-five years immediately preceding such date he has not been imprisoned for a term of five years, with or without hard labour;

(e) that he has not at any time for a period of six months or upwards, if a husband, deserted his wife, or without just cause failed to provide her with adequate means of maintenance, or neglected to maintain such of his children as were under the age of fourteen years; or, if a wife, deserted her husband or such of her children as were under that age:

Provided that, if the pension certificate has issued, the pensioner's rights thereunder shall not be affected by any disqualification contained in this subsection unless the fact of such disqualification is established to the satisfaction of the board;

(f) that he is of good moral character, and is leading and has for the five years immediately preceding such date led a sober and reputable life;

(g) that his income does not amount to fifty-two pounds or upwards;

(h) that the net capital value of his accumulated property does not amount to three hundred and ninety pounds or upwards, computed and assessed as hereinafter provided;

(i) that he has not directly or indirectly deprived himself of income or property in order to qualify for a pension; and

(j) that he is the holder of a pension-certificate as hereinafter provided.

No pension to commence before 1st July 1901.

(2) A claim to a pension may be established and all steps may be taken to entitle the claimant to a pension at any time after the commencement of this Act, but no pension shall commence until the first day of July, one thousand nine hundred and one.

Colonial Treasurer may approve of pensions to persons of sixty years and upwards and physically unfit to earn their living.

10. Where it is satisfactorily proved to the Board that any person of the full age of sixty years, and upwards, and under the age of sixty-five years, is unable from physical unfitness to earn his own living, and that such person if of the age of sixty-five years would be entitled under this Act to a pension, a pension shall be payable to, and the provisions of this Act shall apply in respect of, such person.

Amount of pension in case of husband and wife.

11. (1) Where a husband and wife are each entitled to a pension, the amount of the pension payable to each shall, unless they are living apart pursuant to a decree, order, or a deed of separation, be nineteen pounds ten shillings per year, diminished—

(a) by one pound for every complete pound of income of the husband or wife, as the case may be, above nineteen pounds ten shillings; and

(b) where the husband or wife, as the case may be, have any income, by one pound for every complete fifteen pounds of the net capital value of all accumulated property of such husband or wife, computed and assessed under this Act.

In other cases.

(2) In other cases the amount of the pension shall be twenty-six pounds per year, diminished—

(a) by one pound for every complete pound of income of the pensioner above twenty-six pounds; and

(b) where the pensioner has any income, by one pound for every complete fifteen pounds of the net capital value of all accumulated property of the pensioner, computed and assessed under the Act.

Pension not to vary during year.

12. The rate of each year's pension shall not vary during the year.

Income for purpose of first year's pension.

13. (1) For the purpose of ascertaining whether the claimant for a pension is entitled thereto, and also of fixing the rate of the first year's pension, his income for the next preceding income-year shall be deemed to be his income.

Income for subsequent years.

(2) For the purpose of fixing the rate of the pension for the second and each subsequent year, the pensioner's income for the income-year next preceding such such year shall be deemed to be his income.

Pensions how payable.

14. With respect to every pension under this Act the following provisions shall apply:—

(a) The pension shall be deemed to commence on the date named in that behalf in the pension-certificate issued in respect of the first year's pension, being in every case the first day of the month next after the date of the issue of such certificate.

(b) Each year's pension shall be payable pursuant to a pension-certificate issued in respect of such year, and not otherwise.

(c) Such certificate shall in every case specify the amount of the year's pension, and the instalments by which it is payable, being twelve equal monthly instalments, whereof the first is payable on the first day of the month next after the commencement of the year.

PENSION-CLAIMS.

Pension-claims.

15. (1) Every person claiming to be entitled to a pension under this Act shall, in the prescribed manner, deliver a claim therefor (in this Act called a "pension-claim") to the deputy registrar of the district wherein the claimant resides, or to the clerk of the nearest court of petty sessions, who shall forthwith forward the same to the deputy registrar.

(2) The pension-claim shall be in the prescribed form and shall affirm all the requirements and negative all the disqualifications under this Act.

(3) Every claimant shall, by statutory declaration, affirm that the contents of his pension-claim are true and correct in every material point.

(4) Such declaration may be made before any justice of the peace, solicitor, deputy registrar, or clerk of petty sessions.

Register of pension-claims.

16. The deputy registrar of any district shall file the claim, and number it in the prescribed manner, and shall record it in the prescribed manner, in a book, to be called The Old-age Pension-claim Register of the said district.

Board to investigate pension-claims.

17. (1) The deputy registrar shall, in the prescribed manner, transmit the claim to the board, and the board shall cause the prescribed notice to be given of the day fixed for the investigation hereinafter mentioned, and may require the claimant to attend personally on that day to support his claim.

Provided that where satisfied that the documentary evidence in support of the claim is sufficient to establish it, and also that by reason of physical disability or other sufficient cause the attendance of the claimant should be dispensed with, the board shall not require the personal attendance of the claimant, who shall be notified accordingly.

(2) The board shall on that day, or on the first convenient day thereafter, fully investigate the pension-claim for the purpose of ascertaining whether the claimant is entitled to the pension, and, if so, for what amount in respect of the first year.

Powers of board for purposes of investigation.

18. For the purpose of such investigation, the provisions of section one hundred and forty of the Parliamentary Electorates and Elections Act of 1893 applicable to the commissions mentioned in that section or any member thereof shall apply to the board or any member thereof.

Strict rules of evidence not to be binding.

19. (1) In investigating any pension-claim, the board shall not be bound by the strict rules of evidence but shall investigate and determine the matter by such means and in such manner as in equity and good conscience it thinks fit.

Evidence of claimant to be corroborated.

(2) No pension-claim shall be admitted unless the evidence of the claimant is corroborated on all material points, except that in respect of the age of the claimant, the board, if otherwise satisfied, may dispense with corroborative evidence.

How pension-claims to be dealt with.

30. (1) The board may admit the pension-claim as originally made, or as modified by the result of the investigation, and fix the amount of the pension, or may postpone the investigation for further evidence, or reject the claim, as may be deemed equitable; and the decision of the board shall be notified to the claimant as prescribed.

Board may postpone claim.

(2) If the board is of opinion that, although the claim is not completely established, further evidence may be adduced in support thereof, or it may be amended by lapse of time, the board shall, if the claimant so desire, postpone the investigation, and in such case all matters as to which the board is satisfied shall be recorded as proved: Provided that further evidence may be adduced in respect of any matters recorded as proved.

Mode of rejecting claim.

(3) If the board decides that the pension-claim is not established, and cannot be amended by further evidence or by postponement of the investigation for a reasonable time, the board shall reject it, and when doing so shall specify in writing all the material points which it finds to be respectively proved, disproved and unproved or insufficiently proved.

Matters to be distinguished.

31. (1) In disposing of material points against the claimant, the board shall distinguish between what it finds to be disproved and what it finds to be simply unproved or insufficiently proved.

As to matters disproved.

(2) In respect of matters found to be disproved, the decision of the board shall be final and conclusive for all purposes; unless, on appeal being made by the claimant to the Colonial Treasurer, within the prescribed time and in the prescribed manner, the said Treasurer causes an investigation to be made as to such matters by a District Court Judge named by him in that behalf, in which case the decision of such Judge shall be final and conclusive for all purposes; and such decision shall be remitted to the board and dealt with in the same way as a decision of the board.

As to matters unproved.

(3) In respect of matters found to be simply unproved or insufficiently proved, the claimant may at any time thereafter adduce before the board fresh evidence, and in such case all material points previously found by the board to be proved shall be deemed to be established and the board shall dispose of all other points as in the case of a new pension-claim.

Provisional investigation of pension-claims.

32. In order to facilitate the adjustment of pension-claims they may be delivered filed and provisionally investigated within any period not exceeding two years before the date on which the claimant alleges that his pension should commence; but no pension-claim shall be admitted, nor shall any pension-certificate be issued, until all the conditions prescribed in respect thereof by this Act have been fulfilled.

Pension-claims may be amended.

33. The pension-claim may be amended from time to time on any point which has not been finally disposed of.

Pension-certificate for First Year's Pension.

Issue of pension-certificate when claim established.

34. As soon as the pension-claim is admitted, and the rate of the first year's pension is fixed as aforesaid, the board shall in the prescribed manner certify the same to the deputy-registrar, who shall in the prescribed manner issue to the claimant a certificate (in this Act called a "pension-certificate") in the form prescribed in respect of the first year's pension.

Particulars to be entered in pension-register.

35. (1) The deputy-registrar of any district shall, in a book to be called The Old-age Pension Register for the said district, enter the following particulars respecting each pension-certificate issued by him:—

(a) the number of such certificate, and the name of the district in which it is issued;

(b) the pensioner's full name, occupation, and address;

(c) the amount of his income for the year, and the date on which the income-year ends;

(d) the date on which the year's pension commences;

(e) the amount of the year's pension, the instalments by which it is payable, and the due dates thereof;

(f) such other particulars as are prescribed.

Entries in register to be numbered.

(2) All entries of pension-certificates in the said register shall be numbered consecutively, so that no two entries in the same register bear the same number.

Transfer of pension-certificates to other districts, and issue of duplicates.

36. On application in the prescribed manner and form, and subject to prescribed conditions—

(a) the entry in respect of any pension-certificate may be transferred from the register in one district to the register in another;

(b) the deputy-registrar may issue a duplicate pension-certificate in any case where satisfactory proof is given of the loss of the original.

Pension-Certificates for Subsequent Years.

Statements of income for preceding pension-year to be furnished to deputy-registrar.

37. For the purpose of ascertaining in respect of the second and each subsequent year, computed from the date of the commencement of the pension, whether the pensioner is entitled to any payment in respect of his pension for such year, and if so, for what amount, the following provisions shall apply:—

(a) Within the prescribed period before the commencement of each such year the pensioner, whether claiming any payment in respect of his pension for that year or not, shall furnish to the deputy-registrar a statement in the prescribed form setting forth full particulars of his income for such half (being the income for the last preceding income-year), and also the net capital value of all his accumulated property.

(b) If the pensioner has received no income for the year, and has no accumulated property, the statement shall contain the word "nil."

(c) The board shall investigate the statement, and shall ascertain in the same manner, with the same powers, and subject to the same provisions as in the case of a pension-claim whether the conditions of section nine of this Act have been complied with.

Issue of pension-certificate for year.

(d) The board, when satisfied as to the amount of the pensioner's income, and the net capital value of his accumulated property, and that the conditions of section nine aforesaid have been complied with, shall certify the same to the deputy-registrar, who shall enter the same in the Old-age Pension Register for the district, and issue a pension-certificate, in the prescribed form, in respect of the pension (if any) to which the pensioner is entitled for that year;

Provided that, in lieu of issuing such certificate to the pensioner, the deputy registrar shall forward it to the manager of the bank or branch or the person authorised to pay the pension, and the said manager or person shall issue it to the pensioner in exchange for the continuing pension-certificate.

(c) When forwarding the pension-certificate to the said manager or person, the deputy registrar shall, in the prescribed manner, notify the same to the pensioner.

PAYMENT OF PENSIONS AND FORFEITURE OF INSTALMENTS.

Where pension payable.

28. (1) Each monthly instalment of the pension shall be payable at the Government Savings Bank, or any branch thereof, or at such other bank or such branch of a bank as may be appointed by the registrar for the purpose and named in the pension-certificate.

Change of place of payment.

(2) On application in the prescribed manner, such bank or branch may be changed from time to time, and every such change shall be recorded by the deputy registrar on the pension-certificate and in the pension register for the district.

Instalment to be applied for within twenty-one days.

29. (1) Subject to the provisions of this Act, each monthly instalment shall be payable at any time within twenty-one days after its due date, on the personal application of the pensioner and the production of his pension-certificate to the manager of the bank or the branch appointed by the manager for that purpose and described in such certificate.

When instalment deemed forfeited.

(2) In default of strict compliance with all the provisions of this section, such instalment shall be deemed to be forfeited, unless the forfeiture is waived under the provisions in that behalf hereinafter contained.

When and how forfeiture may be waived.

30. (1) The board, by warrant in the prescribed form, may waive any such forfeiture in any case where, after investigation, it is satisfied—

(a) that the forfeiture was occasioned by default of personal application for payment, or of application within the prescribed time, and that such default was due to the pensioner's illness, debility, or temporary absence from the locality where the application is to be made (but not from the Colony), or other sufficient cause; or

(b) that the forfeiture was occasioned by default in producing the pension-certificate, and that such default was due to its being lost or mislaid:

Provided that—

(c) except in special cases of the pensioner's illness or debility, or by permission of the central board, it shall not be lawful for the board to issue two such warrants in succession to the same pensioner; and

(d) in no case shall any such warrant be issued unless it is applied for within fourteen days after the forfeiture.

Payment under warrant.

(2) The instalment named in any such warrant shall be payable at any time within fourteen days after the date thereof, on the personal application of the pensioner or such other person as is named therein, and on the production of the warrant, and (except where the warrant otherwise provides) of the pension-certificate, to the manager or clerk of the bank at which the pension is payable as aforesaid, or to any person named in the warrant.

When warrant deemed lapsed.

(3) In default of strict compliance with all the provisions of the last preceding subsection, the warrant shall be deemed to have lapsed, and the forfeiture of the instalment named therein shall become absolute.

Payment where pensioner in receipt of charitable aid.

31. No pension shall be payable under this Act to any person who is maintained in any charitable institution, or receives relief therefrom, except where such person is unable, from some physical defect, to take care of himself, and in such case the following provisions shall apply:—

(a) The reasonable cost of such maintenance or relief shall be payable out of the pension.

(b) For the purpose of procuring such payment, instalments of the pension shall be payable to the governing body of such institution in such manner as is prescribed, on production, to the manager or clerk of the bank or branch at which the pension is payable as aforesaid, of a warrant in the prescribed form issued by the board.

(c) Any surplus pension-moneys remaining in the hands of such governing body after defraying such cost shall be paid to the pensioner.

(d) For the purpose of computing the amount of any subsidy or contribution payable by the Government to such governing body under any Act, all instalments so paid shall be excluded.

Pensioner may be boarded out.

32. Any person who, in the opinion of the board, should not receive the pension payment in cash, but who is entitled to a pension under the provisions of this Act, may, at the discretion of the board, be boarded out, and the amount of the pension to which he is entitled may be withdrawn from the consolidated revenue and paid by the board to the person selected to provide for the pensioners' support.

Every person boarded out under the provisions of this section must be inspected periodically by an official appointed by the Government.

Payment to other than pensioner.

33. Subject to the regulations made under this Act, and on production to the manager or clerk of the bank or branch at which the pension is payable of a warrant of the board in the prescribed form, the instalments may be paid to any clergyman, Justice of the peace, or other reputable person named in such warrant, for the benefit of the pensioner.

Such warrant may be issued by the board on being satisfied that it is expedient so to do, having regard to the age, infirmity, or improvidence of the pensioner, or any other special circumstances.

Period for which pension not payable.

34. Every instalment which falls due during any period whilst the pensioner is in prison, in lunatic of a lunatic asylum, or out of the Colony, shall be deemed to be absolutely forfeited.

Procedure as to payments of instalments by banks.

35. With respect to the payment of instalments of pension by the manager or clerk aforesaid, the following provisions shall apply:—

(a) The manager or clerk may, if he thinks fit, require the applicant for payment to prove his identity, but shall not be bound so to do, and may accept the production of the pension-certificate or warrant to which the instalment relates as sufficient evidence that the person producing the same is the person entitled to payment.

(b) When making the payment, the manager or clerk shall endorse on the pension certificate or warrant produced as aforesaid the date and fact of the payment, and shall also require the person receiving the payment to give a receipt therefor in the prescribed form.

(c) Such receipt shall be sufficient evidence that the payment to which the receipt purports to relate has been duly made, and no claim against Her Majesty, or the bank, or the manager, or clerk shall thereafter arise or be made in respect thereof.

(d) Where the warrant produced as aforesaid relates to a single instalment, or to the last of a series of instalments, it shall be delivered up to and retained by the manager or clerk on payment of such instalment.

36. On the issue of any warrant the board shall notify the same to the deputy registrar, who shall record the same. Notification of issue of warrant.

PART III.

Penalties and Miscellaneous Provisions.

Penalties.

37. Every person is liable to imprisonment for not more than six months, with or without hard labour,— Imprisonment for certain breaches of Act.

(a) if by means of any wilfully false statement or representation, he obtains or attempts to obtain a pension certificate, not being justly entitled thereto, or a pension to a larger amount than he is justly entitled to; or

(b) if by any means he fraudulently obtains or attempts to obtain payment of any absolutely forfeited instalment of a pension; or

(c) if, by means of personation or any other fraudulent device whatsoever, he obtains or attempts to obtain payment of any instalment of a pension; or

(d) if by any wilfully false statement or representation, he aids or abets any person to obtain a pension-certificate, or any instalment of a pension.

All proceedings under this section shall be taken in a summary way before a stipendiary or police magistrate or two justices of the peace.

An appeal shall lie from any conviction under this section.

38. In the case of any conviction under the last preceding section, the court, in addition to imposing the punishment thereby prescribed, shall also, according to the circumstances of the case, by order— Additional powers of court when convicting.

(a) cancel any pension-certificate which is proved to have been wrongfully obtained; or

(b) reduce to its proper amount, any pension that has been proved to be too high; or

(c) impose a penalty not exceeding twice the amount of any instalment, the payment whereof has been wrongfully obtained, and, if the defendant is a pensioner, direct the forfeiture of future instalments of his pension equal in amount to such penalty and in satisfaction thereof.

39. If any pensioner is convicted of drunkenness, or of any offence punishable by imprisonment for not less than one month, then, in addition to any other penalty or punishment imposed, the court may in its discretion, by order, forfeit any one or more of the instalments falling due next after the date of the conviction. Additional penalty for certain offences.

Provided that if, in the opinion of the court, any pensioner convicted of any such offence misspends, wastes, or lessens his estate, or greatly injures his health, or endangers or interrupts the peace and happiness of his family, the court may by order direct that the instalment be paid to any clergyman, justice of the peace, or other reputable person, for the benefit of the pensioner, or may by order cancel the pension-certificate: Provided further that it shall not be lawful for any licensed publican to knowingly supply to any person receiving a pension under this Act any fermented or spirituous liquor, and any person convicted of an offence under this section shall be liable to a penalty of not exceeding ten pounds.

40. If any pensioner is sentenced to imprisonment for twelve months or upwards in respect of any offence dishonouring him in the public estimation, the court shall, by order, cancel the pension-certificate. Pension-certificate to be cancelled on imprisonment for certain offences.

41. In any case where any pension-certificate is cancelled by order of a court, the pension shall be deemed to be absolutely forfeited. When pension absolutely forfeited.

42. In every case where any instalment is forfeited or any pension-certificate is cancelled by order of a court, the clerk of the court shall forthwith notify the board and the deputy registrar of such forfeiture or cancellation, and the deputy registrar shall record the same. Notice of forfeiture to deputy registrar.

Miscellaneous.

43. The pension being for the personal support of the pensioner, it shall (subject to the provisions of this Act as to payments, forfeitures, and otherwise) be absolutely inalienable, whether by way of assignment, charge, execution, bankruptcy, or otherwise howsoever. Pensions absolutely inalienable.

44. (1) Every deputy registrar shall, in the prescribed manner and at prescribed intervals, prepare and forward to the registrar a return showing for each such interval— Returns to be prepared by deputy registrars.

(a) all pension-certificates issued and warrants recorded by him;

(b) all forfeitures recorded by him;

(c) such other particulars as are prescribed.

(2) The registrar shall from the aforesaid returns compile a General Old-age Pension Register, containing a record of all pension-certificates for the time being in force and such other particulars as are prescribed. General Register.

45. The registrar shall, at prescribed intervals, furnish to the Colonial Treasurer schedules showing for each such interval— Particulars to be furnished to Colonial Treasurer.

(a) the names of pensioners;

(b) the numbers of their pension certificates;

(c) the dates on which and the banks and branches at which the instalments in respect thereof are payable; and

(d) the amount of the instalments payable.

46. The Colonial Treasurer shall from time to time, without further appropriation than this Act, pay out of the Consolidated Revenue Fund whatever moneys are necessary in order to enable the instalments specified in each schedule in respect of pensions granted under this Act to be paid.

47. All expenses incurred in administering this Act (other than the payment of pensions) shall be payable out of the moneys to be from time to time appropriated by Parliament.

48. The Colonial Treasurer shall, within thirty days after the close of each financial year, prepare and lay before Parliament, if sitting, or, if not sitting, then within fourteen days after the commencement of the next session, a statement showing for such year—

(a) the total amount paid under this Act in respect of pensions;

(b) the total amount so paid in respect of other than pensions;

(c) the total number of pensioners;

(d) the total amount of absolutely forfeited instalments; and

(e) such other particulars as are prescribed.

49. The Governor may make such regulations as he thinks necessary for any purpose for which regulations are contemplated or required, and, generally, for carrying out the intention of this Act, and such regulations upon publication in the Gazette shall have the full force of law, and shall be laid before Parliament within fourteen days after making thereof if Parliament be then in session, and if not within fourteen days after the commencement of the then next ensuing session of Parliament.

50. A copy of this Act shall be posted, so as to be available for public information, at every bank at which instalments of pensions are payable under this Act, and a list containing the names of the pensioners whose instalments are paid at such bank shall be kept thereat.

51. This Act, in so far as it provides for the grant of pensions, shall not apply to—

(a) aliens;

(b) naturalised subjects, except such as have been naturalised for the period of ten years next preceding the date on which they make their pension-claims;

(c) Chinese or other Asiatics, whether naturalised or not; or

(d) aboriginal natives.

52. (1) Every pension granted under this Act shall be deemed to be granted, and shall be held subject to the provisions of any amending or repealing Act that may hereafter be passed; and no pensioner under this Act shall have any claim for compensation or otherwise by reason of his pension being affected by any such amending or repealing Act.

(2) A notification of the last preceding subsection shall be printed on every pension-certificate.

APPENDIX No. 6.

PAPER handed in by the *Chairman*.

COPY, communicated by the Secretary of the National Conference of Friendly Societies, of the Agenda and Resolutions relative to Old Age Pensions of the Conferences of March 1902 and March 1903.

I.—COPY OF SCHEME OF OLD AGE PENSIONS ADOPTED BY COMMITTEE OF THE NATIONAL CONFERENCE OF FRIENDLY SOCIETIES, 1902, FOR SUBMISSION TO THE SOCIETIES CONNECTED WITH THE CONFERENCE.

RESOLUTION OF NATIONAL CONFERENCE OF FRIENDLY SOCIETIES, 1902:—

"That this Conference, representing 2,750,000 of the members of Friendly Societies, are of opinion that it is the duty of the State to provide Old Age Pensions of not less than 5s. a week to all thrifty and deserving persons of 65 years of age and upwards who are unable to work, and are in need of the same; that such a Scheme shall not place any disability of citizenship upon the persons claiming the Pensions; the cost of the same shall be raised without any interference with the funds of Thrift Societies."

SUGGESTED LINES OF BILL TO CARRY OUT THE ABOVE RESOLUTION.

A person (male or female), while in the United Kingdom, shall be entitled to receive a Pension of Five Shillings per week under the following conditions:—

(1) That the applicant is not under 65 years of age.

(2) That the applicant is a British-born subject, or a British naturalised subject of not less than twenty-five years standing.

(3) That the applicant has not habitually received Poor Law relief, has not been convicted of felony within twenty-five years of age 65, has not been convicted of any offence of less gravity than felony within ten years of age 65, and is not leading an immoral life.

(4) That the applicant has, according to the judgment of the Pension Authority, endeavoured, to the best of his or her means or opportunities, to be provident by

(a) Membership in a registered Friendly Society (not being a dividing society) providing Sick, Funeral, or Superannuation, or other benefits, or

(b) A registered Building Society, or

(c) A registered Trade Union having funds kept separate for Sick, Funeral, or Superannuation, or other similar benefits, or

(d) A registered Co-operative Society, or

(e) By deposits in the Post Office Savings Bank or by the purchase of an Annuity through the same source, or

(f) A Savings Bank certified under the Act of 1863, or

(g) By becoming the owner of a house not exceeding £[illegible] in value.

(5) That Clause (4) shall only be modified or disregarded in cases where it is shown to the satisfaction of the Pension Authority that the lack of saving has been due either to continued sickness or disablement, or other exceptional misfortune, or to expenditure upon the education and improvement of applicant's children.

(6) That the applicant is unable to follow his or her usual occupation (excepting females carrying on their ordinary household duties), and is not able to follow or obtain any other employment calculated to produce more than ten shillings per week.

(7) That no Pension be paid to a person whose income is equal to more than ten shillings per week from all sources, or to persons whose joint income as man and wife is equal to more than fifteen shillings per week, subject in all cases to clauses (8) and (9).

(8) That in calculating the weekly income under clause (7) the Pension Authority shall not take into account any sum not exceeding five shillings per week from Registered Friendly Societies or Registered Trade Unions.

(9) That on the Pension Authority being satisfied an Applicant, or a Pensioner, under this Scheme has disposed at any time of any interest or property with intent to defeat the provisions of this Scheme, no claim shall be allowed or the Pension continued, notwithstanding the circumstances of the applicant at age 65 or upwards.

(10) That if a Pensioner under this Scheme receives Poor Law relief (except outdoor medical relief) his or her Pension shall cease, but may be renewed at the discretion of the Pension Authority when Poor Law relief ceases.

(11) That every Pension shall be reviewed every two years by the Pension Authority, but this shall not take away the right of the Pension Authority to review the Pension at any time, provided they have evidence satisfactory to themselves that the Pensioner's income from other sources exceeds the limit laid down in Clause (7).

(12) That where a child or children of a Pensioner are proved to the satisfaction of the Pension Authority to be in good circumstances, they may be called upon to repay the whole or part of the Pension to the Pension Authority at the request of the Pension Authority or upon the order of a Court of Summary Jurisdiction, but this Clause shall not in any way invalidate the rights of the Pensioner as to claiming and receiving the Pension, provided he or she is eligible in all other respects under this scheme.

(13) That for the purposes of any law of settlement, an applicant fulfilling the necessary conditions of this scheme shall be deemed to be eligible to apply to, and receive a Pension from, any Pension Authority provided he or she has resided for not less than five consecutive years prior to age 65 within the area of such Pension Authority; and for the purposes of this scheme the place of residence of the applicant for the said period shall determine the area in which the Pension shall become payable.

(14) That under special conditions a Pensioner may change from one area to another with the consent of the then existing Pension Authority, and the Pension Authority of the new area shall then become liable to continue the Pension subject to the general conditions of the scheme.

(15) That every Pension shall be payable weekly or monthly at the discretion of the Pension Authority, through the office or offices of such authority.

(16) That no person receiving a Pension under this scheme shall thereby forfeit the right of voting in Parliamentary or any election in which he or she would otherwise be entitled to vote.

(17) That in order to claim a Pension the applicant shall fill up and sign a form giving all particulars required (to be vouched for as far as possible by three ratepayers, not being relatives), and the form to be adopted on the lines of this Scheme shall be added, with such other documents as may be necessary, as a schedule to the Bill, provision to be made for penalties in case of an attempt to defraud the public revenue through the application, or during the time a Pension is paid.

(18) That with the application for a Pension the applicant shall forward a certificate of birth, to be provided by the Registrar of Births and Deaths at a cost to the applicant of a sum not exceeding one shilling in place of all fees or payments otherwise payable in respect thereof, but where the Pension Authority are satisfied such certificate is not procurable they shall accept other evidence of age.

(19) That as far as possible inquiries as to applicants shall be made through employers, fellow workpeople, and officers of institutions with which the applicant may be, or may have been, connected.

(20) That in the event of an applicant desiring to appeal against a refusal of the Pension Authority to grant a Pension, such appeal shall be only to the nearest County Court, the decision of the County Court Judge to be final and binding, and the County Court Judge shall have power to charge costs against either the Pension Authority or the applicant.

(21) That no assignment of, or charge upon, a Pension shall be valid, and in the case of bankruptcy of the Pensioner the Pension shall not pass to any Trustee or other person acting on behalf of the creditors.

(22) That the Registrars of Births and Deaths shall give information periodically of the deaths of all persons aged 65 and upwards to the Pension Authority or Authorities in each district.

(23) That neither Parliament, nor any authority constituted by Parliament, shall interfere in any way with the funds or arrangement of any Friendly Society or other thrift institution in the providing of Pensions under this scheme.

(24) That the cost of providing Pensions under this scheme, excluding cost of local administration, shall be met by the Imperial Treasury.

(25) That the Rural District, Urban District, and Borough Councils shall appoint the Pension Authorities subject to the following conditions:—

(*a*) Each Authority shall be elected annually, and shall consist of ten persons appointed by the Council, six of them to be elected from the Council, two from Local Branches of Friendly Societies, and two from Local Branches of Trade Unions or other Thrift Institutions.

(*b*) Where the Council are unable to secure the four, or any of the four, representatives outside their own body, then the whole ten, or as many as may be needed to make up the ten, shall be elected from the Council.

(*c*) The decisions of the Pension Authority shall not be reviewed by the Council or any other body except as provided in clause (20).

(26) That for the purposes of this Scheme, the Rural District, Urban District, and Borough Councils shall be held liable, in the first instance, for payment of the pensions, the amounts expended in Pensions to be repaid annually by the Imperial Treasury to the Local Authorities, but the expenses of local administration shall be borne ordinarily by the said Local Authorities.

19 December 1902.

II.—COPY OF LETTER ADDRESSED BY THE SECRETARY OF THE NATIONAL CONFERENCE OF FRIENDLY SOCIETIES, 1902, TO THE SOCIETIES CONNECTED WITH THE CONFERENCE IN SUBMITTING THE ABOVE SCHEME OF OLD AGE PENSIONS.

119, Stockport Road,
Manchester,
January, 1903.

My Dear Sir,

I beg to hand you a copy of the Scheme drafted by a Sub-Committee of the Conference, in connection with the subject of Old Age Pensions, and in support of the 10th and 16th Resolutions of the National Conference of Friendly Societies, held on the 10th and 11th of March last, at the Co-operative Hall, Manchester.

16. Resolved: "That this Conference, representing 3½ millions of the members of Friendly Societies, are of opinion that it is the duty of the State to provide Old Age Pensions of not less than 5s. per week to all thrifty and deserving persons of 65 years of age and upwards who are unable to work and are in need of same; that such a scheme shall not place any disability of citizenship upon the persons claiming the pension, the cost of the same shall be raised without any interference with the funds of Thrift Societies, but that no particular scheme shall be regarded as the scheme of the Conference until it has been laid before the Delegate Meetings of the various Societies affiliated with the Conference for approval or otherwise, and until the scheme has been finally submitted to a Special Meeting of the Conference, to be held as early as possible after the holding of such Delegate Meetings in the present year."

18. Resolved: "That it be an instruction to the incoming Committee to prepare a scheme of State, or State-aided Pensions, and submit the same to the Societies for their approval or otherwise, and report to a Special Meeting of the National Conference."

The scheme was laid before the Committee of the Conference on Friday, December [illegible], when the following Resolution was passed with two dissentients:—

Resolved: "That the Old Age Pensions scheme presented by the Sub-Committee as now amended, be accepted for presentation to the Friendly Societies for their consideration, in accordance with the Resolutions of the last Conference, and that this submission must only be regarded as discharging the directions of the Conference in this matter."

"I have to request you, in conformity with the preceding Resolutions, to place the enclosed Scheme before the Delegate Meeting of your Society, in order that the question may be discussed at a Special Meeting of the Conference, to be held probably in the month of August. The Scheme, therefore, will not be submitted to the Ordinary Meeting of the Conference in March next.

I remain, yours very truly,
J. E. CLEVELAND,
Secretary to the Conference.

III.—COPY OF RESOLUTION OF THE NATIONAL CONFERENCE OF FRIENDLY SOCIETIES HELD AT CHESTER, MARCH [illegible], 1903.

"Resolved: That a Special Meeting of the Conference be held in Brighton, on Tuesday, October 13th, 1903, to consider the Reports of the several Societies with respect to the question of Old Age Pensions."

APPENDIX, No. 9.

PAPER handed in by the Chairman.

(I.) COPY OF THE AGED PENSIONERS BILL, 1903.

MEMORANDUM.

A.D. 1903.

This Bill proposes to provide pensions for the aged deserving poor, through the existing machinery of the poor law administration, by empowering the pensions committee of the guardians, with the help of Parliament, to grant pensions which shall not involve any electoral disability, nor convey the reproach of pauperism. The Bill is framed on the reports of the Select Committee on "Aged Deserving Poor," 1899, and of the Select Committee on "The Cottage Homes Bill" of the same year.

A BILL TO PROVIDE PENSIONS FOR THE AGED DESERVING POOR.

BE it enacted by the King's most Excellent Majesty, by and with the advice and consent of the Lords Spiritual and Temporal, and Commons, in this present Parliament assembled, and by the authority of the same, as follows:

Pension authority.

1.—(1) The board of guardians in every poor law union shall forthwith after the commencement of this Act, and not later than the seventh day of May in every subsequent year, appoint a committee to administer this Act, and such committee shall be known as the pensions committee. The clerk to the guardians shall act as clerk to such committee, and shall perform the various duties herein after prescribed.

(2) At least two-thirds of the pensions committee shall be members of the board of guardians, but the board may appoint any number not exceeding one-third of such committee from persons selected on account of their special fitness for the work: Provided that the total number of the pension committee shall not exceed one-half of the number of the board appointing.

Amount of pension.

2.—(1) A pensioners' list shall, in every poor law union, be prepared by the pensions committee as hereinafter provided, and every person whose name appears on any such list shall be called an aged pensioner.

(2) An aged pensioner shall be entitled to an old age pension of not less than five shillings or more than seven shillings each week.

(3) An aged pensioner who elects to live in the workhouse, or special cottage homes, or other suitable place provided by the guardians, shall be classified as such, and receive special consideration and treatment, to the satisfaction of the Local Government Board, in lieu of an old-age pension.

Pension age.

3. Any person of the age of sixty-five years or upwards may make application to the pensions committee of the poor law union in which he or she resides, to have his or her name placed on the "pensioners" list, and such application shall be considered and decided by the pensions committee at such meetings, and subject to such conditions and qualifications and right of appeal as are herein-after prescribed.

Mode of application.

4. The pensions committee of every poor law union shall cause to be prepared at least once in every three months for each parish in such poor law union an applicants' list, in which shall be shown the name, age, and place of residence of every person of the age of sixty-five years or upwards who, being resident in such parish, has applied for an old-age pension. The applicants' list shall be divided into two parts:—

(1.) The first part shall contain the names of such applicants as have not been in receipt of poor law relief at any time during the twelve months immediately preceding the fifteenth day of July next previous:

(2.) The second part shall contain the names of such applicants as have been in receipt of such relief, distinguishing the name of any man who might otherwise be qualified to be registered as a parliamentary voter.

Regulations as to procedure.

5. The pensions committee shall cause each applicants' list, within four weeks after the completion of such list, to be submitted to them for examination and revision at a special meeting. Six days' notice in writing of the purpose and date of each special meeting shall, together with a copy of the applicants' list, be sent to each member of the pensions committee by the clerk.

Examination and revision of applicants' lists and qualifications of pensioners.

6.—(1) The pensions committee at each special meeting shall examine and revise the applicants' list.

(2) In every case where the pensions committee are not satisfied that a person whose name appears in the applicants' list:—

(a) Is a British subject:

(c) Has not within the last twenty years been convicted of an offence and sentenced to penal servitude or imprisonment without the option of a fine;

(d) Has not received poor law relief, other than medical relief, unless under circumstances of a wholly exceptional character, during twenty years prior to the application for a pension;

(e) Is resident within the district of the pension authority;

(f) Has not an income from any source of more than—

(1) In the case of a single person ten shillings a week;

(2) In the case of a married couple fifteen shillings a week together;

(g) Has endeavoured to the best of his ability, by his industry or by the exercise of reasonable providence, to make provision for himself and those immediately dependent on him

they shall strike out from the applicants' list the name of such person.

(2) The clerk to the pensions committee shall give notice in writing to any person whose name shall be struck out as aforesaid, and every such person shall be entitled to attend and be heard respecting his case at the next special meeting of the pensions committee, and shall be so informed in the said notice. The decision of the pensions committee at such meeting shall be final.

7.—(1) The applicants' list, to be first prepared after the commencement of this Act, shall, after the completion of its examination and revision by the pensions committee, be signed by the presiding chairman and countersigned by the clerk to the pensions committee, and shall then become the pensioners' list. Pensioners' list.

(2) Each applicants' list subsequently prepared shall, after the completion of its examination and revision by the pensions committee, be signed by the presiding chairman and countersigned by the clerk to the pensions committee, and shall then, together with any existing pensioners' list, become the pensioners' list.

(3) The pensioners' list shall, not later than the twenty-sixth day of July, be sent by the clerk to the guardians to the overseers of the poor of the parish to which the list refers.

(4) Subject to the provisions of this Act and of any Order in Council under the Registration of Electors Acts and this Act, the overseers shall, as regards the publication of and subsequent dealing with the pensioners' list, proceed as nearly as may be, as in the case of the list of Parliamentary occupation electors.

(5) The overseers, when attending the court to be holden by the revising barrister for the revision of the lists of electors for their parish, shall produce and deliver the pensioners' lists to the revising barrister.

8. Where on any representation it appears to the Local Government Board that the combination of two or more unions for the purposes of this Act would tend to diminish expense, or would otherwise be of public or local advantage, the Board may make an order for combining such unions for the purposes of this Act and for constituting for the execution of such purposes a joint committee of the guardians of each of the combined unions, and the powers conferred by this Act shall be vested in such joint committee. Before making an order in pursuance of this section the Board shall satisfy themselves that the financial position, rateable value, and other circumstances of every union to be included in a combination are such as to render the combination of advantage for the equalisation of the burden of the charge in respect of old-age pensions, and any order to be made in pursuance of this section may include all such provisions as in the opinion of the Board are necessary or desirable for such equalisation. Combination of unions.

9. A person whose name is on the pensioners' list shall not be deprived of any right to be registered as a parliamentary or county voter by reason only of the fact that he or she has been in receipt of poor law relief; but such person shall not be entitled to vote at any election for the poor law guardians or for a district councillor in a rural district. Removal of electoral disabilities.

10. It shall be lawful for His Majesty the King, by Order in Council, from time to time to alter the instructions, precepts, orders, and forms under the Registration of Electors Acts, and to vary or modify the provisions of those Acts in such manner as appears to His Majesty necessary for carrying this Act into effect. Alteration of instructions, &c.

11. Every pension to which an aged pensioner becomes entitled under this Act shall be payable at a money order office out of moneys to be provided by the board of guardians of the poor law union in which he or she resides, in accordance with rules to be approved by the Local Government Board and the Postmaster General. Payment of pension.

12. The Treasury, on the certificate of the Local Government Board, shall pay to the guardians of every poor law union out of moneys to be voted by Parliament, a sum at the rate of six pounds per annum for every aged pensioner within such poor law union. Treasury contribution.

13. An old age pension under this Act shall be inalienable, whether by way of assignment, charge, execution, bankruptcy, or otherwise, and any agreement to assign, charge, anticipate, or otherwise deal with a pension shall be null and void. Pension to be inalienable.

14. Any person who, by means of any wilfully false statement or representation, obtains or attempts to obtain an old age pension under this Act, or the payment of any instalment of such a pension, shall be liable, on conviction by a court of summary jurisdiction, to imprisonment with or without hard labour for a term not exceeding six months. Offences.

15. The pensions committee shall, at least once in each year, at a special meeting, revise the pensioners' list, and remove therefrom the names of such persons as may have died or become disqualified for a pension under section five of this Act. Revision of pension.

16. This Act shall not extend to Scotland. Extent of Act.

17. This Act may be cited as the Aged Pensioners Act, 1903. Short title.

(3.) COPY OF THE OLD-AGE PENSIONS BILL, 1903.

A BILL TO PROVIDE PENSIONS FOR PERSONS OVER SIXTY-FIVE YEARS OF AGE.

BE it enacted by the King's most Excellent Majesty, by and with the advice and consent of the Lords Spiritual and Temporal, and Commons, in this present Parliament assembled, and by the authority of the same, as follows:—

1. On and after the appointed day every person of the age of sixty-five years or upwards shall, subject to the provisions of this Act, be entitled to a pension of thirteen pounds a year, to be paid to him in instalments of five shillings each week, as hereinafter provided, during his life.

2. No such person shall be entitled to a pension under this Act unless—

(1) He is a British subject;

(2) He is residing in the United Kingdom on the dates when he claims and when he establishes his claim to a pension, and has been residing therein continuously for not less than twenty years immediately preceding the date when he makes his claim;

(3) He has not, within five years of claiming a pension, been guilty of such misconduct as would, if committed after the claim is established, cause the pension to be forfeited:

Provided that continuous residence in the United Kingdom shall not be deemed to have been interrupted by occasional absence therefrom, unless the total period of such absence exceeds three years, and unless such absence shall have occurred during the five years immediately preceding the date at which the claim is made; nor in the case of a seaman or other person serving on board a vessel trading to and from the United Kingdom, if he proves that during such absence his family or place of residence was in the United Kingdom.

3.—(1) A person claiming a pension shall make his claim (in this Act called a pension claim) in person to the Registrar of births, marriages, and deaths of the district in which the person claiming resides, and in the form, and with the particulars prescribed, and shall personally deliver such claim to the Registrar. If the Registrar requires, the person claiming shall make a statutory declaration that the pension claim is true in every material particular, and shall deliver such declaration to the Registrar.

(2) Any statutory declaration for the purposes of this section shall not be liable to stamp duty.

4. The Registrar shall record the claim in the prescribed manner in a book to be called the District Old-Age Pension Claim Register, which shall be open to inspection on payment of a fee of one shilling.

5. If the Registrar so require—

(1) The board of guardians of the union, or of any union within which the person claiming a pension has resided, shall furnish the Registrar, so far as possible, with such evidence as may determine the poor law settlement of the person claiming, and any expense thus incurred shall be payable out of the poor rate.

(2) The clerk of any parish shall supply certified copies of any entry in a parish register which may be necessary to establish the identity or age of the person claiming a pension.

6. The Registrar may put to the person claiming a pension any question necessary to test the validity of the claim, or the truth of any statement material thereto made by the claimant, and shall record the answers given.

7.—(1) The Registrar, after receiving and considering the pension claim and declaration, if any, and any other evidence, and after personally questioning the claimant, if he sees fit, shall send the whole of the documents, with his report thereupon, to the Superintendent Registrar, who shall decide whether the claim is established or not.

(2) The Superintendent Registrar shall fix a day for inquiry into the claim, not earlier than one week nor later than four weeks from the receipt of the claim and other documents from the Registrar, and shall give the prescribed notice of the day so fixed to the claimant, whom he may require to attend personally, to the clerk of the county council, and to the Treasury.

(3) The county council may, if they see fit, be represented at the inquiry.

(4) Where the Superintendent Registrar is satisfied that the documentary evidence in support of the claim is sufficient to establish it, or that by reason of physical disability, or other sufficient cause, the attendance of the claimant should be dispensed with, the Superintendent Registrar may notify the claimant that he need not personally attend the inquiry, but shall obtain from the claimant any further information, material to the claim in the opinion of the Superintendent Registrar, in such manner as he thinks fit.

(5) On the day so fixed, or the first convenient day thereafter, the Superintendent Registrar shall decide whether the claim is established, but if he is of opinion that further evidence is requisite to establish or to reject the claim, he may adjourn the inquiry for any period not exceeding one month.

(6) The claimant, or the county council, or the Treasury may appeal to the County Court Judge of the district, whose decision shall be final.

8. The Superintendent Registrar shall within three days of deciding on the claim send his decision in the form prescribed to the claimant, to the clerk of the council, and to the Treasury.

9.—(1) If the Superintendent Registrar admits the claim, and no appeal is lodged by the county council or the Treasury against such decision within one month of the date thereof, or, if any appeal is decided by the County Court Judge in favour of the claimant, then the Superintendent Registrar shall forthwith send the final decision to the Registrar.

(2) The Registrar on receiving the decision shall forthwith enter the name of the claimant in the form and with the particulars prescribed in a register, to be called the District Old-Age Pensions Register, and shall issue to the claimant (thereafter called the pensioner) a pension certificate book containing a certified

copy of the entry of his name in such register and of the number of such entry, and spaces for recording the successive weekly payments of the pension and other matters as may be prescribed.

(2) All entries of pension certificates in the Old-Age Pensions Register shall be numbered consecutively.

Transfer of pension certificates, duplicate and application.

10. On application in the prescribed form, and subject to the prescribed conditions :—

(1) Any pension certificate may be transferred from the register of a district from which the pensioner is moving to the register of any district to which he is changing his residence ;

(2) The Registrar shall issue to the pensioner a new pension certificate book when the spaces for the recording of payments in the first or any subsequent book are filled, and may issue a duplicate pension certificate book, where satisfactory proof is given that the loss of the original is not due to the fraud or wilful default of the pensioner, or of any person authorised, as herein-after provided, to receive payments of pension instalments on his behalf.

Payments of pension.

11.—(1) The pension shall be payable at a money order office to be named in the pension certificate book in instalments of five shillings each week on one of two specified days in each week, and upon the personal application of the pensioner, who shall produce the pension certificate book on the occasion of each payment. The postmaster shall stamp the date of each payment in the book as may be prescribed.

(2) The stamp of the money order office shall be deemed to be sufficient evidence that any payment has been made and duly received by the pensioner or any person appointed on that behalf under the provisions of section twelve of this Act.

Payment of pension to other persons.

12.—(1) If the Registrar is satisfied by the personal statement of the pensioner, supported, if required, by a certificate from the medical officer, or by other sufficient evidence, that the personal attendance of the pensioner is impossible, or likely to involve serious risk to his health, he may authorise any one person, being the wife or husband, or son or daughter, or other suitable person of full age, and named for this purpose by the pensioner, to apply personally on the pensioner's behalf for the payment of the pension. In any such case, the Registrar shall enter the name of such person either for a specified period or permanently in the pension certificate book in a prescribed form, and, thereupon, the pension instalments will be payable on the personal application of such person, who shall produce on each occasion the pension certificate book.

(2) If the Registrar is satisfied by sufficient evidence that, in any case, the pensioner, or any one appointed to receive the pension on his behalf, has been prevented from personally applying for the payment of any weekly instalment of the pension solely by illness or by other sufficient cause, he may issue a warrant for the payment of such instalment on the next following day for payment of the pension, but he may not issue two such warrants in respect of the same pensioner in the same year.

Pension to be inalienable.

13. A pension under this Act shall be inalienable whether by way of assignment, charge, execution, bankruptcy or otherwise, and any agreement to assign, charge, anticipate or otherwise deal with a pension shall be null and void.

Suspension of pension during maintenance at public cost.

14. A pension shall not be payable to a pensioner during such period as he may be maintained in any asylum, hospital, infirmary, inebriate reformatory, prison, or workhouse at the public expense, but in case of a pensioner in any such institution other than a prison, the whole or a portion of the pension, as the Local Government Board may direct, shall be paid to the local authority or other governing body of such institution, as the case may be, for and towards the maintenance of such pensioner.

Forfeiture of pension.

15. Any pensioner guilty of the following misconduct shall forfeit his pension :—

Crime (other than a political offence) for which he has been sentenced to penal servitude, or any term of imprisonment exceeding twelve months with hard labour.

Penalties.

16. Any person who by means of any wilfully false statement or representation obtains or attempts to obtain a pension certificate, or by any means obtains or attempts to obtain payment of any forfeited instalment of a pension, or by means of personation or other fraudulent representation obtains or attempts to obtain payment of any instalment of a pension, or by any wilfully false statement or representation aids or abets any person in attempting to obtain a pension certificate or payment of an instalment of a pension to which he is not entitled shall, on conviction by a court of summary jurisdiction, be liable to imprisonment with or without hard labour for a term not exceeding six months.

Court may cancel certificate.

17. In the case of any conviction under section sixteen of this Act, the court shall have power, by order, to cancel any pension certificate which is proved to have been fraudulently obtained.

Suspension of payment of pension by court.

18. If a pensioner is convicted of drunkenness or of any offence punishable by imprisonment of not less than one month with hard labour, then, in addition to any other penalty or punishment imposed, the court may, by order, direct that the pension instalments due to such pensioner shall not be paid to him for any period not exceeding two months, or may direct that the instalment for such period shall be paid to or applied on behalf of any dependants of the pensioner.

Revision of register and returns.

19. The Registrar shall, every three months, revise the District Old-Age Pensions Register, and shall at such times and in such form as may be requested by the Treasury make returns to the Treasury of the number of pensioners upon the register, with such particulars as to the names, ages, places of residence of such pensioners, the registered numbers of pension certificate books issued to them, and other matters relating thereto, as may from time to time be prescribed.

Funds from which pensions are to be paid.

20. The pensions provided under this Act shall be paid as regards two-thirds of the total amount thereof in any year out of the Consolidated Fund of the United Kingdom, and as regards one-third thereof out of the Exchequer Contribution Account of each county, which account shall be from time to time supplemented as may be necessary from the Local Taxation Fund.

Rules and forms to be laid down by the Local Government Board.

21.—(1) The Local Government Board shall, within three months from the passing of this Act, make such rules as in their opinion are necessary for the proper carrying out of this Act by the registrars, superintendent registrars, postmasters, and other officials concerned, and shall prescribe the forms and terms of claims, declarations, pension certificates, pension books, district registers, and all other matters necessary for the identification of pensioners, and the regular payment of pensions, and shall fix the scale of fees for all officials concerned.

(2) The Local Government Board shall prescribe the form of accounts to be kept for the purposes of this Act, and shall make rules as to the audit of such accounts.

Medical officer. 22. Unless the Local Government Board appoint some other qualified practitioner for the purpose, the medical officer of the district shall issue any certificates which may be called for under this Act, and the fee charged for such certificate shall be such as would be charged if such certificate were issued under the provisions of the Workmen's Compensation Act, 1897.

Provision and regulation of funds for payments. 23. The Local Government Board shall, with the assistance of the Treasury and the Postmaster-General, determine all matters necessary for the provision of moneys requisite for the commencement and the regular carrying out of the payments of pensions on and after the appointed day.

Appointed day. 24. The Local Government Board shall, with the assistance of the Treasury and the Postmaster-General, fix a day on and after which claims for pensions under this Act may be made, and the provisions of this Act for payment of pensions come into operation, which day shall be called the appointed day: Provided that such day shall not be later than twelve months from the commencement of this Act.

Commencement of Act. 25. This Act shall commence on the first day of January one thousand nine hundred and four.

Short title. 26. This Act may be cited as the Old-Age Pensions Act, [illegible].

(b.) COPY OF THE AGED PENSIONERS (No. 2) BILL, [illegible].

MEMORANDUM.

The object of the Bill is to provide pensions for the aged deserving poor. The main outlines of the Bill follow the recommendations of the Chaplin Committee's Report.

The chief modifications are:—

(1.) The pensions authority is constructed of representatives of the local authority, the board of guardians, and the local friendly societies in equal proportions respectively.

(2) The total state contribution is limited to the sum of £[illegible] annually, to be apportioned by the Local Government Board, a like amount being obtainable from the local rates.

A.D. [illegible].

A BILL TO PROVIDE PENSIONS FOR THE AGED DESERVING POOR.

BE it enacted by the King's most Excellent Majesty, by and with the advice and consent of the Lords Spiritual and Temporal, and Commons, in this present Parliament assembled, and by the authority of the same, as follows:—

Pension authority. 1. Every county council and every county borough council shall forthwith after the commencement of this Act, and not later than one month before the close of every financial year, cause arrangements to be made for the election of a pensions committee, or pensions committees, within the area of their administration.

Area of pension committee. 2. In every county borough there shall be one pensions committee only, but in a county there shall be a pensions committee for the administrative area of every urban district and rural district council in the county.

Members of committee. 3. The pensions committee shall consist of a chairman and such number of members as may be determined, who shall be elected annually, and a clerk, who shall be appointed by the committee.

Chairman of committee. 4. The chairman of the pensions committee shall be appointed from outside the members of the committee, in a county borough area by the council of the county borough, and in an urban and rural district area by the council of the county.

Number of members of committee. 5. The number of members of the committee shall be determined in a county borough area by the council of the county borough, and in an urban or rural district area by the council of the county, but shall in all cases consist of three or a multiple of three.

Taking of office of committee. 6. The number of members shall be fixed at least one month previous to the assembling of each year's new committee, and such new committee shall take office on the first day of the Local Government Board year.

Committee, how constituted. 7. The members of the pensions committee shall consist of persons nominated, as to one-third by the council of the local county borough, urban or rural district area, as to one-third by the local board of guardians, and as to one-third by the local members of registered friendly societies.

Meaning of "local" council. (1) In this section the expression "local" as applied to county borough, urban or district council shall mean the council within the area of whose administration the pensions committee sits:

Meaning of local board of guardians. (2) In this section the expression "local board of guardians" means that board of guardians having the greatest rateable value within the area of administration of a local council:

Meaning of local members of registered friendly societies. (3) In this section the expression "local members of registered friendly societies" means the members of all registered friendly societies paying sick and funeral allowances and keeping an entirely separate sick and funeral fund, such members being resident within the area of administration of the local council.

Overlapping boards of guardians. 8. Notwithstanding anything in section seven subsection (2) of this Act, where two or more boards of guardians exercise jurisdiction within the area of a local council, in a county the county council, and in a county borough the county borough council shall determine if one board of guardians only is entitled to nominate members of the pensions committee, or if more than one board is so entitled; and if more than one in what proportions such boards shall nominate.

9. The Registrar of Friendly Societies shall within six months of the passing of this Act prepare a scheme by means of which the local members of friendly societies shall be able to select among themselves their allotted number of members of the pension committee, and in preparing such scheme the Registrar shall take into consideration any suggestions which may be put before him by the responsible officials of any registered friendly society. — *Scheme for friendly societies nominations.*

10. All the administrative expenses of the pension committee, including the salary of the clerk, which shall be fixed by the local council, shall be paid by the local council, and the offices of the pension committee shall be at the offices of the local council. — *Expenses of committee.*

11. A pensioners' list shall be prepared by the pension committee as hereinafter provided, and every person whose name appears on any such list shall be called an aged pensioner. — *Pensioners' list.*

12. An aged pensioner shall be entitled, if the funds allowed under this Act are sufficient, to an old-age pension of not less than five nor more than seven shillings per week. — *Amount of pension.*

13. Any person of the age of sixty-five years or upwards may make application to the pension committee of the area in which he or she resides, to have his or her name placed on the pensioners' list, and such application shall be examined and decided by the pension committee at such meetings, and subject to such conditions and qualifications as are prescribed by this Act. — *Age of pensioners.*

14. Every application for a place on the pensioners' list must be made in writing to the clerk of the pension committee, either by the applicant or by some person authorised by him or her, and such application shall be countersigned by two ratepayers residing within the area of the pension committee. — *Application by pensioner to be made in writing.*

15. The names of all applicants shall be reviewed by the pension committee at a special meeting to be held not less than two months nor more than three months previous to the expiration of their year of office, and all such persons who cannot satisfy the committee that they conform to the following requirements, shall have their names removed from the list— — *Qualifications of pensioner.*

(a) That they are British subjects of European descent:

(b) That their age is sixty-five years or upwards:

(c) That they have not within the last twenty years been convicted of an offence and sentenced to penal servitude, or imprisonment without the option of a fine:

(d) That they have not received poor law relief, other than medical relief, unless under circumstances of a wholly exceptional character, during twenty years prior to the application for a pension:

(e) That they are resident within the area of the pension committee:

(f) That they have not an income from any source of more than ten shillings per week, or that they are not possessed of any property which, if converted into cash and laid out in an annuity, would produce a greater sum than thirty pounds per annum:

(g) That they have not disposed of any appreciable amount of their property otherwise than for valuable consideration during the five years previous to their application to be placed on the list of pensioners:

(h) That they have endeavoured to the best of their ability, by their industry or by the exercise of reasonable providence, to make provision for themselves and for those immediately dependent on them.

16. The Treasury shall pay to the Local Government Board, for the purposes of this Act, the sum of two million pounds sterling per annum, and the Local Government Board shall distribute such portions of this sum among the various pension committees as the Local Government Board shall deem equitable after taking area and population into consideration. — *Treasury grant of two millions.*

17. A local council may grant to a pension committee, out of the rates, any sum not exceeding the amount allotted to such committee out of the Treasury grant. — *Local grant not to exceed Treasury contribution.*

18. On ascertaining the amount of money at their disposal the pension committee shall proceed to award pensions to such applicants as may be selected from the list; and of such amounts as the funds provided allow; but all pensions, though renewable, are to be granted for one year only. — *Granting of pensions.*

19. An old-age pension under this Act shall be inalienable, whether by way of assignment, charge execution, bankruptcy, or otherwise, and any agreement to assign, charge, anticipate, or otherwise deal with a pension shall be null and void. — *Pensions inalienable.*

20. A person who is in receipt of an old age pension shall not be deprived of the right to be registered as a parliamentary elector, but such person shall not be entitled to vote at any election for the poor law guardians, or for a councillor in a county borough, urban or rural district. — *Pensioners may vote in parliamentary, but not in local, elections.*

21. Every old-age pension to which a person becomes entitled under this Act shall be payable at a money order office out of moneys to be provided by the pension committee of the district in which the pensioner resides, in accordance with rules to be approved by the Local Government Board and the Postmaster-General. — *Pension payable at money order office.*

22. This Act shall extend only to the kingdom of England and Wales. — *Extent of Act.*

23. This Act may be cited as the Aged Pensioners Act, 1903, and shall come into force on the first day of the Local Government Board year falling in the year one thousand nine hundred and four. — *Short title and time of coming into operation.*

(4.) COPY OF THE COTTAGE HOMES BILL, 190[illegible].

A.D. 190[illegible].

A BILL TO AUTHORISE THE PROVISION OF COTTAGE HOMES FOR THE AGED DESERVING POOR.

Be it enacted by the King's most Excellent Majesty, by and with the advice and consent of the Lords Spiritual and Temporal, and Commons, in this present Parliament assembled, and by the authority of the same, as follows:—

Short title. 1. This Act may be cited as the Cottage Homes Act, 190[illegible].

Power to provide cottage homes. 2. A board of guardians may, with the consent of the county council, from and after the appointed day provide and maintain a cottage or cottages or a suitable house or houses (in this Act referred to as cottage homes) for the use of the necessitous deserving aged poor who have arrived at the age of sixty-five years, under such regulations as shall be approved by the county council.

Application for admission to cottage homes. 3. Any person wishing to reside in a cottage home shall apply to the guardian or overseer of the parish, and the board shall consider the application as soon as possible, and shall, if they are of opinion that the applicant is at least sixty-five years of age and necessitous, and has lived an industrious and deserving life, and that there is room in the home, order such applicant to be admitted to the home.

Powers of county council as to inspection and approval. 4. No such home shall be opened as such until the county council shall have inspected such home and signified their approval of the same in such way as they may direct, and all such homes shall be under the inspection of the county council, who may at any time after three months' notice withdraw their approval of such home or homes, or order such alterations in structure or management as they may think fit, and may enforce the same by withholding the whole or a portion of the county contribution.

Powers of county council as to classification. 5. The county council may direct, whenever in their opinion the number of deserving applicants for admission is sufficient, that separate homes shall be provided for the aged men and aged women, or such further classification as they may think fit.

Treatment of inmates. 6. The inmates of a home shall, so far as possible, be treated with regard to food and other comforts with suitable consideration, but if any inmate prove by bad conduct undeserving or unfit for a home, such person may be discharged by order of the board of guardians.

Inmates not subject to paupers' disabilities. 7. No person admitted to a home shall be considered a pauper or be subject to any such disabilities as persons in receipt of parochial relief.

Contribution by county councils to expenses. 8. The county council shall pay to the board of guardians in charge of a home within their county three-fourths of the cost of maintaining such home out of the general county rate, the county council being hereby empowered to satisfy themselves in such way as they may deem necessary as to the proper expenditure of the money; and the county council shall supply the boards in charge of the homes within their county with sufficient funds to provide, furnish, and fit up the homes subject to their approval, and a county council may for such purposes borrow in manner provided by the Local Government Act, 18[illegible], such sums as may be required.

Case of county boroughs. 9. The council of a county borough shall for the purposes of this Act be in the same position as the council of a county, except that all the expenditure shall be defrayed out of the borough fund or rate, or in the case of capital expenditure out of moneys borrowed on the security thereof; and the council of a county borough may for the purposes of such expenditure borrow, in manner provided by section one hundred and six of the Municipal Corporations Act, 18[illegible], such sums as may be required.

Power to utilise almshouses. 10. In any borough, urban district, or parish where there is an almshouse for the reception of the poor, the council of such borough, district, or parish, and the trustees or other governing body of the almshouse may enter into and carry into effect agreements and arrangements for the adaptation and use of any part of such almshouse as a cottage home, subject to and in accordance with the provisions of this Act, and for the contribution by the council of such annual sum as may be agreed towards the expenses of carrying this section into effect.

Treasury grants. 11. The Treasury shall pay to the council of every county and county borough out of moneys voted by Parliament a sum equal to five pounds per annum for every aged person to whose maintenance such council has contributed.

Appointed day. 12. This Act shall come into force from and after the thirty-first day of March one thousand nine hundred and four, which date is in this Act referred to as the appointed day.

APPENDIX, No. 10.

PAPER handed in by the Chairman.

COPY of REPLIES and RETURNS received (through the Local Government Board, the Secretary for Scotland's Office, and the Local Government Board, Ireland) from certain typical Boards of Guardians in *England* and *Wales* and in *Ireland*, and certain similar Poor Law Authorities in *Scotland*, who were asked to enumerate how many Inmates of their respective Workhouses (over 65 years of age) would be fit and able to live outside with Relatives or Friends, if they had Pensions of from 5s. to 7s. a week.

I.—ENGLAND AND WALES.

STATEMENT showing, according to Returns furnished to the Local Government Board, what number of Aged Paupers over 65 years of age in certain Workhouses (excluding those who, in the opinion of the Workhouse Medical Officers, could not satisfactorily take care of themselves owing to mental or physical infirmity) would be able to live outside the Workhouse with Relatives having suitable accommodation for them, if each had a Pension of from 5s. to 7s. per week, and how many of these would wish to do so.

DIVISION I.

Unions where the necessary inquiries were made of the Relatives of the Inmates referred to in Columns 3 to 6 of the Statement.

UNION OR PARISH.	Total Number of Inmates over 65.		Number complying with above Conditions.				
			Single, Widowed, or with a Husband or Wife not in the Workhouse.		Married Couples.		Total of Columns 3, 4, 5, and 6.
	Male. 1.	Female. 2.	Male. 3.	Female. 4.	Male. 5.	Female. 6.	
Aston Union	247	182	24	27	1	1	53*
	Number who would wish to live outside on the terms mentioned.		24	27	1	1	53*
Bradford Union (Yorks.)	155	135	5	16	—	—	21
	Number who would wish to live outside on the terms mentioned.		5	16	—	—	21
Cardiff Union	204	120	5	—	—	—	5
	Number who would wish to live outside on the terms mentioned.		5	—	—	—	5
[illegible] Union	40	21	5	1	—	—	6
	Number who would wish to live outside on the terms mentioned.		6	—	—	—	6

DIVISION I.—continued.

Unions where the necessary Inquiries were made of the Relatives of the Inmates referred to, &c.—continued.

Union or Parish.	Total Number of Inmates over 65.		Number complying with above Conditions.				
			Single, Widowed, or with a Husband or Wife not in the Workhouse.		Married Couples.		Total of Columns 3, 4, 5, and 6.
	Male.	Female.	Male.	Female.	Male.	Female.	
	1.	2.	3.	4.	5.	6.	
Gateshead Union	[illegible]	[illegible]	2	9	—	—	[illegible]
	Number who would wish to live outside on the terms mentioned.		3	2	—	—	6
Headington Union	55	47	—	1	—	—	1
	Number who would wish to live outside on the terms mentioned.		—	1	—	—	1
Manchester Township	[illegible]	[illegible]	4	11	—	—	[illegible]
	Number who would wish to live outside on the terms mentioned.		7	11	—	—	[illegible]
Kilton Union	[illegible]	84	6	7	—	—	[illegible]
	Number who would wish to live outside on the terms mentioned.		4	5	—	—	[illegible]
Wakefield Union	67	[illegible]	1	6	—	—	[illegible]
	Number who would wish to live outside on the terms mentioned.		1	9	—	—	[illegible]
West Bromwich Union	[illegible]	[illegible]	—	—	—	—	[illegible]
	Number who would wish to live outside on the terms mentioned.		—	—	—	—	[illegible]

DIVISION II.

Unions where Inquiries were made of the Inmates referred to in Columns 3 to 6 of the Statement, but not of their Relatives.

Union or Parish.	Total Number of Inmates over 65.		Number complying with above Conditions.				
			Single, Widowed, or with a Husband or Wife not in the Workhouse.		Married Couples.		Total of Columns 3, 4, 5, and 6.
	Male.	Female.	Male.	Female.	Male.	Female.	
	1.	2.	3.	4.	5.	6.	
Burton-upon-Trent Union	[illegible]	[illegible]	10	3	—	—	[illegible]
	Number who would wish to live outside on the terms mentioned.		[illegible]	9	—	—	[illegible]
Chester Union	[illegible]	47	4	5	[illegible]	[illegible]	[illegible]
	Number who would wish to live outside on the terms mentioned.		4	3	—	—	1

Unions where Inquiries were made of the Inmates referred to, &c.—continued.

Union or Parish.	Total Number of Inmates over 65.		Number complying with above conditions.				
			Single, Widowed, or with a Husband or Wife not in the Workhouse.		Married Couples.		Total of Columns 3, 4, 5, and 6.
	Male.	Female.	Male.	Female.	Male.	Female.	
	1.	2.	3.	4.	5.	6.	
Newcastle-on-Tyne Union	716	[illegible]	41	[illegible]	—	—	[illegible]
	Number who would wish to live outside on the terms mentioned.		41	[illegible]	—	—	[illegible]
Newport (Monmouth) Union	167	[illegible]	47	[illegible]	8	8	[illegible]
	Number who would wish to live outside on the terms mentioned.		[illegible]	4	[illegible]	[illegible]	[illegible]
Portsmouth Parish	[illegible]	[illegible]	46	[illegible]	6	3	94
	Number who would wish to live outside on the terms mentioned.		[illegible]	[illegible]	[illegible]	[illegible]	76
Sheffield Union	361	[illegible]	[illegible]	[illegible]	11	11	[illegible]
					includes four couples of whom one person only over 65 years old.		
	Number who would wish to live outside on the terms mentioned.		[illegible]	[illegible]	8	8	143
					includes three couples of whom one person only over 65 years old.		
St. Thomas Union	44	[illegible]	13	3	—	—	16
	Number who would wish to live outside on the terms mentioned.		13	3	—	—	16
Wells Union	[illegible]	10	[illegible]	[illegible]	1	1	[illegible]
	Number who would wish to live outside on the terms mentioned.		[illegible]	—	—	—	[illegible]
West Derby Union	443	[illegible]	79	44	4	4	[illegible]
	Number who would wish to live outside on the terms mentioned.		79	43	[illegible]	5	[illegible]

II.—SCOTLAND.

ABERDEEN.

Aberdeen Parish Council, Chambers, [illegible], Union Terrace, Aberdeen.
[illegible] October, [illegible].

Sir,

With reference to former correspondence, I am now to say that at a meeting of the Poorhouse Committee held here last night the sub-committee entrusted with the inquiry regarding the above reported as follows:—

"There are [illegible] males and [illegible] females = [illegible] inmates in the poorhouse, of [illegible] years of age and over, and after careful consideration of each case, it was found that there were [illegible] males and five females who might be tried to live with relatives if the Aged Pensioners Bill were passed, but the sub-committee were by no means sanguine that such an arrangement would be either satisfactory or permanent in any of the cases."

The report was approved of, and I was instructed to intimate to you accordingly.

I am, Sir, your obedient servant,

The Secretary, Local Government Board,
Edinburgh.

[illegible] Inspector.

DUNDEE.

EXCERPT from Minute of Meeting of the Sub-Committee of the Poorhouse Committee of the Dundee Combination, of date [illegible] November, [illegible]; Mr. [illegible], Convener, presiding.

In terms of remit to this Committee to investigate the number of aged inmates in the Poorhouse over [illegible] years of age who were mentally and physically fit to live outside an institution, and who have relatives and friends with whom they could live if they had pensions from [illegible] to [illegible] a week, the Committee beg to report to the House Committee that the Register of poorhouse inmates was gone over, and after due investigation the Committee found that on [illegible] September last the inmates of the poorhouse over [illegible] years of age numbered [illegible]; of these [illegible] were in the hospital under medical treatment; [illegible] had no known friends or relatives, and [illegible] had relatives.

The Committee further found that of the [illegible] who have known friends and relatives, [illegible] for various reasons were not suited for residence in private dwellings.

The Committee therefore beg to report that the persons over [illegible] years of age fit for residence outside an institution if suitable provision is made for them numbered [illegible], and they recommend that the Clerk be instructed to report to the Local Government Board accordingly.

[illegible], Convener.

EDINBURGH.

Edinburgh Parish Council, Chambers, Castle Terrace, Edinburgh.
[illegible] October, [illegible].

Sir,

With reference to yours of [illegible] August on the above subject, I now beg to state that the number of inmates in the poorhouses belonging to this Council, over [illegible] years of age, who are mentally and physically fit to live outside an institution, and who have relatives or friends with whom they could live if they had pensions of from [illegible] to [illegible] per week, are as follows:—

Craiglockhart Poorhouse	[illegible]
Craigleith Poorhouse	[illegible]

This has been arrived at by a personal interview with the paupers themselves and inquiry into each of their cases.

I am, Sir, your obedient servant,
[illegible].

G. [illegible]-Stewart, Esq.,
Secretary, Local Government Board,
Edinburgh.

GOVAN.

Govan Combination Parish Council, Chambers, 7, Carlton Place, Glasgow.
[illegible] August, [illegible].

Sir,

I beg to acknowledge receipt of your letter of [illegible] inst., "No. [illegible] Poor Law," enclosing copy of a letter from the Clerk to the Select Committee on the Aged Pensioners Bill to the Secretary for Scotland. On the [illegible] instant the population of the Govan Poorhouse was [illegible]. Of these [illegible] were over [illegible] years of age. Of the [illegible], [illegible] were men and [illegible] women. Of these, [illegible] men and [illegible] women required hospital treatment, leaving [illegible] men and [illegible] women in the ordinary wards of the poorhouse. Of the [illegible] men, [illegible] were between [illegible] and 70 years, [illegible] between 70 and [illegible] years, [illegible] between [illegible] and [illegible] years, and [illegible] between [illegible] and [illegible] years of age.

Of the [illegible] men, [illegible] were widowed, [illegible] had wives alive, and [illegible] were never married. Of the [illegible] who were widowed [illegible] had families and [illegible] had no families alive. Four of the married men had their wives also in the poorhouse, [illegible] being with them in the quarters specially provided for decent married couples. Of the [illegible] men, 7 were bedridden.

Of the [illegible] women in the ordinary wards, [illegible] were aged between [illegible] and 70 years, [illegible] between 70 and [illegible] years, [illegible] between [illegible] and [illegible] years, [illegible] between [illegible] and [illegible] years, and [illegible] between [illegible] and [illegible] years.

Of the [illegible] women, [illegible] were widows, [illegible] were married and [illegible] never had been married. Of the [illegible] widows, [illegible] had families, and [illegible] had no families living.

Two of the married women lived with their husbands in the married couples' quarters.

Of the [illegible] women, 10 were bedridden.

The single men and women and the widowed with no families have really no friends with whom they could reside. Of the widowed with families, a number of the inmates are of intemperate habits, and their families pay to get them kept in the poorhouse, while on the other hand it is the families who are intemperate and their parents cannot reside with them. In quite a number of cases the old persons stated frankly that it was owing to an incompatibility of temper as between sons-in-law or daughters-in-law, as the case might be, that kept them from residing with their families. In the winter, a good number who are at present able to move about, are confined to bed. On the whole, there are very few who are decent and able and have friends willing to allow them to reside with them, even if they had a pension of [illegible] or [illegible] a week.

I am, Sir, your obedient servant,
[illegible], Inspector.

The Secretary, Local Government Board,
Edinburgh.

GLASGOW

TABLE I

[illegible]

[illegible]	[illegible]
[illegible]	[illegible]

[illegible]

TABLE II.

[illegible]		[illegible]	[illegible]	[illegible]	[illegible]	[illegible]	[illegible]	[illegible]	[illegible]	[illegible]	[illegible]	[illegible]	[illegible]	[illegible]	[illegible]	[illegible]
[illegible]	[illegible]	[illegible]	[illegible]	[illegible]	[illegible]	[illegible]	[illegible]	[illegible]	[illegible]	[illegible]	[illegible]	[illegible]	[illegible]	[illegible]	[illegible]	[illegible]
	[illegible]	[illegible]	[illegible]	[illegible]	[illegible]	[illegible]	[illegible]	[illegible]	[illegible]	[illegible]	[illegible]	[illegible]	[illegible]	[illegible]	[illegible]	[illegible]
	[illegible]	[illegible]	[illegible]	[illegible]	[illegible]	[illegible]	[illegible]	[illegible]	[illegible]	[illegible]	[illegible]	[illegible]	[illegible]	[illegible]	[illegible]	[illegible]

[illegible]

[illegible]	[illegible]						[illegible]						[illegible]						[illegible]			[illegible]		
	[illegible]	[illegible]	[illegible]	[illegible]	[illegible]	[illegible]	[illegible]	[illegible]	[illegible]	[illegible]	[illegible]	[illegible]	[illegible]	[illegible]	[illegible]	[illegible]	[illegible]	[illegible]	[illegible]	[illegible]	[illegible]	[illegible]	[illegible]	[illegible]
[illegible]	[illegible]																							
[illegible]	[illegible]																							
[illegible]	[illegible]																							
[illegible]	[illegible]																							
[illegible]	[illegible]																							
[illegible]	[illegible]																							
[illegible]	[illegible]																							
[illegible]	[illegible]																							
[illegible]	[illegible]																							

[illegible]

[illegible]	[illegible]						[illegible]						[illegible]						[illegible]		
	[illegible]			[illegible]			[illegible]			[illegible]			[illegible]			[illegible]			[illegible]		[illegible]
	[illegible]	[illegible]	[illegible]	[illegible]	[illegible]	[illegible]	[illegible]	[illegible]	[illegible]	[illegible]	[illegible]	[illegible]	[illegible]	[illegible]	[illegible]	[illegible]	[illegible]	[illegible]	[illegible]	[illegible]	[illegible]
[illegible]	[illegible]	[illegible]	[illegible]	[illegible]	[illegible]	[illegible]	[illegible]	[illegible]	[illegible]	[illegible]	[illegible]	[illegible]	[illegible]	[illegible]	[illegible]	[illegible]	[illegible]	[illegible]	[illegible]	[illegible]	[illegible]

[illegible]

III.—IRELAND.

WEXFORD.

Union Offices, Wexford, [illegible] September, [illegible].

Sir,

I beg leave to inform you that there are at present about [illegible] old men and women residing in the workhouse who are mentally and physically fit to live outside with friends.

The Committee have seen and asked the Medical Officer's opinion in reference to these [illegible], and he states they are incapable of being removed to places outside if such could be obtained.

The Committee have taken no further steps.

I have, etc.,
[illegible].

The Secretary, Local Government Board,
Custom House, Dublin.

LURGAN.

Extract from Guardians' Minutes of Proceedings, dated 15th October, [illegible].

Aged Pensions Bill.

The accompanying copy of the Committee's report relative to the Aged Pensions Bill was read.

LURGAN UNION.

Males.

No.	Names.	Age.	Observations.
1	Wilson, William	77	A wife and son in England.
2	Wright, Samuel	[illegible]	Prefers to remain in the house.
3	Kennedy, William	77	No friends; remain in the house.
4	Malloy, John	64	Prefers to remain in the house.
5	Hornby, John	[illegible]	Two daughters; prefers to live in the house.
6	M'Quade, John	[illegible]	Three sons and four daughters; would go out.
7	Russell, Archibald	81	Two sons; would go out.
8	Carbery, John	77	Prefers to remain in the house.
9	Burch, Isaac	[illegible]	No friends; remain in the house.
10	Walk, John	[illegible]	Prefers to remain in the house.
11	Malcolm, Robert	[illegible]	No children; remain in the house.
12	Topping, Robert	[illegible]	Two sons in Belfast, but will remain in the house.
13	Hutton, Joseph	[illegible]	One daughter, but says he is better in the house.
14	M'Coy, John	81	Only a brother; remain in the house.
15	Ferguson, William	64	Only a brother; remain in the house.
16	M'Kerr, Hugh	70	Three daughters in Belfast; would go and live with them.
17	Hamilton, William	63	One son and one daughter; live with them.
18	M'Keown, Andrew	[illegible]	Three sisters; would live with them.
19	Reid, William	76	No friends; would remain in the house.
20	Gibson, John	[illegible]	No friends; would remain in the house.
21	Lyons, David	71	Three sons and two daughters in Belfast; go to them.
22	Hughes, John	[illegible]	Prefers to live in the house.
23	M'Court, Charles	73	Refuses to leave the house.
24	M'Geary, John	70	No children; remain in the house.
25	Cowden, John	65	One daughter; would live with her.
26	Ralph, Thomas	70	No friends; prefers to remain in the house.
27	Lavery, Charles	78	No friends; prefers to remain in the house.
28	Rodgers, John	76	No friends; prefers to remain in the house.

FEMALES.

No.	Names.	Age.	Observations.
1	Ryan, [illegible]	[illegible]	No family, has grandchildren in Belfast; go and live with them.
2	Walsh, Sarah	[illegible]	Would go and live with family.
3	[illegible], Alice	[illegible]	Son in Portadown; would live with him.
4	Hall, [illegible]	70	A daughter; would live with her.
5	M'Conville, Jane	70	Sons and daughters; would live with them.
6	Gallery, Margaret	[illegible]	A daughter; would live with her.
7	Wetherall, Abigail	[illegible]	A sister; would live with her.
8	Lunderson, Susan	[illegible]	This woman is paralytic; could not go out.
9	Furley, Mary	[illegible]	A son in Portadown; would live with him.
10	M'Grath, Elizabeth	[illegible]	No children in this country; has a sister, would live with her.
11	M'Cann, Mary	[illegible]	Prefers to remain in the house.
12	Larkin, Elizabeth	65	Has friends she would go and live with.
13	Flanagan, Sarah	70	A friend she would live with.
14	Matthews, Mary	[illegible]	A son and a daughter; would live with them.
15	Watson, Anne	[illegible]	A son and a daughter; would live with them.
16	Sullivan, Ellen	70	A son; would live with him.
17	M'Cabrey, Sarah	70	Three sons and one daughter in Belfast; would live with them.
18	Murphy, Margaret	70	A son and a daughter; would live with them.
19	M'Garvey, Alice	70	A nephew; would keep her.
20	Fulton, Anne	[illegible]	A daughter; would live with her.
21	M'Cullough, Ellen	[illegible]	A niece; would live with her.
22	Kinney, Susan	70	No friends; but if she got enough, would get someone to keep her.
23	M'Teague, Mary	75	A daughter and a son; would live with them.
24	Brown, Ann Jane	80	A daughter and a son; would live with them.
25	Cosgrove, Sarah	[illegible]	One son, but could not keep her; better in house.
26	Cornigel, Sarah	71	No friends; but if she got enough, would go out.
27	M'Kee, Teresa	70	A cousin; would keep her.
28	Robinson, Eliza	65	A daughter; but better in the house.
29	Gibson, Eliza	[illegible]	A son; would live with him.
30	Turvin, Hannah	70	No friends; stop in the house.
31	Rogers, Mary	[illegible]	As well in the house.

Mr. Chairman, Ladies and Gentlemen,

The Committee appointed to inquire and report on the inmates of the house that are 65 years of age and upwards eligible to live outside the house, in case a small weekly pension was granted to enable them to do so, met on Tuesday last, 12th inst., at 3 o'clock p.m.

Present:—John Fleming, John C. O'Reilly, and William John Fleming.

Your Committee interviewed each of the inmates of the house, and beg to hand in the accompanying list of names, with age, and the answers of each as given by them.

Your Committee finds that there are [illegible] males and 31 females over the age of 65 years. Of the males, [illegible] are over [illegible] years, [illegible] over 70 years, [illegible] over 75 years, [illegible] over 80 years, 1 over [illegible] years and 1 over [illegible] years. Of the females, [illegible] are over 65 years, 14 over 70 years, 2 over 75 years, and [illegible] over 80 years.

Only [illegible] of the males expressed a desire to go and live with their friends, in case a small pension was given to enable them to do so; while [illegible] of them expressed the desire to remain in the house.

But the females seemed more anxious to go out and live with their friends, as 23 of them expressed the desire to do so. Only 7 preferred to remain in the house. The remaining one must remain in the house, as she has been afflicted with a paralytic stroke during the week.

Signed on behalf of the Committee,

W. J. Fleming.

14th October, 1899.

WESTPORT.

EXTRACT from Guardians' Minutes of Proceedings, dated 3rd September, 1902.

Inmates over 65 fit to live outside the workhouse.

The report of the Committee appointed to investigate the number of inmates of the workhouse over 65 years of age who are physically and mentally fit to live outside the workhouse, and who have friends or relatives with whom they could live if they had pensions of from 5s. to 7s. per week, was submitted and approved of.

WESTPORT UNION.

The Westport Board of Guardians having appointed us a Committee to make an investigation of the number of inmates of the Westport Workhouse who are over 65 years of age, and who are physically and mentally fit to live outside the workhouse, and who have relatives or friends with whom they could live if they had pensions of from 5s. to 7s. per week, we this day visited Westport Workhouse, and after interviewing all the aged inmates who were able to move about, we came to the conclusion that [illegible] of their number would be able to live with their friends under the circumstances stated.

The following are the names of the inmates selected, and some particulars concerning their cases :—

Michael McNamara, aged 68, of Dooega, W. Achill. He has been an occasional inmate of the house for [illegible] years. Unfit for work. Could live with a cousin, Michael Carey, of Achill, a small farmer.

John McNamara, aged 80, of Dooniver, Bellacorick, Achill. He entered the house about 13 weeks ago. Not being able to manage his small holding of land, he gave it to his grandchildren, the eldest of whom, Bridget Callaghan, of Dooniver, wife of Anthony Callaghan, a small farmer, would keep him if he had a small pension. He is unfit for work.

John Joyce, aged 84, originally from Cloonkeen [illegible], Murrisk, Westport. He is over 17 years in the workhouse. He could live with his cousin, Mrs. [illegible], Cloonpatrick, a small farmer.

Anthony Heneghan, aged 72, of Clownhill. Four years in workhouse. Gave up a small farm, not being able to keep it. His cousin, Mrs. Heneghan, Clownhill, Westport, a small farmer, would keep him. He is a healthy-looking man, who would be able for some years to do light farm work.

John Christie, aged 14 [illegible], of Belclare, Westport. About four years in workhouse. His wife has a small allowance from Mrs. Livingstone, of Belclare House, as gate keeper, and she would be able to keep her husband comfortably if he had the pension mentioned. He is able to do light work.

Martin McGinty, aged 72, of Achill. In workhouse about eight years. Could live with his first cousin, Michael Gallagher, of [illegible], a small farmer. He is strong and healthy, and would be able to assist in farm work.

Martin Malley, aged 76, of Westport. Several years in workhouse. Has no immediate relatives in the county, but could live with a widowed daughter-in-law, Mrs. Dobbyn, Westport. He is able to do some work.

Patk. Gibbons, aged 68, of Murrisk, Westport. Has been an occasional inmate of the house for the last five or six years. His cousin, Patk. Joyce, of Murrisk, a small farmer, would be willing to keep him.

Martin Nestor, aged 74, of Westport. In house about four years. A tinsmith. Could live with his son, Thomas Nestor, labourer, Westport.

Owen McGinty, aged 70, of Ballyveeny. In house about eight years. Strong and healthy. Could live with his nephew, Michael McGinty, Ballyveeny, a small farmer.

Patrick Geraghty, aged 77, of Ballinlough, Knappagh. In house seven years. Bad eye-sight. Could live with his brother, James Geraghty, Ballinlough, a small farmer.

Patrick O'Donnell, aged 70, of Keel, Achill. In workhouse about six years "off and on." His wife and daughter live in Keel, and have a small holding of land. Could live with them, and do some farm work.

Patrick Gallagher, aged 82, of Doughmakeon, Kilgeever. Three years in workhouse. Could live with his nephew, Michael Malley, or other friends, all small farmers.

James Feeney, aged 84, of Croy, Westport. About two years in workhouse. Could live with his niece, Mrs. [illegible], Aughagower, a small landholder.

Michael Moran, aged 77, of Louisburgh. Three years in workhouse. His brother, Martin Moran, of [illegible], a small farmer, would keep him. Inmate could assist at farm work.

Owen Lofton, aged 81, of [illegible]. In workhouse six years. Could live with his daughter, Mary Foley, wife of Patk. Foley, a small landholder of [illegible].

Patrick Glynn, aged 67, of Westport. In workhouse about five years. Formerly a car-driver. Could live with his sons, Peter and John Glynn, car-drivers, Westport. Could do slight work.

Thomas Hastings, aged 68, of Westport. Formerly a dealer in old clothes. In workhouse four years. All his children are away in America, but could live with a friend, John McDonnell, car-owner, Westport.

Mary Newman, 68, of Westport. In workhouse about twelve years "off and on." Has no relatives surviving, but is able to do some work, and could live with friends if she got a few shillings per week.

Anne Gibbons, aged 74, of Kilmeena. Two years in workhouse. Could live with her nephew, Thomas Flynn, a small landholder at Moyne, Kilmeena, Westport.

Ellen Tynds, aged 74, of [illegible]. Could live with her first cousin, John Faherty, of [illegible], a small farmer.

Honor Hastings, aged 80, of Cross, Moyne, Kilmeena. Could live with her cousin, John Reddy, of [illegible].

Mary Gavin, aged 80, of [illegible]. Could live with her brother-in-law, Patrick Kelly, of Westport Quay, shopkeeper and car-owner.

So far as we have been able to judge, none of the parties above mentioned, with perhaps three or four exceptions, have become inmates of the workhouse through any fault of their own.

(Signed) JOHN WALSH.
CHARLES MACDONNELL.
WILLIAM DERR.

Board Room, Westport, 31st August, 1902.

Approved.

(Signed) JOHN WALSH,
Chairman of the Westport Board of Guardians.
(Signed) D. J. O'CONNOR,
Acting Clerk of Union.

3rd September, 1902.

SOUTH DUBLIN.

EXTRACT from Guardians' Minutes, dated 26th November, 1902.

Re Old Age Pensions.

The Master reported in accordance with your order to furnish a return of the aged inmates over 65 years who are mentally and physically fit to live outside an institution, and to have relatives or friends with whom they could live if they had pensions from 5s. to 7s. per week. He found there are in the workhouse [illegible] inmates over 65 years of age each of whom he personally interviewed with regard to their previous history; also if they had friends with whom they could live if assisted by an old age pension. Of the [illegible], he found [illegible] men and 18 women who stated their relatives would keep them if assisted in sums from five to seven shillings weekly. A great number of those who had no relatives but who are able to work stated if they had from 5s. to 7s. weekly, they could live well outside.

Approved.

NAVAN.

Extract from Guardians' Minutes, dated 25th November, 1903.

[illegible] AGED PENSIONERS BILL.

Read letter from Local Government Board, dated 18th November, 1903, requesting to be informed whether the Committee appointed to consider the Aged Pensioners Bill have yet furnished a report, and stating that the information asked for is urgently required by the Select Committee of the House of Commons.

Read Report from Committee appointed to consider Aged Pensioners Bill, dated 25th November, 1903, stating that they visited the workhouse and found therein 65 persons over 65 years of age, 15 of whom had no friends; that they communicated with the friends of the remaining 50, and received the following replies. In five cases the friends were willing to take out the party named; in four cases they were willing to take out the party named, but could not do so for want of house accommodation. In four other cases the friends refused to take out the party named. The remaining 18 sent no reply. Stating further that in their opinion the Act to be of any benefit whatever, should be made to apply to all those in receipt of out-door relief over 65 years of age, and having houses of their own.

Proposed by Mr. Mangan, seconded by Mr. Cronin, and passed unanimously: "That this Report be approved and adopted."

NAVAN UNION.

Result of Inquiries made as to persons over 65 years of age in Workhouse.

Number of Inmates over 65 years having no friends.	Number of Inmates over 65 years having friends.	Total Number of Inmates over 65 years in Workhouse.	Number of Inmates over 65 years whose friends are willing to support them (with pension) and who are physically fit, &c.	Number of Inmates over 65 years of age whose friends refuse to support them (with pension.)	Number of Inmates in Col. 2 whose friends declined to support them owing to want of proper house accommodation.	Number of Inmates in Col. 2 whose friends sent no replies to inquiry.
15	50	65	6	4	4	16

Dated 25th November 1903.

(Signed) *Chas. Lowe*,
Clerk of Union.

Board Room, 23rd September, 1903.

I am directed by the Board of Guardians to inquire whether you would be willing to allow
at present an inmate of this workhouse, to live with you in the
event of being granted a Government pension of from 5s. to 7s. per week.

The favour of an early reply is requested.

(By Order.) Charles Lowe,
Clerk of the Union.

CLONMEL.

Board Room, Clonmel Union, 3rd December, 1903.

Sir,

I beg to reply to your Board's letters of the 15th August, 1903, No. 43,[illegible], etc., requesting particulars for Parliamentary purposes of inmates in the Clonmel Workhouse over 65 years of age who are mentally and physically fit to live outside with relatives or friends, if they had pensions of from 5s. to 7s. per week.

The Committee appointed (four in number) did not at any time meet in full, but singly and in twos, and the following is an abstract of work done:

There are in workhouse 33 males and 22 females of the age of 65 years and upwards. Going carefully over each inmate, there are about 24 males and 17 females who would and could live outside with friends and relatives had they pensions of from 5s. to 7s. per week.

The providing of such persons with the means to live outside is well worth a trial, though it may be anticipated that cases of disagreement and perhaps want of interest and proper care will from time to time turn up, no matter how carefully the business is managed.

It is a difficult matter to arrive at the actual age, as persons with burial insurances are always younger than they actually are, and those uninsured want to be older than what they are.

I am, Sir, your obedient servant,
Timothy Brady.

To the Secretary, Local Government Board,
Dublin.

BELFAST.

Belfast Union, Clerk's Office, 5th December, [illegible].

Sir,

In reply to your letter No. [illegible], dated 15th August, [illegible], and to your telegram of the 2nd instant, relative to the Aged Pensions Bill. The Committee met this day, with the authority of the Board of Guardians, to forward you the information desired. Members present: Dr. John Macintosh (Chairman), Miss F. F. Clark, Messrs. W. O'[illegible], W. Walker, and D. [illegible]. Mr. J. C. [illegible], Clerk of Union, and Mr. R. W. [illegible], Master, were also present. The Committee recommend that the Local Government Board be informed that the number of aged inmates of the workhouse over 65 years of age who are mentally and physically fit to live outside the institution, and who state that they have relatives or friends with whom they could live if they had pensions of from 5s. to 7s. per week, are as follows:—

Classified Infirm, [illegible] men; classified as [illegible], infirm, [illegible] men. Total, [illegible] men.

I am, Sir, your obedient servant,

J. G. [illegible],

Clerk of the Union.

The Secretary, Local Government Board, Dublin.

INDEX.

[*N.B.*—In this Index the figures following the names of the Witnesses, and those in the Digest of Evidence of each Witness, refer to the Questions in the Evidence; the Figures following *App.* refer to the Pages in the Appendix; and the Numerals following *Rep.* and *Special Rep.* to the Pages in the Reports and Proceedings of the Committee.]

A.

B.

Beer Tax. See *Denmark.* *Taxation.*

Belfast Union. Official statement that there are 196 inmates over 65 years of age who state that they have relatives or friends with whom they could live if they had pensions of from 5s. to 7s. a week, *App.* 143.

Boards of Guardians. See *Administration.* *Poor Relief.* *Workhouses.*

C.

Casuals (Poor Relief). Duty of Guardians in London to relieve casuals in the workhouse if the casual ward should be full, though there would be no claim upon the Common Poor Fund in such cases, *Fuller* 1213–1215.

Charity Commission. Total of 638,000*l.* a year controlled by the Charity Commissioners and now distributed among the people, *Sir E. Hamilton* 487–490.

Classification (Workhouses). See *Workhouses.*

Co-operative Union. Explanation that the Union is a voluntary federation of the co-operative societies of the United Kingdom, and embraces 1,169 societies with a membership of 1,834,118 out of a total of about 2,000,000, *Grey* 737–739——Annual Congress held by the Union, about 1,200 delegates attending as representing the various societies; procedure as to the instructions given to the delegates before the Congress, *ib.* 740–743.

First discussion by the Congress in 1893 of the question of old age pensions, a resolution having been adopted in favour of pensions to the employees of the societies; similar resolution at the Congress in 1897, *Grey* 745, 746——Eventual extension of the views of the Congress in 1898 and 1899, it having been resolved in the latter year to appoint a Special Committee to devise schemes applicable to all the members of co-operative societies, women as well as men, *ib.* 746–750.

Summary of the financial proposals of the three schemes first proposed by the Special Committee, showing the suggested contribution by each member, and the estimated total cost of pensions of 5s. a week and 7s. 6d. a week respectively, commencing at the age of 60, *Grey* 748–761——Submission of the foregoing schemes to the Congress held at Cardiff in 1900, and subsequently to the sectional and district conferences all over the country, there having been an overwhelming majority of opinions in favour of a national instead of a co-operative system, *ib.* 762–770——Several causes of the growth of opinion among co-operators in favour of a national system instead of their being called upon to provide pensions for their employees, who are often much better off than themselves, *ib.* 775–786.

See also Trades Unions.

Copenhagen. See *Denmark.*

Cost:

Reference to the Bill before the present Committee as closely following the financial proposals of the Select Committee of 1899 respecting old age pensions, *Sir E. Hamilton* 302–306——Data for former calculation by witness on the part of the Departmental Committee of 1899, that in 1901 there would be 2,016,000 persons above 65 years of age in England and Wales, and that if there were a universal pension of 5s. a week the aggregate charge would be 31,449,100*l.*, exclusive of the cost of administration, *ib.* 307–317.

Calculations made by witness (on the part of the Departmental Committee) that the various deductions to be made in 1901 for want of qualification would reduce the numbers to 655,000 and the cost to 10,300,000*l.*, *Sir E. Hamilton* 327–331. 370–374. 415–418——Conclusion generally that on several grounds the estimated cost of 10,300,000*l.* for 1901 was an under estimate, *ib.* 370–374. 415–418——Calculation by Mr. Brabrook (a member of the Departmental Committee) that on the basis of applying the New Zealand Act to England the cost would be about 13,000,000*l.* instead of 10,300,000*l.*, *ib.* 372–374.

Explanation as to the Departmental Committee not having made any allowance for saving in Poor Law expenditure till 1911, when 615,000*l.* is allowed; statement hereon as to the much larger cost of maintenance in workhouses than is represented by a pension of 5s. a week, *Sir E. Hamilton* 379–397——Question further considered whether there would not be a large saving in Poor Law expenditure by a reduction in the number of indoor paupers if there were an expenditure of some ten millions in pensions, *ib.* 419–438.

Impracticability of ascertaining the total amount that would be required for a scheme of universal pensions at a given age, as large numbers would not claim; objection, however, to

men

Cost—continued.

men being disqualified for pensions if they choose to work, *Steadman* 497–503. 508. 639——Resolution adopted by the Trades Union and Co-operative Union Congress in 1902 that the amount should be at least 5s. a week, an amendment which was moved in favour of the amount being 7s. having been withdrawn, *ib.* 546, 547——Calculation that the cost at 5s. per week under the Bill would be about 6,000,000*l.* instead of 10,300,000*l.*, *ib.* 556–558. 590.

Estimate by Mr. Charles Booth that the cost of the proposed universal scheme would be 26,000,000*l.*; expediency of at once beginning on this scale, *Steadman* 583–594——Very heavy cost entailed under the workhouse system as compared with a system of pensions, *ib.* 673–678.

Calculation that on the basis of relative population in England and Wales and in Denmark the cost for England and Wales would be 3,591,000*l.*, but as the pensions in this country would have to be larger than in Denmark they might cost 7,000,000*l.*, whilst there would be an estimated saving of 3,000,000*l.* on Poor Law expenses, *Miss E. Sellers* 1089–1091.

Inquiry made by the Committee as to the value of the estimate made by Sir E. Hamilton's Committee in 1899, as tested by the Census of 1901, and the extent to which such estimate would be affected by certain variations from the scheme upon which those estimates were based, *Special Rep.* iii.——Modifications suggested in the Bill so as to afford a satisfactory basis for the distribution of the sum required in order to carry out the provisions of the Bill in its entirety, *ib.*

Conclusion that if it be not possible to provide by taxation the full sum required in each year the provision of a much smaller sum would meet many of the most necessitous cases, *Special Rep.* iv. —The foregoing result might be obtained either by raising the age at which a pension might be claimed, or by reducing the amount of weekly income, the possession of which disqualifies for a pension, *ib.*

Opinion of the Committee that for certain reasons the reduction in Poor Law expenditure will be considerably less under a system of pensions than has often been represented, *Special Rep.* v.

See also Administration. Denmark. Married Couples. Number of Pensioners. Taxation. Victoria. Workhouses.

Cottage Homes. Great boon if deserving cases of old people in workhouses could be removed to cottage homes, away from the workhouses; calculation that in all England there would not be more than 4,000 or 5,000 such cases above the age of 65, *Miss E. Sellers* 1143–1161——Calculation that one-roomed cottages built in town, sufficient to accommodate 4,000 old people, could be provided for about 300,000*l.*; less expense if houses were rented for the purpose, *ib.* 1162, 1163——Illustration of the large saving which might be effected in the cost of workhouses if there were cottage homes, *ib.* 1174–1176.

Copy of the Cottage Homes Bill of 1903, *App.* 130.

Strong recommendation by the Committee that the welfare and happiness of many aged inmates of workhouses should be provided for by an extension of the system of Cottage Homes, *Special Rep.* v.

See also Denmark.

Criminals (Disqualification for Pensions). Difficulty in estimating the percentage of disqualification that might escape detection in respect of criminals, *Sir E. Hamilton* 375–380.

Contention that men who have been criminals should not be excluded from pensions, *Steadman* 597–601. 651–658——Approval of disqualification for a pension in the case of men convicted of crime; inadequacy of 5s. a week for their support, in the absence of any other income, *Crooks* 726–732. 733——Grounds for objecting to the proposed disqualification in certain cases of penal servitude or imprisonment, *Grey* 945–948.

Crooks, William (Member of the House). (Digest of his Evidence.)—Witness, who is Chairman of the Poplar Board of Guardians, has had considerable experience of Poor Law administration, 703–706.

Very careful investigation by a Special Committee of the Poplar Guardians in 1899 of the question whether the aged poor in the workhouse over 60 years of age (of whom there are 1,000) could be well cared for out of the house by relatives or friends, 703——Conclusion of the Special Committee, after their first inquiry, that the inmates, many of whom are infirm and helpless, would not be properly cared for if they left the workhouse; reluctance on their part to make the change, 706.

Additional inquiry made in about 1,000 cases, the general result being that not 5 per cent. could with advantage be removed from the house, 706–710——Desire of the Guardians to encourage outdoor rather than indoor relief; very limited extent to which feasible in the

Report, 1903—*continued.*

Crooks, *William* (*Member of the House*) (Digest of his Evidence)—*continued.*

the interests of the aged poor, 703–708——Entire dissent from an estimate that as many as one-third of the aged poor are married couples; very few of this class in Poplar Workhouse, 711–713.

Result of investigation in Poplar Union, that there are 1,824 persons over the age of 60 in receipt of outdoor relief whose relatives or friends might take charge of them if pensioned at 5*s.* a week, some of them having other sources of income, 714–720——Discrimination exercised by guardians and relieving officer in selecting cases fit for outdoor relief; small percentage of selected applicants who have no right to such relief, 720–725——Conclusion that there are many thousands of respectable poor people who with a little relief might remain at home with their friends and relations, 725, 729.

Approval of disqualification for a pension in the case of men convicted of crime; sufficiency of 5*s.* a week for their support, in the absence of any other income, 726–729, 732——Expediency of a maximum limit of income as regards qualification for a pension, 730–732——Strong objections to pensioners being allowed to work for wages or other remuneration, 733, 734.

D.

Denmark:

Statement prepared by witness for the Committee respecting the system of treatment of the poor in Copenhagen and throughout Denmark, *Miss E. Sellers*, 6. 9——Very full control vested in the Third Section Burgomaster of Copenhagen as regards the administration of old age relief in that city, *ib.* 6. 30–36. 56——Division of the city, for poor relief purposes, into 12 districts, each of which is in care of a district superintendent, these being arranged in three groups of four districts each, each group being under a group inspector, *ib.* 6. 102–104——Separate duties of the district superintendents and group inspectors, the former dealing only with the pauper class, whilst the latter deal with the respectable aged poor apart from pauper relief; very careful discrimination between the two classes, *ib.* 6. 9. 56–62.

Fairly satisfactory results at Copenhagen in distinguishing between the pauper class and the deserving section of the community; strict and elaborate investigations made for this purpose, *Miss E. Sellers* 6. 9. 95–100. 109–111——Reference to the questions which applicants for old age relief (as distinct from pauper relief) are required to answer; liability to imprisonment for false information, *ib.* 6–9. 43–46——Limit of 60 years of age in Copenhagen for the commencement of old age relief, *ib.* 9——Strict requirements on the score of moral character; special bar against drunkenness, *ib.* 9. 40–42.

Decision by the group inspector whether applicants are to go before the Old Age Relief Committee, which is presided over by the Burgomaster, and which decides each case, and the amount and form of relief, *Miss E. Sellers* 9——Rule that when a man is strong enough to take care of himself, or has any relatives to take care of him, the relief shall be in the form of a pension, the average pension being about 7*l.* 10*s.* a year, *ib.*——Admission of the deserving poor in many cases to old age homes, these being delightful places and being all over the country, *ib.* 8. 66–70.

Considerable difficulties in connection with a former requirement that applicants for relief must be in a destitute condition, so that there was not much inducement to save; amendment of the law on this point, *Miss E. Sellers* 9, 10——Great importance attached to proposals by Herr Jacobi, Third Section Burgomaster of Copenhagen, that a standard of income shall be fixed below which persons may be qualified for a pension, which should be on a sliding scale according to age, 40 per cent. being added when the man has a wife living, *ib.* 10–12. 83–94. 101.

Explanations with reference to the list of questions which applicants must answer in order to qualify for pensions, *Miss E. Sellers* 13–18——Particulars in connection with certain statistics as to the increased cost of old age relief and old age pensions from 1892 to 1897, and as to the relative decrease in the cost of pauper relief; very satisfactory inferences from these figures, *ib.* 18, 19——Rearrangement by Act in 1903 as to the sources of payment of the cost of old age pensions and relief, one half being borne by the State and one-half by the Communal or local authorities, *ib.* 20, 21——Explanation as to the State contribution being all levied on the beer tax, whilst the Communal moiety is paid out of the local receipts from various sources, there being a poor fund, but no poor rate, *ib.* 21–27.

Concurrence of evidence of representative and official authorities in Denmark as to the very beneficial operation of the law, in respect of the working classes generally, without being any discouragement to thrift, *Miss E. Sellers* 27–30.

Further explanation in detail on various points in elucidation of statement read by witness to the Committee as regards applications for pensions or relief, the qualifications and

Draft

Draft Reports. Draft Special Report, as proposed by the Chairman, *Special Rep.* ix, x.—Draft Special Report proposed by Mr. Channing, *ib.* x, xi.——Adoption of the former, subject to some amendments, *ib.* xi–xiii.

E.

Employment (Pensioners). Strong objections to pensioners being allowed to work for wages or other remuneration, *Crooks* 733, 734——Grounds for the opinion that pensioners should not be debarred from work; practice herein in Co-operative Societies, *Gray* 871–874.

Experiment. View of the Committee that the provision of old age pensions for the deserving poor might well be proceeded with step by step, *Special Rep.* iv.——Further information required on many points on which there is still much uncertainty; actual experiment contemplated, *ib.* v.

F.

Foreign Countries. Very low position of England as compared with foreign countries in respect of the care taken of her aged poor, *Miss E. Sellers* 1165–1167.

See also *Denmark. France. Russia. Workhouses.*

France. Reference to a law passed in France in 1897 whereby the State undertook to contribute, up to half a million francs, towards the cost incurred by the Communal Authorities in granting allowances to poor persons above 70 years; very limited action of the municipalities in the matter, *Miss E. Sellers* 121–127——Recent French law providing that a certain number of hospices or homes should be provided for the aged poor, *ib.* 128–130——Working of the Poor Law in Paris by officials, there being a right to poor persons to claim an allowance at the age of 70, *ib.* 123, 124. 127–131.

Friendly Societies. Reason why the Friendly Societies, with one or two exceptions, were not represented at the Conference of Trades Unions and Co-operative Unions in January, 1903, which adopted, unanimously, a scheme of universal pensions, *Steadman* 503, 504. 659–661——Conclusion that great numbers of unskilled workmen with low wages, who are not members of Friendly Societies, have as much right to be looked after as such members, *ib.* 563, 564. 676–680.

Papers submitted on the part of the National Conference of Friendly Societies in 1902 and 1903, *App.* 121–123——Resolution adopted at Conference in March, 1902, that it is the duty of the State to provide old age pensions, of not less than 5s. a week, to all thrifty and deserving persons of 65 years of age and upwards who are unable to work, and are in need of the same, *ib.* 121——Suggested lines of Bill for carrying out the foregoing resolution, *ib.* 121, 122.

Fuller, S. Drake. Explanation, on the part of the Paddington Board of Guardians, of the amended regulations adopted by the Board since 1880, with the approval of the Local Government Board, in dealing with applications for relief, 1177–1192. 1251——Rule not to grant out-relief except to those who are deserving at the time of the application; details hereon as to the tests applied and the character and mode of inquiry in different classes of cases, the checks upon abuse working satisfactorily, 1179–1193. 1208. 1232–1237——Conditions as to applicants having given some proof of thrift; very rare instances of members of Friendly Societies applying, 1180. 1184–1186. 1208–1210. 1228. 1255–1258.

Practice of the Paddington Board in some deserving cases to obtain assistance or small pensions through charitable societies or from private sources, so that the applicants may not come on the poor rates, 1193–1196. 1205——Grounds for strongly deprecating a system of State pensions, to be worked irrespectively of Boards of Guardians; very prejudicial effect as removing from charity and from the richer classes the duty of helping the poor, 1196–1203. 1205, 1207. 1224–1227——Full powers in Guardians to give liberal weekly relief in deserving cases in addition to incomes of as much as 10s. or 12s. a week, 1198–1201. 1208.

Conclusion, as the result of inquiries, that there are but very few old people in the London workhouses who have relatives with whom they could live, or who would care to leave the workhouse, 1204. 1205——Discouragement to thrift under the proposal for supplementing, in certain cases, incomes of 10s. a week by means of pensions, 1206, 1207.

Liability to abuse under the system of the Common Poor Fund in London; inference as to the temptation to Boards of Guardians to put applicants for relief on a Pension Fund if half the amount were provided by the State, 1211, 1212——Duty of Guardians to relieve casuals in the workhouse if the casual ward should be full, though there would be no claim upon the Common Poor Fund in such cases, 1213–1215.

Outdoor relief up to 7s. or 8s. a week given in some cases by the Paddington Guardians, whose

Fuller, S. Drake—continued.

witness submitting, however, that it is desirable to check much of the outdoor relief now given in some Unions, 1216-1233. 1238-1247. 1261-1263——Conclusion as to the great majority of the inmates being brought into workhouses through their own fault, though there are doubtless large numbers of deserving poor among the inmates, 1228-1237——Care exercised in Paddington in discriminating between the difficult cases of outdoor relief and the varying amounts granted; total of 275 outdoor cases on 1st January, 1903; 1235-1248. 1272-1289.

Further explanations respecting the satisfactory working of the amended rules applied in Paddington, and the staff employed, in testing applications for outdoor relief; discouragement of applications by the undeserving through knowledge beforehand of the efficiency of the inquiries made, 1249-1252——Conclusion as to the limited increase of cost to be incurred generally in carrying out a really efficient administration of outdoor relief; good economy in having an efficient staff, 1253-1267. 1268, 1284. 1270, 1271. ——Very large population in Paddington with incomes up to 21s. a week who are not upon the rates, 1256-1260.

Small proportion of out-relief in Paddington as compared with the majority of London Unions, 1273-1276. 1294-1298——Opinion as to the sufficiency of a period of 10 years instead of 20 as a condition to be required in respect of "deserving" applicants, 1291, 1292——Consideration to be given in cases where men sometimes have to tramp the country in search of employment, and are obliged to occasionally apply for indoor relief, 1293.

Explanation that witness is entirely in favour of the poor being fully considered, but objects to the scheme of the Bill on the subject, 1299.

G.

Glasgow. Return and Tables containing sundry particulars respecting workhouse inmates above 65 years of age with reference to the question of their receiving pensions and living outside with relatives or friends, *App.* 135-137.

Gray, James Clement. (Digest of his Evidence.)—Witness, who is General Secretary of the Co-operative Union, explains that the Union is a voluntary federation of the Co-operative Societies of the United Kingdom, and embraces 1,159 societies with a membership of 1,694,118 out of a total of about 2,000,000; 737-739.

Annual Congress held by the Union, about 1,200 delegates attending as representing the various societies; procedure as to the instructions given to the delegates before the Congress, 740-743——First discussion by the Congress in 1896 of the question of Old Age Pensions, a resolution having been adopted in favour of pensions to the employees of the societies; similar limitation at the Congress in 1897; 743, 746——Eventual extension of the views of the Congress in 1898 and 1899, it having been resolved in the latter year to appoint a Special Committee to devise schemes applicable to all the members of co-operative societies, women as well as men, 746-750.

Summary of the financial proposals of the three schemes first proposed by the Special Committee, showing the suggested contribution by each member, and the estimated total cost of pensions of 5s. a week and 7s. 6d. a week, respectively, commencing at the age of 60; 748-761——Submission of the foregoing schemes to the Congress held at Cardiff in 1900, and subsequently to the Sectional and District Conferences all over the country, there having been an overwhelming majority of opinions in favour of a national instead of a co-operative system, 762-770.

Joint Conference eventually in 1901 and 1902 between the Co-operative Union and the Trades Union, it having been unanimously decided to promote a Bill on the lines of a universal system of Old Age Pensions, 770-776. 962-973——Several causes of the growth of opinion among co-operators in favour of a national system instead of their being called upon to provide pensions for their employers, who are often much better off than themselves, 776-784.

Unanimous adoption by the Co-operative Union of the scheme of universal pensions at the age of 60, irrespective of income and regardless of character, 785-792. 800. 824-828. 968-978——Grounds for objecting to the expense being borne partly by local rates instead of entirely by Imperial taxation, though the administration should be local, 793-798. 837-841——Willingness of witness to accept a modified scheme (as under Mr. Remnant's Bill) if it be found impracticable to obtain a universal scheme, though he submits that the former should not discriminate between different degrees of deserving cases, 799-801. 844-870. 903-908.

Belief that no great difficulty would be experienced, especially in country districts, in discriminating between deserving and undeserving applicants for pensions; absence of

Gray, Jesse Clement. (Digest of his Evidence)—*continued.*

of any great difficulty in Manchester, 802–804. 843–850. 878–882——Thrifty character of members of co-operative societies; doubt as to the proportion of those over 65 years of age who are married couples, but witness will obtain statistics on this point, 804–809. 940–944——Hardship of disqualification in the event of receipt of poor relief during 20 years prior to the application for a pension, even though not applying under wholly exceptional circumstances, 810–813. 867, 868. 909–919. 949, 950.

Objection of applicants to their qualifications being investigated before magistrates, 814——Unfairness of the proposed thrift or savings test as being of very unequal operation, 814–817. 867, 868. 920–926. 951–959——Belief that it would be cheaper and more popular to provide pensions than to compel old people to go into the workhouse; great aversion of the people in some places to become indoor paupers, 818–833. 827–837. 970, 971——Conclusion that large numbers of old and infirm people would find friends and relatives to take good care of them if assisted with a pension of 5s. or 7s. 6d. a week, 827–829. 883–891——Approval of the working classes paying income tax, if fairly levied all round, towards a universal pension scheme, 839. 897. 933.

Grounds for the opinion that pensioners should not be debarred from work; practice hereon in co-operative societies, 871–874——Receipt of poor relief by members of societies without being disqualified as members, 875–877——Further statement in support of the aged poor being under the care of relatives or going into cottage homes instead of to workhouses, whilst some might be provided for in the ordinary hospitals, instead of in the workhouse infirmaries, 883–896.

Non-objection to the Guardians as administrators of a pension scheme, though some representation should be given to the Imperial Exchequer as finding the money, 898–901——Approval of a tax on beer as one of the modes of increased taxation; reference hereon to the excessive expenditure of working men in Manchester on drink, 929–936——Doubt whether workhouses could be entirely dispensed with under a pension scheme, 939——Grounds for objecting to the proposed disqualification in certain cases of penal servitude or imprisonment, 945–948.

Appreciation by the people of a pension system as not conveying any such taint as poor relief, 961, 962——Opinion that the income test could easily be investigated, and that attempts at fraud could be checked, 963–967——View of witness that the only tests should be age, residence, and nationality, 973.

H.

Habitual Paupers. Examination in defence of proposal to pension men who now live upon the rates as habitual paupers; dissent from the view that this would entail an increase of cost, *Steadman* 622–631.

Hamilton, Sir Edward, K.C.B. (Digest of his Evidence.)—Reference to the Bill before the present Committee as closely following the financial proposals of the Select Committee of 1899 respecting Old Age Pensions, 303–306——Data for former calculation by witness (on the part of the Departmental Committee of 1898) that in 1901 there would be 2,016,000 persons above 65 years of age in England and Wales, and that if there were a universal pension of 5s. a week, the aggregate charge would be 26,149,600*l.*, exclusive of the cost of administration, 307–317——Figures to be supplied for Scotland and Ireland; difficulty and probable inaccuracy in respect of the latter country, 318–321. 364–368.

Tendency to error in the Census returns as probably not showing the whole number of persons above 65 years of age; probability on the other hand that some applicants for pensions would send in claims before they had reached the prescribed limit, 322–324——Prospect of an increased proportion of the population being above 65 years of age in accordance with improved sanitary conditions in the future, 325, 326.

Calculations made by witness (on the part of the Departmental Committee on Old Age Pensions) that the various deductions to be made in 1901 for want of qualification would reduce the numbers to 656,000, and the cost to 10,300,000*l.*, 327–331. 370–376. 415–418——Probable increase of the number by aliens becoming naturalised, and thus qualified to claim facilities for this purpose, 332–338——Difficulties as regards the deductions to be made in respect of disqualification for receipt of poor relief or criminal conduct, etc., 339–355.

Conclusion as to the very limited disqualification in respect of the conditions as to residence, 356–358——Grounds for the calculation of the Departmental Committee that 37 per cent. of the population of Ireland (as of England) over 65 years of age would be disqualified as having an income of 10s. a week; whilst only 35 per cent. would be disqualified in Scotland on this score, 359–363——Belief that due care was exercised by the Departmental

Report, 1903—*continued.*

Hamilton, Sir Edward, K.C.B. (Digest of his Evidence)—*continued.*

Departmental Committee as regards the deduction made in respect of persons unable to prove compliance with the thrift qualifications, 367–369.

Conclusion generally, that on several grounds the estimated cost of 10,300,000*l.* for 1901 was an under estimate, 370–374. 415–416——Calculation by Mr. Brabrook (a member of the Departmental Committee) that on the basis of applying the New Zealand Act to England the cost would be about 13,000,000*l.* instead of 10,300,000*l.*, 372–374——Difficulty in estimating the percentage of disqualification that might escape detection in respect of criminals, 375–380.

Explanation as to the Departmental Committee not having made any allowance for saving in Poor Law expenditure till 1911, when 515,000*l.* is allowed; statement hereon as to the much larger cost of maintenance in workhouses than is represented by a pension of 5*s.* a week, 379–387——Reasons for the estimated cost of administration being about 8 per cent., which is far in excess of the proportionate cost in New Zealand; reference hereon to the large expense to be incurred for postal orders in England, 398–405. 409, 410——Considerable reduction of the total charge if existing incomes were only made up to 10*s.* a week, 406, 407——Large saving in administration of the services of Poor Law officials could be utilised, 407–411.

Question further considered, whether there would not be a large saving in Poor Law expenditure by a reduction in the number of indoor paupers if there were an expenditure of some 10 millions in pensions, 419–428——Statement as to the much more liberal conditions of pensions in New Zealand than are proposed for this country, and as to the much smaller proportion of pensioners in the colony than are assumed in the calculations of witness for England and Wales; possible deduction on this score from witness's estimate of total cost, 429–444——Considerations as to the reduction of cost in respect of reduction of pension when husbands and wives are living together; information promised to be obtained from the Registrar-General on this point, 445–464——Deduction allowed in respect of soldiers, policemen, and civil servants, who already have pensions, 465–468.

Explanation that witness has not considered how a sum of 9,000,000*l.* or 10,000,000*l.* might be raised in order to provide a pension fund; reference hereon to the duty on beer, the tea and sugar duties, the taxation of ground values, and the imposition of a duty on corn, as different sources whence the money might be provided, 469–486——Total of 938,000*l.* a year controlled by the Charity Commissioners and now distributed among the people, 487–490.

Letter from Sir Edw. Hamilton, dated 13th July, 1903, enclosing communication from the General Register Office, and further explaining his own views as to the great difficulties in the way of the satisfactory working of a scheme of Old Age Pensions, *App.* 96.

Humphreys, Noel. (Digest of his Evidence.)—Letter from Mr. Noel Humphreys (Chief Clerk in the General Register Office) respecting the total number of married couples in England and Wales, aged upwards of 65 years, who were living together in 1891; calculations thereupon as to the probable charge for Old Age Pensions, *App.* 96.

I.

Income (Applicants for Pensions). Grounds for the calculation of the Departmental Committee of 1898 that 57 per cent. of the population of Ireland (as of England) over 65 years of age would be disqualified as having an income of 10*s.* a week, whilst only 35 per cent. would be disqualified in Scotland on this score, *Sir E. Hamilton* 358–366——Considerable reduction of the total estimated charge if existing incomes were only made up to 10*s.* a week by pensions, *ib.* 406, 407.

Personal approval of the income test of 10*s.* a week, as under the Bill, *Steadman* 633, 634. 689–693——Expediency of a maximum limit of income as regards qualification for a pension, *Crooks* 730–732——Opinion that the income test could easily be investigated, and that attempts at fraud could be checked, *Grey* 963–907.

Conclusion of the Committee that the transfer of property and collusive arrangements as to wages for the purpose of reducing the income of the applicant to a weekly sum below that which will disqualify him for a pension should be guarded against, *Special Rep.* iv.

Indoor Relief. See *Workhouses.*

Ireland. Particulars respecting the inmates above 65 years of age of certain workhouses in connection with the question of their living outside with relatives or friends if they had pensions, *App.* 138–142. See also *Income*, &c.

M.

N.

Mass

NEW ZEALAND—continued.

Main object and provisions of the amending Acts of 1900 and 1901 to strengthen the powers of the Registrar and to provide against fraud in connection with the amount of income and the value of property, *Reeves* 167–188. 238——Total of only 3,553*l.* as the cost of administering the Act in 1902, the Registrar and other officers employed being for the most part Government servants, and the pensions being paid monthly through the local post offices, *ib.* 181–184. 241–251——Considerable number of pensioners in the earlier period of the Act of 1898; total of 12,387 in March, 1903 (including about 550 in homes), the number having slightly fallen since the previous year, owing probably to a more strict administration of the Act, *ib.* 185–191. 234–243. 261–265——Statement required annually from pensioners as to their income and property, *ib.* 190.

Information respecting the population, the Maoris, but not the Chinese, participating in pensions; doubt as to the proportion of those above 65 years of age who are in receipt of pensions or in workhouses, *Reeves* 192–200. 234–243. 261–268——Effect of the Act in reducing considerably the total cost of charitable aid, *ib.* 197. 203. 240——Estimate that about one-third of the aged are almost without means at the age of 65, *ib.* 199–202——Total of 210,000*l.* as the cost of the Act in the financial year 1902–1903, whereas the estimated cost at first was only 120,000*l.* a year, *ib.* 203, 204——Liability of the relatives of the aged poor to make provision for them; relief to this class through the system of State aid, *ib.* 205–208.

Conclusion that there is doubtless some imposture in working the Act, though witness is convinced that the pensioners are on the whole a very decent class, and that the Act is working well, and is deservedly popular, *Reeves* 209, 210. 226–233. 288——Limited extent to which any intense poverty exists in New Zealand, *ib.* 211. 243——Great facility in working the Acts through the towns being comparatively small, and the condition of the people well known to the local magistrates, *ib.* 212——Total of about six and a half millions as the present revenue of New Zealand, there being a surplus of about 350,000*l.*, *ib.* 213–220. 272, 273——Conclusion as to the Act not discouraging thrift, *ib.* 221–224.

Doubt as to much complaint about pensions being spent extravagantly or in drunkenness; check in this respect, *Reeves* 252–254——Searching character of the inquiry further adverted to, the applicants, as a rule, not objecting thereto; advantage of public inquiry, *ib.* 255–260. 274–276——Payment of the full pension at the rate of 1*s.* a day to the Charitable Aid Board in respect of those maintained in workhouses; return of a shilling a week to the pensioner as an act of kindness on the part of the Board, *ib.* 264–271——Absence of any feeling of disgrace in being a pensioner, *ib.* 277.

Great variation in the rate of wages in New Zealand in relation to the amount of pension, *Reeves* 279, 280——Comfortable character of the homes for pensioners, these being chiefly for infirm old people, *ib.* 281–287——Obligation upon the municipalities to relieve destitution; several forms of relief, about half the cost being borne by subsidy, *ib.* 285, 287. 292–297——Expediency of the State, as finding the money, appointing the officers for working the Act, *ib.* 290–291. 297——Belief that pensioners are not disfranchised, *ib.* 298, 299——Explanation that men disabled by accident or otherwise, under the age of 65, are not eligible for pensions, *ib.* 300.

Statement as to the much more liberal conditions of pensions in New Zealand than are proposed for this country, and as to the much smaller proportion of pensioners in the colony than are assumed in the calculations of witness for England and Wales; possible deduction on this score from witness's estimate of total cost, *Sir E. Hamilton* 429–444.

Provisions of the New Zealand Old Pensions Act of 1898, *App.* 83–94——Provisions of Acts of 1900 and 1901 for the amendment of the Act of 1898, *ib.* 95–97.

Calculation by Mr. Noel Humphreys as to the smaller percentage of the white population of New Zealand over 65 years of age than of the population of England and Wales, thus invalidating estimates of the relative cost of old age pensions in the two countries, *App.* 98.

NUMBER OF PENSIONERS:

Reference to a calculation in 1899 that in 1901 there would be 2,016,000 persons in England and Wales above 65 years of age; immense cost if these were pensioned at 5*s.* a week, *Sir E. Hamilton* 307–317——Figures to be supplied for Scotland and Ireland; difficulty and probably inaccuracy in respect of the latter country, *ib.* 318–321. 364–366.

Tendency to error in the Census returns as probably not showing the whole numbers of persons above 65 years of age; probability on the other hand that some applicants for pensions would send in claims before they had reached the prescribed age limit, *Sir E. Hamilton* 322–324——Prospect of an increased proportion of the population being above 65 years of age in accordance with improved sanitary conditions in the future, *ib.* 325, 326——Difficulties as regards the deductions to be made in respect of disqualification for receipt of poor relief or criminal conduct, etc., *ib.* 339–353——Deduction allowed in respect of soldiers, policemen, and civil servants who already have pensions, *ib.* 465–468.

Extract

Report, 1903—*continued*.

Number of Paupers—continued.

Extract from the Local Government Board Report of 1899–1900 respecting the number of paupers of 65 years of age or upwards on 1st July, 1899, and 1st January, 1900, *App.* 72.

Table showing the proportion which the total number of paupers of 65 years of age or upwards, excluding vagrants and insane, on 1st July, 1899, and 1st January, 1900, bore to the estimated population, and to the total pauperism of the country, *App.* 81.

See also Poor Relief. *Workhouses*.

O.

Old Age Pensions Bill, 1903. Copy thereof, *App.* 126–128.

Outdoor Relief (*Poor Law System*). *See Poor Relief*. *Workhouses*.

P.

Paddington. Explanation on the part of the Paddington Board of Guardians of the amended regulations adopted by the Board since 1898, with the approval of the Local Government Board in dealing with applications for relief; satisfactory working thereof, *Fuller* 1177–1197. 1251–1257——Condition as to applicants having given some proof of thrift; very rare instances of members of friendly societies applying, *ib.* 1180. 1184–1186. 1206–1210. 1236. 1285–1288——Practice of the Board in some deserving cases to obtain assistance or small pensions through charitable societies or from private sources, so that the applicants may not come on the poor rates, *ib.* 1193–1196. 1206,

Care exercised in Paddington in discriminating between the different cases of outdoor relief and the varying amounts granted; total of 275 outdoor cases on 1st January, 1903; *Fuller* 1238–1246. 1272–1280——Practice of boarding out children as much as possible, *ib.* 1239. 1241. 1277. 1278.

Further explanations respecting the satisfactory working of the amended rules applied in Paddington, and the staff employed in testing applications for outdoor relief; discouragement of applications by the undeserving through knowledge beforehand of the efficiency of the inquiries made, *Fuller* 1249–1259——Very large population in Paddington, with incomes up to 31*s.* a week who are not upon the rates, *ib.* 1256–1260——Small proportion of out-relief in Paddington as compared with the majority of London Unions, *ib.* 1273–1276. 1294–1298,

Sample of case paper used by Board of Guardians, *App.* 109——Information required in regard to settlement, *ib.* 111. 113——Forms to be observed when first applications are made to the Board, *ib.* 114.

Poor Relief:

Discrimination exercised by guardians and relieving officers, as in Poplar Union, in selecting cases fit for outdoor relief; small percentage of selected applicants who have no right to such relief, *Crooks* 720–725——Conclusion that there are many thousands of respectable poor people who, with a little relief, might remain at home with their friends and relations, *ib.* 725. 729.

Hardship of disqualification in the event of receipt of poor relief during 20 years prior to the application for a pension, even though not applying under wholly exceptional circumstances, *Gray* 810–812. 867. 868. 909–919. 949. 950——Receipt of poor relief by members of co-operative societies without being disqualified as members, *ib.* 875–877.

Very inadequate outdoor relief in some rural districts; circulars of the Local Government Board on the subject not receiving much attention; beneficial results from the proposed Bill in these cases, *Miss E. Sellers* 1137–1140. 1161.

Rule in Paddington not to grant out-relief except to those who are deserving at the time of the application; details hereon as to the tests applied and the character and mode of inquiry in different classes of cases, the checks upon abuse working satisfactorily, *Fuller* 1179–1192. 1208. 1252–1257. 1249–1259——Full powers in Guardians to give liberal weekly relief in deserving cases in addition to incomes of as much as 10*s.* or 15*s.* a week, *ib.* 1198–1201. 1208.

Outdoor relief up to 7*s.* or 8*s.* a week given in some cases by the Paddington Guardians, witness submitting, however, that it is desirable to check much of the outdoor relief now given in some unions, *Fuller* 1216–1223. 1238–1247. 1261–1263——Conclusion as to the limited increase of cost to be incurred generally in carrying out a really efficient administration of outdoor relief; good economy in having an efficient staff, *ib.* 1253–1257. 1263, 1264. 1270, 1271.

Opinion

Poor Relief—continued.

Opinion as to the sufficiency of a period of 10 years instead of 20 as a condition to be required in respect of deserving applicants, *Foley* 1291, 1293——Consideration to be given in cases where men sometimes have to tramp the country in search of employment, and are obliged to occasionally apply for indoor relief, *ib.* 1723.

Copy of replies and returns received through the Local Government Board, the Secretary for Scotland's Office, and the Local Government Board, Ireland, showing for certain unions or parishes the number of workhouse inmates over 65 years of age who would be fit and able to live outside with relatives or friends if they had pensions of from 5s. to 7s. a week, *App.* 131–142.

Recommendation by the Committee as to qualified pensioners being entitled to certain privileges even if they should receive poor law relief, *Special Rep.* iv.——Recommendation that the disqualification arising from the receipt of poor law relief should be so defined as not to exclude from pensions aged persons who are in receipt of such relief at the time of the passing of the Act, but who had received such relief for 20 years before they reached the qualifying age, *ib.*——Further recommendation that a definition of the "circumstances of a wholly exceptional character" under which poor relief may be given without invalidating a subsequent claim to a pension should be inserted in the Bill, *ib.*

See also Number of Pensioners. Workhouses.

Poplar. Very careful investigation by a Special Committee of the Poplar Guardians in 1899 of the question whether the aged poor in the workhouse over 60 years of age (of whom there are 1,000) could be well cared for out of the house by relatives or friends, *Crooks* 706——Conclusion of the Special Committee, after their first inquiry, that the inmates, many of whom are infirm and helpless, would not be properly cared for if they left the workhouse; reluctance on their part to make the change, *ib.* 756——Additional inquiry made in about 1,000 cases, the general result being that not 5 per cent. could with advantage be removed from the house, *ib.* 708–710.

Desire of the Guardians to encourage outdoor rather than indoor relief; very limited extent to which feasible in the interests of the aged poor, *Crooks* 706–708——Result of investigation in Poplar Union, that there are 1,624 persons over the age of 60 in receipt of outdoor relief whose relatives or friends might take charge of them if pensioned at 5s. a week, some of them having other sources of income, *ib.* 714–730.

Popularity (Pension System). Appreciation by the people of a pension system as not conveying any such taint as poor relief, *Gray* 861, 862——Gratitude evinced by old age pensioners in Denmark, though their pensions are very small, through not being treated as paupers or sent to workhouses, *Miss E. Sellers* 1096–1101——Popularity also through the recipients of pensions not being deprived of votes, *ib.* 1097.

Q.

Qualifications and Disqualifications. Dissent from the qualification conditions under Mr. Chaplin's scheme, *Steadman* 559——Great difficulty of the Pensions Committees under the Bill in distinguishing between those who are and those who are not entitled to pensions; ill-will to be created, *ib.* 578–582——Decided objection to any distinction between loafers and industrious workmen as regards a pension, *ib.* 625–639——Difficulties of discriminating between deserving and undeserving applicants; sufficiency of the test of age, *ib.* 641–648.

Belief that no great difficulty would be experienced, especially in country districts, in discriminating between deserving and undeserving applicants for pensions; absence of any great difficulty in Manchester, *Gray* 802–804, 843–850, 876–882——Objection of applicants to their qualifications being investigated before magistrates, *ib.* 814——View of witness that the only tests should be age, residence, and nationality, *ib.* 973.

Conclusion as to there being no great difficulty in arriving at the history of the aged poor either in town or country, *Miss E. Sellers* 1164.

Table containing details regarding the paupers of 65 or 70 years or upwards who were in receipt of relief on 1st January, 1900; *App.* 80.

Conclusion expressed by Sir Edward Hamilton in letter of 16th July, 1900, that any scheme of old age pensions with conditions attached to it must create hardship and inequalities, and be very difficult, if not impossible, to work; whilst any unconditional scheme, which would give pensions to everybody, those who do not want assistance and those who do not deserve it, would be absurd, *App.* 93.

Summary of the qualifications to be required of pensioners dealt with in Clause 6 of the Bill, *Special Rep.* iv.

See also Administration. Age Limit. Criminals. Inmates, etc. Poor Relief. Residence Qualification. Thrift. Ratepayers

Report, 1903—*continued.*

Reeves, The Honourable William Pember. (Digest of his Evidence)—*continued.*

ciency of the State, as finding the money appointing the officers for working the Act, 289-291. 297——Belief that pensioners are not disfranchised, 298, 299——Explanation that men disabled by accident or otherwise under the age of 65 are not eligible for pensions, 300.

Relations (Maintenance of Parents). Conclusion that provision should be made against the transfer of the maintenance of aged parents from well-to-do children to the State, *Special Rep.* iv. *See also Workhouses.*

Residence Qualification. Conclusion as to the very limited disqualification in respect of the conditions under the Bill as to residence, *Sir E. Hamilton* 356-358.

Recommendation by the Committee that if any part of the pension is to be charged on the rates of a Union, the pensioner should have been a resident in that Union for a considerable period, *Special Rep.* iv.

RUSSIA:

Great care taken of the aged poor in Russia in cottage homes and through charitable agencies, there being no Poor Law except in Moscow. *Miss E. Sellers* 1171-1174.

S.

Scotland. Correspondence and returns respecting the number of inmates of certain workhouses in Scotland above 65 years of age who would be fit and able to live outside with relatives and friends if they had pensions of from 5s. to 7s. a week, *App.* 134-137.

Sellers, Miss Edith. (Digest of her Evidence.)—Considerable study devoted by witness to the subject of the treatment of the aged poor in Denmark and other foreign countries, as well as to their condition and treatment in English workhouses, 1-5.

Statement prepared for the Committee respecting the system in Copenhagen and throughout Denmark, 6. 9——Very full control vested in the Third Session Burgomaster of Copenhagen, as regards the administration of old age relief in that city, 6. 30-36. 55——Division of the city, for poor relief purposes, into 12 districts, each of which is in care of a district superintendent, these being arranged in three groups of four districts each, each group being under a group inspector, 6. 103-104——Separate duties of the district superintendents and group inspectors, the former dealing only with the pauper class, while the latter deal with the respectable aged poor apart from pauper relief; very careful discrimination between the two classes, 6. 9. 56-63.

Fairly satisfactory results at Copenhagen in distinguishing between the pauper class and the deserving section of the community; strict and elaborate investigations made for this purpose, 6. 8. 98-100. 109-111——Reference to the questions which applicants for old age relief (as distinct from pauper relief) are required to answer; liability to imprisonment for false information, 6-8. 43-48.

Limit of 60 years of age in Copenhagen for the commencement of old age relief, 9——Strict requirements on the score of moral character; special bar against drunkenness, 9. 40-42——Decision by the group inspector whether applicants are to go before the Old Age Relief Committee, which is presided over by the Burgomaster, and which decides each case, and the amount and form of relief, 9.

Rule that where a man is strong enough to take care of himself, or has any relatives to take care of him, the relief shall be in the form of a pension, the average pension being about 7*l.* 10*s.* a year, 9——Admission of the deserving poor, in many cases, to old age homes, these being delightful places, and being all over the country, 9. 66-70——Considerable difficulties in connection with a former requirement that applicants for relief must be in a destitute condition, so that there was not much inducement to save; amendment of the law on this point, 9, 10.

Great importance attached to proposals by Herr Jacobi, Third Session Burgomaster of Copenhagen, that a standard of income shall be fixed below which persons may be qualified for a pension, which would be on a sliding scale according to age, 40 per cent. being added when the man has a wife living, 10-12. 85-93. 101——Explanations with reference to the list of questions which applicants must answer in order to qualify for pensions, 13-18.

Particulars in connection with certain statistics as to the increased cost of old age relief and old age pensions from 1892 to 1897, and as to the relative decrease in the cost of pauper relief; very satisfactory inference from these figures, 18, 19——Rearrangement by Act in 1902 as to the sources of payment of the cost of old age pensions and relief, one-half being borne by the State and one-half by the Communal or local authorities, 20, 21——Explanation as to the State contribution being all levied on the beer tax, while the Communal moiety is paid out of the local receipts from various sources, there being a poor fund, but no poor rate, 21-27.

Sellers, Miss Edith. (Digest of her Evidence)—*continued.*

Concurrence of evidence of representative and official authorities in Denmark as to the very beneficial operation of the law in respect of the working classes generally, without being any discouragement to thrift, 27–30——Explanations in detail on various points in elucidation of statement read by witness to the Committee as regards applications for pensions or relief, the qualifications and conditions required, the investigations made, and the general working of the system in Copenhagen and in the country generally, 30, *et seq.*

Conclusion as to the expediency and the feasibility of a separate classification of aged poor who should not be treated as indoor paupers in workhouses, 111——Information respecting the system of Poor Law administration in Vienna, with special reference to the forms observed and the investigations made in connection with admission to cottage homes, 112–120.

Reference to a law passed in France in 1897 whereby the State undertook to contribute, up to half a million francs, towards the cost incurred by the Communal authorities in granting allowances to poor persons above 70 years; very limited action of the municipalities in the matter, 121–127——Recent French law providing that a certain number of hospices or homes shall be provided for the aged poor, 122–130——Working of the Poor Law in Paris by officials, there being a right in poor persons to claim an allowance at the age of 70; 123, 124, 127–131.

[Second Examination.]—Explanation that for Copenhagen and the whole of Denmark, respectively, the average pension in the former case for married couples is 9*l.* 3*s.* 6½*d.*, and for a single person 7*l.* 5*s.* 3*d.*, and in the latter case 6*l.* 15*s.* 10½*d.* for married couples, and 4*l.* 16*s.* 9½*d.* for a single person, 1085–1088——Increase from 253,670*l.* in 1895 to 266,491*l.* in 1900, as the total cost for all Denmark, 1088, 1089——Calculation that on the basis of relative population the cost for England and Wales would be 3,591,000*l.*, but as the pensions in this country would have to be larger than in Denmark, they might cost 7,000,000*l.*; whilst there would be an estimated saving of 3,000,000*l.* in Poor Law expenses, 1089–1091.

Very few really poor or destitute people in Denmark, the country being an exceptionally prosperous one, 1092–1096——Gratitude evinced by the old age pensioners, though their pensions are so small, through not being treated as paupers or sent to workhouses, 1098–1101——Popularity also through the recipients of pensions not being deprived of votes, 1097.

Personal inquiry by witness in 1903 into the circumstances of old people above 65 years of age in one large metropolitan workhouse (Newington) and in seven small ones in rural districts in England, 1102–1104, 1141, 1142——Total of 720 inmates of Newington Workhouse (283 men and 437 women), of whom only 196 women and 100 men were strong enough to leave even if they had friends to receive them, 1105–1107.

Result of exhaustive investigations by witness and the relieving officer into the foregoing cases, that for various reasons there were only three women who could leave, though the Southwark Guardians undertook to grant 5*s.* a week to all whom witness could recommend, and who had friends able and willing to receive them, 1107–1115——Result as regards the men (in respect of whom there was no offer of 5*s.* a week), that there were very few, if any, who could go to friends, 1116–1120.

Summary of the results of witness's investigations into the cases of the aged poor in seven rural workhouses, all in the same district; very deplorable condition of the aged inmates, many of them being imbeciles or lunatics, there being practically none whose friends outside could receive them, even if there were small pensions, 1121–1137, 1159, 1160——Strong repugnance to the workhouse in country districts, 1131, 1135–1137——Inspection by witness of a workhouse in a small town in a rural district, the older inmates being generally unfit for removal to cottage homes, 1134, 1135.

Very inadequate outdoor relief in some rural districts, circulars of the Local Government Board on the subject not receiving much attention; beneficial results from the proposed Bill in these cases, 1137–1140, 1161——Great boon if deserving cases of old people in workhouses could be removed to cottage homes away from the workhouses; calculation that in all England there would not be more than 4,000 or 5,000 such cases above the age of 65; 1143–1161.

Entire inadequacy of the limit of age not beginning till 70; illustration in Berlin, 1147–1150——Usually miserable condition of the aged poor in small workhouses where there is no classification; misery also in large workhouses like that at Fulham, 1159——Comment upon the misery of inmates of Newington Workhouse, as being infinitely worse than that of men in Russian prisons, 1160.

Calculation that one-roomed cottages, built in rows, sufficient to accommodate 4,000 old people, could be provided for about 800,000*l.*; less expense if houses were rented for the

Sellers, Miss Edith. (Digest of her Evidence)—*continued.*

the purpose, 1162, 1163——Conclusion as to there being no great difficulty in arriving at the history of the aged poor, either in town or country, 1164——Very low position of England as compared with foreign countries in respect of the care taken of her aged poor, 1165–1167.

Existence in Denmark for the last 600 years of a right to relief in cases of destitution, 1168–1170——Law in Austria, though not enforced, whereby men can claim from the State at the age of 60 one-third of their average past earnings, 1168–1170——Great care taken of the aged poor in Russia in cottage homes and through charitable agencies, there being no Poor Law except in Moscow, 1171–1174——Illustration of the large saving which might be effected in the cost of workhouses if there were cottage homes, 1174–1176.

Steadman, W. C. (Digest of his Evidence.)—Explanation of the origin of the Conference held in London in January, 1902, and convened by the Trades Union Congress and the Co-operative Union Congress in order to deal with old age pensions, witness having presided at the first meeting of the Conference, 491–494. 603——Resolution moved by witness at the Trades Union Congress at Swansea in 1901, and unanimously adopted, as to the legislation required on the subject at issue, and as to the expediency of every citizen having a right to claim a pension at a certain age, 493.

Proposition that it is the duty of statesmen to find the money required, the opinion of witness being that it should come from a graduated income tax, 494, 496——Impracticability of ascertaining the total amount that would be required for a scheme of universal pensions at a given age, as large numbers would not claim; objection, however, to men being disqualified for pensions if they choose to work, 497–502. 563. 639.

Explanation as to the Friendly Societies having taken no part in the Conference of 1902, there having been, however, 394 delegates present from co-operative societies and trades unions, representing a total membership of 2,441,000; 503–510——Circulation of 12 different pension schemes among the members, the Organising Joint Committee having recommended No. 10 scheme to the favourable consideration of the delegates attending the Conference, 503–517. 549——Five principles embodied in No. 10 scheme, viz., that the scheme be non-contributory, universal in its application, that the public (or the Government) should pay, that the pension age be 60, and the amount 5s. per week, 512–519.

Unanimous adoption by the Conference of 1902 of resolution that the scheme should be non-contributory, there having been no adverse discussion, 519–523——Adoption of resolution, with only one dissentient delegate, representing a society with 16,000 members, that the scheme must be universal in its application irrespective of income or character, neither criminals nor immoral people being excluded, 524–533.

Adoption by the Conference, after discussion, of an amended resolution to the effect that the expenditure involved should be borne by Imperial taxation, instead of by Imperial and local taxation; absence of discussion upon the question of the cost of administration, 534–540. 567–569——Very large majority by which a resolution was passed that the age should be fixed at 60, and not at 65; 541–545——Resolution adopted that the amount should be at least 5s. a week, an amendment which was moved in favour of the amount being 7s. having been withdrawn, 546, 547.

Concluding resolution passed by the Conference summarising the results arrived at, and urging the promotion of an Old Age Pension Bill, this Bill now standing in the name of Mr. Channing, 549, 653, 665——Statement as to the Conference not having specially discussed No. 5 scheme (which is similar to the Bill before the Select Committee), the Organising Committee having, however, previously considered all the schemes, and having unanimously recommended No. 10 scheme, 549–556. 570–573——Meeting of the Trades Union Congress in September, 1902, when there were 500 delegates present and the resolution of the Conference in support of No. 10 scheme was unanimously confirmed, 556. 573.

Strong comments upon the proposals of Mr. Chaplin's Committee adopted in the present Bill, as being "a penny wise and pound foolish" policy, and as bearing with extreme hardship upon the poorer class of ratepayers, the rates being burdened under the Bill with more than half the cost involved, 556–560——Calculation that the cost at 5s. per week under the Bill would be about 8,000,000*l.* instead of 10,300,000*l.*, 556–558. 650——Dissent from the qualification conditions under Mr. Chaplin's scheme, 559.

Discussion at the Conference of 1902 as regards not only the thrift tests, but the question of a limit in respect of the income of recipients of pensions, 563, 563. 565, 566——Conclusion that great numbers of unskilled workmen, with low wages, not members of friendly societies, have as much right to be looked after as such members, 563, 564. 678–680——Very general character of the discussion at the Conference as to the mode of raising the money required for the proposed scheme, 574–577. 670–672.

Steadman, W. C. (Digest of his Evidence)—*continued.*

Great difficulty of the Pensions Committees under the Bill in distinguishing between those who are and those who are not entitled to pensions; ill will to be created, 578–582——Belief as to pensions or superannuations existing to a considerable extent in the case of Trades Union Societies; instance in the case of the Amalgamated Society of Engineers, 583–587. 654–669.

Estimate by Mr. Charles Booth that the cost of the proposed universal scheme would be 26,000,000*l.*; expediency of at once beginning on this scale, 588–594——Approval of the qualification that the recipient must be a British subject, 595——Preference for 60 as the age instead of 65; 596——Further contention that men who have been criminals should not be excluded from pensions, 597–601. 681–689.

Examination in defence of proposal to pension men who live upon the rates as habitual paupers; dissent from the view that this would entail an increase of cost, 602–621——Personal approval of the income test of 10*s.* a week as under the Bill, 623, 624. 689–693——Decided objection to any distinction between loafers and industrious workmen as regards claim to a pension, 625–629.

Grounds for disapproving of a tax on beer or sugar as a means towards meeting the large expenditure required; objections by working to contribute by taxation towards their pensions, 632–640. 649, 650. 670–672——Difficulties of discriminating between deserving and undeserving applicants; sufficiency of the test of age, 641–648.

Full powers vested in the delegates to decide at the Conference for the general body of members of the co-operative societies and trades unions, 651–659——Further explanation that friendly societies were not represented, with one or two exceptions, 659–661——Very heavy cost entailed under the workhouse system as compared with a system of pensions, 673–679.

Opinion adverse to the acceptance of Mr. Chaplin's Bill, even though it may seem impossible to succeed in enacting the Bill of Mr. Channing, 694–699——Concurrence with the Conference that the money required should all come from Imperial sources, witness further advocating a graduated income tax for the purpose, 700–702.

T.

Taxation (Cost of Pensions). Explanation that witness has not considered how a sum of 9,000,000*l.* or 10,000,000*l.* might be raised in order to provide a pension fund; reference hereon to the duty on beer, the tea and sugar duties, the taxation of ground values, and the imposition of a duty on corn, as different sources whence the money might be provided, *Sir E. Hamilton*, 469–486.

Proposition that it is the duty of statesmen to find the money required, the opinion of witness being that it should come from a graduated income tax, *Steadman* 494, 495, 511–630, 631——Adoption by the Trades Union and Co-operative Union Conference of 1902, after discussion, of an amended resolution to the effect that the expenditure involved should be borne by Imperial taxation instead of by Imperial and local taxation; absence of discussion upon the question of the cost of administration, *ib.* 534–540. 567–569. 571–577. 670–672.

Grounds for disapproving of a tax on beer or sugar as a means towards meeting the large expenditure required; objections by working men to contribute by taxation towards their pensions, *Steadman* 632–640, 649, 650, 670–672——Concurrence with the Conference that the money required should all come from Imperial sources, witness further advocating a graduated income tax for the purpose, *ib.* 700–702.

Grounds for objecting to the expense being borne partly by local rates instead of entirely by Imperial taxation, though the administration should be local, *Gray* 783–798. 837–841——Approval of the working-class paying income tax, if fairly levied all round, towards a universal pension scheme, *ib.* 839. 897. 935——Approval also of a tax on beer as one of the modes of increased taxation; reference hereon to the excessive expenditure of working men in Manchester on drink, *ib.* 929–936.

Liability to abuse under the system of the Common Poor Fund in London; inference as to the temptation to Boards of Guardians to put applicants for relief on a Pension Fund if half the amount were provided by the State, *Fuller* 1211, 1212.

See also Cost. *Denmark.*

Thrift. Belief that due care was exercised by the Departmental Committee of 1899 as regards the deduction made from estimates of cost in respect of persons unable to prove compliance with the thrift qualifications, *Sir E. Hamilton* 367–369——Discussion at the Trades Union Conference of 1902 as regards not only the thrift tests, but the question of a limit in respect of the income of recipients of pensions, *Steadman* 562, 563, 565, 566——Unfairness

Thrift—continued.

Unfairness of the proposed thrift or savings test as being of very unequal operation, *Gray* 814–817. 887. 888. 920–927. 951–956——Discouragement to thrift under the proposal for supplementing in certain cases incomes of 10*s*. a week by means of pensions, *Fuller* 1205, 1207.

Degree of danger that those who are in a position to save money may be discouraged from saving by the reflection that the more they have the less they will receive in the form of a pension, *Special Rep.* v.——Suggestion as to the pension not being so reduced as to deprive applicants of the fruits of their own thrift, *ib.*

See also Income, etc.

Trades Unions:

Explanation of the origin of the Conference held in London in January, 1902, and convened by the Trades Union Congress and the Co-operative Union Congress in order to deal with old age pensions, *Steadman* 491–494. 503——Resolution moved by witness at the Trades Union Congress at Swansea in 1901, and unanimously adopted, as to the legislation required on the subject at issue, and as to the expediency of every citizen having a right to claim a pension at a certain age, *ib.* 493——Explanation as to the friendly societies having taken no part in the Conference of 1902, there having been, however, 594 delegates present from co-operative societies and trades unions representing a total membership of 2,441,000, *ib.* 503–510. 559–561.

Circulation of 12 different pension schemes among the members, the Organising Joint Committee having recommended No. 10 scheme to the favourable consideration of the delegates attending the Conference, *Steadman* 505–517. 549——Five principles embodied in No. 10 scheme, viz., that the scheme be non-contributory, universal in its application, that the public (or the Government) should pay, that the pension age be 60, and the amount 5*s*. per week, *ib.* 512–519——Unanimous adoption by the Conference of 1902 of resolution that the scheme should be non-contributory, there having been no adverse discussion, *ib.* 519–523.

Concluding resolution passed by the Conference summarising the results arrived at, and urging the promotion of an Old Age Pension Bill, this Bill now standing in the name of Mr. Channing, *Steadman* 549. 562, 563——Statement as to the Conference not having specially discussed No. 5 scheme (which is similar to the Bill before the Select Committee), the Organising Committee having, however, previously considered all the schemes and having unanimously recommended No. 10 scheme, *ib.* 549–556. 570–573.

Meeting of the Trades Union Congress in September, 1902, when there were 500 delegates present, and the resolution of the Conference in support of No. 10 scheme was unanimously confirmed, *Steadman* 556. 573——Belief as to pensions or superannuations existing to a considerable extent in the case of Trades Union Societies; instance in the case of the Amalgamated Society of Engineers, *ib.* 583–587. 664–669——Full powers vested in the delegates to decide at the Conference for the general body of members of the Co-operative Societies and Trades Unions, *ib.* 651–659.

Evidence received by the Committee as to the views of Trades Unions, Friendly Societies, and Co-operative Societies upon the proposals of Mr. Chaplin's Committee of 1899, *Special Rep.* iii.

U.

Universal Pensions. Adoption of resolution at the Conference of Trades Unions and Co-operative Unions in January, 1902, with only one dissentient delegate representing a society with 15,000 members, that the scheme must be universal in its application, irrespective of income or character, neither criminals nor immoral people being excluded, *Steadman* 524–533.

Overwhelming majority of opinions of Co-operative Unions throughout the country in favour of a national system of pensions, *Gray* 763–770——Joint Conferences eventually in 1901 and 1902 between the Co-operative Union and the Trades Union, it having been unanimously decided to promote a Bill on the lines of a universal system of old age pensions, *ib.* 770–776. 958–973——Unanimous adoption by the Co-operative Union of the scheme of universal pensions at the age of 60, irrespective of income and regardless of character, *ib.* 785–792. 800. 824–826. 958–973.

See also Co-operative Union. Cost. Taxation. Trades Unions.

V.

Victoria:

Explanation of the main provisions of the Victoria Old Age Pension Act of 1901, and of the temporary Act passed in the previous year, *Dobson* 974, *et seq.*——Provision of a pension of 10s. a week under the Act of 1900, the estimated total charge having been nearly doubled by the actual expenditure, *ib.* 976–978. 1018–1021. [illegible], [illegible]——Separate Act in 1900 providing for the registration of claimants for old age pensions, this having been the first step taken, *ib.* 979–981.

Condition under the Act of 1901 that the minimum age must be 65, the pension being in supplement of any income from all sources, so as to make the total to 8s. a week, *Dobson* 984. 1039–1043——Summary of qualifications and of the several heads of disqualification, such as drunkenness, break of residence, desertion, etc., *ib.* 987, *et seq.*——Condition as to a man not purposely parting with this income so as to establish a claim to a pension; liability to punishment for fraud on this score, *ib.* 988, 989.

Requirement that a man must have made reasonable efforts to provide for himself, or have brought up a family in decency and comfort; mode of investigation on this point, *Dobson* 989, 990. 1002——Explanation as regards the thrift qualifications and the procedure or test applied on this score, *ib.* 990. 997. 1003–1007.

Large contribution by the working classes of Victoria towards the Government revenue, the Customs revenue being probably three-fourths of the whole; large sums also contributed by the people to hospitals, charitable societies, etc., *Dobson* 990–996. 1070–1075——Obligation upon relatives to provide, if in their power, for applicants for pensions; prejudicial operation of the Act of 1901 on this score, *ib.* 997–999——Important provisions and safeguards as regards continuous residence, *ib.* 1000. 1066–1068.

Information as to the procedure in testing applications, there being local Commissioners for the purpose appointed by the Government, *Dobson* 1001–1005——Valuable check through means of Savings Banks accounts, *ib.* 1006, 1007——Continuance of the pensions without annual renewal, though they are liable to cancellation, *ib.* 1007–1009. 1079–1083——Claim upon pensioners for reimbursement out of any real estate in respect of the amount paid in pensions, *ib.* 1009——Power not to pay to the pensioners directly if not fit to be trusted with the money, *ib.* 1009, 1010——Intention to amend the Act of 1901 in the direction of prevention of fraud, *ib.* 1011——Statement as to the population of Victoria, there being about 50,000 persons over 65 years of age, of whom 16,234 were pensioners, *ib.* 1014–1018. 1023, 1033——Belief that pensioners would be encouraged to work, *ib.* 1027, 1028.

System of payment of pensions out of the general revenue; large State expenditure also in respect of hospitals and charitable institutions, *Dobson* 1029–1036. 1050, 1051, 1064——Special circumstances under which pensions are sometimes granted to men under 65 engaged in dangerous and unhealthy occupations, *ib.* 1058——Several instances of men resigning their pensions and going into charitable institutions, *ib.* ——Relative cost of housing in Victoria and in England; much higher wages in the former case, *ib.* 1036–1052——Further statement as to fraud arising under the present Act as well as under the first Act, *ib.* 1076–1078.

Provisions of the Act of the State of Victoria of December, 1900, for the payment of old age pensions, *App.* 99, 100——Act of December, 1900, making provision for registration of claims for old age pensions, *ib.* 100.

Further Act of December, 1901, providing for the payment of old age pensions and for other purposes; schedules attached thereto, *App.* 101–107.

Further Amendment Act of December, 1901, making additional financial provision and laying down further regulations as to rate of payment, &c., *App.* 107, 108.

W.

Westport Union (Ireland). Report respecting workhouse inmates above 65 years of age in connection with the question of their living with relations or friends outside if they were pensioned, *App.* 140.

Workhouses:

Conclusion as to the expediency and the possibility of a separate classification of aged poor, who should not be treated as indoor paupers in workhouses, *Miss E. Sellers* 111——

Grounds for the conclusion that large numbers of the aged inmates of workhouses would, if they had a pension of 5s. a week, be gladly taken charge of by their relatives, *Sanderson* 678–680.

Relief

WORKHOUSES—continued.

Belief that it would be cheaper and more popular to provide pensions than to compel old people to go into the workhouse; great aversion of the people in some places to become indoor paupers, *Grey* 816–833, 837–837, 970, 971.——Conclusion that large numbers of old and infirm people would find friends and relatives to take good care of them if assisted with a pension of 5*s.* or 7*s.* 6*d.* a week, *ib.* 827–832, 853–891.

Further statement in support of the aged poor being under the care of relatives or going into cottage homes instead of to workhouses, whilst some might be provided for in the ordinary hospitals instead of in the workhouse infirmaries, *Grey* 883–896.——Doubt whether workhouses could be entirely dispensed with under a pension scheme, *ib.* 939.

Personal inquiry by witness in 1903 into the circumstances of old people above 65 years of age in one large metropolitan workhouse (Newington) and in seven small ones in rural districts in England, *Miss E. Sellers* 1102–1104, 1141, 1143.——Details respecting Newington Workhouse, the number of aged poor, the small proportion who could leave under a pension system, and the general condition of the inmates, *ib.* 1105–1120, 1160.——Summary of the results of witness's investigations into the cases of the aged poor in seven rural workhouses, all in the same district; very deplorable condition of the aged inmates, many of them being imbeciles or lunatics, there being practically none whose friends outside could receive them even if there were small pensions, *ib.* 1121–1137, 1159, 1160.

Strong repugnance to the workhouse in country districts, *Miss E. Sellers* 1151, 1155–1157.——Utterly miserable condition of the aged poor in small workhouses where there is no classification; misery also in large workhouses like those at Fulham and Newington, *ib.* 1159, 1160.——Life is, in fact, very much worse than in an ordinary prison, *ib.* 1159.

Conclusion, as the result of inquiries, that there are but few old people in the London workhouses who have relatives with whom they could live or who would care to leave the workhouse, *Feller* 1204, 1205.——Belief as to the great majority of the inmates being brought into workhouses through their own fault, though there are doubtless large numbers of deserving poor among the inmates, *ib.* 1223–1237.

Returns and correspondence respecting the number of inmates over 65 years of age in certain workhouses in England and Wales, Scotland, and Ireland respectively, who would be fit and able to live outside with relatives and friends if they had pensions of from 5*s.* to 7*s.* a week, *App.* 131–142.

Investigation by the Committee as to the number of aged inmates in certain workhouses who could leave if provided with pensions, *Special Rep.* iii.——Steps taken by the Committee for obtaining official information on the foregoing point in respect of England, Scotland, and Ireland; that is, as regards the number of inmates who have friends with whom they could live if they had pensions, *ib.*

See also *Cottage Homes.* *Newington Workhouse.* *Paddington.* *Poplar.*

www.ingramcontent.com/pod-product-compliance
Lightning Source LLC
Chambersburg PA
CBHW020002030726
47500CB00002B/400
* 9 7 8 3 7 4 2 8 1 8 5 5 3 *